## "So what do you want with me? I work for the newspaper now."

"You know what," Diaz said flatly, his eyes hard. "I got two women dead. Maybe there's more and I don't know it. This scene looks just like the other one, and there wasn't a damn bit of useful evidence at the last place."

Without a word, Quinn turned and walked away. Outside, he strode into the darkness, leaving all of it behind—the dead woman, the troubled cops and the curious bystanders who stood around hoping to see something appalling.

"Connor?" Diaz had followed him. "You can't walk away from this. You know that. So what's it gonna be?"

Diaz already knew the answer, Quinn thought. And he began to understand why his boss had been so adamant that he come out here. Everybody would get something out of this—except him. All he'd get were some new nightmares.

Not that it mattered. Squaring his shoulders, he said, "Let's get this taken care of."

With each step he took toward the apartment, Quinn felt himself leaving his newly constructed life behind. He became the hunter. Something was stalking the nights and killing for pleasure, and Quinn could not allow that to continue. But to catch his quarry, he would have to think like his quarry.

To slay the monster, he would have to become a monster.

God, how it sickened his soul.

*Also available from MIRA Books and*
*RACHEL LEE*

A FATEFUL CHOICE

# RACHEL LEE

# CAUGHT

MIRA BOOKS

ISBN 1-55166-298-1

CAUGHT



**Printed in U.S.A.**

To Cris, always, for seeing the
far side of the rainbow.

# Prologue

He woke with a jolt, heart hammering in his chest, blood thundering in his ears, head pounding. The light was bright, too bright, after the darkness of the dream, and he almost cried out at the sudden transition from night to day.

God, not again! Oh, sweet Jesus, not again!

He clawed his way out of bed, past the window through which the morning sunlight poured, and fell to his knees at the prie-dieu in the corner. His hands knotted together so tightly in prayer that his knuckles turned white, and his lungs labored as if he had run a marathon. Dark images from the dream flitted around in his mind, winged images of horror that surely must have been spawned by hell.

Lifting his eyes, he looked desperately at the wooden cross on the wall and begged God to tell him why he was so afflicted.

Dreams. Terrible dreams and visions about which he could do nothing. Dreams that came and went, awful warnings of events to come.

For some reason, he had been cursed by foreknowledge. Or by some kind of psychic connection to a sick mind. It had been bad enough when he believed these visions in his sleep were merely nightmares, but then he had seen things in the newspaper. Photographs. The women he saw in his dreams were real.

And now they were dead.

"Oh, God, please deliver me from this evil...." He prayed wildly, desperately, seeking release, or even a small measure of relief.

And now that he knew the monster of his dreams was real, he needed to do something.

For the monster was stalking again, following a woman. He had seen it in his dream, had seen what the monster intended to do. He had to stop this somehow. But oh, God, he didn't think he was strong enough!

It wouldn't help to go to the police. They wouldn't believe him. They would think he was a crackpot. They would think he was the killer himself. What they wouldn't do was believe him. Nor could they find the next victim any faster than he could.

Maybe...maybe he could do it faster himself. Maybe if he paid attention to his horrible dreams, he could find some kind of clue that would direct him to the intended victim. Maybe he could warn her somehow....

Desperate, more frightened and appalled than he had ever been in his life, he put his head down on his clasped hands and prayed. The headache. The headache was so bad he wanted to cut off his head. Not even aspirin would help.

Only God could help, and God had afflicted him with this. There must be something he could do.

*Something.*

Desperately, he continued to pray.

# 1

The deputy at the barricade lifted a hand. "Nobody goes in there, Quinn. Especially not a photographer."

Connor Quinn recognized the man, but was damned if he could remember his name. "Rick Diaz sent for me."

The deputy hooked his thumbs in his gun belt. "Yeah, and I'm the king of England."

Six months ago, that yellow police tape delimiting the crime scene would have marked Quinn as an insider. Since he'd gone to work for the *Sentinel*, it very definitely marked him as an outsider. "Look, just ask Diaz, will you? I didn't come out here for my health."

The deputy hesitated, then nodded and turned to go inside. With a jerk of his thumb, he told another cop to watch Quinn.

The January night was chilly for the Tampa Bay area, even for this time of year. The cops scurrying around the yard and in and out of the apartment building were all bundled in thick jackets and blowing white clouds with their breath.

In the bright light of the floodlamps the cops had installed, the live oaks towering over the two-story apartment building cast eerie shadows. Like most of the apartment complexes in Suitcase City, this one was surrounded by a high security fence. The fence hadn't done any good.

"Okay," said the deputy, approaching him once again. Burkhardt, Quinn remembered suddenly. The guy's name was Burkhardt. "Sergeant Diaz says to go in. Keep your hands in your pockets, don't touch nothin', and don't use that camera until he tells you."

Quinn ducked under the tape and strode toward the door of the building, hands tucked in his pockets, for warmth as much as anything. Neighbors ringed the perimeter of yellow tape, watching silently like ghouls at a funeral. Christ, he hated gawkers.

The smell hit him in the face before he even stepped through the door, and he almost gagged. There was no mistaking the stench of a decaying corpse. Some of the cops inside wore masks, but he never had. He'd learned a long time ago that his nose became numbed to it in just a couple of minutes, and it was easier to work without a cumbersome gas mask. But, Christ, he'd almost forgotten how awful it could be. Automatically he started breathing through his mouth.

Every light in the apartment was on. Just inside the door was a small foyer, little more than a patch of tile marking the division between the kitchen and bathroom. To the rear was a living room, where crime-scene techs were examining objects and making notes.

A cop standing guard in the kitchen doorway pointed. "To the back and to the right. Diaz is waiting."

Old habits die hard, and Quinn found himself taking a mental inventory as he walked back through the living room. Cheap furniture, dime-store knickknacks, a frayed and tattered rug. At a glance, nothing out here appeared to have been disturbed except by the crime-scene techs, who were tagging and dusting everything.

He knew all of them, of course. Until six months ago, he had been one of them. Those who noticed him nodded, the way people nod to casual acquaintances they don't really want to speak to. He was an outsider now.

Diaz stood in the doorway of the bedroom, waiting for him. The man was small, dark, almost wiry, but with a presence that made up for his lack of height. Nobody messed with Diaz.

"Thanks for coming," Diaz said. Instead of shaking hands, he passed a pair of latex gloves to Quinn.

"I'm not part of this anymore, Rick. You know that."

Diaz shrugged, merely looking impatient. "Fuck, you're not part of it anymore. I think—" He broke off and dropped his voice. "I think I may have a serial here. Now pull on the damn gloves."

Quinn felt a chill trickle slowly down his spine. "How many?"

"Baby makes two."

"You're sure."

"Oh, yeah. C'mere." He drew Quinn away from the bedroom, where the victim was little more than an unspeakable shape on the bed, a shape that Quinn had avoided looking at. He noticed that Diaz wasn't looking that way, either.

Diaz led him over to a dinette in one corner of the living room. On the table were plastic and paper evidence envelopes. Diaz picked up one of them, a clear plastic bag that contained a four-by-five-inch piece of paper. The paper was creased from having been folded, and the corners were dog-eared, as if it had been handled quite a bit.

"We found a half dozen of these," Diaz said. "Basically all the same. Apparently she was saving them."

"Saving them?" He took the bag in his gloved hands and tilted it until the light no longer glared off the plastic. Typewritten words were dark against the paper.

You will be HIS. You will dance for THE PUPPETMASTER.

Detective Ray Matucek joined them. "Hey, Connor," he said with a nod. "How's civilian life?"

"It pays a little better."

Matucek laughed at that. His yellowed teeth always reminded Quinn of a rat's. "You gotta miss the excitement, though."

"That's the one thing I *don't* miss, Mattie. Who found her?"

"Girlfriend. The victim didn't come to work the last two nights—she worked over at one of the clubs on Dale Mabry. Dancer. Anyway, the friend got worried when she didn't answer her phone and didn't show at work. She came over, and the smell hit her before she even knocked on the door."

Quinn nodded, believing that without difficulty. "Sounds pretty straightforward. So what do you want with me?" But he knew. Deep in his gut, he knew, and he was hoping like hell that somebody had made a mistake, and that Rick Diaz hadn't twisted arms at the newspaper to get him over here. It was a vain hope, but he hoped it anyway.

"You know why," Diaz said flatly, his dark eyes hard, defying Quinn to argue. "I got two women dead. Maybe there's more and I just don't know it. This scene looks just like the last one, and there wasn't a damn bit of useful evidence at the last place. No DNA. No hair, no saliva, no semen, no blood except the victim's, no fingernail scrapings, no prints, nada. Unless he fucked up this time, all I got is a file full of shit and no idea how he's picking 'em or why, other than that they were both dancers."

Without a word, Quinn turned and walked out. Outside, he ducked under the tape and strode away into the darkness, leaving all of it behind, the dead woman, the troubled cops, and the curious ghouls who stood around hoping to see something appalling.

He knew he was going to do it, but he wanted a few minutes to try to argue himself out of it anyway. He wanted a few minutes away from the stench of death to let the cold air clear his head. Later, when his soul got dark and he started to feel as if he were lost in a bottomless well with nothing but death and horror for his constant companions, he wanted to be able to remind himself that he'd thought it through first. That he'd taken an opportunity to talk himself out of it. That he was doing it by choice.

"Connor?" Rick Diaz had followed him and stopped a few paces behind him. "You can't walk away from this. If you do, his victims are gonna be on your head."

"Come up with something original, why don't you?"

Diaz came to stand right beside him. "Okay, so you know that already. But time's wasting. The scene's already cold, and it's getting colder while you stand out here and indulge your goddamn angst, or whatever they call it these days. I'm keeping the techs out of the bedroom, so nothing's been touched, but I can't keep them out much longer. What's it gonna be?"

Diaz already knew the answer, Quinn thought as he stared up through the branches of the live oaks as if the smudged clouds in the night sky might contradict him. *He* already knew the answer, too. He knew it in the weight that had settled on his heart.

"I work for the newspaper," he said, holding out anyway.

"Understood. I told 'em you can use anything you learn *after* we catch the creep. Meantime, you get the scoop on new murders first."

Quinn began to understand why Ben Hyssop had been so adamant that he come out here and talk to Diaz. Everybody would get something out of this except him. All he'd get was some new nightmares.

Not that it mattered. Squaring his shoulders, he threw away the lifeline to sanity and turned around. "Let's get this shit taken care of," he said flatly, and strode back toward the apartment. Diaz was right on his heels.

With each step he took, Quinn felt himself leaving his newly constructed life behind. He became the hunter, and his nostrils seemed to flare as he scented his prey. Something was stalking the nights and killing for pleasure, and Quinn could not allow that to continue. But to catch his quarry, he would have to think like his quarry.

To slay the monster, he would have to become a monster.

God, how it sickened his soul.

The room in which Judy Eppinga had spent the last minutes of her life was a study in contradictions. A G-string and fuck-me high heels lay discarded in the corner next to a small dressing table. Cosmetic bottles, tubes and cases covered the scarred tabletop, scattered around a small plastic glow-in-the-dark cross.

Quinn hadn't seen one of those since he was a kid, and he remembered vividly how, at one time, he had desperately wanted one. Looking at it now, he wondered where the victim had come by it, and thought about what it said.

*Shoot the picture.* The urge seemed to spring from some deep corner of his mind, a prodding he could never ignore. Lifting his camera, he photographed the dressing table from a number of angles.

There was a picture of Jesus on the wall over the bed, in a frame so old that he figured it had to be an heirloom. The bed itself was little more than a cot. Not the kind of bed you would expect from someone who entertained male visitors regularly. Not that all exotic dancers were prostitutes.

He avoided looking at the remains. Any information that could still be taken from the body would have to be found by the medical examiner's office. Decomposition was too far advanced.

And as best he could, while he photographed the scene and studied every little nook and cranny, he tried not to think about what all this meant. He tried not to care that a woman had lost her life in some obscene ritual from a sick mind.

But he cared anyway, and he was going to care more by the time this was over. Sometimes he felt as if his soul were a mass of scars left by all the cases he'd worked on. By all the intimate knowledge he'd gathered of the victims.

Judy Eppinga was only a name right now, the name of a person who'd lived in a bad part of town in a small apartment surrounded by cheap furnishings and religious artifacts. Before long, she was going to be as real to him as his own family.

But so was the killer.

He moved around the room slowly and deliberately, noting every photo he took in his notebook, just as he had in the days when he worked crime scenes as a photographer. Just as he had in the days when he was a patrol cop, the first to arrive at scenes like this. He focused on the mechanics and refused to think about the reasons behind his actions.

*Shoot the picture.* The urge guided him, causing him to concentrate on the shoes neatly lined up on the floor of her closet. Squatting down, he tried to stay out of the light as he looked at the shoes—pumps, sandals, flats, of every description. Judy Eppinga had been fond of pretty shoes. One pair in particular caught his eye. Four-inch spike heels, with an ankle strap that had a black satin bow on it. She had probably worn those to work.

He took several pictures of the shoes, heeding an instinct he no longer questioned. Hanging in the closet above the shoes were clothes. Nothing very expensive or noteworthy, and certainly none of the lingerie he might have expected from a woman with her job.

Stepping back to the door, he took in the whole room, snapping photos. The place was surprisingly neat, he realized suddenly. Despite the violence that had occurred here a few days ago, the room looked almost pristine.

Maybe too neat?

He started snapping pictures of the room, feeling that there was something important in the neatness. No blood on the walls, or the floors. No arterial spray…

"How does he kill them?" he asked Diaz.

"The first one was exsanguination. He bled her to death. My guess is this one is probably the same."

No sign of a fight. That always blew him away, the way a killer could intimidate a victim into going to slaughter like a helpless lamb.

What did the guy do with all that blood?

Out in the living room, he looked around some more,

keeping in mind that things were no longer exactly the way they had been found. Someone else had taken the pictures out here, before the techs started cataloging and dusting, and he felt a twinge of regret at the opportunity lost.

He didn't see anything that seemed particularly significant. His guess was nothing had gone amiss until the killer and the victim were in the bedroom. Up until then it had probably seemed like...what? What had it seemed like? A date? A get-together with a friend? Helping out a pleasant stranger? Or had the killer broken in and come upon her while she was sleeping?

"Any sign of forced entry?" he asked Diaz.

Rick shook his head. "Not this time or last time. My guess is he conned his way in somehow."

Quinn nodded, already piecing bits together. A smooth-talker, maybe. Somebody who didn't look at all threatening. Probably very attractive. Somebody with a hang-up about blood.

He turned to one of the techs. "When you do the bedroom, check the shoes in the closet for prints, will you?"

Diaz looked sharply at him. *"What?"*

Quinn shook his head. "I don't know." He was turning away from the couch when he noticed the corner of a book just barely visible under the dust ruffle. "What's that?"

One of the techs, Bill Daley, bent over and looked. "A book."

"I can see it's a book. What book?"

Daley lifted the ruffle and peered under the couch. "Somebody give me a light."

A flashlight was pressed into his hand. He shined it under the couch. "Just a lot of books," he said.

"Can we move the couch?"

Daley looked at the other techs. "Yeah, sure," he said. "I guess it won't disturb anything now."

Together, he and another man lifted the couch and moved it away from the wall. In neat stacks, some dusty and others not, were college textbooks. Reaching down with a gloved hand, Connor picked up a copy of Swokowski's *Calculus with Analytic Geometry,* a standard math text in most colleges.

"She was more than a dancer," he said. "Was the last one a student?"

Diaz shook his head. "Not as far as I know."

"There's got to be some other connection between these women. Some similarity. Some reason these two were picked out of all the other exotic dancers."

"Damn it, do you think I don't know that?" Diaz caught himself. "Hell, they didn't even work at the same club."

"Both clubs on Dale Mabry?"

"Yeah."

Quinn nodded and returned his attention to the books. Judy Eppinga had been a serious student at some point in her short life. An exotic dancer with religious symbols in her bedroom and calculus books under her couch.

He took some more pictures, of the books, of the kitchen and the bathroom, and then he left the apartment once again, this time for good.

He didn't want to be confined right now, not even briefly. He wanted to smell fresh air and wash the stench of death out of his nose, mouth and lungs.

He walked away from them all, past his car, and kept on walking, letting the cold night wind slash at his cheeks and ears. It was bad enough to smell the death in that room, but he did more than smell it. In some strange way, he *felt* that woman's terror, as if she had left some kind of psychic impression on the atmosphere that he was able to sense.

And all he could do was try to walk away from it. Slough it off. Ignore it.

It was never that easy.

Finally, when his ears were so cold that his jaws ached, his legs so cold that every step painfully jarred the frozen skin on his thighs, he headed back to his car. The orange growers were going to suffer tonight, he guessed.

He thought of the plants on his patio and decided he'd better get home and bring them in. His next-door neighbor, an aging woman with long snow-white hair worn loose to her waist, had drawn him into gardening, first by asking him to help with hers when her arthritis flared up, and then by giving him his first two houseplants.

Now he had to worry about whether the damn geraniums and hibiscus would freeze tonight.

His concern for the plants, following so hard on the heels of the horror he had just witnessed, struck him as one of those incredible absurdities that somehow made life easier to take. By the time he got back to the car, his ears frozen, his jaws aching and his cheeks numb, he had shaken off the worst of the horror.

Back at his apartment in St. Petersburg, he carried the planters of geraniums into his living room and set them along the wall. As far as he could tell, they hadn't yet been damaged, and since it hadn't gone below freezing yet, they would probably make it. He hoped so. The last thing he wanted to feel like was a flower abuser.

He threw his clothes in the washer, then took a long, hot shower, washing off the death smells that still clung to him as if they had crawled into his very pores. The hot water felt good beating down on him, so good that he didn't get out until it cooled off.

His thoughts wouldn't leave him alone, though. They were bound and determined to wander down pathways he didn't care to explore. Like the night when he was sixteen and he got rip-roaring drunk with a bunch of his friends. To this day, he couldn't remember how he got home, but he could remember his father knocking him to the floor when he staggered through the door. And no sooner did he drag his thoughts away from that incident than he remembered the time his dad had kicked him down the stairs.

Pleasant stuff to be remembering in the middle of the night, when all he really wanted to do was sink into the forgetfulness of sleep. His brain was playing hide-and-seek, taking drastic measures to avoid thinking of what had happened to Judy Eppinga. If he lay down on his bed and closed his eyes, some horror was bound to be drawn out of the pit of his mind.

The major blessing of his apartment was a view of the sky above the bay. Tonight, high clouds caught the light from towns below and glowed faintly, giving a pinkish cast to the night.

He stood at his open balcony door for a long time, seeking solace from the sky and water, and failing to find it. A sailboat, almost invisible against the dark water, with its sails furled and only its running lights on, swept by in eerie silence. The only sound he could hear was the eternal lapping of the waves.

Finally, abandoning all hope of sleep, he closed the door and went to his office, where he turned on his computer. If there was one thing he could be certain of in this cold, empty world, it was that there would be another night owl out there somewhere he could chat with.

Katydid was on-line. As soon as he saw her handle pop up in answer to his query, he felt a little better. He had no idea who on earth she was, but he was coming to appreciate their exchanges by e-mail and on the public bulletin-board service. He was getting used to finding Katydid somewhere when he got on late at night, unable to sleep because some gruesome image was haunting him.

She said she had a job where she worked late, so he figured her for a waitress. Maybe even a student, although she seemed older than that, to judge by her conversation. It was interesting to speculate, but he had never asked personal questions. Nor had she asked any about him. It was as if the two of them wanted to remain ultimately anonymous, even as they shared some of their deepest feelings.

He queried her for a talk connection, and almost immediately his screen split in two and words appeared in the bottom half as she answered.

"Hi, CQ," she typed. "Long time no talk. Are you okay?"

"Fine," he replied. He had the worst urge to confide what he'd seen tonight and his dread of what was to come, but he kept silent. "Just had a rough photo shoot tonight."

"Crime?"

"What are you—psychic?"

Her response was a little slow in coming. "Just a good guess. I didn't think photographing the local quilting circle would be rough."

"Little do you know." He found himself smiling as he typed. "Those little old ladies can be tough."

"Don't I know it."

There was a pause, as if she had nothing further to say. He couldn't think of much to say himself. His mind seemed to be stubbornly full of images from Judy Eppinga's apartment, and he kept zeroing in on them, as if they were a fractured video playing over and over in his head. Even when he looked away from them, he was aware of them.

Cripes. He almost severed the talk connection, figuring there was no reason to monopolize Katydid this way if there was nothing he could say to her. She might as well be out there surfing, finding some amusement, rather than sitting at her computer staring at a blank screen, waiting for him to say something.

"CQ?" she typed suddenly. "Do you know anything about on-line stalking?"

His heart slammed suddenly. It was as if he were catapulted back to the Eppinga apartment, looking at that obscene note. "Stalking? What do you mean?"

"I keep getting e-mail from somebody who calls himself S.Talker. The notes make me uneasy."

"Threats?"

"No. He just—" The line broke off there, then resumed several seconds later. "I don't know how to explain it. I just don't like it. I don't reply, but he keeps writing anyway."

"Can you forward me one of the notes?"

"I deleted them all."

Another pause. Of course she'd deleted them all, Connor thought. It was the sensible thing to do. "Forward the next one to me. I'd like to see it."

The connection broke. Just like that, she was gone, and nothing he did would reconnect them.

And somehow, in his mind, Katydid and Judy Eppinga began to run together. Sitting alone in the dark and silence of the small hours of the morning, he wondered if reality had somehow torn its fabric, allowing demons to slip through.

# 2

Kathryn Devane watched Connor Quinn stride across the newsroom, and noticed how silent everyone became. As soon as he disappeared into Ben Hyssop's office, Mark Polanski said, loud enough for the whole room to hear, "There he goes, the ace reporter and number one kahuna."

Kate cringed inwardly. The newsroom hadn't stopped buzzing since Mark was knocked off the murder story and replaced by Connor, and nearly everyone was on Mark's side. Mark was the crime reporter, after all, and Connor was a photographer. Polanski had gone out to the murder scene last night when he heard the call on his police scanner, and ordinarily he would have been the one to write the story. But for some reason, Ben Hyssop, the managing editor, had decided otherwise.

"It's because he used to be a cop," Mark had said earlier. "He's probably got some inside track that Ben thinks is more important, but damn it, Quinn isn't a reporter. He couldn't write a story to save his life!"

Everyone agreed that if Hyssop was using Quinn because of his police connections, that was okay, but he shouldn't have taken Polanski off the story. Quinn, they all thought, should have been treated as a source for Polanski to use.

"Dirty dealings," Mark had said several times. "There's something so fishy here it stinks to high heaven."

More than once Kate had wanted to defend Connor, but she couldn't. Turning in her seat, she looked toward the glass-enclosed cubicle where Connor and Ben Hyssop were talking. Every time she saw Connor, she wished she could just call out, "Hi, I'm Katydid." But she didn't do it. She didn't want him to know who she was. Didn't want anyone to know about her secret persona, the woman who seemed not to have a care in the world as she joked her way through on-line discussions about writing. She felt too guilty about that carefree personality, as if she were somehow cheating even by pretending.

Ignoring the tension in the room around her, she tried to return her attention to the story she was editing. Her job required painstaking attention to detail, and she couldn't be mooning about nasty notes from on-line stalkers, newsroom politics, or what life might be like if she really *were* Katydid, instead of Kate Devane, copy editor and divorcée.

The divorcée part was a recent addition to her résumé, and she was far from comfortable with it, so uncomfortable that she still wore her wedding ring. Biting her lower lip, she corralled her thoughts and tried to figure out how to turn the six inches of useful material in front of her into the eight inches of copy she needed.

Around her, other editors worked, performing the same precision tasks, checking the information in stories for accuracy, correcting grammar, shortening or lengthening copy to fit where it was needed. Barring surprises, they would put the paper to bed tonight around eight.

The phone beside her desk rang, and she picked it up. "Devane."

"Kate, get in here, will you?"

She hated the way the managing editor, Ben Hyssop, never identified himself. When she first started working here, his calls had always sent her into a tizzy trying to figure out who he was. Now that she recognized his voice instantly, she didn't like it any better.

Ben's office was a glass-walled cubicle containing a desk, three chairs, and a cot that he used on those occasions when a hot story kept the newsroom busy overnight. Connor Quinn was still in the office with Ben, sitting on one of the chairs, with his arms folded across his chest as if he weren't happy with what he was hearing. His face, a striking blend of Native American and Irish, was as impassive as stone, but his blue eyes contained some emotion that she felt was probably better left unnamed.

"Kate," Hyssop said, looking at her over the top of his glasses. "Sit."

Kate hesitated, not wanting to obey the barked command, but not wanting to start a problem over it.

"She's not a dog, Ben," Connor said flatly.

Ben sighed and scratched his ear. "Would it be better if I said, 'Kate, sit down'? Huh?"

But Kate was already sitting, doing her best to avoid looking at Connor. This close to him, she felt unnerved.

"Close the damn door," Hyssop said.

Connor twisted around and shoved the door shut. The racket of the newsroom was suddenly far away.

"Okay," Ben said, looking at them in turn over the top of his glasses. "You," he said, stabbing a finger at

Kate, "are being exclusively assigned to edit a series of stories that Quinn here is going to be writing for us. Got it?"

"But—" The assignment was highly irregular, at least in the newsroom of the *Sentinel.* And the assignment of a copy editor to a story was usually made by the senior copy editor, Sally Dyer.

Ben read her mind. "I'll take care of Sally. The main thing is that Quinn isn't a reporter, he doesn't have any experience writing anything except police reports—which, if you'll excuse me for saying so, are prime examples of the worst writing ever to deform the English language."

In spite of herself, Kate felt a smile lifting the corners of her mouth. Even Connor looked faintly amused.

"So basically," Ben continued, "Quinn is going to give you a report, and you're going to make a story out of it."

"Why don't you just ask one of the reporters to write the story?" Kate asked him, thinking of Mark Polanski.

"Because a reporter might not stop with the info that Quinn gives him."

Kate stiffened, feeling the first twinges of excitement. "What's going on?"

Hyssop settled back in his chair. "I guess it would help if I explained. Quinn has an inside line with the sheriff's department on a series of murders that have been happening in Hillsborough County. In order to keep his line of communication open, we can't reveal any information the police are trying to keep quiet."

"Why would they keep any of it quiet?"

Quinn looked at her. "So that the real murderer can be identified by what he knows and the phony confessions can be weeded out. And to avoid copycats."

The word *copycat* shivered through Kate's awareness. All of a sudden she realized that when Ben Hyssop referred to a series of murders, he had meant a serial killer. Mark didn't know that. None of them had even guessed it. But it explained why Ben had put Connor on the story. "Oh, God."

Ben leaned forward. "Don't say it out loud, Kate. Not here, not anywhere. For right now, we're reporting them as unrelated killings."

"But why?"

Connor's eyes were bleak as he looked at her. "We don't want to pander to the guy's desire for fame, if he has one, and we don't want him to know we're on to him yet."

*We.* Quinn was talking as if he were one of the cops. She wondered just how involved he was in this case. "Okay, I can keep my mouth shut, but sooner or later it's going to come out."

"When it does, it does," Quinn said with a shrug.

"Look," Hyssop interjected, "this isn't an editorial meeting to discuss strategy on this story. The paper has already agreed to certain restrictions in exchange for inside information. Quinn'll give you what's allowed, Devane, and you'll write the story. Speaking of which..." He tossed a computer disk onto the desk and pointed to it. "That's today's copy. Fix it up. It's going on 1-B."

Without missing a beat, he punched the intercom button on his phone. "Sally, get in here. We're making a change to the front page of section B." He released the button without waiting for Sally Dyer's response. "Kate, after you've read over Quinn's report, get back to me on how many inches you think you can get out of it. We'll have to clear something else out."

As they started to rise, he stopped them. "One other

thing. I want the story under Quinn's byline. Damned if I'll have a woman's name on a story about a killer who's stalking women. Take me to the EEOC if you want."

Kate shook her head. "I assumed from the start it would be Connor's byline. I'm just an editor."

"Just an editor. Ha!" Ben snorted, looking as if he couldn't make up his mind whether to give her hell or laugh. He settled on a scowl. "Get the hell out of here."

Kate nodded and followed Connor Quinn out the door. He stood there and looked at her for a minute while Sally Dyer brushed past them with an inquisitive look. Only when Hyssop's door closed behind Sally did he speak.

"I'll hang around awhile in case you've got any questions," he said. "I'll be in the photo lab."

She nodded and watched him walk away, thinking that there was more to this than that he simply had a good source in the sheriff's department. But it was none of her business, and she'd just been given strict orders not to look past whatever Connor Quinn chose to give her. Without a good reason to do otherwise, she would do as she'd been told.

Back at her desk, she hurriedly finished the intern's article, then gave her attention to reading Quinn's report. Hyssop was right; it was pretty much like a police report. Utterly devoid of feeling, it gave the bald, bare facts. It did, however, give some details that only an artistic eye would have picked out, such as the antique frame on the painting of Jesus over the victim's bed.

Looking up, Kate stared blindly at her monitor when she realized that Quinn had actually visited the scene. He had actually been there, been inside, where no one but the police and medical examiners were ever allowed to go. How had he managed that? Was it just because he used to be a cop?

But she couldn't ask him without disobeying Hyssop's injunction, and she wasn't prepared to do that. Not yet.

By six o'clock, she had pulled over ten inches of copy out of Quinn's report, then cut it back to nine to fit the space being vacated by a story about pollution-cleanup efforts.

Sally Dyer came to look over her shoulder. "Almost done, Devane?" Sally insisted on calling everyone by their last names. "It beats the hell out of me why Hyssop couldn't have arranged to run this damn story earlier and saved me all the trouble of having to yank the pollution story. Hell, they found the body last night! It was old news by the time he decided to run it."

Kate didn't say anything, merely saved the story, then plugged it into its position on the page layout. The headline she had composed ran three lines in the single column: No Leads In Dancer's Death.

Sally sniffed. "You'd think these girls would have second thoughts about dancing in those clubs. Christ, going into combat couldn't be much more dangerous."

"It seems that way sometimes," Kate agreed.

"Seems that way?" Sally sniffed again. "It wasn't that long ago we had that serial killer over in Clearwater, remember? The one who went after prostitutes. Only nobody gets upset when these guys pick on prostitutes. And take Bobby Joe Long. He went after exotic dancers, too. It's almost like they know nobody will care enough to really look hard for them."

"That's probably more of a comment on society than on the killers," Kate replied. Her fingers were stiff on the keyboard as she wondered why Sally was talking about serial killers. Had Hyssop said something to her?

"Mark my words, Devane," Sally said, tapping the

monitor screen with the eraser of her pencil, "this is going to turn out to be some creep who preys on these women. Hell, she's probably not even the first one he killed."

Kate found herself wondering wildly how to reply without lying or giving away something she wasn't supposed to. But Sally didn't wait for an answer.

"Finish up the story about the governor's clemency board and then call yourself done for the day. I can take care of the rest."

Which was Sally's way of reasserting control of the copydesk after Ben Hyssop's invasion earlier. Kate smiled and nodded agreeably, wondering what the hell she was going to do with the extra time this evening. It seemed like she spent most of her life now trying to avoid having time on her hands.

"So you're editing Quinn's story."

Kate looked up and wanted to groan when she saw Mark Polanski standing behind her. Not that she disliked Mark. He was actually a pretty decent person, and a damn good reporter. She just didn't want to get into a tussle about things over which she had no control. She hit a key, saving the story and taking it off the screen. "Yes," she said, volunteering nothing more.

"So tell me, Kate, why are they making extra work for you, when I could do the job better and save you time?"

Kate looked straight at him. "You'll have to ask Ben."

"I *already* asked Ben. He didn't tell me a damn thing."

"What makes you think he told me any more?"

"Because he asked you to do the scut work on this. I want to know why."

"You'll have to ask *him,*" Kate said again, taking the sting out of the words with a smile. "I know you're angry about this, Mark, but I'm as caught in the middle as you are."

He nodded reluctantly. "I just don't think there should be secrets in a newsroom."

"There probably won't be on this, either, not for long."

"Not if I can help it. I mean, what's with this Quinn guy? He's only been here six months. I'll grant you, he's good enough as a photographer, but nobody could mistake him for a reporter."

"Really?" Kate felt her smile stiffening. "I always thought reporters and cops did the same kind of work—investigating."

"Not exactly. Reporters try to uncover the truth. Cops try to make a case against the likeliest suspect."

Kate shook her head. "Reporters are just as likely to go for the obvious as anyone else. You forget, I edit their stories."

"So...what's Quinn done to get on your good side?"

"What do you mean?"

Mark's gaze flickered down to the wedding band on her left hand. "You seem to be defending him."

Kate wanted to slap him, but she restrained herself. "Don't be disgusting, Mark. All I'm trying to do is stay out of politics I have no control over."

He looked down at her for a long moment, then shrugged and nodded. "Okay."

Kate watched him walk away, wondering uneasily if she'd said anything wrong. The last thing she wanted to get involved in was office politics. Her life was already complicated enough.

Her work was done for the day, but it felt odd to be

leaving while the newsroom was still so busy. She snatched up her jacket and purse, nodded to people she passed and took the stairs down to the ground floor.

Darkness had fallen, and the streets of St. Petersburg were already quieting down for the evening. Despite its size, the city felt like a small town. And, at heart, it was.

Since she was out so early, she decided to treat herself to dinner at a small Italian restaurant up the street. It was only a block and a half, and she had never felt unsafe on the streets of St. Pete.

Until this evening. She told herself it was ridiculous to let the story she had just written unnerve her, but by the time she was halfway down the next block, she was battling a compulsive urge to look over her shoulder.

Nerves. Just nerves. Nerves, and the presence of a serial killer across the bay. Nerves, and the nasty notes she was receiving on-line. She tried to ignore it all, but it was a relief when she at last stepped into the cozy little restaurant.

Here everything was warm and friendly, the lamplight golden and inviting. At lunch, the atmosphere was more businesslike and the tables were bare. In the evening, snowy-white cloths covered the tables, and vases held red carnations. She felt conspicuously solitary amid the dining couples and groups. It was another feeling of emptiness she would have to get used to.

The waiter had the sensitivity to put her in a corner, so that she didn't feel as if she were on display. It was ridiculous, she knew it was ridiculous, but there it was. Through most of the years of her marriage she had been alone, so she couldn't understand why the divorce had suddenly made her so conscious of it.

She ordered fettuccine with clam sauce and a small antipasto, and tried not to remember how much Michael had loved garlic bread. God, this was awful. She'd better hit the bookstore on the way home, or she would spend all evening being maudlin, and there was no point in it. No point at all.

Nothing could be changed, she thought, running her finger down the side of her water glass. That was the most awful part of life: Nothing could be changed.

Connor Quinn was on his way to his car when he saw Kathryn Devane hurrying down the sidewalk, away from the *Sentinel* building. To his way of thinking, she was a hard woman to ignore. There was something so…refined about her, some kind of elegance he couldn't quite put his finger on. Even when she came to work in jeans, she managed to seem elegant.

Tonight she was wearing a dress and was hunkered in her jacket against the chilly wind that was blowing from inland. Something about the way she moved disturbed him, and he wondered what was wrong. Was someone following her?

He scanned the streets swiftly, but saw nothing out of place, no one who appeared to be following her. He had been a street cop for a long time, though, and his instincts were kicking into overdrive. Kate Devane was hurrying as if she thought someone were following, and he wasn't prepared to dismiss that.

Instead, he followed her on the far side of the street, and when she darted into the restaurant, he waited to see if anyone followed her in. No one did.

The night wind grew colder, and the streets emptied of life as people accustomed to a warmer climate hid from the bitter bite. An occasional car passed down the street, but as quiet as it had become, it might have been after midnight, not seven-thirty in the evening.

Quinn stood there a while longer, feeling his earlobes grow numb, telling himself to just go home and spend the evening studying the photos he had taken last night. But some kind of uneasiness held him where he was, irritating him with the sense that there was something wrong.

Finally he decided to quit being an ass and crossed the street to enter the restaurant. He might as well have dinner while he assuaged his uneasiness by keeping an eye on Kate.

As he stepped inside, she was the first person he saw. She was sitting in a far corner, head bowed in thought, and he was suddenly struck by how sad she looked. There was something about the tilt of her head and the slender line of her neck beneath her chignon that spoke of sorrow and strength.

He wanted to take her picture. His camera was, as always, in the case hanging from his shoulder, and he was tempted. But it would have been such an invasion of her privacy, one he couldn't justify in any way. As a cop, and now a news photographer, he had learned to ignore the privacy of others, but this time he just couldn't do it. Something about the set of her head made her seem so defenseless....

He shook himself and started across the room. His Irish and American Indian blood had combined their mystical streaks in him to a degree that sometimes seemed almost psychic. Occasionally he saw that mystical bent as a blessing, but mostly he saw it as a curse. Except for it, Rick Diaz would never have dragged him into this case. Without it, he wouldn't have recognized what a sad and nearly disheartened woman Kate Devane was. He could have done without all of it.

"Mind if I join you?"

She lifted her head slowly, and in the moment their eyes met, he felt something, a subtle shift, as if the pressure in the room had changed. Something flickered in her gaze, then was gone. She smiled.

"Sure. I'd enjoy the company."

He took the chair across from her. A waiter appeared instantly with a menu and a glass of water. "What do you recommend?" he asked Kate.

"Anything on the menu is delicious. Their marinara sauce is one of the best I've ever tasted."

"Is that what you're having?"

She shook her head. "Linguine with clam sauce."

"That sounds good, too." He made a pretense of studying the menu, then looked up at the waiter. "Spaghetti with marinara sauce and shredded Parmesan, please."

He looked at Kate again and realized she was still regarding him with that slightly startled, slightly frightened look. He was well aware that he intimidated some women with his size and exotic appearance, but Kate had never appeared intimidated before. "Do I frighten you?"

She blinked. "I... No. Of course not. Why do you ask?"

"Because you look scared. What's wrong? Do you want me to leave?"

"Of course not!" She shook her head and frowned at him. "Why are you attacking me?"

"I'm not. I'm being blunt and trying to figure out if I'm making you uncomfortable by joining you. If I am, I'll move to another table."

She tilted her head, mouth slightly open, staring at him as if she couldn't quite believe him. "Did you learn this conversational technique as a cop?"

He gave in and smiled faintly. "Guess so."

"Well, you're not intimidating me."

"Good." He sat back and regarded her steadily. "I saw you hurrying up the street. It looked like you thought someone was following you."

She looked faintly embarrassed and shrugged one shoulder. "I just got uneasy. I don't know why. I'm not usually skittish." *Not until I started getting e-mails from someone who claims to know everything I'm doing.* She wanted to confide all of that to Connor right now, but she didn't dare. As long as she kept their acquaintance in its proper place, she wouldn't be cheating on Michael. And, divorced or not, she didn't want to cheat on Michael. It was bad enough that she'd had to abandon him.

Another wave of sadness washed through her, and she looked down at the tablecloth. Both her hands lay on the snowy linen, flattened as if she were getting ready to get up. On her left hand, the diamond-encrusted gold band gleamed.

Connor pointed to it. "Why isn't your husband taking you out to dinner?"

Kate's heart slammed, and she compressed her lips, trying to decide whether to equivocate or just blurt out the truth. But who would understand the truth? She wasn't sure she understood it herself. How could she consider herself so completely married to someone she had divorced?

Suppressing a sigh, she looked up and tried to marshal an answer.

"Sorry," he said before she could speak. "It isn't any of my business."

"My husband is sick," she said finally. "Very ill."

Just then, their dinners arrived. Kate leaned back gratefully, relieved that the distraction kept her from feeling the need to explain any further. Usually, when she explained, people backed away as rapidly as they politely could. For some reason, she didn't want Connor Quinn to back away like that. The thought filled her with guilt.

"You're right," he told her after his first mouthful of spaghetti. "This sauce is the best I've ever had." After a moment, he asked, "Do you mind having to write stories that go under my byline?"

Kate shook her head. "It's basically what I do all the time. There's more than one reporter in the newsroom who's great at getting a story but can't write worth a damn."

"Well, I wouldn't blame you if you wanted your name on the articles—although I think Ben is right that it could be dangerous."

"I don't really get that part."

"All we know about this guy is that he probably fits at least part of the serial killer profile. He's probably compulsive, engages in ritualistic behavior, often has brain damage, and feels both powerless and inadequate. The thing he's trying to achieve most from these killings is control. There are other characteristics, of course, but there's no way to know which apply to this guy. The ones I gave you are pretty standard across the board."

Kate nodded, fascinated almost in spite of herself. While she was more familiar than most people with the delusions of mental illness, she couldn't begin to imagine how the mind of a serial murderer must function.

"Otherwise," Quinn continued, "we're blind here. The two women were apparently slightly similar in appearance—but I can't go into that right now. Besides, what I want to get at here is really this—since we don't know exactly how he picks his victims, we can't tell anybody how to stay safe. Meaning you. If you were to put your name on these articles about him, you'd undoubtedly draw his attention. A lot of these types follow their own press very carefully, and you wouldn't want him to be following you. Not for any reason. Once you attract his attention, it would be too easy to do the thing that sets him off."

"And since we don't know what that thing is..." She trailed off, comprehending perfectly.

He nodded. "So a man's name goes on the articles."

"What if he fixates on you?"

He shrugged. "I'm better able to deal with him than you would be. I've had training."

Kate put her fork down and sat back in her chair, her appetite gone. "So there are only two victims? Can you really be sure they were killed by the same person?"

"Only two we know of so far. And yes, there are aspects that are too similar to be coincidence."

A shudder passed through her. "It's awful to think he might be out there stalking someone right now. Awful."

He looked at her but didn't say anything. What could he say? The son of a bitch probably *was* out there right now, stalking someone. Someone who didn't know that she had only a few days or hours left.

All of a sudden he was impatient to get home and get at the photos he'd developed earlier. Impatient to get over to the station and see what Rick had left for him in the way of reports on the two victims. Impatient to get started on finding this creep.

He didn't want to do this, resented the emotional violence this was going to inflict on him, but he couldn't stand the thought that another woman might die while he sat here eating Italian food with Kate Devane.

The shift in him was sudden and sharp, shaking him

out of the reluctance that had been causing his step to drag all day.

And just as suddenly, he had an urgent need to get to his computer and see if Katydid had yet replied to the e-mail he'd sent this morning, when their connection was severed. He'd logged on several times from the office today, but she hadn't replied. Maybe by now she had.

Christ, what if this guy wasn't stalking them in the streets? What if he was stalking them on-line? The Epinga woman had been a student; she'd had access to e-mail through the university. What if that was how he was picking them?

He noticed that Kate wasn't eating, either, and had pushed her plate to one side.

"Come on," he said abruptly. "I'll walk you to your car."

It was as if a clean, cold wind had blown through his head, clearing it of a pervasive fog. With its glacial breath, it hardened his resolve to ice.

Nothing mattered except finding the killer.

# 3

His dream had been true. With trembling hands he cut the article out of the paper, then smoothed it on the table in front of him. He had almost missed it; he couldn't understand why it hadn't been on the front page, standing out like a beacon of warning to other women. Why had they buried it in the second section?

That offended him, for some reason, but he couldn't think about it, not right now. His headache was getting worse, much worse, and if it didn't stop, he would go to the emergency room later to get a shot.

For now, he popped another handful of aspirin and washed it down with whiskey. He had to stop this drinking. Drinking always made things worse. It made the dreams more vivid, and made them happen more often. If God had any mercy at all, he would take away this cursed second sight.

His mother had tried to beat it out of him many times, calling it the devil's gift, but no matter how hard she beat him or how hard he tried to stop the dreams, they came anyway.

He knew things that other people didn't know. He saw

things they didn't see. And he couldn't make them believe him when he tried to warn them.

But that woman he'd seen in his dream last night...somehow he had to find her and tell her that a killer was stalking her. He couldn't make her believe him, of course, but he could at least try. If he tried, maybe he wouldn't have the dream about her death. Maybe God would pity him enough to spare him that.

His hands were trembling worse now, and he looked down at the article before him. He needed to add it to the others he kept as proof that his dreams were real.

He wanted to rise, but somehow he couldn't make his body obey him. Connor Quinn. His gaze suddenly fixed on the byline. Connor Quinn. Maybe he should talk to this reporter about his dreams. Maybe this Quinn would believe him.

But right now he had to get up. At last making his legs obey, he carried the article into his small bedroom and tucked it in the bureau drawer with the others. There were many others. Too many. There was one from South Carolina, where he used to visit family. Two from Miami, where he went to conferences. One from Jacksonville, where he went on vacation.

Then he reached for the Roman collar he wore to remind his growing flock that he was their spiritual leader. In a few minutes, they would all be gathered in the small concrete church next door, and he would give them their Wednesday-evening prayers and sermon. He had no idea what he was going to talk about, but he never doubted that he would open the Bible to some verse that would give him guidance.

The Bible always guided him in everything he did. God always showed him the way, which was why he and his flock were going out to the strip joints and bars on North Dale Mabry after the service to try to get the sinners to repent. God willing, while he was there he would see the woman he needed to save.

And, God willing, she would believe his warning.

"I'm okay," read the message on Quinn's computer screen. "Sorry about my abrupt disconnect last night. The power went out and didn't come back on for nearly an hour. By then I figured you'd gone to bed, so I didn't even log back on.

"As for this stalker…I don't know, CQ. I'm probably making a whole lot more of it than I need to. There's no way the guy could really find me…."

Connor leaned back in his chair and stared out the window beside him. It was still cold out there, and the coldness gave a crystalline clarity to the night sky. His gaze drifted back toward his computer, and as it did, it trailed across the photographs he had taken last night, and across the photos Rick Diaz had given him of the other murder scene.

It was not only a cold night, he found himself thinking. It was a cold world.

Hitting the reply key, he began to write a message to Katydid. Over the past few weeks, they had built an imaginary hideaway where they met in their e-mails, a place of sea, sand and sky, where they had a bungalow right near the water, and a porch swing on which to relax in the evenings while they chatted. She had added the blue heron at the water's edge sometime last week, and he had given them an orange tabby named Tigret. They often sipped glasses of wine and unwound together in a place far beyond the reach of other mortals. It was a pleasant conceit, but he found himself depending on it in the strangest way.

"The waves are quiet tonight," he wrote to her now. "Gently lapping at the shore's edge. The heron flies overhead, crying harshly as it comes to fish for the evening. Tigret is curled in your lap, and I ask if you would like a glass of wine. You nod and smile, and your eyes are as bright as the stars overhead...."

It wasn't even that they shared a whole lot about themselves; it was that they shared a mood. Most of what they had written was descriptions of sitting together on a porch swing and watching the changing moods of sea and sky. It should have been boring, but somehow it wasn't. Somehow it was as relaxing as it would have been to sit there for real. Neither of them was demanding a thing of the other, beyond desultory chat about the weather, the sea, the cat and the gulls.

Escape. It had become an escape where his mind could find refuge at the drop of the hat.

But when he hit the send key, he was cast back into his apartment in St. Petersburg in the dead of a cold, cold night, with only hideous photographs and police files for company.

For a little while he sat, doing nothing, reluctant to get back to the task at hand but aware that each passing minute counted. When he got up finally, it was to go make a fresh pot of coffee. Then he tacked the pictures to his walls and spread the photocopied pages of the police and medical examiner's reports around his worktable, organizing them by victim and type of report.

The first victim hadn't been as badly decomposed as Judy Eppinga. Cause of death appeared to be exsanguination. The victim had been bound with nylon ropes at her wrists and ankles. There was evidence of abrasion and contusion from the ropes, as well as unexplained abrasions of the knees, which contained fibers from the rug in her apartment. There was a ligature mark around her throat, but lack of damage to the hyoid bone suggested she hadn't been strangled. An assortment of other bruises suggested she had been struck a number of times.

But what was conspicuously lacking was the horrible torture and mutilation of which so many serial killers were guilty. Either this guy was different, or he was just getting started and hadn't fully evolved his ritual and fantasy. Or perhaps something had just gone wrong in this instance, something that had made him end it sooner than intended.

At this point they couldn't do much except guess, and Quinn seriously doubted the M.E.'s report on Judy Eppinga was going to be a whole lot more informative, given the state of decomposition.

Having gleaned as much as he could from the medical reports, he scanned the police reports, looking for anything that leaped out at him as being unusual. Rick Diaz had written the report, and Rick knew what he was looking for.

"Organized killer," he had written. "Appears planned well in advance. Nothing is disordered, no sign of struggle, no weapon found." On a self-sticking note, he had added a message to Quinn elaborating on his remarks. "Had this gut feeling at the scene," he had scrawled. "Something about the way it looked. I was sure this wasn't the last one we were going to see. Can you pick it up from the pix?"

Quinn reached for the photos from the first scene, skipping over the pictures of the victim. He had already reviewed them in detail, and somehow he felt the bodies weren't going to give away the killer.

The crime-scene photographer had been a good one and had taken photos of the entire apartment where the murder had occurred. A couple of times he wished the guy had zoomed in closer, but by and large it was all there: the neatly ordered dressing table; the dancer's costume hanging on the doorknob of the closet; the spiked heels lying on their side....

Reaching out, he grabbed a magnifying glass and held it over the photo of the shoes. Black four-inch heels with an ankle strap. Dancer's shoes, the kind that would stay on the feet. Not surprising that both victims had owned some, not when you considered that they were both dancers. He stared at them anyway and finally tacked them to the wall beside a shot of Judy Eppinga's shoes. They were different but the same, and right now he couldn't afford to overlook any similarities.

But finally he had looked all he could and he hadn't found what Diaz had hinted at. His brain was buzzing in circles, hunting answers he didn't have. He grabbed his jacket and headed out, not caring where he went, knowing only that he had to go.

When he found himself crossing the Howard Frankland Bridge over Tampa Bay, he figured he was heading back to the murder scene. Kind of pointless at midnight. Nobody would be there to let him in. Hell. He picked up his cellular phone and punched in Rick Diaz's home number.

"What's up?" Rick asked him. "You hit on something?"

"Not really. If I go up to the Eppinga place, can somebody let me in?"

"I can arrange it. When are you going to be there?"

Connor glanced at the digital clock on the dashboard. "Both these girls worked at clubs on North Dale Mabry, didn't they?"

"Yeah."

"I think I want to cruise past there first. I'll be at Eppinga's around...two."

"You got it. By the way, she apparently didn't pay her utility bill last month. The power's been cut."

"I've got a flashlight."

"All right, then. Two o'clock."

As he drove, the bay was a dark vastness beside him, strung with the lights of the Gandy Bridge to his right and the city lights of Tampa before him. The speed limit was sixty-five, and he was pushing near seventy, but car after car passed him in a rush. Where was a cop when you needed one? he wondered almost wryly, then grinned into the darkness as he saw the familiar flicker of blue and red lights ahead. Got one.

North of I-275, Dale Mabry was wide, a major artery that carried heavy traffic most of the day. Even at midnight it was busy, with traffic moving on and off 275 for gas and lodging, and with people coming and going from the cluster of strip bars. Those businesses had clustered here because it was about the only place far enough from schools, churches, day-care centers and homes to be legal under local ordinance.

He pulled into the parking lot of one of them, a place called Sweet Nights. Nothing looked out of the ordinary, but he wasn't expecting anything to jump out at him. A handful of people milled around; music could be heard from inside, growing louder every time someone opened the door. A patrol car cruised by, slowing down as the cop inside scanned the lot for signs of trouble.

It was a Wednesday night, though, and the crowds weren't that big. Inside, the place appeared to be half-deserted. A half-dozen women in various stages of nudity gyrated suggestively around the room, leaning over the tables of patrons who had tipped them. One dancer stood on the center stage, little more than a raised platform, where she danced and looked bored out of her mind. Her audience looked more drunk than aroused.

Quinn went to the bar and ordered a beer he had no intention of drinking. When it came, he clamped his hand around the mug but never lifted it. He surveyed the dancers, seeking any resemblance to the dead women.

"Hi, sugar. Buy me a drink?"

One of the bar rats climbed onto a stool beside him and smiled, crooked teeth showing between scarlet lips. She leaned toward him, taking care to give him a view of the cleavage bulging out of the skintight red dress she wore.

"Sure," he said, crooking his index finger at the bartender. "If you'll talk to me."

She smiled again. "Talk is cheap."

"Talk is all I want."

"Dirty or rough?"

"Informative." The bartender had come over to them. "Give the lady whatever she wants."

The "lady" decided to get what she could. "Jack Daniels, neat."

Quinn leaned his elbow on the bar and waited.

"You a cop?"

"Not anymore."

She stared at him, her dark eyes intense, measuring him. He would never know what made her decide. "Okay. Whatever."

"Did you know Judy Eppinga?"

"The girl that got murdered?" She shrugged. "No. She worked at After Midnight, didn't she?"

He nodded.

"I saw it in the paper today. They didn't find her body

for days.'' She shuddered. ''That's the worst thing, you know? To think of worms crawling all over your body...'' She lifted the shot glass and downed it. ''Another one?''

''Sure.'' He waited while the bartender refilled the shot glass. ''So you haven't heard anything about what happened?''

''You *are* a cop.''

Quinn shook his head again. ''No.''

''Reporter?''

He cocked his head, considering. Would it hurt anything if word got around? ''Don't tell anybody.''

She put a finger to his lips. ''Sealed. Like the grave.'' She shuddered again and gave a nervous laugh. ''God, I got a case of the creeps! I can't stop thinking about worms. What happened to her?''

''She was killed.''

''I *know* that. It wasn't a boyfriend?''

''Doesn't look that way.''

''So it was a john.'' The woman shook her head. ''I earn my money, you know that? People think it's easy money, but it's not. Creeps pick on us all the time. You never know what's going to happen when you get in a car.''

''It's tough,'' Quinn agreed.

She gave him a crooked smile. ''Like you mean that. So...you want me to get in touch if I hear anything about this girl— What's her name?''

''Judy Eppinga.'' He pulled one of his business cards out of his pocket and passed it to her. ''Or if you run across any john who seems...'' He hesitated, not wanting to put ideas in her head.

''If one gives me the creeps, I'll let you know.'' She shook her head and tucked the card into her bra. ''Not all the dancers sleep around, y'know. Some guys think they all do it for money, but a lot of 'em don't. They just dance. Maybe the guy killed her because she *wouldn't* put out, y'know?"

"Anything's possible."

She laughed at that, then tossed back her Jack Daniels. The look she gave him from the corner of her eye was a definite come-on. "You ever want any, you come look me up, hear?"

She was the last thing on earth he would ever want. When she walked away, he resumed his study of the bar's patrons, looking for something. Anything. Wasted effort.

By one-thirty he'd gone through them all and talked to a couple more bar rats. The dancers were harder to get to, unless he offered them a twenty. Then they would stand at his table, wiggle obscenely and give him bored answers to his questions. It was a great way to go broke, he figured. A couple of them were willing enough to talk when they took their breaks. Only one of them had known Judy. Her name was Doreen.

"Christ, she was just a kid," Doreen told him, taking a deep drag on a brown cigarette. They were standing together in the back lot behind the building, away from the noise. She needed the chilly night air, she'd told him, and wished it got cold here more often. She got too hot dancing, and it was nice to come out here and cool down. It was cold enough out here to do that and more, he thought. She'd barely stopped to pull on a sweater.

"College student, wasn't she?" he asked her.

She nodded and flicked away an ash. "She was gonna graduate in May and be an accountant. Can you believe it?"

"Why'd she dance?"

"To make money." Doreen shook her head. "It's just a job. Just a damn job. Guys'll pay a lot of money to see a naked lady. Why shouldn't a woman take advantage of it? Everybody gets so high-and-mighty about it, but those guys sitting out there are paying good money just to watch me wiggle what nature gave me. I get a couple hundred in tips on a good Friday night. There aren't many places I could do that."

"There sure aren't."

"So she danced, and she didn't have to borrow a whole lot of money to pay for school—if she had to borrow any at all. There's a couple of girls out here who do the same."

"Did she do anything on the side?"

"Nope." Doreen puffed on her cigarette and shook her head emphatically. "She didn't fool around with the customers. Not ever. A couple of 'em complained about it, I guess, but hey, it's her choice, y'know? Over at Breezie's they push the girls to put out, but most of the clubs don't do that. Usually. It'd get them into too much trouble."

Quinn nodded; the local authorities would love an excuse to shut these places down. They'd been trying for years to craft a law that would accomplish it, but so far they hadn't been able to come up with one that would pass the test in court. "You haven't seen anyone or anything unusual?"

Doreen chuckled. "Around here? Everything's unusual. Just look around you. We get every kind of guy from creeps to CEOs. Lately we've had a church group hanging around trying to get all us sinners to repent. It's private property, though, so they usually get run back to the edge of the road, and they don't stay too long."

"And nothing else?"

She tossed away her cigarette and pulled the sweater tighter around her. "What else do you want? These guys who kill us, they always seem so damn normal. The kind of guy you wouldn't hesitate to take home. Hell, if he looked like a killer, nobody'd talk to him."

"So you never heard Judy say she was seeing anyone?"

"Nope. I don't think she dated much. She complained once that the minute she dated a guy, he wanted her to give up dancing." Denise laughed harshly. "Yeah. Right. As if he's gonna pay the bills for her. Listen, I gotta get back inside and drink some water before my next set. You might go talk to Xena over at After Midnight. She's a student, too. She might've known Judy."

"Thanks."

He'd already been to After Midnight, but he decided to go back and ask about Xena. She wasn't on tonight, the manager said, and he wasn't going to give out her address or phone number. Nor would he even say when she was going to be dancing again.

"I read about that dancer in the paper," he said flatly. "As far as this place is concerned, our girls don't have addresses, phone numbers or schedules. Got it?"

"Got it." Connor handed the guy one of his cards, along with a twenty-dollar bill. "Please give her this. She can call if she wants. I'd like to talk to her about Judy."

The man hesitated for a couple of seconds, then shoved both card and money into his vest pocket. "I'll give her the card. I'm not promising anything else."

"Fair enough."

When he stepped outside again, it felt as if the temperature had dropped another five or ten degrees. He figured it probably couldn't have, and his body was just reacting to the late hour, but he sure as hell wished he'd splurged on a really heavy jacket, instead of talking himself out of it because he wouldn't be able to wear it but a couple of times a year.

Dale Mabry had pretty much quieted down. The parking lots of the clubs were almost empty; the only moving car in sight turned into a gas station up the street.

The traffic lights were with him, and it didn't take long to reach the Eppinga apartment. Police tape no longer blocked off the area around the door and sidewalk, but it stretched across the front door in a big yellow X. As he approached, the door of a nearby car opened, and Rick Diaz climbed out.

Together, they walked up to the door.

"Sorry to drag you out of bed," Quinn said.

"Who was sleeping?"

"You could have sent somebody else, or told me to wait."

Rick shook his head as he pulled the tape back and unlocked the door. "I don't want any problems with the chain of evidence. If you find something, I'm going to damn well be here to testify to it."

Rick had brought a battery-powered floodlight that accomplished far more than Connor's eight-cell flashlight, but the light was still lousy. Not that he was really interested in what he saw. He was far more interested in what he felt.

Motioning to Diaz to stand aside, he stepped into the apartment, feeling the walls close around him. The sounds changed instantly, the sigh of the wind and the rustle of the leaves becoming muffled and distant. The apartment still smelled like death, and probably would until the carpet was replaced and the walls and ceilings were painted.

It hadn't smelled like death the night she brought a killer home with her. And Connor didn't have a doubt that she had willingly brought the man home with her. She might not have been in the habit of sleeping with the customers, but maybe this time she had broken her rule. Maybe the guy had just been really nice and personable. Or maybe she'd gotten to know him a little and thought of him as a friend. Maybe he *was* a friend.

Closing his eyes, he stood in the middle of the living room and tried to imagine it. She had worked that night, and nobody had seen her bring anyone home, so it must have been very late. Her car had been discovered in the apartment building's lot, so she had driven herself home. "Did you find anything in her car?"

"No." Rick leaned a shoulder against the wall. "Forensics was all over it today. Nothing that couldn't be traced back to her."

"So he drove his own vehicle."

"Or walked. Or maybe he lived next door."

Connor shook his head. "No. He's too smart to pick a victim he could be easily associated with."

"A lot of these guys want to get caught."

"Not this one. Not yet." He waved a hand, indicating the apartment. "The scene is too organized. He's not dropping any clues yet."

Diaz sighed. "So what are we doing here at two in the morning?"

Connor didn't answer. Instead, he closed his eyes again and let his impressions slowly gel. She'd brought the guy home with her. Either she'd thought he was a really nice person, or she'd felt sorry for him. Ted Bundy had made women feel sorry for him by wearing a cast. Hell, Ted Bundy had worked for a crisis hot line. John Wayne Gacy had been a pillar of his community. The guy they were looking for here might be a news anchor, a member of the city council, a prominent doctor or lawyer, a schoolteacher....

Stifling a sigh, he forced himself to stop thinking about how difficult it was. Instead, he looked around the living room again, trying to imagine what had happened here. Maybe she'd offered him a cup of coffee or a glass of wine. He entered the kitchen and pulled a handkerchief out of his pocket, using it to keep from leaving fingerprints as he opened cabinets and inspected the refrigerator. No dishwasher, and two neatly washed mugs sat on a towel by the sink.

There was a coffeemaker beside the stove, and a canister that contained ground coffee.

"She made him coffee," he told Diaz. "One of them washed the mugs."

"Probably him," Diaz said. "He got rid of all the other evidence. He'd hardly leave his saliva and prints on a coffee mug."

"Probably," Connor agreed. Fingerprint powder on the towel indicated that the techs hadn't overlooked the mugs. And if the killer had spread out the towel to rest the washed mugs on, what did that say about him? That he was fastidious? Anal? "Does she have any family?"

"A mother in Nevada. We're still trying to get hold of her. The next-door neighbor says they aren't close."

"You know what doesn't add up? I was talking to some of the dancers at the clubs over on Dale Mabry tonight. One of them knew the victim. She says Eppinga danced because the money was good and she didn't have to take loans to pay for her education. Does that sound like someone who wouldn't pay the electric bill?"

Rick shook his head dubiously. "Nothing adds up, Quinn. Nothing. Why the hell did this woman get killed?

Why her in particular? You know, I thought it was maybe because she was blonde, like the last victim, but guess what? It was a wig. A goddamn wig.''

''Maybe he didn't know that. So he's picked two blond exotic dancers. That's a starting point. Besides, you have to keep in mind that what seems rational to this guy probably won't make a whole lot of sense to us.''

''Yeah. Yeah.'' He pulled out a pack of cigarettes and lit one unrepentantly, blowing the smoke away from Quinn. ''Come on, hurry up. Believe it or not, I got a family I'd like to see sometime before hell and Tampa Bay freeze over.''

The body was gone from the bedroom, as were a number of items that the techs had figured might be important. He wasn't concerned about what wasn't there. He wasn't here for that.

The mattress was darkly stained and crusted where the decomposing body had lain, leaving a ghastly silhouette of Judy Eppinga's last position.

''Did they find where she knelt on the rug?''

Diaz looked sharply at him. ''What do you mean?''

''The report from the last scene said the victim's knees were abraded and fibers from the rug were stuck to them. I figure he made her kneel for a reason, so he probably made Eppinga do the same.''

''I don't know if anybody looked. There was sure no way to tell from the body.''

''Then have somebody get the luminol out here and see what turns up. If Eppinga had to kneel until the skin was rubbed raw, maybe she left a little blood behind. I'd like to know where he made her kneel, if it's possible to find out.''

''Someone will be here first thing. Anything else?''

Connor didn't answer immediately. Turning slowly, he scanned the bedroom, noting that the clothes that had been in the corner had disappeared, probably into an evidence bag. So had the shoes with the ankle straps and bows. The glow-in-the-dark cross still sat on the dresser, glowing faintly purple.

"No," he said finally, staring at the cross. "I guess not." He turned to Diaz. "About the first murder—"

Diaz silenced him with a shake of his head. "You get nothing but the reports. I don't want my impressions messing you up."

Connor felt frustrated, as if he were missing something that was right in front of him. And, worse, he was afraid it was going to take another murder or two for the pattern to become clear enough for them to nail the killer.

God help them all.

# 4

Kate awoke with a deep sense of dread. When she drank her morning cup of coffee, it settled in her stomach like hot lead, burning and weighing her down. Today was her day to visit Mike, and each time it only seemed to grow harder.

She paused long enough to log on to her computer and see if CQ had sent her any mail. Her involvement in their cyberspace getaway was growing by leaps and bounds, and she was beginning to feel seriously disappointed when he didn't write.

There was a note from him this morning, speaking of warm sunshine and the laughter of children playing in the surf. She felt herself smiling and for a few minutes let go of the anxiety that the thought of Mike always aroused. She typed a quick reply to Connor, suggesting they take a walk on the beach. It was time, she found herself thinking, to leave the porch and explore this world they were making together.

There was no mail from "S.Talker." It had been days since he last sent her anything, and she wondered if perhaps her refusal to acknowledge his notes had finally bored him enough to send him on his way. A tentative relief filled her.

But then she had to climb into her car and go see Mike. It was a duty she set herself; no one else made her go. But even though she made herself do it, she felt it was something she couldn't get out of. Obligation bound her as surely as any law or chain could have. Obligation and loyalty.

It wasn't that she didn't love Mike. To be more precise, she loved the Mike she had married. The Mike he had become was a remote stranger wearing Mike's face. For him she felt nothing except a sense of duty.

And resentment. She was seriously beginning to resent visiting Mike.

Damn it, how much did she owe to a man who had nearly destroyed her life, who had abused her and inflicted all kinds of emotional harm on her? Where was it written that she had to spend the rest of her life feeling guilty because he was sick? She hadn't made him sick, despite what his family thought. All she'd done was try to rescue him.

But when she thought of him sitting in that hospital, so completely lost in his insanity, lacking all the love and warmth that every human being needed, a wave of intolerable sorrow washed over her. How could she possibly abandon him?

When she pulled her car into the parking lot in front of the Cedars, she sat for a few minutes, trying to calm herself down. Every time she made this trip, she wound up feeling as if she were being pulled in a dozen contradictory directions by conflicting feelings. And Mike could sense it when she was disturbed. For his sake, she needed to be calm.

Finally she picked up her purse, climbed out of the car and walked into the building.

The receptionist greeted her brightly. "Hi, Mrs. Devane. How are you today?"

Kate found it almost painful to be pleasant. "Just fine, Rhonda. I'd be a whole lot better if it would warm up a little."

"Hasn't it been cold?" The young woman gave a little shiver. "We're supposed to get a warm front soon, though. It'll be eighty again before you know it."

Yes, it probably would, Kate thought wearily as she stepped into the elevator.

Mike was still withdrawn, and she knew a flutter of panic as she sat across from him and waited for some kind of acknowledgment. What if he stayed gone? What if he never became lucid enough to even recognize her again?

She couldn't tell if the panic was for herself or for him. She couldn't bear the thought that Mike might forever be lost inside the shell of his body, but she also couldn't bear the thought of being tied forever to someone who didn't even know who she was.

But perhaps he knew. Perhaps even in the depths of his present catatonia he was aware that she was sitting there talking to him.

Even as she had the thought, however, she realized how selfish it might be. Maybe it would be better for him if he was aware of nothing at all, rather than aware but unable to communicate. Or, worse, aware of his own madness.

The possibilities were all painful, all useless to contemplate. The very best that could be done for Mike was being done, thanks to his family's money. All she could do was to remain faithful in her visits. Resigning herself, she read quietly to him and tried not to ache too badly over the man who was lost.

An hour later, Mike hadn't even acknowledged her by so much as a blink. She kissed his forehead, smoothed back his hair and told him she would be back next week. At the nurses' station, she asked if she could speak with his doctor, but they told her that Dr. Pritchard was "off campus."

"Mike seems more withdrawn than ever," Kate said, hoping one of the nurses would have something to say about his condition. But, of course, none of them did.

"I'll tell the doctor that you're concerned," one of them said.

Sometimes the thing that upset Kate most about all of this was the lack of information. Everyone seemed to be stonewalling; no one wanted to take the responsibility for telling her anything firm. Even the doctors hemmed and hawed and refused to predict one way or another whether Mike would ever be functional.

Of course, they didn't know. She understood that. No one could know for sure. But it was still maddening the way no one would say, "Well, he'll probably never be much better than this." Or "He might actually come out of this in a year or so. Some people do."

Consequently, she lived in a twilight world, fearing that if she ever walked away, Mike might one day emerge from his illness and find himself abandoned and alone. God knew his family didn't count for much. They footed the bills and showed up once a year, if that often. No, even that was too kind. His mother showed up once a year, for his birthday. His father never came at all, and his siblings had apparently forgotten that he even existed.

He would be so *alone* without her. Every time Kate

thought of that, the ache for Mike became almost unbearable. She couldn't walk away. Ever. Because she couldn't leave him so utterly alone.

But why was she even thinking of this? She'd made her decision. When she had used up all their savings and could not squeeze enough money out of her paycheck to cover the cost of Mike's hospitalization, she had turned to his family for aid. They had agreed to take over payment of the hospital bills, on one condition: that she divorce Mike.

She had struggled with the decision, but in the end she had capitulated. It cost more than she would ever make to keep Mike at the Cedars, and his family could afford it. If she had refused, Mike would have wound up in the state hospital, where the care and conditions were not nearly as good.

She had divorced Mike for his own good, but she felt like a failure for being unable to pay for his treatment herself, and she felt as guilty as if she had abandoned him. And she felt defiant, knowing his family didn't want her to visit. They had tried to prevent it entirely, but his doctor had overridden their order and told the staff to admit her.

The day was warming nicely by the time she left the hospital, promising an end to the bitter cold of the past several days. A glance at her watch told her that she had just enough time to get back across the bay to work.

Instead, she found herself heading toward the university and the area of Suitcase City. She didn't spend much time on this side of the bay, didn't really have any need to, except to come to the university sometimes to take a course or speak to a journalism class.

Suitcase City wasn't really a city, but a neighborhood just outside the Tampa city limits, so dubbed because it was populated largely by transients. Even the tiny little houses that were scattered amid apartment buildings and businesses were rental properties nowadays, and the entire area showed hints of the neglect that came from being tenanted rather than owned.

The apartment houses tried, building high fences around their properties, but the fences shrieked the dangers of the area far more than they protected. Except for those fences, this neighborhood would not have looked so bad to a passing eye.

When she found Judy Eppinga's apartment complex, off Fifteenth Street, she drove into the lot and parked, staring at a door crosshatched with police tape. She couldn't have said why she was here or what she expected to find, but she felt as if she'd *had* to come. Somebody needed to notice this young woman's passing with something other than curiosity or a sense that decent people had somehow been vindicated.

That latter feeling was definitely apparent among the people who had mentioned the murder to her. Even in the newsroom, where nobody would exactly say it out loud, the feeling was present. An exotic dancer had been killed. Those girls just asked for it.

Except nobody asked to be murdered, just as nobody asked to be raped. The serial killer probably picked on dancers because they were easy targets, just as rapists hung around the college campus because there were so many potential targets available.

A knock on her side window startled her. She jerked and looked around to see a middle-aged man in a private security uniform tapping on the glass. With her heart hammering, she rolled the window down two inches.

"What are you doing, ma'am? You don't live here."

"No, I don't." She fumbled in her purse and brought

out her *Sentinel* identification badge. "I'm with the paper."

"Oh." He nodded and pointed toward the apartment. "Can't let you in. The cops haven't released it yet."

"That's all right. I just wanted to get a feel for the neighborhood."

"Well, if that's what you want, I can help you. Folks in this apartment complex are all kinds, you know?"

Kate found herself climbing out and standing beside the car to chat with the security guard. The temperature had risen enough that she unbuttoned her jacket. The January sun felt hot on her face. "Does this complex always have a security patrol?" she asked him. "Or just since the murder?"

"I've been working here for three years," he told her with an emphatic nod of his head. "We have round-the-clock patrols. Two of us on each shift."

"Does it keep down the trouble?"

He gave her a half smile. "Depends on what kind of trouble you're talking about. Mainly we keep an eye out so we can call the cops if something gets out of hand. I guess us being here prevents burglaries. We don't have too many of those. And the women like it that we're here at night to be sure they get inside safely."

"But no one saw Judy Eppinga come home that evening?"

He shook his head. "We can't be everywhere at once. We walk around, you know? She must've come when the patrol was at the other end of the place."

"The guys who are on the patrols—have they been here as long as you?"

"Nah. They come and go. It's not the world's best job, you know. Lousy pay and lousy hours. I like it because I'm pretty much my own boss, but some of the younger fellas got too much fire under 'em to stay for long.'' He looked at her, squinting into the bright sun. ''You sound like the cops. They were asking the same questions.''

''Did you know her?''

''Judy? I knew her pretty good. She was here longer than most people, and she was always friendly. She even made me Christmas cookies.'' His face saddened, and he rubbed the bristles on his chin, as if trying to wipe away an unpleasant feeling. ''Decorated 'em, too. Not just colored frosting, but those little red candies and silver balls.'' He looked away.

''She sounds like she was very nice.''

''She was. Beats the hell out of me why anyone would want to hurt that little lady. Oh, I know what everybody's saying about her being a dancer and all, but she wasn't like that. She was putting herself through school, and dancing was a way to make the money. She used to tell me that the day she graduated, she was going to quit dancing for good. She'd tell me that nobody, nobody at all, was ever going to get her into those high heels again, and that any man who wanted to see her naked again was going to have to marry her first. She used to laugh when she said that, as if she knew she was just going to be so happy....''

His voice trailed away, and he looked at Kate again. ''Why don't you newspaper people ever tell about that kind of stuff? That article in the *Sentinel* didn't say anything at all about what she was really like. It didn't tell anyone what a nice person she was, or how she liked to laugh, or that she was planning to own her own business someday and have four kids. All you said about her was that she was an exotic dancer. Well, she was a whole hell of a lot more than that!''

Kate nodded, resisting an urge to reach out and touch the guard's arm in sympathy. "I'm listening," she said finally.

"Yeah." He nodded, sucked air between his teeth and rocked back on his heels. "You're listening, but are you gonna tell it in the newspaper? Folks are acting like she got what she deserved because she danced."

"I was just thinking about that when you walked up. Her life was just as valuable as anybody else's."

"Yeah. It was. She went to church every Sunday, you know. She was real religious. Her dancing...her dancing wasn't the sin. The sin was done by all the guys that came to watch her. It was *their* sin."

*It was* their *sin.* Those words haunted Kate all the way back across the bay, and were still rolling around in her head when she sat down at her desk and started looking through the assignments that had begun to accumulate.

The guard was right. It *was* their sin. Judy Eppinga had danced because she could make more money doing that part-time than she could working full-time as a secretary or a store clerk, or even as a dental assistant. The sin did indeed belong to men who would pay a pittance for a woman's honest labor but pay her ten times as much to take off her clothes.

Saddened, Kate switched her monitor on and called up the first story she needed to edit, a long piece about a bank robbery the police had prevented.

"You're late today, Devane," Sally Dyer said as she passed by Kate's desk a little later.

"I got hung up in Tampa."

"You go there every Friday morning, don't you?" Sally pulled out a chair from a nearby desk and sat facing her.

"I'm...visiting a friend," Kate replied, wondering if

she was about to undergo an inquisition. "I'm sorry for being late."

Sally waved her apology aside. "You know we don't punch time clocks around here." She hesitated, pulling a pack of cigarettes from her pocket and sticking one, unlit, between her lips. "Jesus, I hate the Clean Indoor Air Act. The one place on earth where smoking ought to be sacred is a goddamn newsroom."

Kate nodded sympathetically, although she was privately glad the newsroom was smoke-free.

"Anyway," Sally said, cigarette bobbing with each movement of her mouth, "I was just being nosy. When you were late, I got to wondering if something was wrong. That's all."

"No, just visiting a sick friend."

Sally nodded again. "Okay, then. Hyssop was muttering something about a follow-up article on the dancer's murder, so Quinn'll be dumping something on your desk. We're saving room for about four inches in section B, okay?"

"All right."

"If it looks like you're going to need more, let me know. I can always yank the story about traffic jams at the airport. That one's just filler, anyway."

As always, the tempo in the newsroom increased steadily as the afternoon wore on. More and more reporters returned from their assignments and began to write their stories, filling the room with the clatter of keys and the murmur of conversation.

Quinn didn't show up until nearly six, and when he did, the look on his face was almost frightening. Instinctively Kate jumped up and followed him into the photo lab. He didn't see her until he started emptying rolls of film from his pockets onto the counter.

"It takes all kinds," he said without preamble. "Some asshole with five DUI convictions and a revoked license was driving drunker than a skunk down 275 at ninety miles an hour. He hit a van carrying a family of tourists and rolled them right off the overpass at Thirty-eighth. Kids are lying like broken rag dolls all over the street below, two more cars collided trying to avoid running over them, and the jerk who caused it all doesn't even have a scratch. You know what he said? He said he only had a couple of beers."

Kate folded her arms, not knowing what to say.

"Christ," Connor said, piling the rolls of film into a basket. "It beats me why they don't give these jerks the death penalty. I saw it happen, Kate. It was a nightmare. The guy was weaving all over the place, driving way too fast, and then he plowed into that van and it flipped—" He broke off and shook his head. "Tell Hyssop I've got a shot for the front page. He won't want to pass it up."

"He's looking for a follow-up on the dancer, too."

"There isn't anything new you can use. I was over there for the autopsy this morning, and they want to keep most of the unusual stuff under wraps. Not that there's a whole lot. I guess you can say they're pretty sure she wasn't raped. And that's about it. Real helpful, huh?"

"I went over to the scene this morning myself and talked to one of the security guards."

He turned his head, his blue eyes truly focusing on her for the first time. The feeling would have been exhilarating under other circumstances.

"Why? Hyssop made a deal with the cops. No investigating in exchange for the inside scoop."

"I wasn't really investigating. I just felt...compelled to go see where she lived."

"Once a reporter, always a reporter."

"Once a cop, always a cop," she retorted.

He sighed and leaned back against the counter. "Look, I have to get these pictures developed. Trust me, Ben is going to want one of them for the front page. So let's just get to the point, huh? What is it you want me to tell you?"

"If I can use what the security guard told me about Judy Eppinga. About how she was working her way through school, and how she made him Christmas cookies, and how she planned to stop dancing forever the day she graduated."

He nodded slowly, something flickering in his eyes. "Go ahead. The only things we're trying to keep out of the press are the details of the actual murder. You can use all the human-interest stuff you want."

"Then I will."

"Good." He picked up the basket of film canisters and started toward the darkroom. "People ought to know that these are real folks dying out here. Nice folks. Damn, I could have killed that drunk!"

She turned to leave, but he stopped her before she got to the door. "By the way, Devane," he said flatly, "don't go nosing around on this case again."

"You can't—"

"Don't bother arguing with me. You know the rules." He took a step toward her, his eyes burning. "You're playing a dangerous game."

"All I did was talk to a security guard!"

"Who might have been the killer. How would you know?"

She opened her mouth to retort, but there was no retort she could make.

"That's right," he said. "This Nancy Drew crap could get you killed. Stay out of it, Kate."

"But..." He was right, but so was she. "It's important to make these victims human to the public. It's all I can do about this terrible crime. I have to make it matter!"

He jabbed a finger at her. "Stay out of it, Kate. You could get into real trouble."

Kate hurried back to her desk, resenting the way he had talked to her and determined to prove to him that the risk she had taken was more than justified by what she had been able to learn.

"I want more space," she told Sally. "Do we have a photo of the victim now?"

Sally nodded. "A high school graduation picture that her mother expressed to the funeral home."

"Well, I'm going to write a human-interest piece about her, and I'd like to run the photo with it."

"I guess I need to yank the article about the airport traffic, then, hmm?" Sally's eyes were almost twinkling, though, and in spite of herself, Kate smiled.

"It's important to me, Sally."

"Then go for it, Devane. Putting a human face on the tragedy is part of what we do."

She went for it, trying to capture the sadness the guard had expressed, trying to bring Judy Eppinga to life for the *Sentinel* readers as the guard had brought her to life. She felt as if it would be an injustice to allow the woman to be remembered only as another dancer who got killed.

"Interesting tie-in, maybe," Mark Polanski said, startling her. She hadn't realized that he was reading over her shoulder.

"What? What tie-in?"

"I was in court today, covering the trial of that guy

who killed those prostitutes in Clearwater. Harold Hammer. Would you believe he told the cops he couldn't understand why everyone was so upset about a couple of prostitutes? After all, he said, they were just criminals."

"That's the impression that I'm trying to shake here."

"I know." Polanski pulled up a chair and sat. "What I want to know is why you're getting so personally involved."

"Someone has to. Otherwise murderers will be free to do whatever they want."

Mark shook his head. "We pay cops to catch them."

"But cops work harder when the public cares."

"True enough. So what are you doing tonight after work? Can I buy you a drink?"

Kate felt as if somebody had just caused the earth to stop spinning. She stared at Mark, wondering what had possessed him. In all the time she had worked here, he'd never shown the slightest interest in her. "Thanks, but...I don't date."

"You had dinner with Quinn last night."

"Oh." She shook her head, wondering just what kind of stories were floating around the newsroom now, especially since everyone believed her still to be married. "It was business, Mark. Just straightforward business."

"Right. Well, that's all it would be if you let me buy you a drink."

The worst part of this, Kate found herself thinking, was that Mark was one of the best reporters at the paper. If anyone could be said to have clout with management, it was Mark. She certainly didn't want to offend him. On the other hand, she didn't want to take their relationship out of the newsroom, either.

"Just a drink," Mark said. "I swear. There's something I want to discuss with you."

She hesitated another second, then nodded. "Okay. After we put the paper to bed."

They went to Cannaday's, a bar two blocks over from the *Sentinel* offices that was frequented by staff members. It made Kate feel secure to know she was going to be surrounded by people she knew. Why the thought of having a drink with Mark should unnerve her so was something she couldn't explain. It just did.

They took a booth near the back. He ordered a gin and lime, while she ordered club soda.

"Not going to drink?" he asked, giving her a mock frown.

"Not when I have to drive." Although the truth was that she rarely drank at all. In her younger days, it had seemed romantic to sip wine with dinner or share a cognac afterward, but then Mike had started to become ill, and Kate had developed an almost pathological devotion to keeping her own head clear. She wouldn't even drink a soft drink that contained caffeine anymore. "Now, what was it you wanted to tell me?"

He shook his head, giving her a wry smile. "What's the rush? You don't have anyone to get home to."

She drew a sharp breath, feeling as if he had just punched her in the stomach. "What are you talking about?"

"I don't know why you wear that wedding ring, but I know you've been divorced for six months."

She hardly noticed when the waiter put her club soda in front of her. All she could do was stare at Mark and wonder why he was bringing this up. It didn't have anything to do with him, and it wasn't as if there were anything scandalous or newsworthy about her situation. "So?"

"So why are you still wearing that ring?"

"I don't see that it's any of your business."

"Maybe I'd like it to be my business."

She didn't know whether to get up and leave or simply tell him to stuff his head where the sun didn't shine. "Look, Mark, whether or not I'm divorced is irrelevant. I don't want to get involved with anyone. Period."

He creased the corner of his cocktail napkin without looking at it. Instead, he stared steadily at her. "I guess I can understand that. It couldn't have been easy being married to a paranoid schizophrenic."

She gasped, stunned. "How...? Who...?"

"I got a call from a member of your ex-husband's family. I won't say which one. The story checks out. You were married to Michael Devane for ten years. For most of those ten years he was getting increasingly sick. More than once you had to have him Baker Acted for his own protection. That had to be difficult."

She couldn't even manage to speak. One of Mike's family had done this to her. Why? She knew they hated her, but she had never imagined they would do something like this. And what did they hope to gain? Did they think she would get fired over this?

"The family claims you drove him insane," Mark continued remorselessly. "My other sources tell me that's impossible. The old stuff about schizophrenogenic relationships applied only to parents—mothers in particular—anyway. What I'm curious about is why these people hate you so much."

"What makes you think it's any of your business?"

He leaned forward, resting his elbows on the table, and cocked his head. "I'm a reporter. Everything's my business until I decide there isn't a story. I ask. You don't have to answer."

"You can't possibly think there's a story in this."

"A pretty harsh accusation has been made. There could be all kinds of stories in that."

She stared at him in horror. "You son of a bitch."

"I could use you as an object lesson in how the Baker Act commitment can be abused by family members."

"My God!" She was unable to believe this was happening. He couldn't really be threatening her like this.

"Look," he said, "I really don't want to slam you. In fact, I'd be really happy if this entire story would go away. If there's any kind of a story here at all, I don't want to involve you personally. But if you're going to carry on like I have no right to ask these questions, I'll have to write the story without your side of it."

Nearly a full minute ticked by while she fought for control. Her breathing wanted to come in ragged gasps, and her hands clenched so tightly that she could feel her nails cutting her palms. But what she couldn't do was just get up and leave. She couldn't let Mike's family win this one so easily.

"What do you want, Mark?" she asked finally, her voice low and tight, sharp as a razor's edge. "What do you think you're going to find? I can show you the police reports. Will that help? Do you want to tell the world about the night the cops found him stark naked in the middle of Central Avenue, lying facedown on the pavement? He was lying there waiting for the aliens to come pick him up."

"Kate..." Mark suddenly looked uneasy.

"Or maybe you want to see the pictures of our house. He had every single window boarded up so the aliens couldn't get in. He put all my pots and pans on the windowsills every night so that if the Venusians tried to get in, they'd knock the pots over and he'd hear them. Maybe you want to hear about how I didn't sleep for months because he would wander through the house at night talking and laughing, carrying on conversations with voices only he could hear. Or maybe you want to hear about the ads he placed in the local papers warning everybody about the aliens' attempts to take over our minds by beaming messages into our brains by way of military satellites."

"Kate—"

"No, you wanted to know about it. I'll tell you all about it. I'll tell you what it's like to live with someone who's losing his mind. I'll tell you all about the aching fear and the constant worry, and the terror when he disappeared again and I'd have to wonder if he was going to get himself killed. Do you know what it's like to try to give someone their medication and have them accuse you of trying to poison them? Do you know what it's like to watch someone you love go crazy enough to finally believe that *you're* the enemy?"

He finally looked down, as if embarrassed. "No," he said. "I can't say that I do."

"I had Mike committed because I had no other choice. And believe me, I tried everything else. I tried to keep him at home, I tried to keep him on his medication, I tried to keep him safe."

"His family tells a different story."

"Of course they do. They believed *him.* But you see, he believed that *everybody* was out to get him. He believed he couldn't trust his doctors, he couldn't trust the cops, and most of all, he couldn't trust me." She had to stop, to catch her breath, to remind herself to keep her voice down. She didn't want the whole world to hear this, because, for some reason she couldn't fathom, there was something shameful about mental illness, and something shameful about not being able to save Mike.

"The point is," she said finally, leaning forward and tapping the table with her forefinger for emphasis, "if I hadn't been able to Baker Act Mike, he'd be dead now. He'd have fallen off the Skyway Bridge trying to get high enough to escape the aliens. He'd have been run over by a truck when he was proving his invincibility in the middle of the road. He'd have gone nuts in the middle of a crowded store and been carted away to jail by the authorities. The Baker Act saved his life. It's too damn bad it can't save his mind!"

Then, without another word, she grabbed her purse, stood up and strode away.

Mark followed her, only one step behind. "Kate, wait. Wait a minute, please."

At the door, she paused and looked at him, wondering if all the anger, hurt and hate she was feeling right now was showing in her eyes. Because right now she hated Mark Polanski.

"Look," he said, "I'm sorry. I had to check it out. I checked it out before I even asked you to come over here with me. But I had to verify it. You can understand that."

"I don't have to understand anything."

He sighed and looked briefly away. "All right. Don't understand my position. But there's one more thing I have to tell you."

She waited impatiently, wanting to be anywhere on the planet other than right here with this man.

"It's about Quinn."

"Oh, for Pete's sake, Mark! You're not going to get petty about that murder story, are you?"

"I'm not being petty. Just watch yourself with him. He was in that apartment where that woman was killed. You know the cops never allow that."

"He used to be a cop."

"Yeah." Mark shrugged. "It's a convenient excuse, isn't it? Just remember, I warned you."

The headache was worse, much worse. They wouldn't give him a shot at the hospital because he'd had a couple of whiskeys earlier, but they gave him some pills and told him not to take them before midnight.

He took them anyway. As bad as his head hurt, he didn't care if they killed him.

But they didn't kill him. They even eased the pain enough that he could see something besides shooting stars and jagged rainbows. By the time he got off the bus, the pain had subsided to a dull pounding in the back of his head.

His skull had been caved in there six years ago, when a car jumped the curb and hit him. The doctors said he was lucky to be alive, but he didn't always feel lucky when the headache got so bad he couldn't even see.

He was a little surprised to see that he'd gotten off the bus on Nebraska Avenue, miles from his house. Why in the world had he done that? He turned slowly, looking around, trying to orient himself. He had only a vague idea of where he was, and the fences that surrounded the businesses here warned him that it wasn't a good neighborhood.

He looked up at the street sign but found no help. Did he turn left or right to head toward his home from here? He hadn't any idea which direction was north, and without knowing that, it was impossible to tell which way to go.

Finally he hunched his shoulders inside his jacket and started to walk along Nebraska. The change in the numbers would tell him whether he was heading north or south, he assured himself.

Finding numbers on the businesses proved difficult, however, and he walked two blocks before he knew he was heading south, into the heart of Tampa—exactly the wrong direction. Turning, he was about to retrace his steps when he noticed the garish neon sign across the street that announced lingerie modeling.

A shiver went through him as he realized that his steps had been guided. He closed his eyes and whispered a fervent prayer of thanksgiving. He had been led to this spot, of that he had not the least doubt. He had been led here to find the woman he was supposed to save. He never, ever would have thought to look here on his own, and so he had been guided.

Quickly he felt in his pockets for money, knowing he would probably have to pay something just to see the woman, confident that the very first one he saw would be the one he was destined to save.

Yes, he had the money. More than enough. He wasn't sure where he had gotten it, but it didn't do to question too closely. He had been guided, and providence had put the money in his pocket. Filled with purpose, he strode across the street to fulfill his mission.

# 5

When Kate got home, she still wanted to smash something. Mark and his damn questions had forced her to dig up things she had been trying to forget for a long time, and she wanted to hurl something just to vent her anger and pain. She didn't do it, though. It wouldn't make anything better, and she knew it.

Instead, she stood in her living room and tried to reach for calm. It didn't help that she could still see the Spackle marks where she had patched all the holes Mike made in the walls when he nailed the boards over the windows. Or that she could still see the faint, snaking trail of the cracks in the drywall from the time he had beaten his head on it until he bled and became dazed enough that she could finally get him in the car and to the hospital. She'd always meant to get those scars professionally repaired, so that they wouldn't be a constant reminder, but she could somehow never find the money.

This house was too big for her anyhow, she told herself disgustedly, and marched into the kitchen to make herself something for dinner. She and Mike had bought it in expectation of the family they planned to start, a family that never happened. That was just another thing his mother held against her.

She heated up some leftover lasagna and made a small salad to go with it. She ate at the table in the kitchen, trying not to remember all the times she had eaten there with Mike. Damn Mark for waking all those memories.

Finally she went to her computer, switching it on and logging on to the local bulletin-board service where she and Connor exchanged e-mail. She was hoping that perhaps he'd had a minute to reply to her note from this morning, but she didn't have very high hopes, not considering the mood he'd been in after photographing that accident.

The first thing she saw was a note from S.Talker.

Her heart slammed uncomfortably, even though she told herself not to let it disturb her. He was nothing but glowing words on a screen. There wasn't anything he could possibly do to her. There was no way he could find her.

Except that she didn't quite believe that. He seemed to know too much about her, and if he knew things about her, he probably knew where she lived.

Not that he had actually threatened to hurt her. Not really. It was just the feeling his notes gave her that made her so uneasy.

Her hand hovered over the delete key, but she stopped herself. No. She would read it, and if there was anything unnerving about it, she would forward it to Connor and see what he thought about it. And if he thought there was something wrong with this guy, maybe she would send his note to the system operator and ask him to do something about it. That was the sysop's role, after all.

Clicking her mouse, she opened the e-mail, aware that her heart had begun to thud.

I know you. I know all about you. I know where you work, and where you live. You can't escape me. You can pretend to ignore my letters, but I know you're reading them, and you know I'm watching you.

I will get even with you.

Kate felt a surge of fury so strong that for an instant she couldn't even see, but then, in a rush, it gave way to icy panic. He was watching her? How could he be watching her? There was no way he could possibly know where she was.

But just as she was getting a grip on herself, she realized that her on-line service provider had her address and phone number for billing purposes. If S.Talker was somehow able to get access to their billing records, he *would* be able to find her.

But what could he possibly want to get even with her for? She had no idea who he was.

She stared at the note on the screen and tried to convince herself that this was just a terror tactic. She'd been getting notes like this for weeks. Surely, if he really knew who she was, he would have done something else by now?

Deciding that she really needed someone else's opinion, because she couldn't look at this objectively, she typed a quick message to Connor and forwarded S.Talker's note to him. He used to be a cop; he would know whether she should be afraid, or if she could safely ignore this guy.

And until then, she promised herself, she wasn't going to worry about it.

Until she remembered Mark's comment about Connor at the restaurant. What had he been trying to insinuate?

That Connor was involved somehow in the murder of that woman?

Every cell of her being resisted that suggestion. She might have known Connor for only six months, but she'd had ample opportunity to observe him, and she'd been corresponding with him now for several months. There was nothing, absolutely nothing, about him that made her uneasy.

It didn't help to recall that most serial killers were personable people who were well liked by those who knew them.

It didn't help at all.

The call dragged Quinn out of a dream about Key West. It tied in to the e-mails he'd been exchanging with Katydid and the walk on the beach she'd suggested earlier. When he opened his eyes, he could almost smell the sea air and feel the warm sand beneath his feet.

The c-phone was shrieking on his bedside table. He snatched it up and punched the button. "Yeah?"

"Quinn, it's Rick Diaz. We got another one, and it's a mess. It's Tampa PD's case, but they asked us to look at it. Put on your best manners and get the hell over here."

It was the address that really woke Quinn up, though. Not another Suitcase City address, but one on Davis Island, where there were a lot of exclusive homes. It couldn't be the same guy, he told himself as he jammed his legs into jeans. No way. These guys didn't just suddenly switch from exotic dancers to the Junior League.

*But they could,* his mind argued back. *Don't forget Ramirez, the Night Stalker.* His victims had ranged from impoverished elderly women to the teenage daughters of upper-middle-class households. He'd killed men and women both, and sometimes he'd even permitted his victims to live.

God help them if the Puppetmaster was as unpredictable as Richard Ramirez had been.

The trip across the bay seemed to take three times as long as usual. By the time he pulled up in front of the house, it looked as if the media people outnumbered the cops. All four local TV stations were represented, as were all the newspapers. He recognized the faces as he walked by, and saw some of them look questioningly at him as he crossed the police line. They knew he was no longer a cop. Damn, that was going to make for some awkward questions.

Rick was waiting for him just inside the door. He was talking to Bob Silva of the Tampa Police Department. Connor had worked with Bob in the past on cases that crossed jurisdictional boundaries, and was glad to see him. Silva wasn't quite as certain.

"Diaz tells me you're working with him on this."

Connor nodded.

"And I'm supposed to believe that none of this is going to come out in the paper?"

"That's the agreement we have," Connor said flatly.

Silva looked at Diaz. "Do you know the kind of trouble I'm going to have with the rest of the media if I let him in here?"

"Fine," Connor said, starting to turn away. "I don't need any more nightmares."

"Wait," Diaz said sharply. "Damn it, don't get difficult on me now, Connor. Bob, you know Quinn is the best profiler we have. Either he does it or we call the feebs. Take your pick."

Nobody really wanted to call the FBI. They would, as a last resort, but despite all the efforts the Bureau had made to repair relations with local law enforcement since Hoover, resentments still lingered.

"We're probably going to have to call them anyway," Silva said. "If this really is a serial murder." He ran his fingers through his steely-gray hair and glared at Quinn. "All right, I'll try you first. God knows what I'm going to tell all those reporters out there."

Diaz shrugged. "Just tell 'em Quinn's back with the sheriff's office. We won't tell 'em it's only temporary." He turned to Quinn. "This one's fresh. Real fresh. She must've been killed just before her husband came home."

"The husband found her?"

"Less than two hours ago."

Quinn glanced at his watch and was surprised to realize it was already five-thirty. "Where was he when she was being killed?"

Silva's look was sharp. "He said he was in Orlando, visiting his sister. We're checking it out."

"It doesn't fit," Quinn told Diaz. "The victim doesn't fit."

Diaz shrugged one shoulder. "But the murder does. So we have to figure out why he picked a banker's wife this time."

Quinn stepped over the threshold, wishing he could see the place with no one else around, get a better idea of what might have happened here. Where had the Puppetmaster found this woman? And why had he picked her? She was so different from his other two victims. Things didn't seem to be adding up, and Connor hated it when things didn't add up. The only thing he had to count on when tracking a serial killer was that the murderer had a ritual, that his victims were always similar in some way.

The foyer was large, and he found himself wondering if the killer had hesitated here, questioning whether he should go ahead with his plans. He must have paused and wondered, must have guessed that picking a victim from this kind of background was going to intensify the hunt for him.

Maybe that was what he wanted?

Quinn stood in the middle of the foyer, turning slowly as he looked around, trying to imagine the killer's reaction.

"No sign of forced entry?" he asked.

"None," Silva answered. "And believe me, we've checked. This place is outfitted with a damn good security system. It didn't even give a squawk tonight, and it's not disabled."

So she had let him in. What kind of guy would know both exotic dancers and bankers' wives? Quinn turned around one more time, then looked at Silva. "Where's the body?"

"Upstairs."

"I want to look around down here first."

"Go ahead."

The house wasn't terribly big, although compared to the boxes that were being built in most subdivisions, this was a spacious house. On the ground floor there were a moderate-size living room, a galley kitchen, a large dining room, one bedroom and a spacious family room.

The husband was in the family room, sitting on the edge of the couch. His elbows rested on his thighs, and his hands were clasped tightly, as if he were afraid to let go of himself. He rocked back and forth steadily, endlessly, with his head bowed and his eyes staring blankly.

When he heard Connor's step, he looked up, his face

a mask of anguish. "I knew I shouldn't go. I knew I should stay home. But tonight was her night to go out with her friends, and my sister needed me—she's getting divorced, you see. Her husband is being such a bastard about it—" He broke off abruptly, shaking his head as if to clear it. "I should have stayed home. If I'd just stayed home, she'd be okay—" His voice broke on a smothered sob.

Connor started to turn away but stopped himself. "It wouldn't have made any difference," he told the man. "If you'd been here tonight, he would have killed her another night. Once he picks them, nothing stops him."

The man looked at him, taking Quinn's words inside himself like hammer blows. He flinched. "I could've saved her."

"You couldn't have saved her. Nobody could save her. We've got to catch this bastard before he picks somebody else."

The banker nodded at that, solemnly, as if he had just accepted a serious charge. "Find him. What can I do?"

"Tell me if anything, anything at all, is out of place in the house. If anything doesn't look right to you."

He nodded. "Okay. But...I can't go back in...that room."

"No. No, you don't have to. But you can check the other rooms for me, okay?"

The man nodded and got quickly to his feet. He still looked dazed, but he had something to do, and purpose gave him the strength to take the first step. He halted in front of Connor.

"Her car wasn't in the garage," he said. "I noticed that when I got home. She always puts her car in the garage, but not tonight."

"Can you think of any reason she might leave it out?"

"No." A shudder passed through the banker. "The alarm wasn't on. That's when I got scared. She always puts it on. I used to tease her about it sometimes, because she'd even get out of bed to go check it at night if she couldn't remember turning it on. And when I'm away she keeps it on, even in the daytime."

"So tonight was different."

The man nodded. "Very different. The house smelled funny when I came inside. That's the other thing I noticed, how funny it smelled. Like...shit. And something else..." He shook his head again, as if trying to shake loose of something. "As soon as I smelled it, I knew. I knew." He walked away, breathing raggedly.

The place did smell like shit, Connor thought. He'd noticed it the minute he stepped inside: feces and urine and fear, the signature of violent death. The smell wasn't overpowering, and it was mixed with the scent of the spicy potpourri that was kept in a small bowl in every room he'd entered.

The house wasn't huge, but out back there was a large wooden deck that led to a boathouse, and moored there was a cabin cruiser, glowing palely in the light that reached it from the house. Life-styles of the wealthy, he thought. People like this didn't expect violent death to visit them. But then, who did?

He didn't see anything obviously out of place, and maybe that made sense. Maybe when the killer realized what kind of tiger he had by the tail, he'd hurried up. Maybe they hadn't indulged in any socializing beforehand.

Maybe the victim had been having an affair with him.

It wouldn't be the first time a killer had been having a relatively normal relationship with a woman while he was killing others. There was Bundy, who'd had a girlfriend, and Gacy, who'd been married, and what's-his-name up in Georgia who'd been dating a policewoman and a psychiatrist the whole time he was killing little old ladies.

So what if the killer had been dating the banker's wife? What if her night out with the girls hadn't been a night out with girls at all?

He found Silva standing in the kitchen, having a heated discussion with a technician over a piece of paper in a clear evidence bag.

"Did he write notes to this woman, too?" Connor asked.

Silva nodded, waving the tech away and holding up the envelope so that Quinn could see it. "Damned if I know. What do you make of this?"

Quinn took the bag and held it so that the light didn't glare off the plastic.

He found you. He's watching you. Run for your life.

"That's nothing like the notes the other two got."

"That's what Diaz said." Silva sighed and rubbed his eyes with the heels of his palms. "Fuck it. Maybe somebody else is messed up in this somehow. Because the killer did her just like the others."

Upstairs, Quinn found a scene very much like the last one, except that this time the victim looked almost as if she might wake at any moment.

She was pale, too pale, and a mark on her arm indicated that she, too, had been bled to death. What did the perp do with all that blood? It didn't make sense. Why would he want to cart a couple of gallons of blood away from the crime scene?

She was tied like the other ones, too, at her wrists, knees and throat. That was interesting, the ropes at the knees, and Connor stood there for several long minutes, looking down at her, trying to imagine why anyone would want to tie her up this way...and wondering what the ropes had been tied to. Right now, they lay loose, trailing off the bed to the floor.

"This isn't her bedroom."

Silva's voice startled him, and he turned around quickly. "It's not?"

Silva shook his head. Behind him was Diaz. "Husband says this is the guest room. Nobody uses it except his mother when she comes from Miami for a visit."

Quinn looked at the body again. "She used it," he heard himself say. "She used it all the time."

"What do you mean?"

"Check it out. You're going to find things in here that belong to her."

Silva was looking irritated. "What things? You haven't even looked. You don't know this."

But Quinn was absolutely certain. "She brought the killer into this house. There aren't any signs of overt violence anywhere, so they got to the bedroom without a fight. Which means, since this was her house, that she led the way."

Diaz looked at Silva. "Makes sense to me."

"Sounds like a bunch of Indian hocus-pocus to me," Silva groused.

Connor didn't take the comment amiss. Silva's grandmother was Seminole.

"Okay, okay," Silva said. "I'll check it out. But it beats the hell out of me how I can prove she ever used this room!"

Quinn took a pair of latex gloves out of his pocket

and pulled them on. "You'll find things," he said. He went straight to the dresser and began to pull open drawers. In the first one, underneath a neatly folded electric blanket, he found lingerie, the kind of things that a woman wore to please a man. Piece by piece, he pulled them out and tossed them toward Silva.

"A regular goddamn love nest," Diaz drawled. He couldn't quite hide the smile in his eyes as he looked at Quinn. "Got any more rabbits?"

"It's possible she was having an affair with this guy and stumbled on something she shouldn't have. It would explain why he switched his usual victim type."

Diaz looked at Silva. "*That's* why I wanted him here."

"I could be wrong. It's possible she was in the habit of bringing strangers home."

"The point," Diaz said, "is that she was in the habit of bringing *any* man home. This is going to kill her husband."

"Maybe *he's* the one who played little games in this love nest," Silva remarked. "Maybe she was getting even."

But it was all a lot of speculation, and the three of them knew it. The point was, this woman had let a man into the house tonight and had brought him to this room, where he had proceeded to kill her.

"Do you think these broads are letting this guy tie them up before they realize anything's wrong?" Silva asked.

"He talks them into it somehow," Connor agreed. His gaze suddenly fell on the items in the corner of the room, almost hidden behind the dresser. He walked closer and drew a deep breath. G-string and high heels. Just like at the Eppinga place. "Rick?" He pointed.

Diaz came to stand beside him. "Well, shit," he said.

"What's that?" Silva asked, joining them.

"Another one of his signatures," Rick Diaz replied. "The last two had worn theirs. I'll bet we find out this one wore hers, too."

"And her knees," Connor said, turning and pointing. "Her knees are abraded."

"Just like the first one."

Something, Connor never could have said what, dragged his gaze to the wall over the bed. Hanging there was a crucifix carved out of wood. It wasn't very big, and it didn't especially show up against the busy rose-covered wallpaper, but all of a sudden it seemed to stand out like neon.

What the hell did it mean?

"It was all over the morning news."

Connor was checking out the negatives of the photos he'd taken at the Davis Island house when Kate Devane entered the photo lab.

"I figured it would be," he replied without lifting his head. It suddenly struck him that he was losing patience with all this shit, and all he really wanted to do was go find Katydid and abduct her to the Florida Keys for a week. Or a month. Or maybe the rest of his life. Spend his days on the sand or in the water and just forget the whole rest of the world existed.

"They know there's a serial killer, and they're calling him the Puppetmaster," Kate continued, leaning back against the counter and folding her arms. "Where did they get that name?"

"Probably from the notes he wrote to one of them."

She drew a sharp breath. "Tell me."

"He just referred to the Puppetmaster. He didn't say

it was him, though. I don't remember it exactly, and I'll need to clear it with Diaz before I release the exact text of those notes to anyone."

"Then call him, will you?" She bit her lower lip and looked at him with concern. "I saw you on one of the video clips they played this morning. What were you doing there? You went right past the police line."

He still didn't look at her. "I know people" was all he said.

"Know people? *I* know people. So does Kerry McCue, the Channel 9 anchor. *She* didn't get past that line, and neither would I."

"She didn't use to be a cop." Now he straightened and looked straight at her. He was an intimidating sight, with his burning blue eyes sunken from lack of sleep and his long black hair trailing over his shoulders. His entire posture defied her to pursue this line of questioning.

"True," she said finally, letting it go. For now. "Last night's murder doesn't add up. The other two were exotic dancers. Marceline Whitmore was Junior League and Daughters of the American Revolution—or something like that. We're talking old family, old money, and a rising-star husband. Women like that don't get killed by men who prey on exotic dancers."

"You wouldn't think so."

"So tell me what I'm missing here."

"I don't know yet."

She frowned at him. "Yeah, right."

He gave a disgusted sigh and slapped his palm against his thigh. "Look, Kate, I honestly don't know. Something's missing, I'll grant you that, but I don't know what it is. Nobody knows what it is."

She stepped farther into the lab, and he picked up the

negatives he'd been looking at and slipped them into an envelope.

"I need to write an article about this killing, and I need to write it by seven o'clock," she told him. "So I need a story, Quinn. You're supposed to give me a story, remember?"

"I'll get the information to you."

"I can't wait indefinitely. This is going on page one."

"Naturally." In spite of himself, he felt a wave of bitterness. "It's always important when one of the influential people gets hurt. An exotic dancer goes in the second section, but the banker's wife gets the front page."

"It's making the front page because it's a serial killer."

"Oh, come on," he said. "You weren't born yesterday, Kate! What about that serial killer in Clearwater two years ago? He made the second section, too. I don't think he ever made the front page until he escaped from the sheriff and they had to hunt him down. But what the hell, he was only killing prostitutes."

"More people will want to read about the banker's wife. She makes more interesting copy. It's not a comment on the value of these lives."

"You think not?" He shook his head sharply. "Forget it. I'll get the information to you, but all I have right now deals with the murder. If you want information about the woman, you'll have to get it yourself."

"Then I will."

He watched her walk away, then had a sudden thought. He went to the door and leaned out of the lab, calling after her, "But if you get any harebrained ideas about going out to talk to people like last time, you come to me, you hear?"

"Stuff a sock in it, Quinn."

"Like hell!"

But he let it go, figuring he'd better keep an eye on her. Especially now that the killer had broken his pattern.

By early afternoon, Kate had pulled everything out of the paper's morgue about Marceline Whitmore. The woman had been exceptionally active in local clubs and committees until a little over a year ago. Then, for some reason, she had disappeared from the social pages and wasn't even mentioned in connection with fund-raisers for two or three charities in which she had previously been prominent.

Kate pored over the copies the researcher had brought her, seeking something, anything, that might connect this woman to a serial killer who had hitherto hunted exotic dancers. Finding nothing, she ran checks on the backgrounds of the first two victims, hoping to find some point at which their paths intersected Marceline Whitmore's. Nothing again.

Frustrated, she sat back in disgust and drummed her fingers on her desk. Could it really be possible that the *only* connection between these women was their killer? That they had no other similarities at all?

Well, that wasn't exactly right, she reminded herself, rubbing her temples with her fingertips. They were all blond. Maybe this guy stalked blondes, and the first two just happened to be exotic dancers. Maybe all the blondes in the Tampa Bay area were at risk.

The thought made the back of her neck prickle with awareness that she, too, was blond. And with that thought came remembrance of the e-mail message from S.Talker. What if the guy wasn't harmless? What if—?

With a sharp jerk, she pulled her thoughts back to

work. There was a lot she needed to accomplish between now and putting the paper to bed tonight, and no time to waste worrying about extraneous matters.

By four, she had written a background piece on Marceline Whitmore. She was just sending it over to Sally Dyer for insertion when Connor Quinn pulled up beside her desk and straddled a chair.

"Okay," he said, and handed her a sheet of paper. "Here's what the police are releasing to the press."

Kate looked at him. "Well, thanks a lot. Where's the inside scoop we were promised?"

"One tidbit," he said, leaning close.

For an instant, just one instant, Kate's thoughts scattered like autumn leaves in the wind. She was drawn to this man in ways that were beginning to terrify her, and she refused to acknowledge it. Denial had been her strongest ally during the years of her marriage, and denial came to her rescue now. "What is it?" she asked, as if she had felt nothing at all.

"The house was unlocked, and the security system was turned off. There was never a peep out of it. There's no sign of forced entry and no sign of a struggle. Marceline Whitmore invited her killer into the house."

"My God," Kate whispered. "She must have known him!"

"It looks that way. Either that or he has the world's best con. It's been the same at all the scenes. These women are inviting this bastard in. Anyway, there's the scoop for the paper. No one else has that information yet."

She nodded. "Anything else?"

"Only that the information about the Puppetmaster came from a leak in the sheriff's office. But that's covered in the press release I just gave you. If you need me,

I'll be in the lab. And don't leave without checking in with me first. I might have something more for you."

The rest of the day sped by in a rush. She finished the article on the murder just in time, then waited patiently for Sally to check it over. The senior editor didn't make any changes.

"That's it," Sally said. "Get out of here, Devane. You're done. Unless they need you to write another article on this killer, you'll do layout tomorrow." Then she flashed a grin. "I was right, wasn't I? It *was* a serial killer." She tapped her nose. "I still got the old sniffer."

Kate gathered up her purse and sweater, and was halfway to the elevator when she remembered that Connor had wanted her to stop in the lab before she left. Had it been anybody else, she would have kept walking. Since it was Connor, she turned around and headed back.

Besides, now that it was time to head home, she found herself reluctant to step out into the dark evening. The note from S.Talker, which she had hardly let herself think about since she forwarded it to CQ, now insisted on thrusting itself to the forefront of her mind. Maybe it was time to think about getting a roommate. Living alone suddenly seemed like a damn-fool thing to be doing.

Just inside the lab, she drew up short and felt a smile tug at the corners of her mouth. Connor Quinn, all six-foot-something of him, was stretched out on the floor, sound asleep.

She hesitated, not wanting to wake him, yet reluctant to just leave him. He must have wanted to talk with her about something, she reasoned, but she was damned if she was going to stand here until he woke up.

"Connor," she called quietly. "Connor, wake up."

His eyes opened instantly, and in a single fluid movement he rose to his feet. ''Sorry. I was dozing.''

She cocked her head and gave him a smile. ''Wish I could wake up that quickly.''

He flashed an unexpected, breathtaking grin. ''Some of us got it, and some of us ain't.''

She couldn't afford to let herself fall into casual conversation with him. That had to be reserved for their computer chat, where distance could keep her safe when she let down her emotional barriers. ''So,'' she said firmly, ''you had something you wanted to see me about before I left?''

''Yeah. Let me buy you dinner, and then we're going to do a little investigating.''

# 6

Tonight they didn't dine in the ambience of the Italian restaurant with the snowy linen tablecloth. Instead, they went to the nearest fast-food joint, where Kate ordered one double cheeseburger and Connor ordered three. They sat together in a booth and gorged on grease.

It made Kate feel like a reporter on the beat again, the way she had been before Mike's illness forced her to move to a position with more regular hours. Without a thought for calories or grams of fat, she savored every single mouthful of her burger.

"What are we going to investigate?" she asked him. What she really wanted to know was why he was taking her along. He didn't seem like the kind of person who would want company on a mission like this.

"I need to interview a friend of Judy Eppinga's. A dancer who worked with her. The woman called me today and asked me to meet her. I'll ask her the cop questions, you ask her the reporter questions. Maybe we'll even rustle up a lead."

Her heart accelerated. "And if we do? Can I write about it?"

He shook his head. "Not until it's cleared by the cops."

"Damn it, Connor!"

"Kate, come on. You know perfectly well that we have to be careful about what we let out to the public about these killings! In the first place, with all the publicity the guy is getting, there's a serious risk of copycats. But worse, if the killer reads enough details about the killings in the press, he might change his routine to confound us. It wouldn't be the first time."

She should have nodded or agreed or something. Anything but ask, "Why'd you quit the police force?"

He was taken aback. For a few seconds, he simply stared at her. "What does that have to do with the price of peas?"

"Nothing. Everything. I'm sitting here listening to you, and I'm listening to a cop. You're not a reporter on a story, you're a cop on a case. So tell me, Connor, why'd you quit the force, and why'd you join the newspaper?"

His jaw worked tensely, but his eyes never left her. She had a strong feeling that he was going to get up without a word and just walk away. She would have bet her next two paychecks that that was exactly what he wanted to do.

"I quit because I couldn't stand the nightmares anymore."

The starkness of his statement left her feeling as if she'd been punched. She didn't even know what to say.

"I quit," he continued, "because I was fool enough to think working for the paper would be more creative and less disturbing. Because I wanted to take pictures that said all that needed to be said, so I could leave the images at work when I came home, instead of having to carry them with me for weeks or months while I tried to figure things out. I wanted to put some distance between me and all the shit the world is drowning in."

She caught her breath. "Did it work?"

"What the hell do you think?" Rising, he took his coffee cup up to the counter for a refill, leaving her to pick at cold french fries and wonder if everybody on planet earth had private demons.

When he returned, his face was set as hard as a stone mask. "I figure since Xena called me, she probably has something she wants to share."

"Why did she call you?"

"One of the dancers told me she was a good friend of Eppinga's. I left my card with her boss."

It sounded good, Kate thought. And people who wanted to talk to the press always had plenty to say.

"Of course," Connor continued, "it's possible she's just a publicity hound."

"There is that," Kate agreed.

Thirty minutes later, they were standing in front of a lounge called After Midnight. Kate suddenly found herself filled with qualms. She'd never been in an establishment of this sort before, and she didn't particularly want to go into a place that was advertising lap dancing.

Connor noticed her hesitation and looked down at her from eyes that seemed to see every thought in her head. "It's not that bad, Sister Kate. Just look straight ahead."

"Do we have to talk to her here?"

His response was dry. "For reasons I can only guess at, she doesn't seem real eager to meet a strange man in a private place."

"Oh." There was nothing she could say to that.

Inside, the music was only moderately loud, but the beat was driving and hard. The lounge was hardly more brightly lit than the night outside, and the figures moving around were merely shadows, except for one girl dancing in the middle of the room under a spotlight. All she wore was a G-string and high heels, and she moved her body in ways calculated to make everything sway. Kate felt her cheeks redden.

In darker places, the shadows of nearly naked women could be seen sitting on the laps of men and moving in ways that made Kate's blush deepen. The urge to leave nearly overwhelmed her.

"The bar," Connor said, pointing.

As she followed him across the room, Kate wondered if he had brought her along on this jaunt simply to embarrass her to death and teach her her proper place. It was an unworthy suspicion, and one she was ashamed of almost as soon as she had it. Mark Polanski might do something like that to her; Connor wouldn't even think of it.

At the bar, they sat on stools and ordered drinks—Connor a beer he didn't touch, Kate a glass of wine she didn't want.

"Xena asked me to meet her here," Connor told the bartender when he delivered the drinks.

"Her break is in ten minutes," the man replied. "She'll find you."

Kate kept her attention fixed on the bottles behind the bar, not wanting to think about what was going on behind her. She simply could not imagine why anyone would want to do such things in public.

"Prudishness is an odd quality in a reporter," Quinn remarked. "About as odd as it would be in a cop. We see everything sooner or later."

"This is a later for me. I've never been in one of these places."

"And you don't intend to come back would be my guess."

"You got it."

He chuckled quietly. "It's not my idea of a night out, either."

"Really?" She looked him up and down with a dubious eye, teasing him.

A snort of laughter escaped him. "Well, not since I was sixteen and it was *all* that interested me."

It was her turn to laugh, and some of her discomfort fled. She was a reporter, she reminded herself, and started pretending that she was tough as old shoe leather and inured to everything. Playing that role had gotten her through more than one tough spot in her career. Lifting her glass of wine to her lips, she let it just barely wet the tip of her tongue. In a movie, she would be knocking back the hard stuff.

"Are you Connor Quinn?"

Kate swung around on her stool and saw a tall woman with skin the color of milk chocolate standing beside Quinn. She was breathtakingly beautiful in a red caftan, and Kate felt a serious twinge of envy.

"I'm Xena," the woman said, and slid onto the stool beside Connor.

"This is my partner, Kate," Connor said by way of introduction. "She'll probably ask questions, too, okay?"

"Sure," Xena said. "But listen—I don't want my name in the paper or anything. I'm planning to go to medical school, and I don't think this kind of work would help my chances any with the admissions committee."

"I don't have a problem with that," Kate assured her.

"If we publish anything, we'll just refer to you as a friend."

Xena tilted her head to one side, taking Kate's measure, then nodded. "Okay." From a pocket she pulled a pack of cigarettes and lit one, blowing a cloud of smoke. "Judy and I were good friends. We met the first week of our freshman year. We talked about living together, but I smoke and Judy has asthma. She can… I mean she could barely stand the smoke in here. She had to take medicine before she could dance. I thought about quitting…." Xena's voice trailed off, and she looked down at the cigarette in her hand for long, silent seconds. "Maybe if I had, she wouldn't be dead now."

Kate didn't know what to say to that. All that occurred to her were worthless clichés. Apparently Connor felt the same, because he pressed on.

"Judy never dated customers, did she?"

Xena looked up from the cigarette and shook her head. "Never. She was willing to wiggle her bod for bucks, but she wasn't a whore. Never."

"What about boyfriends?"

"She was pretty hot and heavy with this guy for a while, but they split when she started dancing. She had one more boyfriend after that, but then she quit dating permanently. They always wanted her to quit, she said. What is it about men, anyway? I've seen it with the other girls, too. They come in here and watch us dance, practically slobbering all over themselves, then, when they start dating one of us, they want us to quit."

"I think they get possessive," Connor said.

Xena laughed shortly. "Right. Well, if you start dating a dancer, you're a fool if you think she's going to quit."

Kate spoke. "I heard that Judy planned to quit eventually."

Xena nodded and blew another cloud of smoke. "Right after graduation. She was only doing this to get through school, same as me. Then she was going to work for an accounting firm for a couple of years. She figured that in five years she'd have her own business."

"So she really wanted to go places," Kate remarked.

"That's part of what we had in common. We both wanted to go places, and neither of us was going to let anything get in our way. Both of us were poor kids, you know? I grew up in south St. Pete. I guess I don't have to tell you guys about the neighborhood. There wasn't a whole lot of money floating around, but I had good family. Judy didn't have much of anything. Her parents divorced when she was little. Her dad never paid a penny of child support, and her mom was always moving from one city to another trying to find a better job. When her mom left Tampa and headed west, Judy stayed behind so she could go to college. She never saw her mother again." Xena shook her head. "I can't imagine that. I see my mother every weekend."

"How's she feel about your dancing?"

Xena took a long drag on her cigarette and stubbed it out. "She hates it. She's afraid I'll get hurt. This stuff on the TV this morning about Judy being murdered by a serial killer is probably going to send her through the roof. She'll be screaming for me to quit."

"Could you?" Connor asked.

Xena looked at him. "Oh, yeah. I could right now. I've got enough saved. But you know what? I don't want some dumb-ass white boy driving me out of my job. I've had enough of that kind of shit."

Connor nodded. "He might not be white."

"Serial killers almost always are." Xena lit another cigarette. "I read, too."

"I didn't mean to imply that you don't."

"Maybe not. Look, I know enough to know these killers have a type. I couldn't be more different. I'm not blond, and I'm chocolate besides. His flavor is vanilla." She shrugged. "I'm more at risk from other kinds of jerks around here."

"You're probably right." Connor shifted on his stool and scribbled something on a pad he'd pulled from his pocket. "Now, what about the last night Judy worked here. Were you here?"

"I was. So was Mary Ellen. In fact, Mary Ellen is the one who...found her, I guess you'd say. They were friends here at work. You might want to talk to her, too."

"Maybe. But about that night. Did you see anything unusual? Did she act differently? Spend time with a customer?"

"No. Sorry. The only unusual thing was that she left about an hour early. That would have been around midnight, I guess. Her asthma was kicking up, and even the medicine couldn't control it, so the boss let her go."

"Did anybody go with her to make sure she was going to be all right?"

Xena cocked her head. "You know, I honestly don't know. I was busy dancing at a table, and my back was to the door. I knew she was going, but I didn't watch. I don't think her attack was so bad she needed help...." She slid off the stool abruptly. "Let me go talk to the boss. He might know about that."

Kate looked at Connor. "Wouldn't the police have asked her these questions?"

"Maybe they stopped at the part about Xena not seeing her leave."

Xena returned a few minutes later. "Bob says she left alone. She said it wasn't that bad, even said she'd hang around in the parking lot for a few minutes and see if that helped. Sometimes just getting away from the smoke for a little while was all it took."

"So somebody could have grabbed her in the parking lot," Connor said.

Xena shook her head. "I've been thinking a lot about that since the cops were here. I don't think that could have happened."

"Why not?"

"Because that minister was here that night. You know the one. He and a bunch of his missionaries hang out down here, trying to talk us girls out of dancing and shame the men into not coming inside. Anyway, his whole crew were out there when I took a break at ten, and they were just leaving when I got off at one. The parking lot was safe that night."

Kate exchanged a look with Connor. "That would fit with the newest one, wouldn't it?" Kate asked him. "Judy Eppinga probably wasn't grabbed. She probably knew the guy and let him into her apartment."

Connor nodded agreement.

"Well, she did know a lot of people," Xena agreed, lighting yet another cigarette. "She had plenty of friends on campus, students and teachers alike, and there were probably dozens she wouldn't hesitate to let into her apartment, especially if they said they needed help. She was like that, you know?"

When Kate and Connor stepped outside, after leaving Connor's card for Xena to pass to Mary Ellen, neither of them felt considerably more enlightened than before they had talked to Xena.

"It's great human-interest stuff," Kate said. "But it doesn't get us any closer to the killer."

"I guess not. Except that we know she was probably safe when she left here, otherwise the people in the parking lot would know about it. I suppose the police have questioned them, too?"

"You can bet on it. I'll check on it tomorrow, anyway." He rubbed his eyes with the palms of his hands and sighed heavily. "The only thing I can think is that the asthma medication she was taking may have affected her judgment. Maybe she picked up a hitchhiker. Maybe she let somebody into her apartment that she shouldn't have trusted. Maybe she got sicker on the way home and needed to ask for help and just asked the wrong person."

Kate nodded, feeling a stirring of excitement. "Maybe that's what happened with Marceline Whitmore. Maybe she was out somewhere and got sick and needed help. Or her car broke down, and somebody offered to follow her home to make sure she made it safely. Maybe the guy never was stalking exotic dancers. Maybe all his encounters with his victims have been accidental, and something about the victims just triggered his urge to kill."

"That could be." He scuffed his toe over the parking-lot gravel and sent a few pebbles flying. "These killers experience a kind of aura. It comes over them, and they lose their connection with reality. Once the aura starts, they begin their hunt, and when the right victim turns up, *pow!* That's it."

"But what sets a serial killer apart from someone who kills several people?"

"The serial killer has a ritual of some kind involved

in the killing. I'm still trying to figure out the ritual in this case."

For some reason, it didn't occur to her to ask him why he should do such a thing. "What have you got so far?"

He unlocked his car and opened the door for her. "Very little," he said as he closed it. He didn't want to discuss it with her. Couldn't, actually. After all, anything he told her might well end up in the paper.

Another wave of longing washed over him, bringing a powerful urge to escape to his computer and Katydid. She wanted a walk on the beach. He wanted to hold her hand. She spoke of feeling the sand between her toes. He wanted to feel her skin beneath his palm, even it if was only in his imagination.

Christ, he was losing it! They were e-mail friends, nothing more, and the thoughts that were dancing around in his head were crazy. He'd heard of people writing erotic e-mails to one another, indulging in pretend relationships, but he'd always thought that was...nuts. He'd never had the least desire to do any such thing, but here he was starting to dream of it with an intensity that should have been reserved for a woman he was dating.

He glanced uneasily at Kate Devane as he slipped in behind the wheel and wondered what she would think of the thoughts that were dancing across his brain synapses and irritating his nerve endings. She would probably think wanting to hold an e-mail friend's hand was tantamount to mental illness.

And maybe it was. Why the hell didn't he just find himself a real woman, someone like Kate Devane here? She was married, but there were plenty of women who weren't, and it wasn't very hard to find one. So why was he living a monastic existence filled with nightmares and horrifying photos, cut off from damn near everything except an ephemeral relationship by electronic mail?

For the first time, it occurred to him that all the years he had spent as a cop might have made him unfit for other relationships. He still related to cops; so far, he'd done a lousy job of relating to his new colleagues.

And he had to get his mind off this before he blew a gasket. Grasping at straws, he asked a question.

"Is your husband feeling any better?"

She was startled. He could feel it clear across the car, and he glanced her way, surprised to find her facing him, her eyes dark shadows in her pale face.

"Is he still sick?" he asked, repeating it because it occurred to him she might have been lost in thought and not really heard him.

But she didn't answer immediately, and he began to get the feeling that he had just put his foot in something deep and dangerous. "Kate? Sorry. I guess it's none of my business." Although he couldn't begin to imagine why that should be.

"No, it's not that," she said finally. "It's just that… Oh, hell. I don't like to talk about it. He's very ill."

"And you worry about that?"

"All the time."

He decided this would probably be a good time to drop this entire conversation. Raking up people's divorces and marital problems was rarely a smart move. Often as not, you wound up neck-deep in garbage. Besides, he was getting the definite feeling that Kate didn't want to discuss it, either.

By the time they got back to the newspaper offices, the silence between them was so thick that he was beginning to wonder just what he'd stepped into. The cop in him wanted to ask questions until he had answers.

The more sensitive part of him recognized that that could be hurtful.

And he didn't want to hurt this woman. As he pulled into a parking slot near her car, he looked over at her and thought how defenseless she appeared. She wasn't, of course, no more than anyone else, but she looked so...fragile, somehow, as she sat with her arms tightly folded and her head ever so slightly bowed on her slender neck.

The nape of her neck caught his attention, and he zeroed in on the fine honey-blond hairs that had escaped her chignon and were gently caressing her nape. Desire awoke in him with a sudden hot tingle, and he looked quickly away.

The problem, he told himself, was simply that he needed to get laid. It had been too long, and now he was fantasizing about a woman he'd never met and feeling a strong urge to make a pass at a co-worker.

He was in serious danger of fucking himself.

The thought made him suddenly want to chuckle, and he almost grinned as he climbed out of the car. Before he could get around to help Kate out, she'd already climbed out and was heading toward her car.

"I'll follow you home," he called after her. "To make sure you get there okay."

Her back stiffened a little. "That's not necessary. Really."

"Sure it is," he said. "We have a serial killer stalking blondes. I'll follow you."

This time she didn't argue.

Connor's mother was a full-blood Crow who had worked as a waitress at a truck stop on U.S. Highway 2 in Montana. His father had been an Irish immigrant working as a long-haul trucker. He'd eaten at the truck stop every time he came through, and while he waxed maudlin about missing Donegal, she'd waxed miserable about the endless bitter winters and the way her people were treated.

Misery loves company, and Diurmuid Quinn and Anna Eagle Bear had been two miserable people. Connor had never understood how or why the urge hit them, but they'd decided to get married and move to Florida, where at least it wasn't cold. Diurmuid had said he needed to be near the water. Anna had said she never wanted to see another snowflake. They had hardly arrived in Florida before Connor was on the way.

Now their son stood on the balcony of his small apartment and watched the inky waves lap at the seawall below. It was warmer tonight, and he decided he'd better put his geraniums and hibiscus outside again in the morning, before they started believing they were houseplants.

His heritage from his parents included a strong mystical streak that he was forever trying to bury. He definitely didn't like the feeling that he saw things in ways other people couldn't, that he sensed things that were beyond ordinary understanding. That sense was part of what had made him so good at hunting killers, but he didn't like it at all. He didn't want to slip into their depraved minds and view things from their perspective. Even less did he want to slip into the victims' minds.

But tonight, after he'd left Kate safely at home and before he permitted himself to relax by reading the mail from Katydid, he let his mystical streak come to the fore. The sea-softened breeze from off the bay blew his hair about and whispered gently in his ears. The stars above were stark and cold, clear as pinpricks in heaven's dark cloak. It was a beautiful night, but the beauty couldn't touch the core of coldness that was growing in him.

He could see Judy Eppinga so clearly in his mind's eye now. Her pictures hung on his wall, pictures from before her death, taken by friends, taken by her bosses. She had been a beautiful woman, with eyes full of life and a smile that invited the world to laugh along with her.

She hadn't deserved to die.

Except that one killer had thought differently. One man had felt she most definitely needed to die. Her death had been strangely nonviolent, to judge by the death scenes of the women who had been killed before and after her. Strangely nonviolent for a serial killer. But clearly ritualistic.

So the killer hadn't wanted to make them suffer horrible agonies, hadn't wanted them to scream in pain for his satisfaction. He hadn't even seemed to be especially angry with them. Perhaps all he had wanted was their fear?

And what had he done with all that blood? Blood loss from both the first victim and Marceline Whitmore was estimated to be about five quarts. Enough to kill them through massive shock. Once their hearts stopped pumping, the killer had apparently stopped draining the blood. What did he want it for?

The inescapable conclusion seemed to be that he wanted it for some further ritual after he left the scene. It was certainly common enough for serial killers to take trophies, which they customarily used to relive the killing, but blood was the most unusual trophy he'd ever heard of, and it was a trophy that wouldn't keep well or long. And that complicated the whole damn question about what demons the killer was trying to appease.

Finally Connor turned and went back inside, letting the feelings and half-formed impressions roil around in the back of his mind while he gave himself permission to think about something else.

Katydid had e-mailed him twice, he saw. The first note he opened was her suggestion that they take a walk on the beach. It still amazed him how quickly a few words from her could make his imagination carry him off to the Florida Keys and a beach that was empty save for himself and Katydid.

She wrote that the kitten, Tigret, was tumbling down the beach after them, stumbling in the sand. She painted the picture of a tangerine-and-turquoise sunset, a sailboat out beyond the reef on darkening waters.

He could see it, smell it, feel it. And when his heart started to thud in a slow, steady rhythm, he found himself writing back, speaking of the soft breeze and the sparkle in her eyes. And then, holding his breath even as he wrote it, he reached out and took her hand, touching her for the very first time. His fingers flew over the keys as he felt the warmth of her palm pressing against his.

And gently, daringly, he turned her toward him and drew her to him for a kiss. He felt it all, and wrote it all, and his heart beat as heavily as if he were actually holding her.

Then he hit the send key, before he could take it back, and sat there wondering how she would react, hoping against hope that she would respond in kind. Katydid was becoming the center of his private life.

After a bit, his sense of having taken a great risk subsided, and he opened her second note.

"I'm forwarding the latest communication from the

e-mail stalker," she wrote. "See below. Let me know what you think."

He read the note, and his heart thudded again, differently this time. He didn't like the way it sounded, didn't like the implication that this guy actually knew where she was. But maybe he was just bluffing?

He looked at the note for a long time, feeling that the threads of fate were running together somehow. It was an uneasy, anxious feeling that he couldn't quite get a grip on. He was probably just so disturbed over the Puppetmaster that he was making more of Katydid's e-mail stalker than was necessary. After all, the guy had never done anything but send her obnoxious notes.

He saved the forwarded message and sent her a brief, reassuring note saying he thought the guy was a bag of wind and not to worry until he wrote something more specific. Meanwhile, he made a mental note to talk to a friend of his about finding a way to trace this guy.

Just as he was turning off his computer, ready to call this too-long day over, his phone rang twice and his answering machine picked up. Moments later, he heard a strained male voice speak.

"Mr. Quinn... Mr. Quinn...you don't know me, but I read your articles in the paper about the...killer. The serial killer. I... You'll think I'm crazy, but...I have these visions.... I know who he's going to kill next...." A pause, then *click.*

Quinn was halfway to the phone when the guy hung up. A dial tone filled the apartment for a few seconds before the answering machine cut out.

Swearing savagely, Quinn grabbed the phone and dialed star 69. Moments later a canned voice was telling him that the last call received was from 555-1032. He scribbled it down and dialed it back immediately. The phone on the other end rang and rang, but no one answered.

"God damn it!" Quinn slammed the phone down and yanked the tape from the answering machine so that it wouldn't get erased accidentally. Then he picked up the phone and called Rick Diaz, dragging him out of bed.

"Rick? I think I've just had a call from the Puppetmaster."

# 7

"The number is a pay phone on Fletcher," Diaz said. "It could have been anybody in the world calling you. It was probably just some crank. We've already had five different people turn themselves in and confess to the killings. Why shouldn't you get your share of weirdos?"

"I guess." The guy really hadn't said anything, except for his claim to have visions about who was going to be killed next. Anybody could say that.

"But you don't believe that," Rick said after a moment. "So okay, why don't you believe this is some weird publicity hound?"

"Because he didn't leave his name."

The detective rolled his eyes. "He didn't leave his name."

"Exactly. If he wanted publicity, or any other kind of attention, he sure as hell would have left his name."

"Granted. So you got a plain old weirdo who doesn't want publicity. Somebody with half a loose cog instead of a whole one."

"Maybe."

Rick shook his head impatiently and poured more sugar in his coffee. They were sitting side by side at a lunch counter just off Fowler. Quinn had needed to come over here to do a photo spread about a new exhibit at the Museum of Science and Industry, referred to by locals as MOSI, and Rick was taking care of some business at the university right across the way.

"Bobby Joe Long used to prowl the same area," Quinn remarked.

Rick took a big swig of coffee and made a face. "This damn stuff tastes like burnt rubber." He poured more sugar into it. "So what if Bobby Joe Long prowled the same area? Christ, Quinn, what with all the transients, the college students, the lingerie-modeling shops, the X-rated video stores...this end of town is a serial killer's dream. You could say it's overflowing with potential victims."

"But our killer moved down to south Tampa."

"Don't remind me." Not that Rick had any intention of forgetting about it. It just didn't make the cops very happy when wealthy, influential people were the victims, because they made a lot of ruckus and generally made life hell until the bad guys were caught. "That was his first mistake."

"Maybe." Connor pushed his coffee away, signaled the counterman and asked for water. "These guys want to get caught, Rick. You know that. Sooner or later, they start to leave a trail."

"That's a nice theory."

"It works a lot of the time."

"So you think this guy wants to be caught?"

"I don't know. I'm thinking about it. He changed his modus—or at least it looks that way—and that could be because he wants us to work harder at finding him. Or it could be because he wants to show us how smart he is."

Rick snorted. "Yeah. Thumbing his nose at us. That's my take on it."

"Except that he gave us a very big clue. Our killer is a guy who apparently had the trust of Marceline Whitmore, as well as the trust of some exotic dancers. That's a broad range of friends."

Rick shook his head. "Not for some of the young bloods I know around here. Too much money and not enough to do with themselves."

"Exactly."

Rick turned on his stool and looked at him. "That's not for general distribution."

"People will think of it themselves. It's the only logical fit. Some young guy who hangs around strip bars and knows bankers' wives. Sounds to me like the country-club set."

Rick grimaced. "Don't say that out loud. The TPD have enough problems with the Whitmores breathing down their necks. They don't need half of south Tampa in a panic."

But Quinn was unrelenting. After all, he'd been dragged into this mess to do just what he was doing. "It goes with the phone call I got the other night. A cultured, educated-sounding voice."

"Well, as a lead it's useless."

"Not really. If I go with the assumption that the guy who called was the killer, I've got another insight. He thinks he has visions."

"And if he's not the killer?"

"I'll figure it out soon enough. But damn it, Rick, I've got next to nothing to go on here! Ropes, abraded knees, exsanguination, no sign of struggle... It's not a whole hell of a lot. So if the guy has visions—"

"Yeah," Diaz said, interrupting him. "What if he has visions? What the hell does that tell you?"

Connor looked at the water glass in front of him. "It tells me," he said after a minute, "that this guy is seriously dissociated."

"Well, hallelujah! Every serial killer is seriously dissociated. Isn't that one of the hallmarks?"

"This guy is more so than most, if that was him on the phone."

"Look," Rick said, facing him again. "I know how you work, and I'm trying real hard not to get in the way of your instincts, but if you go running off after a decoy, we could be in serious trouble here. And so could some young girl who at this moment doesn't know she's only got a few days to live. You be real damn careful about what you make out of that phone call last night."

Connor nodded, accepting the justice of what Rick was saying, even if he wasn't prepared to dismiss the phone call. "When are you calling the FBI in?"

Rick looked down. "We started talking to them this morning. They're going to send down a couple of profilers to look over the evidence."

"Good. We need all the help we can get."

Rick looked at him. "It doesn't mean we don't have confidence in you."

Connor smiled. "You know what, Rick? The more the merrier. The faster we find the guy, the better. And besides, you bring in the feebs and I don't have to carry the whole damn mess on my own shoulders. And that's just fine with me. Maybe I'll even be able to get a little sleep."

"I know, Quinn. I know."

"No, I really don't think you do," Quinn said. "I quit, remember? I quit this shit because I had enough nightmares to last a lifetime, and then you dragged me right back in. You know what my nightmare is these days, Rick? I keep having this dream where I'm looking at the killer through the lens of my camera, and all I can do is photograph what's happening. I can't stop the guy. I can't save the girl. All I can do is keep on taking the pictures."

He stood up and threw some money on the counter. "I've got to get over to MOSI. When the feebs show up, have 'em call me. I'll be more than glad to tell 'em what little I've come up with."

The newsroom was abuzz with activity when Kate arrived for work at noon. There had been a police shooting in northwest St. Petersburg in the early hours of the morning, and reports were sketchy. Some claimed the woman who was shot had been drunk and had threatened a police officer with a knife. Other witnesses claimed she'd been unarmed.

"Depends on who you want to believe," Mark Polanski told Kate. "Sally says you're handling the story. Unfortunately, all we have are conflicting eyewitness accounts. And, of course, as we all know, if the woman wasn't armed when the cop shot her, she probably got armed real fast."

Kate looked up at him, unable to suppress a wry smile. "Don't be so cynical."

"Who's being cynical? I'm just a realist. There's a real big fudge factor when cops tell you what happened."

"So do an investigative piece on the subject."

"Ha. Right. Like anybody can ever prove it. Anyway, there's the story, as much of it as we have. Conflicting opinions and descriptions everywhere, but basically this woman got drunk, assaulted her husband, chased him out into the yard, woke the neighbors, threatened to kill the hubby and one of the neighbors. Somebody called 911, the cops arrived, tried to talk her down, but something went wrong. One way or another, the woman is dead and her husband is screaming for the cop's blood."

"The *husband* is?"

"Oh, yeah." Mark grinned wryly. "Typical abused-spouse response. That's one that cuts across gender. Anyway, I wanted to talk to you about something else."

Everything inside Kate tensed. She hadn't felt comfortable with Mark since his accusations about Mike, and she kept waiting for the next development.

"I got another call from that family member who called before," Mark said. Kate opened her mouth, but he held up his hand, silencing her. "Just wait, Kate. It's bullshit, and I know it's bullshit. I did a little investigating and discovered this is a tempest in a teapot, so far as scandal is concerned. So I figured I'd just let you know that this person is still gunning for you, and you'd better watch your back."

"Thanks, Mark." Her stomach eased a little, but she couldn't have said it was unexpected. The Devane family had been nothing if not persistent in their belief that she was responsible for Mike's illness. Sometimes she thought they were all just as ill as Mike.

After Mark left, she tried to turn her attention to the work that was piling up in front of her, but instead she found her thoughts straying to the e-mail she had found from Connor this morning. It was reassuring that he didn't think she had anything to worry about from the e-mail stalker.

But his other note... Her heart skipped a beat, and her hands clenched over her keyboard as she thought about the kiss he had described. At first she had been shocked, but then she had discovered just how very much she wanted CQ to kiss her. Her mind had no trouble filling in the picture, and for long moments this morning she had clearly imagined how it would feel to be pressed to him, to have his arms around her. Her pulse had accelerated, and her breath had quickened, and suddenly she'd been alive and aching.

And she almost hated him for that. Hated him for reminding her of all the things she was missing and had been missing since Mike became so ill. She also hated it that for a few painful, stark moments this morning she had acknowledged all the yearning she felt. It was as if she had opened Pandora's box, and now she couldn't close the lid on all the feelings that had escaped and forced themselves to her notice.

"You okay?" Sally Dyer sat beside her and touched her shoulder. "Devane, you look like hell. Don't tell me you're getting the flu."

Kate managed a smile. "No. I had a flu shot in November along with everyone else. Remember?"

"Yeah, but we get so many tourists here, you never know what kind of germ one of them is going to bring in. Did I tell you about that guy from Michigan who got in front of me yesterday on Gulf-to-Bay and kept hitting his brakes? It was like watching a strobe light. And every time I tried to get around him, some jerk in the other lane would speed up. Do you know, this is the only place I've ever lived where a turn signal is a challenge to other drivers to speed up and pass you before you can change lanes?"

Kate nodded sympathetically. "I've noticed that, too."

"I'm thinking about getting one of those bumper stickers that says, 'Not all of us are on vacation.'"

"That wouldn't have helped with the guy from Michigan."

"No, or with the jerk from New Hampshire who pulled out right in front of me the other day. I swear he never saw me. He almost had me in the side of his head."

Almost in spite of herself, Kate laughed. Everyone around here complained their way through tourist season. Lines grew too long at all the stores, dining out in a restaurant required both waiting and planning, and traffic was heavy all day long. It wouldn't improve until after Easter, and by then the natives would have become as rude and impatient as the tourists they loved to complain about.

"What really kills me," Sally went on, "is their attitude. Where do they get off acting like we only exist for their convenience? I can see them feeling that way at the hotel where they're staying, but in a drugstore or supermarket? Please."

"I don't know what to tell you, Sally. I don't mind it too much, except for the crowding and the rudeness that seems to come with it. I just try not to think about it."

"Exactly," Sally said, patting her shoulder. "And that's what you're going to do right now. You're going to forget about all the troubles you were worrying about a minute ago, and you're going to focus on this shooting story. It's going to get interesting. The husband is now claiming that neither he nor his wife ever owned a knife like the one the cop claims she was threatening him with."

"Is that in Mark's story?"

Sally shook her head. "The call just came in. He's taking it now."

"He'll want to rewrite his story, then."

"Probably. Depends on what he thinks of the source and whether he can back it up. Anyway, hold up on the editing until he gets off the phone and lets us know what he wants to do. In the meantime, take a look at the layout on section B. Something about 1-B is bothering me."

Kate nodded agreeably and promptly called up the layout on her large monitor. Ten minutes later, she had reordered two of the articles, giving the page a more balanced appearance and putting a more important story above the fold. Even as she did it, she wondered why Sally was even bothering with it now. Chances were, something would happen to change the whole layout before the day was over.

"Hey, Devane," Sally said, "there's a call for Quinn on the Puppetmaster story, but Quinn isn't here. You want to take the call?"

"Sure." Kate snagged the receiver and brought it to her ear. "Kate Devane," she said.

"I want to talk to Connor Quinn."

"I'm sorry, he's not here. I'm working with him, though. Can I help you?"

There was a long hesitation, and just about the time Kate decided the guy must have hung up, he spoke. "You know about the murders?"

"Yes, I'm working with him on that. Do you have some new information?"

Again a long hesitation. "You won't believe me."

Kate's interest immediately perked up. In her experience, people who were about to lie didn't say that. Of course, she could always be wrong. "Try me."

"Well, I...keep having these dreams."

Dreams? Her pencil paused over her pad. "What kind of dreams?"

"Dreams about the killings. I...didn't believe it at first, but I...see the women he's going to kill before he kills them."

"In your dreams? You see them in your dreams?" Half of her was convinced this guy was a nut, and the other half was terrified that he wasn't.

"Yes. I...see him following them. I can't see *him*, of course, but I see them. And then...then I see their pictures in the newspaper. And they're the same ones I saw in my dreams...." His voice was growing thin, almost anguished. "Oh, God, I have to find a way to stop him!"

Kate's mind was scrambling around wildly, seeking some kind of response. She didn't know whether to dismiss the guy out of hand as a nut or to suggest they get together and discuss it further. Or even whether to offer to help him find these women. A good artist might be able to draw pictures of the women from his descriptions...if he was really seeing them.

But before she could say another word, he spoke again, his voice rising. "I'm sorry," he said. "You don't believe me. Why should you? I can hardly believe it myself." Then, with a sharp click, he hung up.

Kate immediately checked the Caller ID and swore under her breath when she found out the number had been blocked. In all likelihood, the man had been a crackpot, but she still had the feeling that something important had just slipped through her fingers.

"Anything useful?" Sally asked.

"No." Kate shrugged a shoulder. "Some kind of crackpot talking about visions."

"That we can do without. Until the cops hire a psychic, anyway."

"Are they going to?"

"I don't know. The pressure's getting pretty heavy, though. Have you scanned Gerry's article about the mayor's press conference this morning? Apparently the natives are restless and want a quick resolution. Especially now that one of their own has been killed."

"Who doesn't?"

Sally cracked a dry laugh. "Yeah."

Kate called up Gerry Aldrich's article and read it quickly. The mayor's office expressed concern and assured the public that the police were sparing no effort in finding the Puppetmaster. The sheriff and the chief of police stood shoulder-to-shoulder with him and described their joint task force. To her surprise, no mention was made of calling in the FBI. After this latest murder, she would have figured someone would be demanding it.

"Politics," Connor said later, when he came in with several rolls of film to develop. "Politics, pure and simple. Somebody isn't ready to turn the spotlight over to the feebs." He didn't tell her that Rick was already talking with them.

"I would have thought after the Whitmore killing that they'd be eager to shed the responsibility."

"I am," he replied.

"You are?" Confused, she stared at him. "What responsibility?"

He hesitated as he dumped a roll of film into a basket. "I mean, I *would* be eager to turn it over. Christ, this thing is a political hot potato that's getting hotter by the minute. But apparently somebody thinks he stands to gain more by handling it himself."

"Isn't catching this guy more important than politics?"

He regarded her from beneath a lowered brow. "You would think so, wouldn't you?" He entered the darkroom through the revolving door, and she followed him, blinking with surprise at the brightness of the light. She had thought darkrooms were always dimly lit with red.

"I got an interesting phone call," she told him, watching him as he laid out cassettes of film in an orderly row. Then he took down metal developing tanks and laid them out in a neat sequence. Beside them he placed stainless-steel spools, a pair of scissors and a can opener.

"I'm going to turn out the lights for a couple of minutes," he told her. "Just lean against the wall so you don't get disoriented."

"Okay."

She listened to the sounds, trying to tell what he was doing in the pitch darkness, but she could only guess. "About the phone call—"

"Wait until I turn the lights on," he said, interrupting her. "I need to pay attention to what I'm doing."

"Sure." It was then, as if it exploded out of some crypt in her mind, that she remembered the e-mail he had sent her earlier. The e-mail in which he had kissed her. She had been so focused on that damn phone call that she had forgotten it.

And now she was standing here in the dark with him, and the sounds of the things he was doing receded until all she could hear was her own heartbeat.

"Are you all right?" he asked abruptly.

"Uh...yeah. Sure. Why?"

"Because you're breathing so heavily. Does the dark bother you? Do you feel claustrophobic?"

"No...no, really. I'm fine." But she wanted to crawl under something and hide from embarrassment. She'd been thinking about him kissing her. What if he just walked over here and kissed her? But of course he wouldn't. He could kiss Katydid by e-mail, because it meant nothing. He couldn't kiss Kate Devane, who was his colleague, because it would create all kinds of difficulty. How could he even know that she wouldn't scream sexual harassment or something?

But, oh, it had been so long since she had been kissed! And to be kissed by Connor Quinn... Guilt jabbed her sharply.

All of a sudden the lights came on, nearly blinding her. The film cassettes lay scattered on the counter, their ends pried off. He picked them up and tossed them in the wastebasket, then turned his attention to the constant-temperature bath. He filled it with warm water from the sink, checked the temperature, then set the developing solutions in it. When he was satisfied with the temperature of the solutions, he poured developer into the canisters, closed their vents and set a timer. Picking them up, one in each hand, he rapped them once sharply against the counter, then gently began agitating them with a twisting motion of his wrists.

"What did you do while the lights were out?" she asked him.

"I opened the film cassettes, wrapped the film around the metal spools and put it all in the developing tanks."

"You did all that in the dark?" The idea astonished her.

"I've done it so many times now, I could do it standing on my head."

"I suppose. But it was hard at first?"

"Not as hard as you'd think. So what about this phone call you mentioned?" he asked her. The timer beeped. He set the developing tanks in the constant-temperature bath and reset the timer.

She hesitated, suddenly feeling almost foolish for taking it seriously enough to mention it. "Well, it was probably nothing, but this man called for you. I took it because you weren't here."

"Sure," he said, as if in answer to her unspoken question. "That's okay."

"Anyway, he said he...was having visions about the killings."

He turned sharply to look at her. "What exactly did he say?"

She shrugged. "It was all confused. He was apologizing for even calling, telling me he knew I wouldn't believe him. Anyway, before I could find out any more, or get a number, he hung up. I checked Caller ID, but the number had been blocked."

"Christ." The timer beeped. He picked up the developing tanks, rotated them a couple of times, then returned them to the bath and reset the timer.

"What?" she asked, when he said nothing more.

"The same guy called me at home last night. He hung up before I got to the phone. At least, I think it was the same guy."

Something cold seemed to trickle down her spine. "You think he could be for real?"

"That's the sixty-four-thousand-dollar question, isn't it? What if he's the killer?"

"Oh, God!"

"Pleasant thought, hmm?" He shook his head. The timer went off again, and he reached for the developing tanks. "Give me some time to think about this and what we need to do about it. I'll let you know if I have any brilliant ideas."

"Sure." She turned to the door.

"Kate?"

"Mm?"

"Did you give this guy your name?"

The chill grew deeper, penetrating to her very bones. "Yes. Of course. When I answered the phone. I said I was working with you."

"Hell."

He didn't say another word. He didn't need to. She left the darkroom and went back to her desk, feeling as dislocated as she had the day she committed Mike to the hospital for the first time.

It was hard. Harder than he had thought it would be. How was he supposed to call total strangers and tell them he was having visions? How did he make them believe he wasn't just some kind of crank? Twice now he'd called, and both times he'd panicked, certain that he would be dismissed as a lunatic—or, worse, that they would think he was the killer.

He prayed about it. He prayed until the words of his prayers were buzzing like angry bees in his head. If he called them and went through with it, they were going to want to know who he was. And if he told them, it wouldn't matter whether they believed he was crazy or that he was the killer. His ministry would be ruined. His flock would consider him an embarrassment and abandon him.

Then what? How could he find another church? Who would want him?

He would have to explain about the visions and how they had gotten worse since the accident. And about the headaches that so often laid him up. Nobody would want him. Even Mrs. Hebert, his housekeeper, didn't know about the visions, and she thought the headaches were just ordinary migraines. Nobody knew about the visions.

If he told them about the accident and the headaches and the visions, they would probably want to put him in a hospital, and he didn't think he could face that again.

But his own whining was disgusting him. He took out his well-thumbed Bible, the one his mother had given him the day he was confirmed, and read the Gospel about the betrayal of Jesus, about His mistreatment at the hands of the Romans. And he read about Peter's betrayal of Jesus, when Peter thrice denied Him.

His own name was Peter, and he found himself wondering if he was following in his namesake's footsteps by refusing to take up the burden that had been thrust upon him. He needed to stop worrying about himself. What did it matter if he was reviled and spit upon, if he did the right thing? What did it matter how much humiliation he suffered? Could he suffer worse than He had when they crucified Him?

But the flesh was weak, and the headache was so bad, and he feared that if he got driven out of his church, he wouldn't be able to afford the doctors who could ease his pain. Sometimes the pain was so bad he honestly thought he could cut off his own head. What if it drove him to suicide, which was one of the deadliest sins, and would cost him his own salvation?

Oh, God, these questions were too difficult, and the answers so elusive!

Near to despair, he sent Mrs. Hebert home. Then he went to the church, where he knelt and prayed the night away.

He had to believe that God would not abandon him. He had no other hope.

# 8

"Yeah, of course we talked to the picketers," Rick Diaz told Connor. "It's in the report."

"It's not in my copy of the report."

"Then turn on your damn fax machine and I'll send it over right now."

"It's on."

"Two minutes."

Connor hung up the phone and loaded the fax software on his computer. Fifteen seconds later, he was up and running. A little over a minute later, his phone rang. While he waited for the transmission to finish, he wandered over to the window and looked out. The sun was bright today and glistened off the water of the bay so brilliantly that it hurt his eyes. Days like today were rare, even in beautiful Florida, he thought—so dry and breezy, and just the right temperature. The kind of day that made him want to go out and run for miles.

A beep signaled that the transmission was done. He called it up on his screen and cursed at the poor quality. No chance he could print it out; he would have to make do with an enlarged video image.

The religious group had been interviewed, all right,

the very next day, after the body was found. They had been questioned first singly and then as a group as they picketed a different strip bar. None of them had retained a very clear memory of Judy Eppinga's last night alive. They had vaguely remembered that she might have left the bar before it closed. One of them had been absolutely certain she had left alone. Two others hadn't been sure, and three more couldn't remember her at all. The minister, Peter Masterson, had said that if it was the same girl, she had stopped and talked to them for a few seconds, complaining about the cold and her asthma. Then she had gotten in her car and driven away.

Useless, thought Connor. Utterly useless. And he was beginning to get very tired of beating his head on this particular brick wall.

What had he gotten so far? Not a damn thing that mattered. Not one.

Grabbing a pad of paper and a pen, he itemized the things he felt he could say with any certainty.

One: The killer was organized. He left nothing at the scenes that could identify him. At least, nothing they had so far found.

That bothered Connor. Tipping back in his chair, he closed his eyes and thought about that. How could the killer leave nothing at all, not even a hair? Certainly these women weren't letting a man into the house who was wearing some kind of hood or mask. So what did he do? Shave all the hair from his body? But that would make him remarkable-looking, so remarkable-looking that somebody would surely remember having seen him.

Two: The attacks weren't overtly sexual. He was reluctant at this time to say there was nothing at all sexual about them, but there was certainly no evidence of rape, or of masturbation at the scene. If the guy got off on this, he did it somewhere else.

Three; No evidence of trophy taking, other than blood. None that they could find, anyway. Which meant next to nothing. No one was likely to know if any of these women was missing something so small as a hairpin or a pair of panties. Not even Marceline Whitmore's husband claimed to be sure of that.

And speaking of Marceline Whitmore's husband, the man was in danger of being arrested for his wife's murder. There was a theory floating around that he might have staged the first two murders to cover the murder of his wife. The suspicion was aided by the fact that his sister said he'd left Orlando early in the evening, which meant he should have arrived home before midnight. Further questioning of Alan Whitmore had resulted in contradictory stories about how he'd spent the time. Quinn suspected he had a girlfriend. So did the cops. None of that helped Whitmore.

But Quinn was convinced the man hadn't killed his wife. None of the murders displayed any of the anger he would have expected in such killings. If anything, the murders were strangely passionless...which made them all the more disturbing.

The killer had a reason for what he was doing, but whatever it was, it didn't involve anger. In fact, Quinn would have bet his next two paychecks that the killer of these women wouldn't harm his own wife or mother. Most serial killings displayed rage, but the hallmarks of anger just weren't there, and that was very troubling.

So many serial killers used their victims as stand-ins for the person they were really mad at. Ted Bundy had killed women who resembled his ex-girlfriend. It was chilling to Connor how similar all the victims were in appearance.

A more common focus of the anger was the killer's mother—Ed Kemper and Henry Lee Lucas being prime examples. But if this killer felt any anger toward his mother, he was not displaying it in his murders.

Or perhaps he was. They still didn't know what the guy was doing with all that blood.

It dawned on Connor suddenly that the killer must be older than most. That would explain why the rage was so well controlled. Why the whole scene was so well controlled. He was compelled to kill, but he wasn't acting on impulse. Everything was very carefully planned, and the planning had taken place over years of fantasizing.

So he was older. Thirty. Maybe even more. Personable, well-spoken, unthreatening. He had to be, in order to convince all these women to trust him. Every one of them had invited him into her home, and in this day and age, that was something no sane woman did with a stranger. Hell, it was getting hard even for cops in uniform to get across a threshold.

No one had seen the first victim after she left the club that night. The same for the second victim. Marceline Whitmore, the banker's wife, hadn't been seen by neighbors, friends or family after four o'clock the afternoon before her death. The last person known to have seen her, a girlfriend with whom she had gone shopping that afternoon, said Marceline had talked about spending the evening working on a newsletter for one of the charities she aided. If she had done so, there was no sign of it at her house.

Marceline's white Lexus had been in the garage when her girlfriend dropped her off after their shopping expedition. No one knew how or when the car had been moved into the driveway. She had probably gone out somewhere during the evening.

Things weren't adding up. The first two victims had been stalked and had received notes from the stalker. Presumably the person who wrote the notes that referred to the Puppetmaster was also the killer. If Marceline Whitmore had received any notes, she had mentioned them to no one and had kept none of them, except that lone anonymous note of warning.

It appeared that she had ignored it, but why? A woman who was as paranoid about turning on the alarm system as her husband claimed should have been terrified, should have told someone about the warning note. And that, like it or not, was another strike against her husband. Perhaps he was a copycat killer who had heard some loose talk among cops or prosecutors about the two earlier slayings, and had left the note to cover his tracks, to make it look as if someone else had committed the crime. If so, he'd made a big mistake, because the absence of notes referring to the Puppetmaster made him look even likelier as a suspect. Connor made a note to check if Whitmore had friends in the police or the State Attorney's office.

But her murder was similar in every detail to the other two, and the likelihood that anyone could have independently arrived at anything this unusual was highly unlikely. Not just the exsanguination and the ropes, but the abrasions on the knees, as well.

He kept coming back to those abrasions, sensing that they held a vital clue, but damned if he could figure it out. The ropes, of course, were obvious, given the killer's attachment to someone he called "the Puppetmaster." There was no question in Connor's mind that the killer was tying these women as if they were marionettes, probably even forcing them to "dance" for him in some way.

Dance, dancer, puppet. It all fit together beautifully, except for the fact that one victim was not a dancer. Otherwise, it would have fit together too perfectly, and he would have been as suspicious as hell. It was rare indeed that a serial killer's ritual was that transparent.

But even though it was only a glimpse, it *was* a glimpse, and it kept him puzzling the puzzle. He studied the photographs again, with every light in the room blazing. He studied them with magnifying glasses, hunting for details the camera had caught that the human eye might miss. He paid particular attention to those photos that his inner voice had prodded him to take. It was often as if his unconscious mind recognized important details that his conscious mind missed.

But not always. It was never that simple.

Finally, bleary-eyed and frustrated, he sat down at his computer and logged on. Two e-mails from Katydid awaited him, and it suddenly hit him that the last note he sent her had contained the kiss.

It was as if a rope lassoed all his scattered thoughts, drawing them back from the killings and all his other preoccupations, tightening until every bit of him was centered on this moment, on the screen before him. His heart gave an uneasy lurch, and he wondered if he was going to open her mail and discover that she was furious with him. To discover that he had just lost a friend because of an errant moment of need and sensuality.

But finally he clicked his mouse and watched the first note from her appear on the screen.

"Thanks, CQ. You're right. There's no way the guy could know who I really am. I checked with the service, and they said none of my personal info is available online. I feel better now. Thanks again.''

Feeling oddly let down and relieved, all at the same time, he clicked on the next note from her. When it appeared, he felt as if all the air had just been sucked out of the room.

''CQ,'' she had written, ''you take my hand and it feels so good to have a friend like you, someone with whom I can be so comfortable. Your palm is warm against mine, and I squeeze your fingers, wanting you to know how much I appreciate your touch.''

Well, that's not so bad, he thought, moving on to the next screenful of words. Apparently she wasn't going to hate him forever.

''Then you tug me gently and turn me to face you,'' she continued. ''I know what is coming. I can feel it about to happen. Part of me is terrified that we'll lose something precious if we become more involved. Friendship is a delicate thing, meant to be nurtured, and man-woman attractions can ruin it. But part of me...part of me wants this as much as I have ever wanted anything. I can see the glimmer of the moonlight in your eyes, can see the dark strands of your hair moving gently in the breeze, caressing your shoulders.... Oh, yes, I want this, too!''

A pent-up breath escaped him in a rush. He leaned forward a little and read more eagerly, as every cell in his body seemed to leap with nervous excitement in response to her admission that she wanted this, too.

''It feels so good,'' she wrote, ''to lean against you and feel your strength. So good to feel your arms close around me and know that for these few moments I am safe. I almost feel as if I could stay here forever. Vain wish!

"And the touch of your lips...oh, have lips ever felt so warm, so gentle and yet so compelling? I rise on tiptoes, wanting even more, wanting never to stop...."

And there she stopped. Connor's heart was beating rapidly, and he almost felt as if a gauntlet had been thrown. She was daring him, but he wasn't sure exactly what she was daring him to do. Take the kiss further? Or back away from it now, before it became something more?

*Wanting never to stop...* He read the words over and decided to take them at face value. He started typing a reply almost before he knew he was doing it, taking the kiss farther and deeper, so intensely involved in what he was writing that nothing else seemed to exist. He felt the kiss vividly, and he wanted her to feel it, too. Wanted her to feel him pressed against her the way he felt her pressed against him.

He was just sending the message when the phone rang.

"Well, Quinn," said Rick Diaz. "What the hell have you got for me?"

"What makes you think I have anything?"

"The fact that we're at murder number three, that he's taking these women out at a rate of one every ten days— Well, that's the average—"

"It's hard to make an average when you've only got two periods to compare."

"I'm making the average anyway. Now it's three days since Whitmore bought it, and probably only seven or so until the next girl gets it— You know, he's probably stalking her even as we speak."

Connor didn't say anything. He didn't have to. Rick was stating the obvious. But then, Rick had always had a penchant for stating the obvious. Sometimes Connor thought he did it just to fill up dead air while his mind was racing on to something else altogether.

"So what have you got?" Rick asked again.

"Nothing earth-shattering. He turns those women into puppets."

"Yeah. So why does he think he's the Puppetmaster?"

"He doesn't think he is."

There was a silence. "What are you saying?"

"Read the notes again, Rick. He's not claiming to be the Puppetmaster. In my opinion, he's trying to appease this Puppetmaster with these murders."

Rick was silent for a while. "Are you saying someone else is involved? Or are you saying this guy is schizophrenic?"

"Neither. Yet. I'm just telling you the way I picture it from the notes and from the murders. He's trying to appease someone or something he calls the Puppetmaster. I'm beginning to wonder if this guy is practicing some basic form of sympathetic magic."

"Whoa. Hey, there. Magic? What are we talking about here? Covens? Satanism?"

"No. I don't see it being anything like that. I'm talking about something very basic here. It's almost instinctual in the human race. A lot of cultures believe that a person can take on the characteristics of a particular animal by eating its flesh or by using implements made from its skin or bones. Another example is sticking pins in dolls."

"So these girls are some kind of voodoo doll for him?"

"I wouldn't go that far. I don't know enough yet. But I would guess that if he's trying to appease this Puppetmaster by turning these women into some kind of puppet, then he's using sympathetic magic to make himself more like the Puppetmaster, whatever that is. The blood could also be part of the sympathetic-magic thing. Maybe he drinks it to take on some characteristic of these women. Or he could have some other use for it. I'm not real sure of any of this yet."

"I could do without the blood part, y'know. If the papers get hold of that, there'll be talk of vampire cults, and the politicos will raise one hell of a stink. Investigating this stuff is hard enough without city hall breathing down our necks."

"I remember."

Rick gave a short laugh. "I suppose you do."

"What about the FBI?"

"We're consulting by phone, but all their guys are seriously tied up. In case you haven't heard, serial killings are on the rise. At the moment, Tampa's problem is taking a back seat to problems in Chicago, Newark, Des Moines and Missoula."

"Missoula? Missoula, Montana?" He had family living up there. "What's going on?"

"I didn't ask. I got enough problems of my own. Hey, did you hear the new lawyer joke? I picked it up over at the courthouse earlier."

"What's that?"

Rick chuckled. "How do you get a law school graduate off your front porch?"

"Hell, I don't know."

"Pay for the pizza."

Connor laughed, even though he didn't feel much like laughing about anything. When Rick hung up, he was again alone with the murderer and his victims. And not even a brilliantly sunny day could drive away the darkness inside him.

* * *

The trip to see Mike drained Kate, as always. This time she found herself wanting to rant at him, to demand that he come back from his oblivion just long enough to explain it to her.

Why? she wanted to demand. Why did you have to go away from me? Why did you have to get sick? Why the hell did you have to marry me?

The last question yanked her up short and flooded her with guilt. Oh, God, how could she even wonder such a thing? How could she resent Mike for something beyond his control?

Besides, it was her fault for not having recognized that something wasn't quite right about him from the very start. Instead, she had found his volatility exciting, and the strange notions he took from time to time had been exhilarating. It had never once occurred to her that they were harbingers of something far, far worse. Mike, she had believed, was simply imaginative.

They had met in college, and things had been wild enough for both of them that a little wildness in one another had simply seemed like part of all the rest. His suspicions of people had always been justifiable, and his sudden interest in alien abductions had seemed like a great lark.

Even after they married, even when it began to worsen, she had been able to explain it away as a vagary. Because back then there had been long periods when Mike was just fine.

And during those times when he was fine... She looked at him now, and her heart squeezed. Oh, God, how she had loved him. He had made her whole world bright and vibrant, had turned every day into a wonderful adventure. Had made every morning feel like Christmas.

Until the nightmare began. And it was the nightmare that colored every memory she had of him. The fear. The lying awake all night listening to him talk to people who weren't there, wondering if tonight would be the night he decided to leave the house and do something totally insane.

During the early periods, she had shared his delusions, simply because there was no way to fight them. She had kept silent even when she felt he was wrong, because he wouldn't hear her arguments, anyway, and he'd only become extremely agitated. Agitated and sometimes threatening.

Because no matter how hard she tried to shelter him, no matter how much she loved him and cared for him, there had come a time when he began to see her as a threat. He had begun to believe the medication she gave him was poison. He had begun to suspect the meals she cooked were meant to kill him. He had even come to believe she was one of the aliens he so feared, and that she was trying to seduce him to get his seed to raise a race of slaves.

He had torn her into little pieces, twisting her in ways she could hardly comprehend even now. He had wounded her, though of course he had been wounded even more. And perhaps worst of all was that no matter how badly she was hurt, no matter how terrible her life became, or how many dreams she watched die, she never felt she had the right to be hurt, because Mike's condition was always so much worse.

So instead of acknowledging the price she paid, she felt terrible for feeling that she paid any price at all. She hid her hurts and felt embarrassed by them. She denied that she suffered, even when her days felt like living hell.

All so that years later she could sit in a mental institution and stare at a zombie and wonder if she was even entitled to have a life.

"It's not fair, Mike," she heard herself say. "It's not fair that you're sick, and it's not fair that your sickness has blighted my life, too."

It was a blunt, bald statement, and as soon as she spoke, she wished the words unsaid. Where was it written, after all, that life should be fair?

She looked past him out the window at the sunny day and wondered if he even knew the sun was shining, or if he was so lost in his delusion that he was completely out of touch. Or if the medications that calmed him had simply turned his mind into an empty slate where nothing was ever written anymore. How could anyone know?

She looked into his eyes, seeking signs of life and finding nothing but bland indifference. Finally she gave him a kiss and departed, wondering if he even knew she was there. Or if he cared. Or if he was on a medicated buzz that precluded any kind of caring.

He ate when food was put in front of him. He went to the bathroom when he needed to. Apart from that, he did nothing but sit and stare. Except, of course, for the periods when he became agitated, periods during which she wasn't allowed to see him. That bothered her, that they refused to let her see him when he was upset.

But that was what happened when the medical establishment took over. They ran the show, and everyone else had to make way for them.

Outside, she took a deep breath of fresh, dry air and felt a sudden wild wish to do something crazy. Something fun. Something just for herself. To cast off the psychological widow's weeds she had been wearing and be young again.

It was a pretty sorry thing to realize that you had forgotten how to have a good time.

But at this point, she didn't even have friends she could call. Mike had driven them away with his madness, and since his last commitment, she hadn't made any effort to find new ones.

The pier, she decided. She would take herself to the St. Petersburg Pier and watch the sun glint on the waves as boats sailed by. Maybe she would even feed the pelicans. She didn't have to work today, and after her visit to Mike, the empty time seemed to loom large and threatening. She had to fill it up somehow.

Driving down Sixty-sixth, she saw a group of police cars pulled into a knot around the front of a strip shopping center. She slowed down to look and realized that a car had driven through the front of a business. Before she reached a complete stop, she picked up her c-phone and called the paper.

"I need a photographer," she told Mary Carmichael, and gave her location. "A car ran into the front of a store here and crashed through the windows. There's no ambulance, but there are seven police cars."

"Call me back when you've got the story," Mary told her. "I'll get someone out there."

Kate nosed her car into a neighboring parking lot and climbed out even as she pawed through her purse for her notebook and tape recorder. They were at the bottom, of course, since she hadn't used them in a while. A quick check of the recorder told her the batteries were still good. Holding it near her mouth, she gave the date and location and walked over to the nearest cop.

"Hi, I'm Kate Devane of the *Sentinel,*" she said with

a pleasant smile as she flashed the identification badge that was clipped to her purse. "What happened here?"

The cop, a young man named Wexler, shook his head. "It'd be funny, except we already had to send a woman out in an ambulance. It's a warranty dispute."

"It was done deliberately?"

"Kinda takes your breath away, doesn't it?"

"What about the woman who was taken away? Was she badly hurt?"

"You'd better talk to Sergeant Yost, ma'am. He has more information than I do."

The young officer obligingly pointed out the sergeant who was in charge, and she made her way over to him. Yost was a handsome man of about fifty, with salt-and-pepper hair and a trim figure that would catch any woman's eye. He glanced at her badge with resignation but perked up a little when he took another look at her. She recognized the look; it said he found her to be what Mike used to call "eye candy." Well, that was certainly something she could use. She gave Yost a smile.

"Sergeant, I was hoping you could tell me what happened here."

"The owner of the vehicle has been involved in a prolonged dispute with the owner of the business. There was some disagreement about whether a piece of furniture needed warranty repair or replacement. The driver of the vehicle felt the business owner wasn't listening to him and apparently decided to get his attention."

Kate looked at the car that was sitting half in and half out of the store. "That would be hard to ignore."

Yost cracked a smile. "Just slightly. We are arresting Mr. Kazajian, the driver of the car, for attempted murder, criminal mischief, battery and reckless driving."

"And the woman who was injured?"

"Janine Armbruster. We haven't notified her family yet, so don't release her name. We don't know the extent of her injuries yet, but she was conscious when we arrived. She's been taken by ambulance to Bayfront."

The owner of the store, John Belfort, proved to be voluble. As soon as he was through talking to the cops, he was only too glad to talk to Kate. Connor Quinn arrived with his camera just as Kate was getting all kinds of personal information from Mr. Belfort about Mr. Kazajian. Mr. Belfort wanted to make very sure that the whole world knew who Albert Kazajian was.

"Can you believe the guy?" he asked Kate as Connor snapped photos of the car and the damage to the store. "He thinks I should buy him a new couch because the fabric didn't stand up good enough! Well, of course it didn't! He has three cats and two dogs, and they made a mess out of the fabric. You should smell it. Phew! And the cats, they clawed it all to shreds. Now how am I supposed to be responsible for that, I ask you?"

Kate clucked sympathetically and steered him to the events that had led up to Kazajian driving into the shop. The dispute had begun nearly three months ago, and had been escalating steadily. Kazajian had filed suit in small-claims court against Belfort, and Belfort had responded with a countersuit. Yesterday had been their day in court, and Kazajian had lost both cases.

Apparently he couldn't accept defeat. Just a little while ago, he had shown up at the store and told Belfort he was giving him one last chance "or else." Unimpressed, Belfort had told him to get lost or he was calling the police. Not five minutes later, Kazajian had driven his car through the front of the shop, injuring Mrs. Armbruster, one of Mr. Belfort's oldest and dearest customers.

Kate took that last with a large grain of salt. Belfort Furniture didn't look like the kind of place that would develop old and dear customers. In fact, it looked like exactly the kind of cut-rate easy-financing place that would develop customers like Mr. Kazajian. She didn't say so, of course.

Connor snapped a picture of Belfort, who swelled his chest as much as possible for the camera. A few minutes later, he waited by her car while she phoned in to tell Mary they had photos and a story. She gave Mary the gist of what had happened, then agreed to stand by.

"I was heading out to the beaches," Connor remarked, shaking his head a little as he looked around.

"I was heading to the pier," Kate retorted.

He glanced at her and smiled. "It's your day off, isn't it? Mine, too. Some luck."

"Actually," Kate told him, "I'm enjoying myself. I'd forgotten how much fun it is to be a reporter." Tinny sounds started coming out of her c-phone. "Mary? Yeah. Sure. I'm on my way in." She looked at Connor. "So much for days off."

What she would never have admitted was that it was a relief to be busy.

It was after four by the time they were finished with the article and photos. Side by side, they walked out of the building and over to the parking lot.

"It's getting late," Connor remarked. "It'll be dark in another hour or so."

"Unfortunately."

"We can still go out to the pier. You can feed the pelicans an evening meal, and then I'll buy you dinner."

All of a sudden she found herself remembering their e-mail kiss, and how it had made her feel. Guilt immediately surged in waves, casting up the memory of Mike on the shores of her mind. She knew she should say no. This was getting dangerous. The closer she grew to Connor in real life, the more likely it was that their e-mail relationship would spill out into the real world, and now that they had taken the step of that cyberkiss, that would be very dangerous.

But Connor didn't know she was Katydid, she reminded herself, and his ignorance would keep her safe. As far as he was concerned, they were just colleagues who had worked on a couple of stories together.

"Sure," she said, trying to sound brisk. "Sounds like fun."

But deep inside, she knew she was taking a dangerous step down a dark road.

# 9

"Pastor? Pastor, are you all right?"

The knock on the door of his study disrupted his meditations, and he had to battle an urge to tell Mrs. Hebert to get lost. It wasn't like him to be so impatient, but he hadn't been feeling very much like himself lately. One more aberration was hardly noticeable in the sea of aberrations in which he seemed to be swimming. The pounding in his head was like the background roar of the surf.

Rising from the prie-dieu, he went to open the door. "What is it, Mrs. Hebert? I was praying."

Mrs. Hebert flushed faintly, but her kindly face remained concerned. "Pastor, you haven't eaten enough to keep a bird alive these past several days, and now—well, people have been waiting to speak to you since early this morning. We're all getting a bit concerned that you're not well."

Since early this morning? He glanced around at the clock on his desk and was appalled to see it was nearly four in the afternoon. What had happened to the day?

"I'm sorry, Mrs. Hebert," he said finally. "I've been having some trouble with headaches...."

Her expression grew worried. "Maybe you should see a doctor. I can call and make you an appointment."

"No...no..." He waved the idea away. "God will heal me in due course. In the meantime, I must endure."

The housekeeper clucked and shook her head. "God helps them what helps themselves, I always say. He put doctors here to help with things like this, and you mustn't be letting it go on for too long. Now, I've sent everyone home and told them to come back tomorrow. I'll go make supper, but you have to promise me you'll eat some of it."

"Yes. I promise."

The headache was like a burning brand right behind his eyes, and as he closed the door, he had to resist an urge to slam it on the old busybody. As soon as he had the thought, he felt guilty and wondered what was wrong with him, that he was being so uncharitable these days.

His temper had grown entirely too short, and thoughts of violence never seemed far away. It was all a test, he believed, and he spent many hours praying for the strength to triumph.

And, of course, there were the dreams. They haunted him almost nightly, warning of horrors to come, horrors he didn't seem to be able to prevent.

He thought of calling those reporters again and wondered if all his problems of the past days didn't arise from his cowardice. Maybe he was being punished for failing to do the one thing that might actually help save these women.

He looked at the phone again and thought about calling Connor Quinn, or perhaps that woman he was working with. What was her name? He'd written it down somewhere, and he started pawing through the scattered papers on his desk, trying to find it. It would be easier to talk to her, he thought. Women were always easier to talk to. Men, on the other hand, always seemed to have something to prove.

The pounding in his head suddenly strengthened, and he straightened, grabbing his skull between his hands and squeezing, as if he could crush the pain out of his head. Nothing helped. Nothing. As he squeezed his head, he felt the plate that had replaced a section of his skull, and he wondered wildly if pulling the plate out would end his pain.

But of course it wouldn't. He'd seen enough doctors to know they didn't have any answers, and half of them hadn't even believed he was experiencing this much pain. Having someone tell you that you were imagining it was like adding insult to injury. And the pain made him so angry. So very angry...

He sat down at his desk and leaned back, closing his eyes. Gradually, as he sat perfectly still, the pain subsided enough that he no longer felt like tearing off his own head.

Maybe what he needed to do was send an anonymous note to the reporter. He could write down all the information he had—not that it was very much—just as easily as he could tell it to the man over the phone. What was more, he could tell the entire story without the risk of being interrupted or getting confused, so that he didn't explain properly.

The more he thought about it, the more the idea appealed to him as a no-muss, no-fuss, no-misunderstanding way to deal with the problem. Just as importantly, if they misinterpreted his note as coming from the killer, it wouldn't matter, because they wouldn't know who he was.

Yes, that was how he would do it, he thought, sitting

up and swiveling his chair to face his computer. He would send a letter describing his dreams in detail and how he had learned from the newspaper stories that he was not just having nightmares. He would tell them that he could see the women who were being stalked. He would promise to describe the next victim to them just as soon as he dreamed of her.

And maybe he would even tell them that according to his dreams there had been more than three murders.

"Pastor?" Mrs. Hebert peered around the door. "Supper's ready."

He thought about killing her. For just an instant, a bloody picture sped across his synapses, showing him Mrs. Hebert lying beaten to death on his study floor. Really, he thought, he had to get his temper under control. He squeezed his eyes shut and breathed a brief prayer for forgiveness.

"Thank you," he said, managing a smile. "I'll be right there."

He could write the letter later. There was no hurry, after all. The killer wasn't stalking anyone right now.

The St. Petersburg Pier, stretching east into Tampa Bay, was one of those landmarks that everyone felt obliged to visit, though no one could really say why. The walk out to the end of the pier was pleasant, there were restaurants out there, a few shops, an aquarium and an adventure golf course. Depending on the weather and what special events were occurring, the crowds could be large or small.

This afternoon they were small, and with no distractions except for a couple of kids with in-line skates who needed lessons in courtesy and safety, Kate and Connor were able to stroll easily out to the pelican feeding station.

"You like to feed the pelicans?" he said, looking amused.

"Sure. They're so greedy and pushy, I always have to laugh."

"But it's not good for them. They need to know how to find food on their own."

"These birds have been hanging around the pier since birth. They're hardly likely to change their life-style now."

She paid a few dollars for a small bucket of fish and climbed onto the block that kept her high enough that the horde of pelicans couldn't push her over. They were such funny-looking birds, she thought, as she tossed the first fish. Pear-shaped and potbellied, with short little legs and huge webbed feet, they had eyes that were as soft and sad as any puppy dog's. Making a horrendous racket, they waddled as close as they could and opened their beaks as she tossed another fish. A couple of passersby took photos.

When she finished, the birds waddled away to await the next feeding. Her hands smelled like fish, but she didn't care. She was smiling and feeling really good for the first time in days, or maybe even weeks.

"I better find the rest room and wash my hands," she told Connor as they resumed their walk.

"There's one inside."

One of the highlights of the pier was a towering superstructure that always reminded Kate of the bridge of a large ship. Inside were shops and the aquarium, and a number of restaurants. When she came out of the ladies' room, Connor suggested they get a sandwich and watch the sunset.

"We should have gone out to the Gulf, if you want to watch sunsets," she said.

He shrugged a shoulder. "We'll be able to see enough."

They found a table looking south over the bay, from which they could see most of the sky, both east and west. It was still early, but the clouds to the east, over Tampa, on the far side of the bay, were already turning golden and pink.

"The sunsets are always more spectacular in the winter," Kate remarked. "One of these days I'm going to have to find out why."

"It'd make a good article for the paper."

"Whether it does or doesn't, I'm curious."

He sipped his coffee, then began to unwrap his sandwich. "You looked like you were having fun this afternoon, chasing those cops and that store owner for the story."

"I was." She smiled again at the memory. "I'd forgotten how much I love being a reporter."

"Why don't you go back to it?"

She started to tell him about Mike, then realized that was no longer a valid concern. She didn't have to plan her life around Mike's needs any longer, because Mike was never coming home. "Maybe. I'm certainly going to think about it." She reached for her sandwich, then paused and looked at him. "Do you ever want to go back to police work?"

"I don't know." He looked away from her, as if taking an interest in the rosy clouds to the east. "I don't think I'm a cop type at heart."

"But you did it for so many years."

"Yeah." He shrugged again and bit into his sandwich. It was a good excuse not to say more.

"Mark said you went from being a patrol officer to being a crime-scene technician. Why was that?"

Now he looked at her, his eyes like chips of blue glass. "Is this an interview?"

"No. I'm just...interested." More than interested, since their e-mail kiss. "Sorry if it seems like I'm prying."

"I got tired of in-your-face police work," he said finally, by way of an answer. "I got tired of the screaming and shouting and weeping, the constant confrontation. So I volunteered for the lab. Eventually that got to be just as bad. I...get too involved."

"And you thought it would be easier working for the paper?" she asked in disbelief.

"Not easier. Different. And it is. Or it was," he added, as if to himself. "I thought it would let me use my photography more creatively."

"Has it?"

"Sure. Except for straight news stories, that is. But I do a lot of other things, like going over to MOSI the other day, or taking pictures of herons wading in Lake Maggiore. There are advantages." And fewer nightmares...until lately.

It was true that the newspaper nurtured creativity among its photographers, encouraging them by publishing their artistic work from time to time. It was bound to be a better creative atmosphere than the police department.

"Why don't you go into business for yourself?" she asked him.

He gave her a wry look. "I'm fond of eating, and sleeping indoors when it rains. And I wouldn't be happy doing portraits and weddings."

She could understand that. People were always asking

her why she didn't use her writing ability for something else, like writing a novel. The truth was, she needed the excitement and stimulation of the newspaper. "What does it feel like, though, working on this killer story and watching other people do what you used to do?"

He didn't answer for a long time. When he did, he surprised her with his candor. "I wish to God nobody had to deal with this kind of shit. I'm having nightmares about these women. I'm having nightmares about the creep who's killing them. The more I learn about these murders, the better I know him, and I don't want to know him at all."

"Know him? What do you mean?"

His gaze bored into her. "I'm starting to know what he thinks. How he feels. What drives him. He's a man with incredible intelligence and charm, and he uses it as a weapon against unsuspecting women. He doesn't deserve to breathe the same air as the rest of the human race."

He waved a hand toward the people walking by. Above them, the thin, high clouds were turning tangerine against a turquoise sky. "He could be walking by us right this instant, scanning the crowds for his next victim. He looks perfectly normal, the kind of guy anybody would feel comfortable talking to. He's friendly, inoffensive. Hell, I wouldn't be surprised if he had the face of an angel. After all, he sent notes to two of these women that should have put them on their guard, yet both of them took him home with them. Both of them trusted him enough that they never fought him."

"Maybe they were just too terrified to fight. I mean...if somebody told me they'd let me go if I just cooperated, I'd probably cooperate a whole lot."

"Maybe. Probably. But he still has to get past the

natural caution of these women to get inside their homes. The first dancer may have taken him home for money. We don't know. But the second one—she wasn't like that. Everyone is adamant about that. So why did she let a man into her apartment?"

"She knew him."

"Obviously. So did the banker's wife. They recognized him at least well enough to consider him trustworthy." He shook his head. "And now he's probably out there stalking another one. Christ!"

But Kate's thoughts had run in a different direction. "If he sent notes to the first two, why not to the third one?"

"I don't know. Maybe he did and she threw them away. Maybe she was a target of opportunity, not somebody he'd stalked in advance."

"Mm." She didn't like the way that sounded, and she thought about it for a while, but she couldn't make anything useful out of it.

"Kate?"

"Hmm?"

"Truth for truth. What is your husband ill with?"

She felt almost as if she'd been punched, the question was so unexpected. "Why...do you ask?"

"Because you never talk about him, and because you're here with me. I'm just wondering."

It was a fair question, especially after the questions she had asked him, and as much as she wanted to tell him to mind his own business, she couldn't. The rudeness would be unforgivable. Her fingers knotted together, and she looked down. "He's...he's in a mental hospital."

For a long time, neither one of them said another thing. The brilliant colors of sunset gave way to duskier tones, and night slowly settled over the world. The lights from the pier soon washed away the sky and winked off the waves below them.

Finally Connor spoke. "That's tough."

There didn't seem to be any answer except to agree. She wanted to stop there, but instead she found herself confiding even more. "Actually," she said, her voice tremulous and her heart racing as if she were about to bungee-jump off the Sunshine Skyway Bridge, "we're divorced."

There. She had said it out loud. Finally. The words that had never crossed her lips had crossed them now. Instead of feeling as if she had just freed herself from the shackles of a horrible secret, she had a sinking sensation in the pit of her stomach. She had said it out loud. She had volunteered the information to someone who hadn't known. In so doing, she had somehow made the divorce more real.

It was as if she had laid bare her deepest shame, and she couldn't bring herself to lift her eyes while night settled around them. She needed his reaction, yet she feared it.

He stirred, and his chair creaked a little. The waves lapped tirelessly at the pier, a gentle, forlorn lullaby. "Now that *is* rough," he said. "Really rough."

She dared to lift her gaze, but his face was unreadable. Impassive. In the strange light from the lampposts, he looked exotic and wild. He leaned forward and touched her wedding ring with one finger. "It hurts, doesn't it? You don't feel good about it at all. You didn't want to do it, did you? And you didn't do it for yourself...."

How did he know? Was she wearing a sign on her forehead? How could he know such intimate things about her?

"You wear the ring because you feel guilty. Very guilty. You feel as if you've failed." He stopped suddenly and looked away.

Kate stared at him, disbelieving. Part of her was offended at his invasion of her most personal feelings, and part of her was terrified. How did he do it?

He looked at her. "I shouldn't have gotten so personal. Unfortunately, it's something I do. That's one of the reasons I had to get out of police work. I start thinking about what motivates people, and I get too deeply into it."

Still feeling stunned, she didn't know quite what to say or how to react. "You did this as a police officer?"

He nodded slowly. "Yeah. I was a profiler. I looked at crime scenes and got into the heads of the criminals. I got too good at it."

"Too good? How?"

He didn't answer for a long time. The waves continued to lap, and the breeze strengthened. He almost seemed to sigh, but if he did, it was lost on the breeze. "Like I said, I got into their heads. I started to think like them. It affects me."

Understanding struck her. "You're doing that with the Puppetmaster, aren't you? That's why you were talking about him that way. My God, how do you get into a mind like that?"

"I don't know. I just do. Only this one is more difficult."

"Difficult? Why? What's different about him?"

"He's so passionless...."

*Passionless.* The word hit her with a cold chill. Somehow it was easier to think of an angry killer, or even one driven by some twisted sexual need, than to think of one without any passion at all. "Are you sure?"

"That's the impression I get. I could be wrong."

She hoped he was. She'd felt drawn to this man almost from the moment he started working at the paper, sensing in him a kindred spirit. Now she knew why: They were both isolated. Both of them were set apart by experiences they could not share because other people couldn't understand them.

He rose suddenly and scooped up the remains of their supper. "Come on. Let's walk before we get stiff from sitting."

She was only too glad to oblige.

When they left the pier, Connor drove Kate to her car, then followed her home to make sure she got there safely. When she waved from the porch, he waved back, waited another five minutes, then called her on his c-phone to make sure everything was okay.

It was a ridiculous amount of caution, she thought. She'd been coming home to an empty house for a long time.

There was a message on her answering machine from an old girlfriend she hadn't seen much since Mike became so ill. Jacqueline wanted to get together for lunch. Kate hesitated, then copied down her number. On the one hand, she felt hurt by the way her friends had drifted away during Mike's illness; on the other, she knew she hadn't done very much to prevent it. Mike had consumed nearly her entire life with worrying about him and taking care of him. There hadn't been any energy left for another soul.

Grabbing a glass of orange juice, she headed into her study to check her e-mail. Anticipation filled her as she wondered if Connor had responded to her continuation of his kiss. At this moment, she didn't particularly care whether she was being disloyal to Mike. These e-mails were nothing but fantasies, and surely she was entitled to her fantasies.

Connor had replied to her. Her heart tapped rapidly and she licked her lips nervously as she clicked on the button to read the message.

"Katy, holding you close fills me with the deepest sense of contentment, as if every unsatisfied yearning is suddenly fulfilled. I draw you closer and feel your heart pound against me. Your mouth is so sweet, and I want to drink of you forever.

"But there's a danger here, a danger that I will yield to my need for more and transgress too far. Our friendship could be destroyed, and I never want to do that.

"Slowly, reluctantly, I release you and step back. Around us the starlight settles gently on dew-kissed grass and sand...."

Kate felt tears trembling on her eyelashes, and she drew a shaky breath. It would be so easy, she realized, to love this man. Too easy. Fear and guilt yanked her back from the precipice, and she decided not to respond to the note until she'd had time to distance herself from the feelings he had evoked.

She had mail from other on-line correspondents, people she had met on various bulletin boards and discovered common interests with. She replied to them as soon as she read them, brief notes that gave her back her sense of equilibrium.

She was hitting the Next-message button as she finished each note, not really paying attention to how many she read. She hadn't seen a note from S.Talker on the index list, so she was stunned when one suddenly popped up on the screen before her.

"I don't like being ignored," he wrote. "I know

you're getting my mail. Answer me, or I'll have to teach you a lesson."

Her stomach rolled, and she reached out to delete the message, as if erasing it would take the fear and disgust away. But it wouldn't. She stayed her impulse and logged off. Moments later, she was dialing the number of her on-line service provider. Enough was enough.

Unfortunately, no one was on duty, so she had to leave a voice mail message about her problem with the stalker. Then she logged on again and forwarded S.Talker's note to the sysop with a request for help in dealing with the problem.

"Surely," she wrote, "there's some way to block his e-mails. Or some way to find out who he is so he'll have to stop. What can I do?"

Then, in a burst of discomfort that reminded her miserably of her ex-husband, she went through the entire house, checking locks on windows and doors, and pulling all the curtains so that she would not be visible from outside.

It was inescapable that she felt as if she were under siege. Just the way Mike had felt. Only Mike had imagined it. Kate wasn't imagining a thing.

The phone rang in the small hours of the morning, dragging Kate out of a restless sleep. She picked up the receiver and put it to her ear almost before she realized what she was doing. The voice that spoke was slurred, difficult to understand. Strained. Almost singsong.

"He's following her."

"What?" Groggily, she tried to follow what he was saying.

"He's following another woman. I had a dream. A dream... I saw her in the dream...."

"Who? Who did you see?" Suddenly she was awake and alert, remembering the call she had had the other day at the office. How had this guy found her at home?

"The killer...he kills them.... I saw it.... He follows her, he follows her he follows her...."

"Who does he follow? Who?"

There was a sound that might have been a sob. "I don't know...I don't know. I see her in my dreams.... He'll hurt her, hurt her hurt her hurt her...."

"Please," Kate implored, sitting up and feeling for the light switch. "Can you describe her? Tell me what she looks like!"

"The same. She looks the same. All the same. Same...same...same... He hunts the same to save."

"To save? To save what? What do you mean?"

But all she heard was a click and a dial tone.

Finding the light switch, she flipped it on and hugged herself, feeling cold and frightened. Had that been the voice of the killer? Or the voice of some poor tormented soul who was troubled by nightmares? There had been an eeriness to the voice that unnerved her, but minutes passed before she realized what it was.

Mike had gotten the same strange quality in his voice when he was deeply in the grip of a delusion. It had been as if his voice were somehow attenuated by the problem of communicating across a nearly impenetrable barrier of madness.

This man had sounded very similar. So he was some ill soul who was suffering a delusion. Someone who was as sick as Mike. She hesitated a moment, then lifted the receiver again and dialed star 69. Moments later, a recorded voice recited the phone number the man had called her from. She dialed it and got nothing but an endless ringing. If he was still there, he wasn't going to answer.

She wrote the number down and waited, wondering if he would call back. When he didn't, she finally decided to call Connor. As a former cop, he might know of some way to trace the number so that they could find the caller, and if he could do that, they didn't want to wait until morning, when the man might have gotten far away.

Connor answered on the second ring, and he sounded fully alert. "What's up?"

"I just got a phone call from that guy who claims he sees the victims in his dreams. Can you trace the number he called from?"

"Give it to me."

She recited it.

"Hang on," he said. "I'm going to call a friend on my cell phone. Just don't hang up."

"I won't." She didn't want to. The night seemed threatening, and Connor's voice was a reassuring link to the normal world. She could hear him talking to someone on his cellular phone, but he'd muffled the receiver somehow, so she couldn't make out his words. After a couple of minutes he came back on.

"Listen, Kate, I'm going to come over there, okay? I want you to write down all your impressions of the guy's phone call, okay? Then we'll take it to the police."

"The police? There really isn't anything to go on."

"We don't know that yet. But we sure as hell can't afford to pass up any possibility. Write it down for me, okay? I'll be there in twenty minutes. Don't open the door until you recognize my voice."

Kate hung up and realized with the most awful, creeping sense of dread that he was afraid for her. That he was afraid the caller was the killer.

# 10

Kate had donned jeans and a black cotton sweater and was sitting curled up on her couch, feeling cold to the bone, although it wasn't especially chilly. Just the hour of the night, she told herself. Connor, who had arrived fifteen minutes ago, had gone to answer the door.

"Kate?" Connor returned to the living room accompanied by a small, dark man. "This is Rick Diaz. He's with the Hillsborough sheriff."

Kate shook the man's hand and invited him to sit. "I can make coffee...."

But Rick Diaz smiled and shook his head. "I had a cup on the way over here. I don't think my stomach could face another one. Thanks. Now, about this phone call..."

Connor handed him the pad on which Kate had written as much as she could remember of what the man had said, and of her impressions of him. Rick read it over, his lips pursed thoughtfully.

"Sick?" he said suddenly. "You think this guy's mentally ill?"

"I don't know." Kate felt a flutter of nerves. She *hated* discussing this. "My husband—my ex-husband—

is hospitalized with chronic paranoid schizophrenia. Something about the way the caller sounded reminded me of the way Mike used to sound when he was having a particularly strong delusion. Sort of distant and... attenuated. As if he were far away. Oh, it's so hard to say exactly what I mean."

Rick nodded. "Take your time. There's no hurry."

Kate closed her eyes and made an effort to let go of her nervousness and reluctance. What she needed right now was the clinical detachment she had learned as a reporter. Feelings would only get in the way.

"Okay," she said finally. "It sounded as if he were trying to be heard through a barrier. The overriding impression was that it was difficult for him to communicate these things. My guess would be that he was losing touch with reality and was making a last attempt to reach out before he lost himself in a delusion. That's how it used to be with Mike. As if there was this last, tenuous thread of sanity..."

She opened her eyes and looked at them, wondering if she sounded crazy. But Rick was nodding, and Connor had an arrested look, as if he had just thought of something. Neither one of them seemed to think she had taken leave of her senses. Rick glanced at the pad again.

"'He hunts to save.' Hunts what to save? Them? To save them? Save himself?"

"He didn't say. That's what was so odd about it, and why it stuck in my head."

"But those were his exact words?"

Kate started to answer affirmatively, but paused. Closing her eyes, she tried to remember exactly how the phone call had progressed. "He said they were all the same. When I asked him what the woman looked like, he said, 'The same.' And...that's right. His exact words were, 'He hunts the same to save.'"

"'He hunts the same to save?'" Rick sighed and wrote it down. "Could we get any more cryptic here? This guy might just be some kind of nut who's been following the story in the papers. Maybe—pardon my bluntness here, Kate—maybe the guy's already under treatment. This kind of talk sounds..." He waved a hand, lacking a descriptive word.

"It sounds," Kate said, "as if he's having trouble making the logical connections we ordinarily recognize. That's what I was trying to get at. When Mike would start to get really sick, he'd begin making what they call 'loose connections' in his thinking and speech. Connections that are skewed from the ones we would normally make. Sometimes it used to feel as if we were using languages that were slightly different. As if there was a translator somewhere in the middle who was garbling things just enough to make them feel off kilter. And that's what this guy reminded me of. He was really struggling to make the connections he needed to convey his message."

"So we have, 'He hunts the same to save.'"

"It isn't exactly useless," Connor said. "In fact, it's not useless at all. So the guy says all the victims are the same. Or look the same. I wish I had his exact words. And he says the killer hunts the same to save. That could mean a number of things, all of them very interesting. Let me think about it, Rick. Maybe together with some of the other evidence it'll give a clue."

"Fine." Rick closed his notebook, stuffed it in his pocket and lifted the pad on which Kate had written the substance of the phone call. "Can I keep your notes? Not the pad, just the notes."

"Sure." She didn't have any use for them. The call certainly wouldn't make a story for the paper.

"On the off chance that this guy is our killer," Rick continued, "I'm going to talk to local law enforcement. If he's reaching across the bay for any reason, they should know about it. Especially if I have to spend any time over here investigating." He stood up.

"Did you find out where he was calling from?" Kate asked.

"A phone booth on Busch Boulevard."

She felt deflated. The most important part of this was the possibility that they could find this guy and learn something useful about these killings.

"I know," Rick said, a faint smile softening his features. "I keep hoping, too."

Connor lingered after Rick left. "Are you going to be okay?" he asked her.

"I'll be fine. It was only a phone call."

He hesitated. "Are you in the book?"

"No. He didn't get my phone number from the book."

"The question is, where *did* he get it from?"

Kate shook her head. "God knows. It isn't exactly a state secret. I even used to put it on my business cards, back when I was a reporter and didn't want to risk missing a story."

He smiled at that. "Yeah. I quit doing that finally." He walked over to the window and looked out. It was after five, but dawn was still more than an hour away. "Why don't you go up to bed?" he said over his shoulder, suddenly not wanting to look at her. "I'll just hang around."

There was a long silence from her, so long that he finally turned around to look at her. "Kate?"

Her green eyes looked lost and sunken in her face. "You think he's after *me*."

"No!" He didn't know whether it was hearing her voice, the possibility or the way she looked, but he felt his heart clench almost painfully. "No, I don't think he is. You haven't gotten any threats or any warnings like the other women."

She saw right through him and gave him a small, sad smile. "Right. But I'm blond, and he always goes for blondes." She looked away and sighed. "I don't feel like sleeping."

He didn't either. Turning back to the window, he tried to ignore the sense of impending doom that had been deepening for days now. He was sure it sprang from his preoccupation with the murders, but that didn't make it any less oppressive. It was as if a darkness were creeping into his mind, eating away at the edges of normalcy, leaving him somehow hollow. Hollow and uneasy.

Christ, he didn't need an attack of his mother's damn Indian mysticism now! Or an attack of his father's Irish melancholy, either. And for some unknown reason, he suddenly found himself telling Kate about it.

"My parents were two of the unhappiest people I've ever known," he said.

"Why?" She actually sounded interested.

"I used to wonder that myself, especially when I was a kid. If you didn't know how miserable they were, you'd have thought they had everything they wanted. Mom got away from the reservation and the miserable Montana winters, and Dad escaped being landlocked and got back to fishing. He was from Ireland and had grown up on the coast. When he got to the U.S., the first job he could get was driving a truck. Unfortunately—from his perspective, anyway—they had him driving U.S.

Highway 2, from Duluth to Spokane. He missed the water, and he missed fishing for a living."

"That's understandable. And your mother?"

"She's a Crow Indian. Raised on the res, which she hated. She was working at a truck stop when she met my dad, and all she wanted to do was get away to someplace where she never had to feel cold again. They made it. Right after they married, they moved down here. Dad worked on a fishing boat until he retired, and Mom hardly ever got cold again." He shrugged and looked at her once more. "They should have been happy, right?"

Kate shook her head. "We take ourselves with us, wherever we go."

"Exactly." A faint smile creased the corners of his eyes. "They're a pair of perpetual malcontents. I finally realized they both liked it that way. Dad lived in a cloud of Irish melancholy that used to pervade the house like cigarette smoke. It drove Mom nuts, so she was always nagging him about it. And her... Well, she had a streak of mysticism that drove him nuts, because he thought it was heathen."

"Must have been fun for you."

He saw sympathy in her gaze, and he wasn't sure he liked it. Uncomfortable, he looked away. "It was... interesting. Both of them had a tendency to drink too much, which was even more interesting. I guess I took care of them at least as much as they took care of me. Dad had an explosive temper, too, and Mom was hot-blooded. Christ, could the two of them fight."

He shoved his hands in his pockets, trying to remember why he'd brought this all up. Oh, yeah. "Anyway, this is all leading up to explaining about me. I tend to be...melancholy, too. And a little mystical. Kind of a mix of Irish and Indian. I get these feelings.... Oh, hell,

I don't know exactly what I'm trying to say, except that I have this feeling of, well, foreboding. I don't like it. I don't know if it has any basis in fact, or if my ancestors' genes are just acting up, but..." He shrugged.

"But you can't ignore it." She nodded slowly. "I can understand that, Connor. Really. I have those feelings, too. Being a woman, I can call them intuition." The smile she offered him was small. "Or paranoia."

"Yeah." He gave a short laugh. "Except that I don't dare dismiss them."

"Of course not." She rose from the couch. "I'm going to make some coffee, and then I'm going to figure out how to keep this day from turning into a total waste. Would you like some eggs and bacon?"

"Sure. Thanks."

In the doorway, she paused and looked back. "Connor? Did you get your dad's temper, too?"

He hesitated, then nodded slowly, never taking his eyes from her. He wasn't sure exactly what he expected by way of response, but he was surprised when she appeared to accept the news without a ripple. Giving him a nod, she turned away and went to the kitchen.

He was used to feeling alone, but her silent departure left him feeling even more alone than usual. He thought of Katydid and wished he was at his computer, writing her a long letter. In their cyberspace getaway, he had found the one place where he could be himself without fearing himself.

Christ, what a comment that was!

Sally Dyer took one look at Kate and shook her head. "You need to take up smoking. You look like hell."

"What good would smoking do?"

"It gives you something pleasurable to do when everything else in life goes to hell."

"Gee, thanks, but my life went to hell years ago. At least my lungs aren't going to hell, too."

Sally snorted. "Something has to kill you sooner or later. And right now, you look like you've been rolled over by a Mack truck."

"That'd still be quicker than lung cancer."

Sally leaned confidingly toward her. "Haven't you heard? Only ten percent of smokers get lung cancer. The odds are higher that a woman will get breast cancer."

"Which cigarette company have you been talking to?"

Laughing hoarsely, Sally returned to her own desk.

Kate tried to focus on the screen before her but found it difficult. Something about staring at the monitor made her even sleepier, and she wondered what Ben Hyssop would say if he found her snoozing over her keyboard. It hardly bore imagining.

Mark Polanski interrupted her before she had managed to do more than scan the first paragraph of a story she was editing. "Got a minute?"

"Do I have a choice?" Each time he approached her, ever since the night he had confronted her about Mike, she liked Mark less. He grinned at her now, refusing to let her ill-tempered response disturb him. Of course, Kate thought. He was a reporter and had been treated far worse by people he needed to talk to.

Pulling up a chair, Mark leaned close enough to make her uncomfortable. She tried to draw back but couldn't do so without tipping her chair.

"I don't want anybody else to hear," he said in a low voice, as if realizing how uncomfortable he was making her. "You know how Quinn is so deeply involved with this serial killer case?"

"He's been assigned to it."

"I know." Mark glanced over his shoulder—an almost theatrical move that would have been funny if he hadn't seemed so genuinely concerned. "Listen, he knows more than he should. More than he's putting in these stories."

"He used to be a cop, Mark. They talk to him."

"But pictures... Kate, they don't let just anyone take pictures of the scene. And they don't give out copies of the ones their investigators take. They don't want them in the press, and they don't want them feeding prurient interests, particularly the interest of the killer himself."

"I know all that."

"You do? Then maybe you'll wonder why Quinn has pictures of the scenes."

"Well, he..." She trailed off. "He's helping the cops, I think."

"Yeah? Why? What do they need him for that somebody else can't do? And why would they let him have evidence photos in his personal possession? I'm telling you, Kate, his interest in this case, those pictures—either Quinn is a sicko or he's... Well, you figure it out."

Kate was horrified, but she couldn't have said whether she was horrified by Mark's behavior or by the possibility he was suggesting. She couldn't even think of a thing to say as she watched him rise and walk away after giving her a significant look. The only thing she knew with absolute certainty was that she hated Mark Polanski.

One thing she could say for him, though: he had succeeded in fully waking her up. Anger had a way of doing that.

She edited three stories in rapid succession and inserted them on their assigned pages. Sally commented on the speed with which she was working and asked where the fire was.

Kate shrugged. "I just want to get everything done before I collapse."

"As if that's really possible in a newsroom," Sally retorted dryly. "There's a new story every five minutes. If you need to collapse, just let me know. Somebody else can cover for you."

When she took a break around three, she treated herself to an illicit log-on to her private Internet account and checked her mail. There was a note from Quinn, and she opened it eagerly. God, she thought, it was terrible how involved she was getting in their correspondence. It wasn't even real, it was just words on a screen, but it was becoming incredibly important to her.

"Katy," he wrote, "it's been hectic, and I'm so glad to escape to our world of sea and sand. Coming home to you is becoming the high point of my day."

*Me too, Connor,* she thought. *Me too.*

"In the last couple of days, I've thought more than once about taking you away with me to the Keys. Do you suppose we could make our fantasy real?"

A sorrow seemed to grip her then. It wasn't possible, she thought. No way. Reality could never be as sweet as the world they were building in cyberspace.

"Probably not," he continued. "So we'll hide out here and build our castles in the air...or in the sand. Knowing you're here waiting has become the anchor of my days.

"You smile at me as I come down the beach toward you. You and Tigret have been playing in the gentle waves. The sand is as white as snow, and the water behind you is a deep aquamarine, so smooth and gentle today that you can almost forget there's an ocean out there.

"You smile, and I love the way it lights up your whole face. No one's ever made me feel so welcome...."

Kate felt her throat tighten with a yearning so intense that it was almost painful. What was happening to her? Quickly, almost afraid of the door that seemed to be opening before her, she closed her mailbox and logged off the network. Later. She would think about it all later. Right now she had to get back to work before she lost it in front of the entire newsroom.

A short while later, Connor arrived with his camera slung around his neck, and his bag of lenses and other accoutrements slung over his shoulder. He gave her a nod as he passed by on his way to the photo lab. There were a couple of the other photographers in there, and she heard them exchange friendly greetings as the door closed behind him.

Mark was just a snake in the grass, she told herself when she realized she was staring blindly toward the lab. Just a snake trying to stir up trouble. If Connor had pictures of the crime scenes and the victims, he had a good reason for it.

But the snake had done its work, and her mind wasn't quite ready to let go of the possibility. After all, she didn't trust her own ability to judge people anymore. She'd made entirely too many excuses for Michael all those years. As the old joke went, she'd been Cleopatra, queen of denial. She had been able to explain away just about everything until it started to endanger Mike. So she was perfectly capable of ignoring every warning about Connor.

Of course, there wasn't much to be nervous about. If

he had pictures, he probably had a good reason. She had definitely gotten the feeling from his interaction with Diaz last night that they were working together, however unofficially. And there was no other reason to think...

Except that the person who called her last night had had her phone number, and Connor claimed to have gotten a call from the same person. What if Connor hadn't received a call at all. What if he had *made* it?

As soon as she had the thought, she recoiled sharply from it. No way. Absolutely *no way!* The man who wrote her those gentle descriptive notes couldn't be capable of such duplicity. How could she let Mark poison her thoughts this way?

Realizing that her fingers were frozen on her keyboard and that her monitor was blinking the information that another article had been shunted to her for editing, she shook herself back to reality. Mark was nothing but a snake, and she damn well wasn't going to take a bite of his poisoned apple.

Just then the newsroom door swung open and admitted Rick Diaz, who was wearing a visitor's badge. Kate instinctively turned toward him, wondering what he could possibly be looking for here. Her first thought was that there had been some kind of bomb scare—the paper had been through three of them in the past year—but then she remembered that he was out of his jurisdiction here in St. Pete.

He spied her and came straight toward her. "Where's Quinn?" he asked.

"In the lab. I'll show you." She certainly had no intention of being cut out of this conversation unless she was told to get lost. Whatever Diaz was here to say, she wanted to hear it. Her reporter's instincts were going into hyperdrive.

So were Mark Polanski's. He started to rise from his chair, but Kate waved him back with a sharp movement of her hand. No way did she want that man in on anything.

Quinn was in the lab with Dick Helmut and Barb Swart, two of the paper's other photogs. They were discussing last night's basketball game with good-humored heat but broke off when Rick and Kate entered. Quinn stood up immediately, reaching for a plastic bag that contained a white sheet of paper.

"See you guys later," he said to Barb and Dick, and stepped out into the newsroom with Rick and Kate. "Let's go someplace where we can talk privately."

Diaz nodded, and Kate followed them. In the elevator, he punched the button for the next floor, and Kate presumed they were heading upstairs to a seldom-used conference room. Connor handed the plastic bag to Diaz.

"When did you get this?" Rick asked.

"In today's mail. I picked it up on my way out of the apartment and opened it when I got here."

"Your fingerprints are all over it?"

"Of course. I didn't know it was anything special." His tone became dry. "I'm not exactly in the habit of putting on rubber gloves to open my mail."

They stepped out of the elevator and crossed the hall to the small conference room. As soon as he stepped inside, Diaz held the bag up to the light and examined it. "Christ."

"What is it?" Kate asked, taking a chance that they wouldn't tell her to get lost.

Rick answered. "It appears to be a letter from the guy who called you last night."

"Can I see?"

He hesitated, glanced at Connor, then shrugged. "As long as you don't put it in the paper until I say so."

"That's been the deal all along," Kate readily agreed, even though she hated having to do so. It went against her every instinct to stifle the news. Taking the bag gingerly, she tipped it until she could read the typewritten note.

> He's stalking her. Right now. I see him in my dreams. You have to stop him. Please believe me. My dreams are true.
>
> A woman. Maybe 5'6", 120 pounds, blond hair, dark eyes. Bleached blond. In my dream, I can see the dark hairs on her lip. She's walking down a dark street, and she thinks she knows him.
>
> He's nice to her. He's always nice to them. They like him. She's a dancer. Look for the mole on her left earlobe.
>
> Please find her before he hurts her. Please.

"My God," Kate whispered as an icy chill made her shiver. "My God. Do you suppose he's right?"

"We can't run the risk that he isn't," Rick said flatly. "It shouldn't be too hard to find out which dancers along Dale Mabry have moles on their left ears. We'll get on it right away." He took the bag from her and looked at the note again. "It doesn't sound like the killer."

"No?" Connor shook his head. "Don't leap to that conclusion, Rick. Kate told you the guy sounds delusional, and a lot of these killers strongly dissociate, anyway. He might very well have dissociated to the extent that he thinks someone else is responsible for the killings."

Rick looked at him squarely. "Is that what you think?

Come on, Connor, give me a goddamn profile I can work with, will you?"

Kate wouldn't have been surprised if Connor snapped back at him, saying something to the effect that he wasn't a miracle worker. Diaz's demand seemed unreasonable to her. Connor surprised her, however. Instead of snapping, he leaned a shoulder against the wall, stuffed his hands in his pockets and looked at Rick almost sadly.

"I've told you," he said. "You're not looking for the usual young loner. You're looking for a charming, attractive man in his thirties. Mid- to late thirties, I'd say, since he's strongly controlled in his actions. He's patient, extremely bright, well liked by everyone who knows him. He is most definitely not a loner. The lack of anger in his killings leads me to believe he's atypical, in that he hasn't been nursing a rage all of his life. Something happened—probably a head injury—that turned him into a monster. If he's the guy making the phone calls, then he has a serious moral problem with what he's doing."

Diaz was nodding, taking notes swiftly on a pad.

Connor continued, his gaze distant. "He's so horrified by what he's doing that he can't acknowledge that he's the one doing it. He's completely dissociated and has convinced himself that the snatches of memories he can't suppress are some kind of psychic dreams. He wants to be stopped, but since he has himself convinced he's not the killer, the only way he can help us stop him is to share his so-called dreams with us."

Kate watched as Connor's eyes closed and his voice grew quieter, thoughtful and almost distant. He was giving them stream of consciousness now, and it chilled her to watch him talk about this killer as if he knew him.

"When he starts decompensating—starts giving in to

his killing impulse—he rationalizes it. He tells himself he's saving these women by what he does. That's what he meant on the phone. He saves them, maybe even convinces himself that he's saving himself, as well, through whatever ritual he practices. He excuses his actions as benefiting them or himself, or both. Maybe even convinces himself he's benefiting society."

He passed his hand over his face and sighed, but he didn't open his eyes. A moment later, he continued. "He's had violent impulses for years. When he felt himself in danger of losing control of them, he tried to get help. For whatever reason, he didn't get it. He's been compensating somehow for a long time. Leading an exemplary life. He's probably a person who holds a prominent position and is considered a good example in the community. Then he started decompensating, and the only help he can hope for now is to get caught."

Diaz mumbled something that Kate didn't catch.

"I don't feel a whole lot of sympathy for him, either," Connor said, his eyes opening, "but sympathy isn't the issue here. Understanding is. This guy needs help. He needs to be saved from himself."

He lowered his head for a few seconds, then looked at Diaz again. "He looks prosperous. Not necessarily wealthy, but his image is the kind that wouldn't be associated with any kind of crime. It's part of how he gets these women to trust him. If he drives a car, it's reasonably new and large, though probably not brand-new. That would make him too identifiable. It's a conservative color. Gray, probably, or maybe beige, but nothing metallic or bright. It fits his image as a conservative person and would never stand out parked along the street or in a parking lot. He dresses conservatively, too, probably in suits or slacks, shirt and tie, depending on the weather.

He not only looks like a pillar of the community, but those who know him believe he is."

"Like Gacy," Diaz remarked.

"Like Gacy." Connor straightened and removed his hands from his pockets. "He's very controlled, and his mask is a good one. Nobody suspects he's capable of any kind of violence, and I'd bet no one has ever seen him get seriously angry. The guy appears to be a saint."

"Great," said Rick. "That's really helpful. I'm looking for a saint who is a respected pillar of the community. That should knock the suspects down to about three hundred thousand."

Connor flashed an unexpected smile. "Well, he doesn't lisp."

"You're sure of that?"

"Positively."

Kate thought he was kidding, then suddenly realized he wasn't. "How can you know whether he lisps?"

"Con artists don't lisp, and this guy has developed the ultimate con."

"I always wind up wondering how people can be so gullible," she admitted. "Why do they trust this guy?"

"These women only look gullible because they got killed. Other people do thousands of gullible things a day but get away with it. That's the only difference. If nobody picks up hitchhikers anymore, how come there are still so many people hitchhiking?"

She could see his point and nodded. "You're right."

But Rick's mind was running on different lines. "Do you think this guy has a police record?"

Connor shook his head. "No. He's way too controlled, and these murders are planned rather than opportunistic. This guy doesn't mess up."

"Marceline Whitmore was opportunistic."

Connor shook his head slowly. "I thought so at first, but...no. No, it was planned, too. Just like the others. My guess is that this woman was up to some things that absolutely nobody else knew about."

Rick shook his head. "TPD hasn't been able to find out a thing."

"Then check outside Tampa, in the county. Let me show her picture along Dale Mabry. Or maybe even at those lingerie-modeling places on Nebraska. Maybe Marceline Whitmore knew one of those women."

Rick hesitated.

"Look," Connor said, "people are more willing to talk to me now that I carry a press card instead of a police badge."

The other man snorted. "Yeah. They really want everything smeared all over the papers."

"With me, they can at least remain anonymous," Connor reminded him.

"I'll go with you," Kate said. "Sometimes women are more willing to talk to women. Besides, you don't want them wondering if you're the killer." Even as she said it, she felt a pang of fear but dismissed it.

"Okay," said Rick after a moment's thought. "Okay. But anything you find out comes straight to me. I better not wake up and read all about it in the morning *Sentinel.*"

# 11

"Marceline Whitmore went somewhere during the evening she was killed," Connor told Kate. "That's why her car was out in the driveway. And when she went out, she probably picked up the killer. It makes sense to me that we should ask our questions during the evening."

"Sure." It made sense to her, too. "I need to finish my work, anyway."

"So, plan on leaving here around seven? Will you be done by then?"

"I can arrange it." She had not the least doubt that Ben Hyssop and Sally would be willing to let her go. The paper was praying for a blockbuster exclusive to come out of this, or they wouldn't be agreeing to such restrictions on their current articles. Right now, the other area papers were beating the socks off them in the scoop department, and that was hard to swallow under any circumstances. "But we'd better tell Ben what we're going to do."

From the way Connor hesitated, she gathered he didn't feel really comfortable with that. "I'll be doing it on my own time," he said finally.

"You still feel like a cop, don't you? Well, I've got news for you, Quinn," she said with forced lightness. "You're working for the *Sentinel* now, and Ben would feel justifiably annoyed if we didn't clue him in to what we're doing with the biggest story of the quarter."

Unfortunately, Ben was not in the most amenable of moods. "Quinn can go," he said, "but not you, Devane."

"Why not?" Annoyance surged in her. "I'm a capable reporter."

"You sure as hell are," Hyssop agreed. "You're also a blond female, and like it or not, I don't feel right about you snooping around in places that might bring you to the attention of a killer."

"Damn it!" she said hotly. "I'm sick of fighting these battles with you. Either I'm a reporter or I'm not, but you can't keep holding me back because of my sex!"

"You're not a reporter anymore," he reminded her bluntly. "You're a goddamn copy editor. And if you ever want to rise to news editor, you'll need to live long enough!"

"On this story I'm a reporter," she retorted. "If it'll make you happy, I'll dye my hair, but I *am* going out on this investigation!"

Hyssop leaned forward. "Look, haven't you already got enough problems? I've had four phone calls in the last two weeks from some member of your ex-husband's family saying all kinds of nasty things about you. The guy has called Mark Polanski, too. Mark dismissed the whole thing, and I'm not paying any attention to it, either—Jesus, Kate, I *know* you—but the other papers might feel differently. Maybe you ought to be spending your time mending some fences before you find yourself front-page news."

Kate sat back in her chair, disbelieving. Part of her was embarrassed that Connor—of all people—was hearing this, but mainly she was furious at Mike's family, and at Ben for throwing this up like it meant something. "I don't have any fences to mend with anyone," she told him flatly. "And I can't believe you're sticking your nose in my personal affairs."

"I kind of had my nose shoved into them," he told her. "Four phone calls in two weeks. And you're probably going to have them shoved in *your* face if this guy convinces anyone else that there might be a story here."

"There is no story," Connor said, surprising her by intervening. "Mike Devane has chronic acute paranoid schizophrenia. From the sound of it, this phone caller is probably suffering from a case of it, too...which wouldn't be surprising, since there's some evidence the disease is inherited."

Kate gaped at him. "How do you know that?"

He shrugged a shoulder. "I looked into it after you told me about your ex. I like to know what I'm dealing with."

"You're not *dealing* with anything!"

"I'm dealing with *you*, and you're dealing with it." He appeared totally unrepentant.

"Well," said Hyssop, intervening, "that was kind of what I thought after I listened to this guy...that he's sick, too. It did sound paranoid, all this stuff about how you drove your ex crazy and had him committed."

"Oh, I had him committed," Kate said tightly, ignoring the pain that seemed to be squeezing her heart. "Make no mistake about that. I had him committed several times. It was the only way I could keep him from getting himself killed."

Ben waved a hand. "That goes without saying. I'm

just concerned about you winding up in the middle of a controversy over the Baker Act and how it can be abused. That's what this caller is after."

"Did he give you his name?"

"No." Ben shook his head. "Just said he was a concerned relative."

There were several of those, Kate thought, not the least among them Mike's parents, his two brothers and a sister. None of them wanted to believe they might be carrying a genetic defect any more than they wanted to believe that something they had done might have contributed to Mike's illness. It was so much easier for them to blame it all on Kate, whom they had disliked from the outset.

"It'll take more than me to make a story," she said presently. "And there's no way I can stop these people from saying anything they want."

"You might consider an injunction," Ben suggested. "It *is* slander, and the guy is both trying to embarrass you and trying to get you fired."

"Like he'd pay any attention." Kate shook her head. "You couldn't even prove who it is on the phone, Ben. An injunction would be a waste of paper."

"You're probably right." Ben looked glum, but he'd been a reporter for too long to have a rosy view of what a piece of paper from a court could do to protect someone. Generally, injunctions worked only on people who were law-abiding to begin with, and they seldom made serious threats. "Hell."

"Now, about this investigation," Kate said. "I'm going out with Quinn tonight. It's my neck, Ben."

He scowled at her. "I told you at the beginning that I didn't want you doing anything that would bring you to the attention of this maniac."

"It's already too late."

"What?" Ben sat forward as if he'd been propelled by a spring. "What the hell are you talking about? Did you get some kind of threat?"

"No, no threats."

Connor spoke. "No threats, but he may have called her early this morning." Swiftly he outlined what had happened.

"Damn it!" Ben slapped a hand on his desk. "Damn it! How'd he find out about you?"

"He called here a couple of days ago, asking for Connor," Kate explained. "He wasn't here, so I took the call."

"And let me guess. You gave him your name and told him you were working on the story with Quinn."

"You got it."

"Sometimes I wonder if you have the brains God gave a duck, Devane. I warned you about this!"

"You did. But I was hardly expecting the killer to call."

Ben sighed exasperatedly. "Christ, what do I have to do to keep you out of trouble? All right! Go out with Quinn. But it's on *your* head if anything goes wrong!"

Feeling energized, Kate finished her work early. Since she'd agreed to leave with Quinn at seven, and he was tied up enlarging and cropping some photos that had been requested at the last minute, she took the opportunity to log on to the bulletin-board service and answer CQ's e-mail from earlier. In some corner of her mind, she knew she was becoming too involved with Quinn, but she didn't want to think about that right now. Life was suddenly too much of a mess in other areas for her to be worrying about a phantom love affair.

Because that was what it was becoming. Steadily and surely, she and CQ were moving their cyberrelationship into deep waters. She was feeling as romanced as she ever had in her days of dating, and feeling the same leaps and tumbles she had felt before when she fell in love, high one second and low the next, over something as simple as whether or not he wrote.

All of this was a warning, and she knew it, but she just didn't feel able to do the wise thing at the moment. Later, when things settled down, maybe. But right now she couldn't give this up. It ran at the back of her mind all day, like a pleasurable buzz, making her feel lighter, younger and happier than she had in so many years. No, she would indulge herself for just a little longer. Besides, as long as CQ didn't know who she was, she was safe. The relationship would never move out of cyberspace.

She was beginning to repeat that as if it were some kind of mantra: their relationship was safe because it would never move into the real world. Shaking her head at her own foolishness, she nonetheless replied to CQ, returning the hug he had sent earlier. What she wanted to do was expand the embrace, turn it into something erotic, to use her imagination to travel down pathways that she had been denied for years now. Acutely aware that her large monitor could be easily scanned and read by anyone who happened by, she confined herself to something innocuous.

What she really wanted to do was throw Connor Quinn down on the sand of their island hideaway and have her way with him. And after that, she wanted him to have his way with her.

A giggle almost escaped her, born of embarrassment and her own silliness. She hit the Send key and watched the screen clear. A moment later, a flashing message told her the note had been successfully sent. She logged off and willed herself to ignore the yearnings that CQ was awakening in her. Marriage to Mike had eventually become celibate, and since their divorce, she had been living like a nun. She had, in fact, begun to believe that all her sexual needs and desires had vanished somehow. Now she knew otherwise and wasn't at all sure that she was glad of it.

"Kate." Mark Polanski squatted beside her. "I hear you're going out on an assignment with Quinn tonight."

She swiveled her chair so that she could look straight at him but didn't answer.

Mark shook his head and sighed. "Okay, okay. I'll mind my own business. Just don't forget what I told you earlier. There's something wrong there. Be careful."

She watched him walk away and wondered why Mark was getting so involved in her life all of a sudden. He'd talked to her more in the past few days than in the entire three years since he blew into the newsroom from Jacksonville. She knew he didn't like being cut out of the serial-killer story, and he didn't like Quinn, but whether that was motivating him, she honestly didn't know. Nor did she want to believe the things he said about Connor.

Quinn emerged from the lab about ten minutes late. "Sorry," he said to Kate.

"No problem." She gathered up her purse and jacket, and walked out into the warm evening with him. She opened her mouth to say something about the notes they were exchanging and the world they had created in cyberspace, then caught herself in the nick of time. Oh, hell, she thought, this was one complication she hadn't imagined. It had never occurred to her that she might actually give herself away.

And now she discovered she had twin pangs of guilt,

one for Mike and one for Connor. In different ways, she was cheating on them both. She owed it to Mike to be faithful—although it was getting harder and harder to remember why she had made that vow to herself—and she owed it to Connor to be completely truthful with him. But if she told Connor she was Katydid, their e-mail relationship might move into the real world. She absolutely couldn't permit that. Besides, he would probably be angry with her for not having told him right away who she was.

"Something wrong?" he asked as they walked to his car.

"No," she responded quickly. "Not a thing. Just thinking."

Just trying to find the loophole in a mess of her own making, she thought miserably. Of course, Connor had never exactly told her his name during this entire correspondence. Katydid theoretically knew him only as CQ. But he had an excuse, in that he was talking to someone he thought he didn't know outside the Internet. She, on the other hand, had been guilty from the moment she connected CQ and Connor Quinn. She'd had an obligation right there and then to tell him, "Hey, guess what? We work together!"

But she'd kept her mouth shut, both because she felt guilty about having a friendship with a man and because she had talked herself into believing it was okay since CQ was just a pen pal. Because she had fooled herself into believing that distance somehow kept her safe and pristine.

Well, guess what, Devane? she told herself sourly. The distance has almost vanished, and there's nothing pristine about the thoughts you're having!

And now that things were moving in a romantic direction, she was even more reluctant to tell Connor the truth. She was just getting in deeper and deeper.

Connor's voice intruded on her thoughts. "Any preferences for dinner?"

"Japanese, but who has the time?"

A laugh escaped him. "Some night when we don't have anything else to do. It would be a crime to turn sushi into fast food, though."

They settled on a fast-food place that promoted chicken. "Hey, it's healthier than a burger, right?" Quinn said with a twinkle in his eye.

"It was before they fried it," Kate agreed. She peeled most of the batter off hers, then ruined her diet by eating two biscuits with gravy.

Thirty minutes later, they were pulling up in front of After Midnight. This time, when she entered the club, Kate didn't feel as uncomfortable or as squeamish. It was a weeknight again, a Thursday night. The same night of the week on which Marceline Whitmore had been killed. They showed her picture around, but no one recognized her, except one guy who said, "Wasn't her picture in the paper?"

"We're wasting our time," Kate told Connor as they moved on to the next place. "Why in the world would Marceline Whitmore come to a place like this? This stuff is for men."

"It's also a great place to pick up men."

Kate faced him, squinting as a passing car shone its headlights right in her face. She needed to get a grip, she found herself thinking. She needed to focus on the hardness of the pavement beneath her feet and the coolness of the breeze that was blowing her hair around. On anything except the horror of these murders and the ugliness of Connor's suggestion. Damn it, she'd been a reporter for eight years before she moved into editing, and she knew the dark side of people and life. Why was she feeling as if this time were different? As if she were in danger of getting some of the muck on herself?

"Connor..." She hesitated, trying to collect her thoughts. "Marceline Whitmore was a pillar of this community. Her face was splashed all over the society pages. Why in the world would she want to risk everything by picking up strangers in places like this?"

"I'm not saying she did. I'm just offering it as one reason she might have come here. There has to be a link, Kate. Think about it. There has to be some link between a banker's wife and two exotic dancers. Either they frequented the same kinds of places, or they knew the same person. Either way, we might find out something here."

"But if that's the only reason she might have had to come here—"

He silenced her with a shake of his head. "She was a do-gooder, Devane. Don't forget that. How many charities was she involved with? How do you know she wasn't down here trying to talk these women into a better way of life? Trying to save them, just like that preacher and his gang?"

She nodded reluctantly. "It's a point, but would she come here alone?"

"I don't know. What I do know is that if we're to have any hope of catching this guy before he kills again, we need to find out what the link is."

They kept on looking, checking earlobes and asking the dancers about the earlobes of women who weren't working that night. Nobody knew anybody with a mole on the left ear.

"It's not like a mole on the ear is so uncommon,"

Kate said in frustration as they exited the second establishment. "Dozens of people have moles on their ears!"

"Yes, but this is apparently one that people notice."

She couldn't argue with that. In fact, she was feeling pretty irritated with herself for being so impatient. She had known this would probably be a wild-goose chase. It was the kind of footwork she was accustomed to from long years as a reporter, but time hadn't made her any more comfortable with dead ends.

Before going to the last club, they detoured for coffee at a doughnut shop. Kate couldn't help teasing him as they settled at the counter. "Old cop habits die hard, huh?"

He flashed her one of those smiles that nearly took her breath away. "You try patrolling the graveyard shift and see what your body is screaming for at two in the morning. Sugar and caffeine."

She glanced at her watch. "It's still a couple of hours until 2:00 a.m."

"I'm building up my reserves."

The shop was nearly deserted. Only one other patron sat at the counter, nursing a cup of coffee. The clerk, a woman in her fifties, was sleepy-looking but pleasant as she poured coffee for them and brought Connor a couple of doughnuts.

"When I was on patrol, I used to stop in once or twice a week," Connor said.

"Has the neighborhood changed much?"

He cocked a brow at her. "It hasn't been *that* long."

"I didn't think it had been. But the area is growing so fast that a lot of neighborhoods are changing almost overnight."

He shook his head. "Right around here, it's pretty

much the same. Even the crimes are pretty much the same."

How depressing, Kate thought.

"I think after we finish the last club here we ought to go over to North Nebraska and check out those businesses."

She looked at him. "Why? The first two victims were from businesses along here."

"That doesn't mean he exclusively stalks over here. I'd be surprised if he did. The kind of women he's generally after are easy to find in a number of places."

"Including the homes of the wealthy, it seems."

Twenty minutes later, they entered the last club on Dale Mabry. The third man they spoke to recognized the photo.

"I know her," he said, tipping the photo to catch as much of the dim light as he could. "Yeah. Yeah, I seen her before."

"You're sure?" Kate asked, refusing to let her hopes rise.

"Yeah, I'm sure."

"Where?"

The man sucked air between his teeth, making a little whistling sound. "She's a working girl, know what I mean? But I go to so many of these places...."

"Was it here or right around here?" Quinn asked him.

He shook his head slowly, giving a long-drawn-out "Nah..."

"Any idea where? Just an area will do."

The guy tilted his head back and looked up at them. "What difference does it make? You trying to arrest her for something?"

Sensing that they were about to lose their only source

of information, Kate stepped forward. "We're not cops."

"No? Then what are you so interested for?"

Kate hesitated, unsure whether to tell the truth. Connor had no such qualms.

"She was killed," he said to the man. "We're trying to find out what she did in her last few hours."

"You *are* cops."

Quinn shook his head and pulled out his press badge. "No."

The man hesitated, then shrugged. "I guess. When I saw her, she was modeling lingerie. I don't remember where. I just remember she looked incredible in black."

"North Nebraska," Connor said as they climbed into his car. "There're a bunch of those so-called modeling places over there, and a lot of bars besides."

Kate was still mulling over what the guy had said. "He could be mistaken. Can you see Marceline Whitmore as a *working girl?*"

"I never met the woman, but she wouldn't be the first society woman who went slumming for sexual thrills."

"I suppose not. God, what this is going to do to her family if it's true..."

"Pardon me for saying so, but it couldn't happen to a nicer jerk."

She turned to look at him. "What do you mean?"

His face appeared strange in the yellowish glow of the streetlights and the quick, bright flashes from passing headlights. "Just that I'm not real impressed with the woman's husband. He claimed to be out in Orlando helping his sister with her divorce, but he left his sister's in the late afternoon. There are six or seven hours that can't be accounted for. Now, either the bastard killed his wife or his alibi is going to take the shape of a mistress. Either way, he deserves this little piece of news."

"Are you usually vindictive?"

"I'm not vindictive at all. If I were, I'd want to give him the news myself. No, I'd almost be willing to bet that the vindictive one in this equation was Marceline herself."

"You think she did this to hurt him?"

"I'd almost be willing to bet on it."

"But wouldn't she need to tell him? He doesn't know about this, does he?"

"If he does, he's keeping mum. But no, I don't think he knew yet. I think she was saving it up."

"God!" All of a sudden, Kate felt very little sympathy for the dead woman. "I just can't imagine people acting that way!"

"No? What about a certain member of your ex-husband's family?"

"That's different. He's obviously sick."

"Is it?"

"Just what are you trying to get at here, Quinn?" she said irritably.

"Nothing major. Just a lesson I learned as a cop, one you should have learned as a reporter—there's no limit on the kind of shit people will do to each other. And it gets really bad if they care."

Kate pressed her cheek to the cool glass of the window and watched yet another traffic light turn red before them. "Hell hath no fury—is that what you're saying?" She wondered why this conversation was making her so uncomfortable, why she felt compelled to defend Marceline Whitmore and the rest of the human race from Quinn's cynicism. Or maybe she was just disturbed to discover that Connor was a cynic.

"Basically. Look at all the things people are capable of doing to each other on a daily basis. I don't have to give you the laundry list. Why would it be so impossible that Marceline Whitmore, finding out that her husband is having an affair, decides to do the most hurtful thing she can think of?"

"It's not impossible. But why would she turn herself into a whore? That would hurt *her* more than him."

"Not necessarily. That would depend on how he viewed her and how she viewed herself. Maybe he's extremely possessive."

They raised eyebrows, entering the lingerie "studios" as a pair. They raised even more eyebrows when they refused to take a look at the models. The immediate assumption was that they were cops, and mouths clamped tightly closed.

"Look," Quinn said repeatedly. "All I want to know is one thing. Did this woman work here recently? Answer that and I'm on my way."

The answer was a shake of the head.

"They're certainly paranoid," Kate said finally.

"With good reason. What they're doing is illegal."

But finally they got a nod, at a place called Renoir's Studio. Kate was getting used to the squalor of these places, but this one was even worse than most. A negligee hung on a hanger from a hook in the wall. Clearly, it wasn't meant to be worn; it was covered with dust. The little entry in which they stood was approximately four feet by six and hadn't been swept in recent memory. Through a bead curtain, they could see into a room where three women lounged on cheap chairs in low-cut leotards. All of them were smoking.

"She worked here," said the manager. "For the last eight months. Real popular with our customers." He shook his head and handed the picture back. "She's the one who was killed, isn't she? I thought so when I saw her photo in the paper. She used to wear a lot more makeup when she was working. It changed her face a little, but I still recognized her."

Kate felt the unmistakable tingles of excitement that always came when she knew she was on the brink of discovering something important. "Did she work here the night she was killed?"

"That was last Thursday, right? Yeah, she worked here. Left at about one o'clock."

"Did any customer show special interest in her?"

The manager grinned. "They all do. I mean, did. She was dynamite. She was one of the ones who *liked* this job."

Connor smothered a sigh. "But did any customer that night stand out?"

"Oh." The manager looked at him. "You mean like maybe she met the killer here?"

"It could have happened."

"Are you sure you're not cops?"

"Positively."

"You sure sound like a cop."

"I used to be one before I quit and signed on with the newspaper." Connor gave the guy a smile. "The pay's not as good, but the hours are better."

For some reason, that relaxed the manager. "Yeah, right," he said, laughing. "That's why you're talking to me at two in the morning. No, I don't remember any customer who seemed special in any way. But I don't think she could have picked up the guy here. We take real good care of our girls, you know? They're never alone, and we always walk them to their cars. We don't want nobody hurting them."

"So she left here alone?"

He nodded. "Absolutely. I walked her out to her car myself. You know she drove a white Lexus? She sure didn't make all her money here." Then he laughed. "'Course she didn't. Her old man is some kind of big bank guy, right? Hey, did he get off on knowing she did this? Some guys do, y'know. They *like* having their women sell it for money. I can't figure it, myself."

"I don't know anything about her husband," Connor said. "So she left alone."

"I already told you that."

"And you didn't notice anything at all unusual that night?"

"Nope. Look, we're equal opportunity here. Anybody with fifty dollars or more gets to view the merchandise. So we get all types. Some are strung out on drugs, or drunk, some are lowlifes, and some are the hoity-toity rich guys. A little of everything. I just didn't see nothing no different from usual."

Quinn nodded, looking around. "You offer a full menu?"

"Of course."

"What was her specialty?"

"British."

Kate wondered why Connor's eyebrows suddenly rose so high.

"Interesting," he said. "Do you have a policy on the girls meeting customers away from here?"

"Yeah. We don't allow it. We catch anyone doing that and they're fired."

They didn't say anything when they got back in the car. Connor drove them toward the university until he found an all-night sandwich shop. "Let's get some coffee," he said.

Kate followed him in and ordered a small milk shake. If she drank coffee at this time of night, she would never get to sleep. Connor, however, didn't appear to be concerned. He ordered a large coffee and an Italian sub, which he insisted on sharing with her.

Kate could no longer contain her curiosity. "What's British?"

"British?"

"You know. Marceline's specialty."

"Oh." He hesitated, and Kate could have sworn he almost blushed. The realization amused her no end, and she had a hard time concealing a smile. "Evidently she was, um, into dominance and submission."

"Oh." Kate felt her own cheeks heat. "A dominatrix."

"Well, sometimes. It certainly would explain how she came to be tied up without a struggle."

"Oh. Oh!" The picture was suddenly clear to Kate. "You know, I've always wondered why anyone would let a total stranger tie them up. It seems so...risky."

"No kidding. But sexual gratification is a strong drive, strong enough to overcome common sense."

"But why do they call it British?"

"It's a code system. I don't know if they use it because the customers are more comfortable with it, or if they actually think it's concealing what they're doing. But British is dominance and submission, French is oral sex, and Greek is...well, Greek is self-explanatory, I imagine. Everybody's heard that."

Kate nodded. "How is it you know these codes?"

Now he did color. Visibly. Kate was enjoying herself hugely. "Don't get the wrong idea," he said. "I don't patronize these places. But I was a cop, remember? I heard just about everything."

She let him off the hook then, but she felt she'd gotten even for his patronizing attitude about her naiveté. Cheerfully she stole a huge bite of his sandwich.

Then another thought struck her. "So Marceline was operating on the side."

"So it would appear." He sipped his coffee and swallowed another mouthful of sandwich. "But you know, Judy Eppinga was known *not* to do tricks on the side. Nobody's sure about the first girl, but everyone was sure about Eppinga. Now we have Marceline, who was turning tricks in a brothel but was forbidden to turn any on her own. Why would she want to, anyway? These women must turn eight or ten tricks a night. Why would any of them want to do more?"

"Since I don't understand why they want to do any, I can't begin to venture a guess as to why she might have done more." She sipped her milk shake while she thought about it. "Maybe this guy was special to her. It would fit with all of them, wouldn't it, the way these women let someone into their homes? It had to be somebody they knew and trusted."

"We're pretty much agreed on that."

His tone irritated her. "Sorry. I haven't been privy to your discussions with Rick Diaz."

"Hey, don't get your feathers in an uproar."

But she was still annoyed. "It is technically impossible to get feathers in an uproar."

"You know what I meant." A smile suddenly creased the corners of his blue eyes. "Are you cranky because you're tired?"

"I'm cranky because you make me feel like I'm stating the obvious. It may be obvious to you, but not all of us are gifted with your abilities or your connections."

His smile deepened. "You're tired. I wasn't insinuating that you were stating the obvious. I was *agreeing* with you. I guess my choice of words was poor."

"Actually, it was your tone of voice." But now she was beginning to feel foolish, as if she were exaggerating the whole thing. "Look, let's forget it. I *am* tired."

"Sure." He waved the waitress over and asked for more coffee. When she had refilled his cup, he pulled his cell phone out of his pocket and began to punch in a number.

"You're never going to sleep tonight," Kate remarked.

"Probably not." He lifted his phone to his ear and waited. "Rick. Connor. Listen, I've got some big news about number three. You want to meet someplace, or talk in the morning?" He paused. "I'm on the cell phone. Right. Okay. I'm at Johnny's Place. Right."

He turned off the phone and slipped it back into his pocket. "He'll be here in twenty minutes."

"Let me guess. He doesn't sleep, either."

"Not when something like this is coming down. We never did. Just kind of napped here and there as we could."

"Running on adrenaline." She'd done that quite a few times herself. It was what she was doing tonight, in fact, only the adrenaline had begun to wear off. Her surroundings were beginning to look as if she were seeing them through water, and she kept getting the feeling that she was phasing in and out.

Reaching out, she grabbed Connor's coffee mug and took a deep swallow. He laughed, but it was a friendly sound. "Let me buy you a cup," he said.

She was just starting her second cup when Rick Diaz arrived. He slid into the booth next to Connor. He looked as rumpled as Kate felt. A brush hadn't quite managed to tame his hair, and his cowlick was standing up. His shirt looked as if he'd pulled it out of an ironing basket.

"So okay," Rick said. "What's up?"

"Marceline Whitmore had a secret life."

Rick's eyebrows rose, and his dark eyes grew suddenly animated. "Well, hot shit," he said. "What was it? Wild parties? Orgies?"

"She was a working girl."

Rick blinked. "Oh, hell. I was hoping you were going to give me some bored-little-rich-girl story. Christ. A working girl. This is going to create a scandal of epic proportions."

"Not your problem."

Rick eyed Connor wryly. "You know better. I can hear the noise already. They'll be claiming we're making up evidence." He shook his head. "How did you find this out?"

Connor took him step by step through their evening, and Rick wrote everything down. "The manager is sure it's the same woman?"

"He identified her photo. He also mentioned that she drove a white Lexus."

"Hell." Diaz made a few more notes, then slapped his notebook closed. "Sit on this, will you? I need to verify this stuff, and I want to do it before word gets out. Then I'll need to break the news to the family before you print this."

"*Should* we print this?" Connor asked.

"It's going to come out one way or another. We still haven't plugged the leak in the department. And you guys *did* uncover this."

Connor hesitated. "But the story is brutal, and I don't see that it's really necessary to embarrass the family."

Kate sat up straighter. "Wait a minute. This is *news.*"

"This is tabloid journalism," he argued.

"No, it's not. It's important to the public to know that the victims are a certain kind of woman. Middle-class matrons have a right to know they can sleep safely in their beds. And we have a responsibility to print the story to ease their terror."

"That's one way of looking at it."

Kate didn't bother arguing further. She would be the one to write the story, anyway, and she knew what Ben Hyssop's decision would be. "I won't sensationalize it."

"It doesn't need to be sensationalized."

Kate looked at Rick. "Just let me know if it's okay before five today."

He nodded, then looked at Quinn. "She might as well print it, Connor. If you guys don't, the leak will pass it to one of the other papers."

Quinn nodded, but he didn't look happy.

"I also won't tell anybody else in the department until tonight," Rick said. "I promised you guys would get exclusives, and so far you've gotten zip, while everybody else is getting info that isn't supposed to be on the street." He shook his head. "When I find the bigmouth, his career is over."

Kate wrote the story about Marceline Whitmore as soon as she and Connor got back to the *Sentinel* offices. Then she stored it in a password-protected file, left a note for Sally explaining why she would be late and headed home to bed. She had no idea where Connor had disappeared to.

It was noon when she awoke, feeling as if she had hardly slept at all. The only thing that mobilized her was the realization that she was supposed to be at the copydesk. She made a pot of strong coffee and wondered when she had become so old that a disruption of her sleep schedule could throw her off all day. Back when she was a reporter, last night would merely have energized her. Now she felt like something the cat had dragged in.

Speaking of cats, maybe she ought to get that dog she had always wanted. The non sequitur made her smile wanly into her coffee cup as she wandered into her office and powered up her computer. Five minutes to check mail, and then she would jump into some clothes and head to work.

Leaning against her desk, waiting for her system to log on to her network provider, she felt a slow, deep pulsing begin inside her. She wanted Connor to be waiting for her on-line. She wanted him to be there with one of his magical notes in which he touched her and held her close and made her feel like a woman.

His ID was at the very top of her mail queue, and she leaned forward eagerly to see what he had to say.

He astonished her. He had changed the setting from early evening to late night, and had moved them indoors so that they were sitting before a fire sipping white wine. He put his arm around her shoulders and held her close to his side.

And suddenly, in her mind, Kate was there. With every nerve in her body, she could feel Connor beside her, feel the heat of him and the strength of him. Tears began to run down her face as yearning gripped her heart. God, how she wanted him. How she wanted to be with him, away from everything. Away from guilt and fear and violence and all the rest of it.

He turned to her and put his other arm around her, drawing her mouth to his. She felt the heat of his lips, the warmth of his tongue, felt his broad chest hard against the softness of hers. His hand rubbed her back gently, driving away all the tensions of the day, softening her until she leaned against him, all warm and yielding.

Then his hand slipped around until it cradled her breast....

And there he stopped, leaving her wanting more, so much more.

There was another note from him, this one prosaic, talking about things in his life, mentioning that being a news photographer had its downs, almost as many as being a cop. He used to be a cop, he said. Had he ever told her that?

The question pierced her with guilt, because she still had not told him who she was. Before she carried this e-mail love affair any further, didn't she owe it to him to tell him? To be honest?

Why? So that he could back away the instant he learned she was a colleague? To disrupt the delicate balance they had achieved, which allowed them to be so achingly honest with one another? Would they be this honest face-to-face? *Could* they be?

She doubted it. When they were face-to-face, all the inhibitions and prohibitions would be in place. He would never say things to her such as he had just written.

Nor, probably, would he tell her what he told her in his next note.

"I had a nightmare again. This case is waking up all those dormant terrors I thought I'd finally managed to leave behind me. I jolted out of sleep at dawn, covered in sweat, with visions of mutilated bodies. In my hand was the knife that had killed them.

"I know I would never hurt anyone that way, but...when I do the profiling my mind starts to follow strange, sick pathways, and I become almost afraid of myself. My dreams reflect the transformation, bringing the killer I construct inside me to life.

"I hate this. I can't tell you how much I hate doing this and hate what it does to me. This is why I quit the police force. But what choice do I have? More women will die...."

She replied to that message, telling him that he was taking too much responsibility for events that weren't in his control. Telling him that she was so sorry he was having nightmares. Seeking and failing to find any words that might actually give him comfort.

To the embrace he had described, she didn't reply at all.

# 12

"There's been another murder."

Connor wanted to hurl the phone across the room and smash it against the wall so that he couldn't hear what was coming.

"Pinellas County Sheriff's Office just contacted us," Rick continued.

"Pinellas?" Connor froze. Pinellas County was on this side of the bay, encompassing the peninsula that contained St. Petersburg, Largo, Clearwater and an assortment of other communities.

"Yeah." Rick's voice sounded heavy. "All that time we spent looking for a dancer with a mole over here in Hillsborough, and this time he killed a dancer over there. Not too far from U.S. 19, just outside the Largo city limits."

"Christ!"

"Nice, huh? Listen, I'm getting all the reports faxed over here, but I told 'em you might come by to look over what they have. They agreed to let you see the file, so I'd really appreciate it if you'd stop by the main office before too long."

"How far along is the investigation?"

"They found her yesterday afternoon. She was killed the night before."

"Before I got the letter." That disturbed him, but he couldn't put his finger on why, so he set it aside for later consideration.

"Apparently so," Rick agreed. "Maybe our guy is just playing with us."

"Were there any notes?"

"I don't know. Like I said, I'm waiting for the fax of the reports, but I'm counting on you to get over there and get all the info you can."

"Hey, I've got a job. I've got two shoots scheduled for this afternoon."

"I'll call your boss. He can find somebody else to do it. Quinn, I *need* you."

In the end, Connor called Ben himself and told him what was coming down. Ben told him to take the afternoon, just bring in another story like the one Kate had written about Marceline Whitmore.

Bill Kittrick, an old acquaintance of his, was heading up the investigation. His greeting was friendly. "Hey, it's about time you dipped your toes back in the water, Quinn."

"Believe me, I'd have preferred to stay dry."

"From what Diaz told me, this case is a bitch. What's this about you getting phone calls and notes from this guy?"

"I'll show you my photocopies if you'll show me yours."

"Deal. Look, I really don't have time right now," Bill said, "but we can get together this evening, if that's okay. Instead of you driving up here to Largo, why don't we meet somewhere in between? You can scan the file and tell me what you have on this guy."

"Fair enough."

"And let's have dinner while we do it. I haven't eaten anything but a couple of doughnuts since we found the body."

The comment about doughnuts suddenly reminded Connor of Kate and her querulousness that morning. For some reason, he smiled. "Listen, if it's not too much trouble, why don't you just come to my place instead? I've got all the crime-scene photos from the first three victims tacked to my wall, and I could get some take-out Chinese."

"Even better. Seven?"

"Seven is great. Meantime, can I check out the crime scene?"

"Sure. I'll call up there right now and tell 'em to let you in. Just promise me it won't be on the front page of tomorrow's *Sentinel*. So far, we've managed to keep word of this killing out of the press."

"No problem. I've got an agreement with Rick. I don't print anything until he clears it."

"Okay, then. See you tonight."

Quinn hung up the phone, considered going in to work, then found himself gravitating to his workroom, where the crime-scene photos were pinned to the walls and the reports were in neat stacks on a table. He turned on all the lights, including a halogen torchère and the rack-mounted spotlights, brightening the room almost to daylight.

Something was nagging at him, beginning to tug uncomfortably at the edges of his thoughts, demanding his attention. Something he was overlooking. Sitting in his deep leather chair, he leaned back and swiveled slowly, scanning the pictures as if they were a collage, pieces that somehow made up a whole. What he was missing was the larger picture....

The doorbell rang. His mind still on the murders, he went to answer it and found his next-door neighbor, Sophie Butler, standing there with a stern look on her face. "Shame on you, Connor," she said, waggling one arthritic finger at him. "Have you looked at your poor hibiscus? The damn thing is dying for lack of water. I looked over from my balcony and thought for sure you must have died!"

"Oh." Quinn meekly stepped back and allowed the eighty-year-old woman to march into his apartment, her fuchsia broomstick skirt swirling around her ankles. The apple-green smock she wore over it was spattered with bright splotches of the oils she preferred to paint with. Her snow-white hair tumbled unrestrained to her waist, and unless Connor missed his guess, it contained some cadmium-yellow and cobalt-blue splotches, too.

"What have you been painting?" he asked her as she strode to the kitchen and rummaged around for his watering can.

"The bay. It's been absolutely incredible the last few days. There must be a hundred different colors in the water in the morning." She found the pot and straightened, pausing just long enough to glower at him before she filled it. "When did you become a plant murderer?"

He shook his head. "I'm sorry, Sophie. Things have been going on."

"Nothing takes precedence over the care of a living thing that one has taken responsibility for."

"Of course it doesn't."

"Well, then, I suggest you apologize to that poor hibiscus."

He followed her out onto the balcony and winced

when he saw how ragged the hibiscus looked. It had dropped most of its lower leaves, and one forlorn red blossom was all it displayed.

"For shame," Sophie said, and gently touched one of the branches of the bedraggled plant. "The geraniums are more forgiving, but they're unquestionably thirsty, too. And when was the last time you fertilized?"

He tried to remember but couldn't, not because he hadn't done it recently, but because his mind was refusing to focus on the problem. "I have, but I can't remember if it was two weeks ago or three."

"Well, if it was that recent, I won't do it again today." The breeze tossed her long white hair, dragging strands of it across her face. She brushed them impatiently aside. "If you're too busy, just give me your key and I'll take care of the poor dears."

"Maybe that would be a good idea."

She looked sharply at him then, her blue eyes as bright as the bay on a clear, warm day. "Are you working on those serial murders?"

"What gives you that idea?"

"The hours you've been keeping. Since you started working for the paper, you've usually finished up at a reasonable hour."

He looked at her and almost smiled. "You'd make a good detective."

"I know. I pay attention to things…like these plants."

"Oh, for Pete's sake, Sophie. I said I'm sorry."

"Just think about how you'd feel if you were all dehydrated and had to depend on someone else to remember to give you water." But suddenly she chuckled and gave him a grin. "Just give me the key. Then you don't have to worry about being planticidal."

"Planticidal?" He couldn't help it. He cracked up.

Maybe he cracked up more than he ordinarily would have, because of all the strain he'd been feeling lately, but he started laughing and laughed until his sides ached. Sophie kept right on watering his plants, pausing once to give him a benevolent smile.

"You needed that," she said when he caught his breath.

"I sure did."

"So what's happening with these serial murders?"

"Sophie..."

"I know, I know. You can't discuss it. Are you working for the paper or the police on this one?"

He couldn't see any reason to lie. Sophie wasn't a gossip, anyway. "The police."

She nodded approvingly. "Good. You haven't been exactly happy since you left the force. I know you said you couldn't stand the violence anymore, but I don't think you feel as useful now, do you?"

She might as well have slapped him on the side of the head with a wet dishtowel. Startled, he stared at her...and found himself wondering if she was right.

But, God, he couldn't stand the nightmares. He couldn't stand waking up in the dead of night with a victim's screams loud in his brain and his heart racing as he wondered if he was somehow part of the madness that killed these people. It didn't haunt him when gang members gunned each other down, or when arguing spouses shot each other, but when some innocent woman was attacked in her bed, or some child was injured or killed in an accident... Then the images refused to go away.

And when it came to this kind of crime...well, he started feeling as if he were somehow part of the process. The letter from the killer this time had made him feel even more so. It was as if it had somehow dragged him into the crime as a participant. It had made him feel dirty in his soul.

Nuts. He was nuts.

"Well, you'll do what you think best, dearie," Sophie said. She pinched a couple of yellowed leaves off a geranium, then patted the plant almost maternally. "Why don't you come over for dinner? I'm making manicotti."

"I'd love to, but I'm having company for dinner tonight."

She perked up. "A woman?"

"'Fraid not. Colleague."

"You need a love life, Connor Quinn."

"Nobody needs that kind of pain in the ass."

She put her hands on her ample hips and frowned at him. "Your parents weren't the only married people on the planet, you know."

"Who said my parents have anything to do with it?"

"You! In a thousand ways. So they fought all the time? So what? Not everybody does. I was happy with Edgar, God rest his soul. We had thirty wonderful years together."

"So wonderful that you never wanted to remarry. So wonderful that you never painted a picture until you were widowed."

She scowled. "I just never thought about painting before."

"Right. The urge just sprang full-blown to life after your husband died."

"It did!" She waved a dismissing hand. "You're impossible, you know that?"

He grinned. "I know."

"So die a bachelor. See if I care. Never know the warmth of a woman's love—"

"Hey, I've had my fill of women. And believe me, there's nothing in their love worth giving up my freedom and sanity for."

She sniffed disparagingly and stalked toward the door, grabbing the spare key off the hook in the kitchen on her way. "I'll look after the plants, Quinn, but who the hell is going to look after you?"

"Me," he replied, but he doubted she heard it over the slamming of the door. Too damn bad, he thought, that Sophie wasn't thirty or forty years younger. He might consider sacrificing his solitude for her.

With a glance at his watch, he realized he'd lost a half hour since he told Bill he was going up to the crime scene. Grabbing his camera and bag, he headed out.

The house was little more than a four-room bungalow in a run-down section of subdivision between U.S. 19 and the Bayside Bridge. When Connor got out of his car, he paused to look around, seeing the decay and neglect that probably made this an unhealthy place to live. The houses were farther apart than more recent construction, the lots almost lavish in size, but the buildings themselves had been allowed to go to seed as rentals. It wouldn't be long, he figured, before the insatiable appetite for land leveled this place and replaced these aging bungalows with four or five times as many very expensive houses, creating yet another bedroom community for Tampa.

For now, though, this area looked as if it had been forgotten. Yards were little more than bare dirt and patches of grass under the Spanish-moss-laden arms of live oaks. Rusting cars and battered garbage cans added to the charm.

The crime-scene tape was bright yellow, jarring against the gray, green and brown backdrop of this forgotten piece of Pinellas County. Instinctively he lifted his camera, checked the light and began to shoot. There was a story here that went far beyond the dead woman. Absentee landlords, primarily, and low-income tenants who couldn't afford to care.

He ducked under the tape and walked up to the front door. There was a police lockbox on it, and he looked around, wondering what he was supposed to do. Bill had thought someone was going to be up here for most of the afternoon, but apparently he had been wrong.

Deciding to wait a few minutes, in case the crime-scene tech had merely gone off to get some coffee and sandwiches, he wandered around the yard, peering in windows. Beside the back door, there was a window with part of a pane missing.

His heart slammed, and he stood frozen, staring at it. It looked as if it had been removed with a glass cutter. The hole was in exactly the place that would allow someone to reach in and unlock the back door.

Had the killer done that? If so, he was escalating to a new type of victim, or to a new stage in his fantasy. The cooperation of people who trusted him was giving way to something even darker. Or maybe this was a copycat killing. Sufficient details of the first killings had been held back from the public that there was no possibility anyone could simulate the first murders exactly. Theoretically, it shouldn't be hard to sort this out.

But if he was escalating somehow... The thought, even incomplete, chilled Connor.

He shifted his attention to the door and saw that the

frame had been broken. Someone had broken his way into the house using force. The killer? But that was so unlike the man who had committed the first murders. Damn, where was the forensics team?

He pulled a pair of latex gloves out of his jeans and slipped them on. Then he pushed gently on the door and watched it swing open. The hinges groaned, almost as if the old house were weeping.

*Don't get fanciful now.*

The interior of the house was dim, and it took a few seconds for his eyes to adapt. He was standing in a small kitchen with a stove and refrigerator that looked to be forty years old. The linoleum was cracked, and the floor sagged and creaked. Termites. This old house didn't have a whole lot of life left in it.

On the counter, neatly rinsed and turned upside down on a dishtowel, was a mug. He remembered the two mugs in Judy Eppinga's apartment and suddenly wondered if they'd found a mug beside the sink in Marceline Whitmore's kitchen.

He stepped through into a living room with a vinyl-covered couch, a twelve-inch TV and a beanbag chair. Nothing appeared to be disturbed, but he found himself wondering why this woman had been living this way. He would have expected her to have made more money than this would indicate.

The bathroom had been disturbed. A towel lay on the floor, and in the sink there was a rusty stain that suggested watered-down blood.

This wasn't right. This wasn't like the other scenes. Stepping into the bedroom, he noted the stench of feces and urine, and the stain on the stripped mattress. If there had been linen on the bed, it was gone, and so was just about everything else that might have been useful as evidence. He wished he could have gotten here sooner.

Then, on the floor, he saw a six-inch splatter of dried blood. Squatting, he stared at it and wondered what had happened here.

He took a roll of photos, logging them as meticulously as he had when he was working crime scenes as a cop. There was little enough left here, but he took the photos anyway, knowing how even something seemingly insignificant could turn out to be important.

Afterward, as he was coming around the outside of the house to get back in his car, he saw another car parked out front. A tall man with blond hair stood outside the police line, beside a gray Seville. He wore gray clerical garb and was holding what appeared to be a small prayer book.

The two men looked at one another. Connor halted a few steps away. "Did you know the victim?" he asked.

The man nodded. "I was her pastor. Are you a police officer?" He looked pointedly at the camera dangling from the strap around Connor's neck.

"I'm working with them."

"Oh." He looked down at the yellow police tape. "I'm Peter Masterson, pastor of the Church of the Holy Fellowship."

"That's over in Tampa, isn't it?"

Masterson nodded.

Connor looked back at the house, then at him. "She drove all the way over there for church?"

"Sometimes. We didn't ostracize her because of her profession."

Quinn nodded, meeting the man's eyes. "I'm Connor Quinn."

Masterson's eyes widened. "You... Your name is familiar. Have we met?"

Connor shook his head. "I'd remember. Did you ever think she'd get into this kind of trouble?"

"Are you saying this was her fault?"

"I don't blame the victims, Pastor. I never have."

Masterson nodded slowly, his expression faintly doubtful. "Crystal had her failings, and certainly we at the church tried to persuade her to find another means of earning a living, but..." He trailed off and looked sadly at the house. "If only she had heeded us, perhaps she wouldn't have come to the killer's attention."

"If it hadn't been her, it would have been someone else." The pastor looked a little surprised at that, so Connor elaborated. "These people kill because they're compelled to kill. If this woman hadn't come to his attention, another one would have."

Masterson nodded. "I see. How...depraved."

"They're sick. Most of them have measurable brain damage. That doesn't justify their actions, of course, but it helps to explain them."

"Explanation," the minister said slowly, then went on, spacing out each word as if he were thinking this through, "is the first step, perhaps, to understanding."

"I don't ever want to understand one of these sons of bitches." And maybe that was what terrified him most when he started to profile a killer—that he might actually begin to understand this.

"But perhaps understanding is necessary to forgiveness in this case."

Connor looked down at the prayer book in the man's hands. "Maybe. If you really want to forgive this bastard. Look, I'm afraid you can't come past the line."

"I don't want to. I just thought...a prayer might not be amiss."

"It's about all any of us can do for her now."

"Exactly." Masterson opened the book to a marked page and bowed his head, reading silently, moving his lips.

Connor considered joining in, then rejected the idea. The only prayer he had to offer for the dead was to catch the killer.

While he was waiting for the dinner delivery and for Bill Kittrick to arrive, Connor called the Church of the Holy Fellowship and asked who their pastor was.

"Reverend Peter Masterson," said the woman who had answered. "He's a good pastor."

"I think I met him today. Tall man with blond hair, maybe thirty?"

The woman laughed. "He's closer to forty, but he has a youthful look. Would you like to leave a message?"

"No, no. I was thinking about coming to service on Sunday. He seemed like such a nice man."

"He certainly is. One of the kindest men I've ever known."

Quinn ended the conversation as quickly as he gracefully could, satisfied that the man who had come to the latest victim's house was exactly who he said he was.

The Chinese food he had ordered was delivered, but Bill still hadn't arrived, so he got on-line and looked for mail from Katydid. She still hadn't responded to his escalation of their kiss, and he was beginning to feel like a grade A shit. Obviously he'd gone too far.

On the other hand, she'd written him a note about ordinary things, signaling that she wasn't breaking off their relationship but hinting that she did object to the direction he'd taken. Which, of course, he could understand. He thought about apologizing, then dismissed the idea. No, she'd been playing along right up until that point. He was damn well not going to apologize for taking the next, inevitable step. What really bothered him, though, was how much he found himself caring. How much it hurt that she had suddenly put this distance between them.

He dashed off a note to her, keeping to an innocuous discussion of his neglected plants and his next-door neighbor, figuring that he'd let her set the limits on this relationship for a while. Funny, he thought as he logged off, but in his mind, Katydid was beginning to look like Kate Devane.

Well, of course, he thought after a moment. They had similar names, and it was only natural that he should fuse them in his mind. Besides, he liked the way Kate Devane looked. His eyes liked tracing her contours.

The bell rang, and he went to open the door to Bill Kittrick. The detective was carrying a thick expandable file under his arm and tossed it on the dining room table.

"Tell me that's food I smell," Bill said. "I still haven't eaten." He was a tall, thin man with reddish-blond hair and a thick mustache.

"Let me just heat it in the microwave. The guy delivered it about twenty minutes ago."

"Sorry I'm late, but you know how that goes. Some schmuck decided to beat his wife to death with a tire iron and claim some marauding thief did it. Unfortunately, the tire iron had his prints all over it. Got any beer?"

Connor pointed to the fridge while he put the various entrées into bowls for heating. Bill opened two long-necks and set one on the counter beside Connor. "So what did you think of the scene?" he asked.

Connor slid the first bowl into the microwave and turned it on. "There wasn't a whole lot left to look at, but what I did see bothered me."

"Such as?"

"Such as the hole in the window, the shattered door frame, the bloodstains in the bathroom sink and the bloodstain on the bedroom floor."

Bill nodded and took a long swallow from his bottle. "Go on."

"Our killer has so far worked with women who trusted him enough to let him into the house. He didn't have to break in. The scenes were always spotless. No blood on anything."

Bill nodded. "We *do* think the killer cut the windowpane to unlock the door. He didn't smash the door frame, though. The boyfriend did that when he got home from work at 7:00 a.m. and she wouldn't answer the door."

"Why the back door?"

"Because they always entered by the back door. It was the first place he knocked."

"It was locked?"

"Yup. Doesn't mean anything. It was one of those locks you can set to lock after you."

"What about the window? Did the boyfriend do that, too?"

"He denied it. Said he didn't even notice it at first."

Connor nodded. "So the killer entered surreptitiously. He never did that before."

"You *think* he never did that before. What if he found all these other places unlocked?"

The microwave beeped, and Connor removed one bowl and replaced it with another. "It's possible. Not very likely, though. The Whitmore woman was evidently a security nut. Her husband said she *never* went to bed without making sure the alarm system was on."

"Interesting." Bill sat down at the table and pulled a legal pad out of the expandable folder. He scrawled a few notes with a ballpoint pen. "Now, about the bloodstains. Prelim from our guys says it was spilled. There's no sign of arterial spray. In fact, except for that stain and the stains in the sink, there's no blood anywhere. The victim, however, appears to have bled to death."

Connor nodded. "That fits with the others." The microwave beeped, and he switched bowls, turning it on again. "Pictures. What I really need are pictures, Bill."

"Like I said, you show me yours and I'll show you mine."

"How about we eat first?"

"Fair enough."

The snow peas weren't as crisp as they probably had been when they left the wok originally, but everything else had heated up perfectly. Connor opted for chopsticks and Bill for a fork.

"Not bad," Bill said as he tasted the Szechwan beef. "So, how do you like the newspaper business?"

"Most of it's not bad. Most of the people I see actually *want* to get their pictures taken. I meet some interesting folks, and few of them are in trouble with the law."

Bill chuckled. "How dull can you get?"

"It's not dull very often. It's the people who make any job, Bill. You know that. I was getting sick of stiffs, and I'd heard every story Dave Plummer had to tell at least a dozen times."

"He's still telling the same stories."

"I imagine so."

Bill bit off half an egg roll, chewed and swallowed. "A little more ginger than I like. Let me know when you want to come back to some real work. I can get you into forensics easy. Or maybe you'd like to work homicide. Either way, I'd sure like to have you."

"Thanks." Connor found himself remembering what Sophie had said earlier, and felt something inside him make an infinitesimal shift, as if his perspective were undergoing a permanent alteration. As if someone had changed the focus on the lens.

"I saw the crime-scene photos you used to take," Bill went on. "You've got one hell of a talent for highlighting the important stuff. I don't know how you do it."

"Neither do I."

Bill looked at him, disbelieving.

"I'm serious," Connor said. "After it's all over, it's as clear as crystal, but when I'm taking those pictures, before we know what's going on, it's just an instinct. Damned if I can explain it."

"You get in their minds, Quinn. Somehow you make a leap and get in their minds at a level you aren't even aware of. You walk into the crime scene and something about the way things were left triggers something inside you, and you know. You just know what the bastard was thinking."

Quinn was beginning to lose his appetite. "I left all that shit behind for a good reason, Bill."

"Of course you did. It's a terrible burden. But once you've rested enough, you'll be back."

"Says who?"

"Says me. I know you. You'll rest awhile, and then some case will break, and you'll start to get feelings about it, and you won't be able to stand the thought that someone else might get hurt if you sit on your duff. When you start to get that feeling, give me a call."

Connor found himself wondering why he'd ever liked this man.

After dinner, they went into the workroom. Connor pointed out which section of the wall was devoted to which crime and explained the organization of the papers on the tables. Bill handed over the expandable file and told him he could keep the photos, because they were duplicates.

Sitting at his desk while Bill perused the photomontage on the wall, Connor worked his way through the Pinellas County file. The initial police report bore out what Bill had said about the boyfriend and how he had discovered the body. The cop had further indicated that the body was lying supine on the bed with ropes tied around the wrists, neck and knees, but the ropes were attached to nothing else. He had also noted the blood splatter on the floor beside the bed.

After that, Connor looked at the photographs, seeing the scene the way the crime-scene techs had when they arrived a couple of hours later. Theoretically, nothing had been disturbed in the interim.

The body looked like all the others, and even in the photos he could see the abrasions on the knees. The victim had been blond and pretty, and far too young to die in such a squalid way. Her age, the M.E.'s report said, was only twenty-three.

"They did the autopsy this morning," Bill volunteered as he sat at the worktable and prepared to start reading the reports on the other cases. "A lot of the test results are still pending."

"Sure."

But as he scanned the reports and the photos, and

noted the M.E.'s mention of the knees and how the abrasions contained some splinters that appeared to come from the wood floor of the bedroom, and when he saw the panties and high heels in the corner, he was sure this was the same man. The differences were not nearly as significant as the similarities.

Victim four. And plain as day, on her earlobe was a large, dark mole.

Two hours later, Bill pushed his chair back from the worktable and stretched widely. "Damn!" he said, and stood up, putting his hands on his lower back and walking to the sliding glass doors. The bay was almost invisible tonight, a blackness bounded by the lights of the Gandy Bridge to the north, the city of Tampa to the east and the Sunshine Skyway to the south. Tonight the air was so clear that it was even possible to make out the twin peaks of the Skyway's suspension system. Above, thin, high clouds reflected the city lights, giving the sky a pinkish cast.

Connor leaned back in his chair, taking in the view, waiting for the other man to speak.

"It has to be the same killer," Bill said finally.

"It sure looks like it."

Bill nodded, rubbing his lower back and staring out into the night. "You only found notes with the first two, though."

"My guess is that Whitmore probably threw them away as meaningless trash."

"Could be. As far as I know, we didn't find any notes with this one."

"No." Quinn had read every line in the murder file for Josephine Gumm, a.k.a. Crystal. There were still significant gaps, however, but it hadn't even been forty-eight hours since the discovery of the body.

"Well, I'll question the boyfriend about it. Maybe he'll remember something once we ask him. Quinn?"

"Yeah?"

"What's this creep doing with the blood?"

"I figure he's using it in some kind of ritual. Either drinking it or bathing in it."

Bill looked over his shoulder. "Why?"

"I think it's some kind of sympathetic magic, but I can't quite get what trait these women have that he's hoping to endow himself with."

"Big breasts?" Bill's tone was sarcastic.

"I doubt it's that simple."

"So exactly what kind of profile have you got so far?"

Quinn sketched out what he had previously told Rick Diaz, adding one new detail. "I think he's impotent."

Bill came back across the room and sat facing him. "Why?"

"Because the scenes are overtly sexual, but there's absolutely no sign of sexual activity."

"Or mutilation," Bill argued. "The impotent ones usually sexually mutilate."

"That's the reason I've been so reluctant to tie the killer's sexuality to these crimes. But the sexual tone is there. For one thing, the women are always nude. For another, in a corner of the room we invariably find a G-string and spiked heels, usually of the fuck-me variety."

Bill nodded. "We sure did here."

"Exactly. But the other signs are missing. I've been thinking about that a lot, wondering why the pieces weren't fitting. I can only conclude that the man is impotent but has buried his negative feelings about it to the point that he believes his impotence is a good thing."

"Now how could he believe that?"

Connor shrugged a shoulder. "Maybe he believes it makes him more powerful. Or more pure. Either way, he's not sweating it, and he's got himself convinced enough that he doesn't feel angry about it. These scenes are amazingly passionless." He frowned thoughtfully, then ran his fingers through his long black hair, pushing it back from his face. "I don't know. This guy is a new wrinkle on an old problem."

"New varieties all the time, eh?"

"It seems like it."

"What about the abrasions on the knees?"

"He makes them crawl on their knees. Maybe he makes them beg for their lives. Maybe it's for some other reason."

"And the broken window glass?"

"That really bothers the piss out of me," Connor admitted, staring past Bill at the night outside. "Why in the *hell* did he have to break in this time?"

It was Connor Quinn's fault, Peter decided. Standing outside the apartment building, he looked up to the third floor, where Quinn had a balcony overlooking the bay, and told himself he was glad the man had company. Otherwise, he might have done something rash.

Good God, how much more did he have to tell Quinn, anyway? He'd told him about the girl, warned him that the killer was stalking her, and still the girl was dead. If that damn Quinn had done his job, he could have saved the girl. Could have prevented the murder. So it was all Quinn's fault that Crystal was dead.

The question now was what Peter was going to do about it. Quinn needed to be punished. Severely. Through simple laziness, he had cost a woman her life.

But he deserved a second chance. Everyone, Peter believed, deserved a second chance.

He would have to think about it, find some way to get Quinn's attention. Maybe if he entered Quinn's apartment when he wasn't at home and left a message of some kind. Maybe that would convince the newsman that Peter Masterson wasn't kidding.

In the meantime, maybe he would tell the woman reporter about his new dream....

# 13

Kate couldn't sleep. The house felt bigger and emptier and scarier than it had at any time since Mike was committed. The night she had sent him to the hospital the last time, knowing it would be permanent, she had cried her eyes out and then sat up all night, listening to every little sound and wondering how a house could seem to have become so huge and so vacant.

Tonight she felt something similar, but tonight she was also afraid. The phone call from a man who might be the killer had left her on edge, whether she wanted to admit it or not. If he could find her phone number, he could find her address.

And when she wasn't thinking about that phone call, she was thinking about the vendetta against her by some member of Mike's family. She got angry every time the memory of her conversation with Ben flitted across her mind, but there was no one to get angry at, so the feelings just roiled helplessly around in her gut.

So what? she asked herself now. So fucking what? If she knew who was behind it, what could she do, anyway? Get a restraining order he would most likely ignore? Sue him? Not likely. There wasn't a damn thing she could do about any of it except trust in the goodness of her colleagues.

She hated being helpless. She hadn't felt this helpless since Mike's descent into madness.

For the third or fourth time, she checked all the windows and doors to make sure they were locked. That, she thought bitterly, was all she could do about any of this.

Finally she went to her computer, logged on and, in a burst of frustration and daring, answered Connor's e-mail.

"Your hand cups my breast," she wrote, "and I suddenly feel so languid, so warm, so...tingly. An unmistakable wave of desire washes through me, and I want more. Oh, please, don't stop here. Don't leave me this way...."

She went farther, pressing her body to his, holding him closer, running her hands over his back. And then, before she could change her mind, she sent the note on its way.

Then, desperate to keep herself distracted, she called up her web browser and went surfing the World Wide Web. There were some sites out there dealing with serial killers, and she found herself reading an in-depth discussion of their characteristics—not that it told her much about the man who was stalking women in the Tampa Bay area. When she finished reading, she jumped back to her mailbox, not really expecting to find anything, but delighted when she saw a note from Connor.

"Thank God," he wrote. "I thought I'd offended you. Instead...instead I'm grinning wickedly and thinking about all the other places I can put my hands, and my mouth. If you want to set limits, set them now, sweetheart."

Sweetheart. She would have given a great deal if he had really meant that, and if he'd been saying it to her instead of Katydid. She felt another twinge of guilt over her secrecy but shoved it aside. Right now, all she wanted to think about was all the wonderful heaviness he had set loose in her womb and the way she was aching between her thighs. The feeling was as strong as if he were really touching her, and she could no more have called a halt to what was happening than she would have backed away if they had really been touching one another. All thoughts of her vow to remain faithful to Mike fled before her absolute need for Connor Quinn.

His hands wandered farther, so she wrote back to him, allowing her mouth to travel across his chest and explore. Impatiently she waited a while, hoping he was still on-line. He was. She caught her breath and hardly dared breathe as he wrote back. He was removing her clothes, guiding her to lie down in the sand, bringing her close to him while the sky purpled with tropical sunset and the waves lapped nearby.

She was there. She was *there.*

A beep announced a new e-mail, and she opened it eagerly, without even reading the header on the index. But this time it wasn't Connor. This time it was her stalker.

"I'm going to get you. And when I do, you'll dance to my tune. Soon. It will be soon."

When she saw the figure so painstakingly typed out in slashes and *O*s across the bottom of the screen, her breath locked in her throat.

Beyond a shadow of a doubt, it was a puppet on strings.

Connor was enjoying his e-mail exchange with Katydid. Whatever had persuaded her to pick up where he'd left off the other day, he was glad of it. He was beginning to feel seriously aroused, beginning to wonder if they should carry this all the way. Or maybe not. He wasn't exactly comfortable with this milieu for this kind of activity. He knew plenty of people who enjoyed reading and writing erotica, but still...

When Katydid's next e-mail came through, he opened it in a flash, wondering if she had chosen to go farther. It was incredible, this nearly real-time conversation they were having and the way they were creating a shared dream experience. The Keys were looking better by the minute.

"Connor, I just got this message and I'm terrified! What should I do?"

He was so astonished that he didn't immediately notice that she addressed him as Connor rather than CQ. Nor would it have mattered. He couldn't remember exactly what he had shared with her and what he had not, and he might well have given her his real name at some point.

What rattled him was the note she had forwarded. He read it and felt his heart lurch when he saw the crude drawing of the puppet. Without wasting another instant, he e-mailed right back,

"Call the cops at once. And e-mail me your phone number. Or call me at 555-3012. Otherwise I'll go out of my mind worrying about you."

The next ten minutes passed like an eternity as he waited for her to write back or call. When his cell phone shrieked, he jumped in his chair, then knocked the phone over when he reached for it. Fumbling as if he were all thumbs, he managed to turn it on and get it to his ear.

"Katy?" he barked.

"Yes." Her voice was little more than a hushed whisper.

"Did you call the police?"

"Yes."

"Are they coming over?"

"They didn't sound exactly excited. I...I guess I'm not in any kind of immediate danger."

"Shit!" He wanted to grab somebody by the throat and shake some sense into him. "Which police department did you call? What city are you in?" And why does your voice sound so familiar? But he didn't ask that, because it sounded so much like a line.

"St. Petersburg."

"Look, I want to bring someone over to your place, a Hillsborough County sheriff's investigator who's a friend of mine. He's working on this case, and I know he'll want to see that note. Will you let me do that?"

There was a long silence from her end of the line. Too long.

He thought he understood. "Katy? Katy, I realize you don't feel you know who I really am. I guess I can understand that you don't want to tell me where you live."

"It's not that...."

"Don't worry, you're not offending me. Listen, maybe you'd feel better if you called the Hillsborough Sheriff's Office yourself. They'll put you through to this friend of mine, and you can tell him where you live. I can stay out of it, if you prefer."

"I... Thanks. What number do I call?"

Disappointment speared him, but he told himself not to be ridiculous. This woman didn't know who he really was, only that he was someone with whom she corresponded by e-mail. For all she knew, he could be Jack the Ripper.

He gave her the sheriff's office number and told her to ask for Rick Diaz, that it was urgent. Or, if she preferred, she could call Bill Kittrick at the Pinellas Sheriff's Office.

"Thanks." She hesitated, and he hoped she was going to tell him her address, but she didn't.

"Call me after you talk to them," he asked. "Let me know what's happening. I'm going to be sitting here worried out of my mind."

She gave a little laugh. "Okay. I'll call."

When she hung up, he pressed star 69 on his phone and waited for the recorded voice to recite her number.

What he heard made him livid.

When Kate heard the knock at her front door, she peered out through the peephole, expecting to see Rick Diaz. Instead, she saw Connor Quinn.

Flinging the door open, she stepped back to let him in. "Connor, what—"

He grinned down at her, but his eyes remained hard, like twin chips of ice. "Hello, Katydid."

She lost her breath as surely as if he had punched her. He knew! How? Oh, God, he was furious! "Connor..."

"Your phone number," he said. "I hit the automatic callback code to get your number because I knew I was going to sit up all night worrying about you, and I at least needed to know I could call you. Funny, but I recognized it."

She didn't know what to say. Suddenly an apology seemed like empty words, and there was no conceivable way to make up for this.

"Were you ever going to tell me? Or were you enjoying the fact that you knew who I was and I didn't know who you were?"

She wanted to deny that she had known who CQ was, but she couldn't bring herself to lie. Words, any words, seemed to be stuck in her throat like glue.

"Yeah. I thought so. I figured it out right away. I wanted to believe you were as much in the dark as I was, but then I remembered that you'd called me Connor. And you always did seem to know a little more about me than I'd ever told you."

"Connor, I'm...I'm..."

"Speechless?" he suggested. He stepped inside and closed the door behind him. "I feel...betrayed, I guess is as good a word as any. It'll do. But don't worry. You've got time to put together a good story, because we've got more to worry about right now than the fact that I've been played for a fool. Is Rick here yet? Or did you call Bill?"

"I called Rick."

"I thought so."

"He, um, he's not here yet."

"Then I guess we'll just have to wait for him." Connor walked into the living room and sat down. He wouldn't even look at her.

Kate felt something inside her ripping painfully, as if her heart were being torn out by the roots. She told herself that it didn't matter, that they never could have been more than friends, anyway. After all, she couldn't allow herself to care—because of Mike. But right now she knew just how much she had been deceiving herself, and she knew exactly how much she was losing.

She couldn't think of a single thing to say. Not that she could mend this, but there had to be something that would ease his sense of betrayal. Unfortunately, she couldn't think of a single thing. Her own iniquity loomed before her like a brick wall, and she was sure there would never be any way to breach it.

It was a relief when the doorbell rang.

"That has to be Rick," she said inanely. She turned to answer it, but Connor suddenly stood up.

"Let me get it," he said. "In case it's not Rick."

She hadn't thought of that, and right now she was in such an emotional turmoil that she couldn't even respond. She just stood there mutely and let him go to the door. At this point, she couldn't be sure which catastrophe was worse: the e-mail from the killer or the rupture in her relationship with Connor. Either one seemed equally dire.

Rick strode into the living room and took her hand immediately. "This is a good thing," he said to her. "You realize that, don't you?"

It required some effort, but she pulled herself out of her morass of misery enough that she could actually use her brain. "I'm the cheese in the trap, you mean."

Rick shook his head. "I hope to God not. No, I mean e-mails are traceable. We'll find this guy pretty quickly now. This is a whole lot better than if he'd mailed you a regular letter."

"Oh." The relief should have felt a whole lot better than it did, but she was hurting too much over Connor's anger to really feel it.

"Let me see what you've got."

She took him into her home office and bumped the mouse to turn off the screen saver, which currently had colorful tropical fish swimming across her monitor. Her mail menu came up immediately, and she moved the mouse to click on the appropriate letter. Oh, God, she thought with a sudden jolt, she hadn't removed Connor's letters to her. What if Rick read them?

But Rick was interested in one letter only. He read the note over and studied the drawing of the puppet for nearly a full minute. "It sure as hell looks like it might be him, Connor. It even has the phrase about dancing to his tune."

"Yeah. That was my reaction."

Rick selected a different setting on the options menu, then commanded the system to print several copies of the note. Looking over his shoulder, Kate saw that he had printed an expanded header to the message showing all kinds of additional information about the message routing.

"That information," Rick explained, pointing to the header, "should be enough to nail the guy. We'll have him within twenty-four hours."

Then he swiveled the chair and looked up at Kate. "Now, when you called, you said that he'd been sending you these notes for a while. Do you have any of the others?"

"Just one. I deleted all the rest as soon as I read them." It was the note she had forwarded to Connor what seemed like ages ago. She brought it up now for Rick to read. "After I got this one, I called my sysop and asked him if he could block mail from this guy. I thought he had, because until tonight, that was the last one I'd received."

"There are ways around things like that." Rick shook his head as he told the computer to print out the note. "My son is kind of a computer geek. He can practically make the damn thing stand up and whistle 'Dixie' when he wants to. Me, I'm happy if I can get my mail and write reports on it. So this is the first time you saw that puppet drawing on one of these notes?"

"Yes."

"Weird." He swiveled the chair around and stood up. "I wonder if he contacted the other women by e-mail. Whitmore had a computer at her place, and Eppinga was a student. She would definitely have been able to get e-mail on campus. Jeez, you can't even go to college anymore without a computer." He shook his head. "It used to be typewriters. Now these kids gotta have computers. Something, huh?"

Back in the living room, he took up a position near the fireplace with his hands in the pockets of his slacks. "Okay, so here's the drill. You can't stay alone here. Not until I've got this guy in a cell. Which, like I said, should be in less than twenty-four hours. Could you maybe go to a hotel?"

"She can come to my place," Connor said flatly. "She'll be safer with me."

"It'll save the trouble of trying to coordinate protection with the St. Pete police," Rick agreed. "Not that they aren't cooperative or anything, but..." He shrugged. "It'd probably take almost as long to get the okay as it will to track this guy down. So, you go to Connor's. Just for tonight, probably. Go pack a bag."

She wanted to object, but there was nothing to object to, other than their high-handed settling of matters. Raising a ruckus, when she didn't have an alternative to offer, would only make her look foolish. Besides, there might be an opportunity to make things better with Connor.

Turning without a word, she went to pack.

Kate wanted to take her car, but Connor insisted she ride with him. "It's too risky if we get separated," he told her.

It was only for a day, she reminded herself. Just one

day. But, God, how she hated not having the freedom to come and go as she pleased. It carried her right back into the worst days of Mike's illness, when she hadn't even been able to go to the grocery store for fear he would get into trouble while she was gone. She had worried constantly and felt trapped, and she had resented the hell out of Mike for it. Sometimes she had nearly hated him for the way he was destroying their lives. And then she had felt so guilty. He couldn't help it, after all. He was sick. His illness had become the trap that imprisoned them both.

The streetlights created a collage of light and darkness, seeming to hold the shadows at bay. It was like the shadows in her mind, she found herself thinking. Her mind contained dark places that she forced into the background by keeping herself busy, but tonight those shadows were looming, threatening to break free of the constraints she had put on them.

"Why did you lie to me, Kate?"

Her heart began to pound. She turned to look at him, trying to read his face, but it was impossible, as light and shadow moved across it. He looked like some pagan warrior, she thought, with his long black hair and hawkish face. "It's hard to explain. When I realized that CQ was you, I just...felt it was better if I didn't tell you who I was. I mean...we worked together. I was afraid."

"Of me?"

"No. Not you. Of me."

"Oh, come on!"

She averted her face and looked out at the passing buildings. Tears prickled her eyes, and she had to blink them back. "Then don't ask me to explain."

For a long time, there was no sound except the slap of tires on the pavement and the rumble of the motor.

"Forget it," he said finally, in a tone that filled her with despair. "It doesn't matter."

For some reason, she was surprised to discover that he lived right on the water in a high-rise apartment building. While they were riding up to his floor in the elevator, he said, "I have two bedrooms, but I'm afraid one of them is a workroom. You can have my bed."

"I'll sleep on the couch or the floor," she said stonily. "I will not sleep in your bed."

"Kate—"

"Forget it. It's only for one night, anyway." But she absolutely was not going to sleep in the bed of a man who thought she was a liar. Even if she was.

Oh, God, why had she been so stupid about that? Distance hadn't spared her a damn thing, and now it had cost her something she had begun to feel was very precious.

His apartment made no particular impression on her, except that it was clean. He spread sheets and blankets on the couch for her, found a spare pillow and showed her where to find the bathroom. Then he very pointedly disappeared into one of the bedrooms and closed the door firmly.

Earlier, they had begun to embark upon something very special. Now it was shattered beyond repair. Kate sat down on the couch, buried her face in the pillow and let the tears come.

"I'm going out to get some bagels for breakfast."

The sound of Connor's voice dragged Kate up from sleep. The sun was shining brilliantly through the east-facing sliding doors, and she blinked against its strength. "Okay," she managed to mumble.

"I'll be back in twenty minutes."

Was that some kind of hint? she wondered as she heard the door close behind him. Or some kind of warning?

Sitting up, she pushed her hair back and looked around. The apartment had a very different character this morning. It looked cheerful and comfortable, well lived in. Like a home. Her own house hadn't managed to achieve that feeling in all the years she lived there.

She folded the blankets and sheets, then looked around for somewhere to put them. The bedroom, of course. On Connor's bed. Then he could decide what he wanted to do with them.

Arms full, she pushed open the door through which Connor had disappeared last night. She was three steps into the room before her brain registered what was all over the walls. Drawing a sharp breath, she took an instinctive step backward and dropped the bedding.

"Oh, my God," she heard herself whisper. Mark had been right! Panic lanced her, and she quickly scooped up the bedding, backing out of the room as fast as she could. My God! Why would he have those awful pictures plastered all over the walls? And where had he gotten them?

Shivering, she huddled on the couch and wondered what to do. He worked with the police, she reminded herself. Look at his relationship with Rick Diaz. And he'd admitted he was helping the police on this one. But those pictures... Surely they ought to be in files or envelopes and not on his wall? And even if the police had given them to him, why would he pin them up? It seemed sick, so sick.

She was still huddled on the couch when Connor returned.

"Are you sick?" he asked. "You don't look good."

"I'm...just tired," she managed to say. She'd slept in her clothes last night because she felt so uncomfortable, but she had planned to change this morning. Now all she wanted to do was get out of here, because the suspicions that Mark had planted in her mind were writhing like snakes in a pit. This was not good, she told herself. Not good at all.

"The bagels are fresh," he said, placing the white bag he'd brought on the table. "I've got butter or cream cheese and jam. Coffee?"

How would she swallow it? she wondered desperately. Her throat felt as if it were locking up on her.

He'd walked into the kitchen, but now he leaned back and looked around the corner at her. "I may be mad at you, but I don't bite or kick. You can answer without worrying about your safety. Coffee, yes or no?"

"Yes. Please." She was going to need something wet if she was to choke down a bagel.

Moments later, he had set the table with plates, flatware and steaming mugs of coffee. She joined him, feeling as if she had just crawled out from under a rock. Heck, she hadn't even combed her hair.

"You're welcome to use my shower," he told her as she sat across from him.

She was taken aback. "Do I stink?"

He looked up, and one corner of his mouth lifted. "No. I just thought you might want to clean up before we go to work."

"Work. Oh." God, work! It was the last place she wanted to go.

She took a bagel and started to split it, but her fingers wouldn't work right. The knife clattered from her hand, and the bagel seemed to squirt from between her fingers, coming to land in the middle of the table.

"What's wrong?" he asked.

"Nothing." Except all those photographs in his workroom. Except Mark and his damned suspicions. Was this what life had been like for Mike? All the paranoid suspicions that he knew were false but couldn't suppress, until finally they became real?

"Kate?"

She jumped up from the table and hurried over to the sliding glass doors, looking out at the brilliant day, trying to find a thread of sanity in a mind that seemed to be losing it. "I'm sorry," she said. "I'm sorry. I think I'm going nuts."

"What do you mean?"

"I just feel so...paranoid." She had to squeeze the word out past lips that were refusing to move. "I've begun to check my doors and windows three or four times at night before I can go to bed, and then again before I leave for work in the morning. Getting those e-mails started it, and it's worse since the phone call the other night. I keep my curtains closed so no one can look in. I'm almost afraid to answer the phone, and every time I log on to the Net, my heart climbs into my throat."

She wrapped her arms around herself as tightly as she could, trying to hold in the fear that had been steadily growing in her for weeks. "I tell myself I'm being ridiculous and to stop it, but then something else happens. Somebody calls Mark Polanski and makes accusations about me. Somebody calls Ben Hyssop and says terrible things about me. A strange man, maybe a serial killer, calls me on the telephone, and then I get an e-mail that must have come from him. I mean..." She trailed off, unable to collect the rest of her thoughts.

"So maybe you have reason to be paranoid," he said

after a moment. "Not everybody who thinks someone is after them is wrong, you know. And you've certainly had cause, between the e-mail and the phone calls."

"Mike thought he had cause, too. He used to pick up the telephone and hear voices in the dial tone. To him, it was as real as that phone call I got the other night. He believed messages were being beamed into his head, and those messages were every bit as real to him as this conversation we're having is to me. But how do I know this is any more real than what he heard?"

"Questions like that can drive you nuts."

"No kidding." She shivered with apprehension and tried to focus on the bright red blossoms of the geraniums on the patio. "Now I know how Mike felt."

"Except that you have other people who can confirm what's happening."

"Oh, Mike always found confirmation, too. Whenever I tried to argue with him, he'd come back in a little while with something to confirm his story. Of course, the confirmation was real to him and useless to me. I don't read letters in the cracks in the pavement or hear the whisper of voices in the rustling of leaves. Or whatever. Once he came to me with a crayon drawing on a paper plate, something a child had done, and insisted it was a coded message. How do you argue with that?"

He rose from the table and came to stand behind her. "Kate, we're not reading coded messages here. Believe me. We're all seeing it as plainly as you do. You're being stalked not by one, but by two people."

"Two?" Her voice caught on the word.

"Yeah. Two. One of them is a relative of your ex-husband's. The other is the guy who's been e-mailing you. I'm not sure how you came to be so popular, but what difference does it make, anyway? You're in trouble, and your paranoia is justified. You're not losing your mind.''

''I'm not?'' She hesitated, wondering about the pictures on the walls of his workroom and about what Mark had said. She ought to just let it go, but she couldn't. Her paranoid mind kept turning it up and taunting her with it. She had to get it settled, even if she made him furious.

She turned then and looked at him. ''Mark Polanski told me you have pictures of all the killer's victims plastered all over the walls in one of the rooms here. He said...he suggested...'' She couldn't even bring herself to say it.

Connor's gaze darkened. ''Mark is a slime, you know that? He may be a damn good reporter, but he envisions the worst possibility in every little damn thing.''

Was he evading her question? Her heart began to hammer.

''Yeah, I've got pictures. Photos from every conceivable angle, in gory living color. And yes, they're plastered all over the walls of my workroom. I sit in there and look at them for hours, trying to get into the mind of the lunatic who hurt those women. I sit in there and try to get in touch with feelings that make me want to puke!''

She stepped back instinctively as his voice grew louder. ''Connor...''

''Would you like to see them, Kate? Huh? Would it satisfy your curiosity? And when I'm not staring at the pictures, I'm reading the damn police reports and autopsy reports over and over, until I could almost rewrite them from memory. Come on. I'll show you.''

He took her arm in a grip that was as unbreakable as it was painless. He threw open the workroom door and drew her inside. "Here," he said. "Look. And while you're at it, take a good long look at what's on the table. You might find the autopsy reports particularly stimulating. Personally, I think these photos violate those poor women as badly as their murderer did, and I kind of think they should only be seen by sympathetic, caring eyes. But what the hell. You might as well satisfy your curiosity!"

She whirled around, crying his name, but he'd already stormed out of the room and slammed the door behind him.

Oh, Christ, what had she done?

# 14

In the grip of a cold, dark rage, Connor stormed out onto his balcony, into the cool morning air. Bright as the sun was, it still hadn't burned off the night's chill. The cold, fresh air was a tonic that helped him hold on to his control.

He wasn't really angry with Kate's suspicions, he realized. All she had done was set off an explosion that had been building for a long time. For weeks now, he'd been going along with Rick and this investigation, facing all the nightmares he'd tried to leave behind, dealing with the crazy guilty feeling that if he didn't exist, neither would those killers. That was nuts, of course, but every one of those killers needed someone who could appreciate what they did.

Although the word *appreciate* suggested approval, and Connor sure as hell didn't approve of what those guys did. But he gave their actions an attention, and their fantasies a comprehension, that few others could. And serial killers, by and large, were seeking some kind of admiration or understanding. After they were caught, a surprising number of them proved willing and eager to spill their guts to investigators and psychologists. Sometimes, even before they were caught, they contacted the press or the police with hints and clues to show how smart they were.

But that left Connor wondering if they would kill if there was no one to look at their handiwork and study it so assiduously. If they didn't know they were going to grip the attention of entire cities, totally absorb the profilers and cops who were trying to catch them.

Stupid thoughts, he told himself. But he couldn't escape the feeling that the killer and the profiler were two sides of the same horrific act. Two sides of the same coin. The longer he worked the problem, the thinner the coin got and the closer the two sides became. And the worst of it was, he could never turn the coin over to see the other side; he had to work his way through it. Until he was *on* the other side.

Standing there watching the sun rise higher over the bay, he also admitted to himself that he had been resisting this case from the outset. He didn't want to do this. Hell, he'd quit the police force to avoid having to do any more of this. So instead of throwing himself into this investigation wholeheartedly, he'd been blocking himself, allowing perceptions to come in dribs and drabs. Christ, he would have no one to blame but himself if this lunatic killed another woman.

Anger surged and ebbed in him like the waves below, and he knew it wasn't going to go away until this case was over. The false calm he'd been forcing himself to feel, the distancing from this case, was gone. In one giant crash, he was in it up to his neck and likely to drown in it.

Behind him, he heard his cell phone shriek. As he went to answer it, he felt a pang when he saw that the workroom door was still closed. Kate was still in there with all those horrific pictures. Still in there, probably too terrified to come out, after the way he'd been acting. Hell, he was mad at her, but he certainly hadn't hurt her. And wouldn't.

Grabbing the phone, he hit the button and answered it. "Quinn." Then he opened the door of the workroom and looked in. Kate was sitting at the table, head bowed over police reports. Ever the reporter, he thought, almost cynically.

"Connor Quinn?" asked a male voice. "This is Keith Shepherd of the FBI. We've been working with Rick Diaz on the Puppetmaster case, and he's been feeding us your impressions of the killer. I understand you're working as his unofficial profiler."

"Yes, I am."

"I'd really like to talk in more depth to you in person about this, but I'm tied up on some other cases and can't get down there. Are you on a regular phone or a cordless phone?"

"My c-phone."

"That won't do. Anyone could listen in. Have you got another number where I can reach you?"

"Sure." He gave Shepherd the number of his regular phone.

"I'll call you back in thirty seconds."

That was exactly when the phone rang. Connor picked it up at once.

"Okay," said Shepherd, "let's talk. I got what you think about the guy being passionless and well-controlled, and I agree. I also agree with your suspicion that he uses the blood in some kind of ritual after he leaves the scene, and that there's some kind of sympathetic-magic-type thing going on. I agree he's older than most killers, maybe around forty, that he drives a conservative car...." Item by item, he ran down the whole list of characteristics that Connor had so far suggested.

"Now, this impotence thing you suggested most recently," Shepherd added. "Absolutely. He's impotent, and he's sublimated his anger until he believes his impotence gives him power. Power and purity. I think we're looking for a religious nut."

As soon as Shepherd said it, Connor felt the shift inside himself, the recognition that this was right. "Yeah," he said. "I've been getting that feeling, too. But there's a problem with making that assumption. Kneeling isn't necessarily a religious activity. It could simply be forced submission. And nothing else is overtly religious." He thought once again of the crucifixes, but didn't say anything. At this point, for all anyone knew those crosses might well have belonged to the victims. The second victim had even had a picture of Jesus over her bed, so much as the darn things kept snagging his attention, he was reluctant to place too much emphasis on them. A profiler could get easily misled by things like that.

"Religion doesn't necessarily have to be conventional, or even recognizable," Shepherd said. "Even the most rudimentary religions incorporate purification rituals. But we've got a problem with the different modus operandi on this Pinellas County murder. He never broke in before."

"And there's his new stalking," Connor said. "Maybe you haven't heard, but it appears that he e-mailed one of the reporters at the *Sentinel*."

"No, I haven't heard that. Does she fit his victim type?"

"Only insofar as she's a blond female."

"Can you forward me a copy of the e-mail?"

"Just give me your address. I'll send it off to you as

soon as we get off the phone." He grabbed a pencil and pad from the breakfast bar and wrote the address down. "This time he signed it with a drawing of a puppet."

"Mm." Shepherd fell silent.

"It's different," Connor said finally. "I'm not comfortable with it. But I'm not willing to take the chance that it isn't the same guy."

"No, that could get expensive. But I'm with you—it doesn't feel right."

"It's possible he was e-mailing some of the other victims," Connor said. "One of them owned a computer, and another one was a student."

"Possible. I guess it would explain the lack of notes at the last two murders."

"Bill Kittrick is going to question Josephine Gumm's boyfriend about that in more detail today. He thinks it's possible they got notes and just threw them away."

"Could be." Shepherd was silent for a moment. "Do you have any feeling about the different mode of entry?"

Connor closed his eyes for a moment, letting impressions sift around and slowly emerge. "One. The first two women weren't involved with anybody on a regular basis. The third woman was cheating regularly on her husband. This last victim had a live-in boyfriend. Maybe it's only the last woman who wouldn't let the guy in. Maybe she said no."

"Bingo," said Shepherd. "That's exactly what I was thinking. So their cooperation isn't necessary to his fantasy. That opens a few doors. Then we've got the ropes, which apparently *forced* some kind of cooperation. There's an interesting conflict between the notes we have from him and the murders themselves."

"You mean that he refers to the Puppetmaster as a

third person but apparently assumes the role of Puppetmaster during the slayings?"

"Bingo," said Shepherd. It was apparently one of his favorite words. "I'm going to like working with you, Quinn. That was exactly my thought. So, is this guy dissociating to that extent? Does he feel he's being directed from without by some entity he calls the Puppetmaster?"

"Actually, I was wondering if he isn't assuming the role in some kind of magical ritual that's supposed to make him more like this Puppetmaster he referred to."

Shepherd was silent for a minute. Connor noticed Kate standing in the doorway of the workroom, listening to his end of the conversation. He should have felt irritated, but he didn't. Somehow, he didn't at all mind that she was listening in.

"I like that," Shepherd said abruptly. "That's good. It would fit with the blood, too. First he makes them dance to his tune, then he takes their blood for a purification ritual. What is he purifying? Himself? But wouldn't he need to do that beforehand, rather than after the puppet ritual?"

Connor's thoughts were racing down the same path. "Maybe he uses the blood from the previous killing to purify himself for the next killing."

"Great! So where did he get the blood for the first one?"

"I don't know. A hospital? A funeral home?"

"Maybe. Maybe."

"On the other hand," Connor said, "maybe what he's doing to these women supposedly purifies *them* in some way, so that their blood is then clean enough to purify him."

"Good. That's good." Again Shepherd paused.

"You're going to send that e-mail along to me, right? And I need to get more information on this latest killing. Right now I'm going on a sketchy verbal report. Why don't we make this morning phone call a ritual every day, just to touch base and see what's coming down?"

When he hung up the phone, Connor felt that he'd regained a little of his perspective. He might be the other side of the coin working as a profiler, but he would be the killer's side of the coin if he didn't use every skill he had to stop this guy.

He looked at Kate. "I'm sorry," he said.

"What for?"

"Dragging you into that room and forcing you to look at those pictures."

She shrugged. "It was a little Neanderthal, but I'd already seen them. This morning, when I went to put my bedding away, I went in there by accident. It kind of blew me away."

"It blows me away, too."

"So who was on the phone, and is the offer of a shower still good?"

"The FBI was on the phone, and help yourself to the shower."

She apparently realized he wasn't going to say any more, because she grabbed her overnight bag and headed for the bathroom. She was wearing jeans, he noticed. He didn't think he'd ever seen a woman who looked better in jeans. Then he went into the workroom to forward the e-mail to Shepherd.

The newsroom was abuzz with the information that Kate had received an e-mail from the killer. Word had probably come from the same leak in the Hillsborough Sheriff's Office, Connor thought sourly. He made a mental note to give Rick a really hard time about catching the scuzz before he let out something really important.

He was still mad at Kate. Wounded, even. He felt bruised by her dishonesty with him, all the more so because he had been coming to care for her in both her guises. The sense of betrayal was sharp and painful.

But mad at her or not, he felt really sorry for the scrutiny and questioning she was getting now from her colleagues. If this guy only targeted dancers and prostitutes, why was he interested in Kate? Some of them were even asking slyly if Kate had a part-time job.

"Devane! Quinn!" Hyssop called from the door of his office, raising his voice to be heard over the early-morning racket of the newsroom. "In my office," he growled, jabbing his thumb over his shoulder.

When the door was closed and they were both seated facing him, he glared at them. "You're supposed to be investigating the news, not making it. Damn it."

Kate's chin thrust forward in a way that Connor had come to recognize. "I didn't exactly ask this scumbag to write to me."

"I hear you've been stringing him along for some time."

"What?" Kate nearly leaped from her chair. "Who the hell is saying that?"

"I'm not naming any names. Is it true?"

Connor interrupted. "No," he said sharply. "It's not true. Kate's been getting some threatening e-mails for the last couple of weeks from somebody she doesn't know. She even asked me for help with it. She hasn't been stringing anybody along."

"Well, thank God for that! You hear all kinds of stuff about the Internet these days. There's that cop over in Clearwater who poses as a young girl so he can catch the pedophiles who prey on them. I'm damned if I want to find out any of my people are involved in anything disgusting like that."

"This guy is *stalking* her, Ben," Connor said, forestalling the impending eruption that was written all over Kate's face. "You can't blame the victim because some creep she doesn't even know has decided to make her life hell."

"Of course not. I wouldn't think of it. I've just been hearing other things...."

"Like you heard all those rotten things about her from that phone caller last week?"

Ben nodded, looking disturbed. "Kate does seem to be getting a lot of negative press from a lot of different directions."

"Yes, I do," Kate said, reminding them that she was in the room and capable of speaking for herself. "Anyway, they think they'll have this creep by tonight."

"I hope so," Ben said fervently. "This has been nothing but a pain in the ass since the beginning. I'd like this story to blow wide open and then fade away."

Almost in spite of himself, Connor felt amused. "Hey, this is a big story. Easy news. You don't have to sweat what to put on page one."

"No, I just have to sweat that every other paper in town has a direct line to the latest developments, and I'm sitting on my thumbs, tied to the official version of events. See if I ever agree to anything like that again! God, this is sinking us!"

"You'll make it all back," Connor assured him. "I'll see to it."

Ben simply shook his head. "I've been hearing that all along. At this rate, it'll be too late to recoup."

"No, it won't," Connor said firmly. "This paper is

going to get exclusive, in-depth coverage of the hunt for this guy. Trust me."

Ben nodded morosely. "If we haven't lost our entire readership by then."

"Hey, you're not being cut out of the stuff, you're just not scooping it. And some of what's being printed in the other papers is inaccurate."

"As if readers remember that from one day to the next." Ben sighed. "I'm getting some pressure from upstairs, but nothing more than I can handle. It's just a pain in the butt. So okay. What the hell is happening with this e-mail, and what the hell are you going to do to make sure that nothing bad happens to Kate?"

Connor shook his head. "I can't discuss that right now. But we ought to have something within the next twenty-four to forty-eight hours."

Forty-eight hours now? Kate wondered uneasily. When had the time been extended? But she didn't ask in front of Ben, who at the moment looked perfectly capable of sending her on assignment to Tierra del Fuego just to get her out of the way.

Ben leaned forward in his seat. "Something? What do you mean by something? You gonna catch the guy?"

"It's possible," Connor said.

"Possible." Ben grumbled the word, but subsided. "Just don't get her killed. That's one story I can live without." He wagged a finger at Kate. "Do whatever the cops tell you, hear? The job takes second place. Now get the hell out of here."

After its noisome beginning, the rest of the day passed ordinarily. Connor was out most of the afternoon, but came back and hung around until the newspaper was put to bed, then came to get Kate.

"Let's get out of here," he said.

She grabbed her bag and went with him, surprisingly glad to escape.

They stepped outside to discover that nature had played a winter trick on them. Sometime during the day, a cold front had moved in, with clouds, rain, falling temperatures and high winds. Neither of them was dressed for it.

"Wait inside," Connor said. "I'll bring the car around. No point in both of us getting soaked."

He left her standing in the lobby and dashed off into the darkness. Behind her, the guard at the security desk answered the phone and fell into a conversation she couldn't quite hear. At least she wasn't alone. Because suddenly she was terrified of being alone. Terrified of what the night might hold.

A fist grabbed her heart and wrenched it, bringing Mike to mind. He must have felt this way almost all the time. Maybe he still did. Maybe beneath his drug-induced calm, his mind was still screaming wildly in fear. Maybe it seemed to him that he was imprisoned by aliens who kept him paralyzed while they did whatever they wanted to him. Maybe he wasn't any better or any more comfortable at all. How would anyone know?

When Connor pulled up, she dashed out into the rain and climbed in beside him. The heater was on, but the air it was blasting wasn't yet a whole lot warmer than the air outside. She shivered.

"You look like you've seen a ghost."

For some reason, she told him what she'd just been thinking about Mike. "How would anybody know how he's feeling? He can't talk!"

"Christ!" He braked for a light and looked at her. "Have you ever asked his doctor?"

She shook her head. "I always just assumed that since he's so quiet now, he must be feeling calm inside. This is the first time it occurred to me."

"Well, I think this is something we need to check out first thing in the morning. I'll drive you up to the hospital."

She was touched that he would do that for her. "Thanks, Connor. But really, I can drive myself."

He shook his head and accelerated as the light turned green. "You're not going to be alone, remember? Besides, if you feel like you're not getting a straight story, I can be a little more forceful. I've noticed that men sometimes brush women off when they won't brush a man off."

She had noticed that, too. It amazed her, however, that Connor had. Men tended not to notice things like that. "Thank you. It might help. I don't feel I'm always getting a straight story, but, of course, I'm not his next of kin anymore. They don't have to tell me a thing."

"They don't have to let you see him, either, but they do."

"I know." She bit her lip, then said, "His family tried to keep me away, but the doctor insisted I be allowed to continue to visit."

"What a bunch of scum." His grip on the steering wheel was white-knuckled. "What did you see in this guy, with a family like that?"

"He was...exciting. Mercurial. Passionate. He was always taking off on these flights that I thought were just fanciful. He had a unique way of looking at things. Then it got worse." She turned her head and looked out at the passing buildings so that she wouldn't know if he was looking at her while she talked.

"At first the paranoia wasn't nearly as scary as the

times he would become—oh, I don't know exactly how to describe it. It's called flattened affect. It was like he had no emotions, as if they were cut off somehow. Or, just as bad, they would be totally inappropriate to what was going on. Of course, in *his* world, other things were going on that I couldn't perceive."

"Of course," he said, his tone gently encouraging.

"But the hardest thing to live with was the apathy. The way he just...became mechanical. The fear I could relate to. Difficult as it was to live with, I could handle the times he stayed up all night in terror of something he couldn't even describe. But when he felt nothing at all...that was hard to take. It's so hard to communicate with someone who feels absolutely nothing. Who doesn't care about anything. Who doesn't want anything."

"I can imagine."

"No," she said shakily, "I don't think you can. I don't think anyone can, unless they've actually seen it. It's so alien to our way of thinking of ourselves and others. He would become almost robotlike. Empty. There was a terrible emptiness in him when he couldn't feel anything, as if a significant part of him had gone away. He even told me once that he'd rather be afraid than feel nothing at all."

"So maybe what you're seeing now is just an extension of that."

"Maybe. It could be. I just need to be sure. If they've simply got him so drugged that he can't express himself, and he's sitting there in terror—well, I can't stand the thought of that."

"Of course you can't. We'll go up there first thing in the morning."

A few minutes later, he pulled up in front of her house

and parked. "The bad news is, they haven't got the guy who wrote to you. Rick said he was using a phony name and a phony bank account when he set up his account with the Internet provider, so now they're trying to track down who he really is."

She nodded slowly. "So what's the good news?"

"You get to sleep on my couch again. Let's go in and get you a change of clothes."

It was cold, so very, very cold. He stood outside Quinn's apartment building while the wind and rain lashed at him, and he wondered if the man would ever get home.

This is stupid, he told himself, but he waited anyway. Icy water trickled off the brim of his hat, and a drop landed on the end of his nose. He hunched deeper inside his inadequate clothing and tried to pull the collar of his raincoat higher around his neck.

Quinn hadn't paid attention to the letter, so he had to do something to get his attention. He had to get somebody's attention, so that the madman wouldn't kill any more women. It was as simple as that.

He was dreaming of stalking again, although he hadn't yet seen the victim clearly. Maybe the killer hadn't yet settled on a victim. Maybe he was only searching for the appropriate woman.

But either way, it meant that time was growing short. The killer was hunting, and his prey was in danger.

A chill ran through him that had nothing to do with the weather. It always chilled him to think about the cold, calculating way the killer hunted. When Peter dreamed, he saw things from within the killer's mind, and the coldness he felt there terrified him almost as much as the scenes that would eventually be played out.

The killer didn't even see the women he stalked as human beings. They were merely a means to an end, and he felt nothing about them one way or another.

As coldly as if he were shopping for socks or shoes, the killer wandered the streets, passing in and out of the clubs where women danced and men slavered. He kept going from club to club until he found the shoe that fit. And he had no more feeling about it than that.

Peter struggled with that coldness as if it were a living demon. He would have found it easier to understand this killer if he had felt something. If he had been hunting these women out of anger, or hatred, or some kind of twisted need. But as far as he could tell, this killer felt nothing at all, except a compulsion. The same kind of compulsion that drove people to have a drink or smoke a cigarette.

That terrified him more than he could rightly explain. He believed in forgiveness, and he was finding it impossible to forgive this man for the things he was doing. How could he forgive someone who acted as if no one and nothing mattered?

Shivering again, he stepped back farther into the shadows and realized that at least part of the reason he was standing out here like this in the cold rain was that he was afraid to go home and be alone with his thoughts, afraid that he might fall asleep and dream again. It was easier, far easier, to stand out here and freeze than to face the looming nightmare.

A car pulled into the lot, and he turned his attention to it, hoping it was Quinn. Because if it was, he was going to step forward and tell Quinn about the dreams. He was going to do what he should have done long ago, to prevent these horrible crimes.

It was Quinn, but he wasn't alone. Peter stepped even

farther back, until a royal palm almost completely hid him. A woman. A woman with blond hair walked quickly beside Quinn. In her hand was a small bag, like a duffel.

He watched them move swiftly across the parking lot and disappear into the building. Quinn wasn't alone. He couldn't speak to him now, when someone else would be there. It just wasn't possible.

He had to find another way to get Quinn's attention, so that he would heed the warnings. Some way to make him understand the seriousness of this situation.

The woman. He thought about the blond hair, the way it had gleamed in the streetlights and sparkled with rain drops. He wondered if she was going to spend the night with Quinn. If she was cheap.

And something within him began to shift....

# 15

Connor's apartment was frigid, only slightly warmer than the air outside. He went to turn on the heat while Kate kept her jacket on and took the opportunity to study the nighttime bay. Even with the rain and wind dulling the lights from the bridges and Tampa, it was beautiful. On the porch, she saw the rapidly bobbing heads of the geranium blossoms, and the hibiscus looked as if it were about to be stripped of leaves.

"I'd better bring those in," Connor said as he came up beside her. "They'll freeze, and Sophie will kill me."

"Sophie?"

"My next-door neighbor. She's an artist."

Even as he spoke, there was a knock on the door. He went to answer it, and Sophie sailed in, today wearing a purple velvet skirt and a cloth-of-gold shirt with an emerald butterfly pin.

She was talking as she entered the apartment. "I just came over to make sure you got your plants inside—" She broke off sharply as she saw Kate. "Oh! You have company. I'm sorry."

Connor shook his head, smiling. "I was just telling

Kate about you. Kate, meet Sophie. She's the lady who coaxed me into houseplants, geraniums and hibiscus."

"Next it's begonias. Ridiculously easy to grow," Sophie said as she smiled at Kate. "So Connor actually has a female friend! I'd begun to think he was hiding them from me."

"No such thing," Connor said, looking embarrassed and unsure how to handle this.

"Don't mind him," Sophie said to Kate, taking her by the arm and drawing her a few steps away from Connor. "Do you two work together?"

Kate nodded. "I'm a copy editor at the *Sentinel.* Connor tells me you're an artist?"

"He *was* talking about me. Well, I'm certainly flattered. Yes, I paint oil landscapes...or seascapes, depending on which way I'm facing when I take up the brush." She gave a smiling shrug. "Wherever the whim takes me. But I don't want to intrude on the two of you. I just wanted to make sure that Connor hadn't forgotten his plants."

"You're not intruding, Sophie," Connor said. "Kate's just staying with me for a few days while...her house gets painted. I was just about to make us dinner. Why don't you join us?"

Sophie looked from Connor to Kate, and Connor could have sworn that her wise eyes took in the tension between the two of them. "Depends on what you're having," she said finally. "At my age, I don't eat that much, and I figure I should only eat things I really like."

"I'm making lo mein. You know, the frozen thing you get at the supermarket, add your own chicken?"

"Sounds good, dear, but entirely too healthy. I think I'll just stick with my plan to eat chocolate mousse for dinner."

A grin began to dawn on Connor's face. "You're kidding, right?"

"Absolutely not," Sophie said, drawing herself up. "Today I eat chocolate. Tomorrow I may well go on a broccoli kick. It all evens out sooner or later." With a wave, she walked out the door.

"What a character," Kate remarked.

"She's the best thing that happened to me. I got lucky the day she moved into this building. Does lo mein sound good to you?"

"Wonderful. What can I do to help?"

"Not a thing. This is bachelor fare, remember? I can whip it up in just a few minutes."

The worst part of sharing quarters with Kate Devane, Connor thought later, was that he was now aware that he knew her far better than he had thought before he discovered she was Katydid. Now she wasn't simply an attractive woman, she was someone with whom he had shared intense emotional intimacy through their e-mail exchanges of the past months. She was a woman with whom he had built a fantasy escape and with whom he had come very close to making love in words. The Kate Devane he had come to know and like during the time they worked on the Puppetmaster story was blending with the Katydid he had very nearly come to love in their fantasy world.

The problem was that he couldn't get over the hurdle of her having lied to him. Nor did he especially want to. Sophie was right; he was totally down on marriage, because of his parents, and he didn't think he was mistaken. Every relationship he ever had with a woman had eventually wound up with her being dissatisfied. Of course, a lot of that had had to do with his hours as a police officer and the way he couldn't be relied upon to show up as promised. But was it really so different now that he was working for a newspaper? The job seemed to consume him just as much, and the hours could be just as irregular.

So to avoid finding himself hog-tied to a woman in a mutually conceived hell, he simply kept his relationships light and brief. It was the only sensible way to do it.

With Katydid, he'd thought he'd found the ultimate way to have a safe relationship. As long as they were nothing but glowing words on a screen, how seriously involved could they become?

Quite seriously, he decided now, as he thought about how betrayed he felt by her dishonesty. He wouldn't be angry and hurt if he hadn't come to care a whole lot. A hell of a lot more than he would have believed possible from a simple correspondence.

He watched her now, being careful not to stare too intently as she washed the dishes. She had insisted on cleaning up to thank him for his hospitality, and he had let her, because he didn't want to be bumping into her in the narrow confines of that tiny kitchen.

He'd never really had the opportunity to observe her this way before, and he found himself noticing the graceful line of her neck and the slenderness of her waist. She didn't look strong enough to have withstood all that life had dealt her, yet somehow she had. He suddenly had the worst urge to put his arms around her and just hug her.

As soon as he felt the urge, he backed away from it. In the first place, she had deceived him. In the second place, they were co-workers who had been thrown into close quarters. If he did something she took amiss, the repercussions could be bad indeed. And he certainly wouldn't want her to think he was taking advantage of the situation.

Rick Diaz called around ten, just as Kate was putting away the last dish. "Nothing yet," he told Connor. "The e-mail stalker somehow managed to open a bank account with a name and social security number that don't match up. And we can't find a driver's license or anything else for this guy. There is, however, a ray of hope. The bank account is almost tapped out. The guy needs to make a deposit soon, or his next electronic draft to cover his Internet account is going to bounce. We've stationed a couple of guys at the bank to keep an eye out."

"How soon does that next draft come due?"

"In seven days."

At least it wasn't a month, Connor thought. "Anything else?"

"Yeah. Bill Kittrick says Gumm's boyfriend recalls her receiving some notes at the club. They threw them away, thinking it was just a crackpot. Neither of them reads the newspapers or watches the TV news, and neither of them got unduly disturbed by the notes. Seems she used to get notes from crackpots all the time. Apparently they didn't think these were special."

"Maybe they weren't, then."

"No, actually, the boyfriend remembers them saying something about dancing to the Puppetmaster's tune. He thought it was some kind of joke."

"Apparently not." Connor thought for a few moments, then said, "I think maybe it's time to go proactive."

"Why? We know his next target, and we'll probably catch him within the next seven days, when he comes to make a deposit to that account."

"What if he sends someone else to do it, someone

who doesn't know who he really is? What if he doesn't come at all, because he no longer cares whether the account gets canceled? What if we *don't* know who his next target is? We're making some very broad assumptions here that I'm not comfortable with, Rick. The guy who wrote the note to Kate might not be the killer."

"That's a remote possibility."

"But it's still *a* possibility. Then there's the possibility that even if the e-mailer is the killer, Kate isn't slated as his next victim. We can't afford to stand around waiting to find out. If we do something proactive, it won't mess up the bank deal anyway, so why not go for it?"

"You think you know enough now?"

"I think we know enough to write an article that pushes his buttons and maybe makes him mad enough to do something to defend himself. Something that might give him away. If I can draw his attention to me, he might even want to get in my face to correct my misimpressions."

"Maybe." Rick was silent for a minute. "Okay, talk it over with Keith Shepherd when he calls in the morning. If the two of you feel this is right, we'll do it."

When Conner hung up, he found Kate standing in the kitchen doorway, a dishtowel in her hand, watching him.

"That was Rick Diaz," he said.

"I gathered that. I also gathered that you're planning something to get the killer to expose himself. Excuse me if I don't feel thrilled at the idea of this lunatic wanting to get in your face, as you put it."

Connor shrugged. "Better my face than yours."

"Maybe. Maybe not. But don't expect me to act like it's nothing." She tossed the dishtowel onto the counter and faced him with a squared chin. "Damn it, Connor, that could be really dangerous! You could get hurt!"

Something in her expression looked wounded and frightened, as if she were suddenly desperate to escape.

"Hey," he said, in what he hoped was a soothing tone. "You've been calmer about being the target yourself. This might distract his attention from you."

"I know. That's exactly what worries me." She turned to walk away from him, although he couldn't imagine where she hoped to go in this tiny apartment.

"Kate..." But he didn't know what to say. She wasn't really making sense. What he couldn't stand, however, was watching her walk away from him angry, and maybe hurt. He reached out and caught her arm. "Kate..."

She whirled and glared at him. "Maybe you don't care what happens to you, but I do! You've got no business deliberately putting yourself in harm's way! And certainly not in an attempt to protect *me!* If you think I want to live with that, you've got another think coming!"

"Kate, he won't try to kill me. It wouldn't serve his purpose! He'd need to get his story out, to correct the record, and he couldn't do that by killing me."

Her glare faded, and she looked uncertainly at him. "Is that what you think? That he'll only want to use you as a mouthpiece?"

"Believe me, it wouldn't be the first time a serial killer has tried to use the press. If he's the guy who's been calling us, then that's exactly what he'll want to do. He'll want to correct the misimpressions, to try to make himself look better, because believe me, sweetheart, he hates what he's doing."

God, he couldn't stand it anymore. She looked so lost and alone, as if she were reaching the end of her tether. Not that he could blame her. No one lived a life without problems and pain, but Kate Devane had taken an awful lot on the chin over the past few years.

In his need to comfort her, his anger at her seemed to vanish like smoke on the wind. He drew her against him and hugged her tight, tucking her head under his chin. And God, oh, God, it felt exactly as he'd imagined it would when he was writing to her of their fantasy hideaway. It was as if everything inside him softened and relaxed, as if tensions he had hardly been aware of let go.

"If I could," he heard himself whisper, "I'd take you to the Keys right now and find some isolated little bungalow where no one could find us." He heard her sigh softly as she nuzzled his shoulder, and it touched his heart.

"But you're mad at me," she murmured. "Furious."

"To hell with that," he said. "I can be mad at you again later."

A little laugh escaped her, followed by a gasp as he lifted her into his arms.

"Enough games," he said hoarsely as he carried her to his bedroom. "I've had enough of games and subterfuge. God knows whether we'll even be alive tomorrow."

The connection wasn't clear to her, but she didn't care. As an excuse, it was good enough.

His bedroom was simple—a king-size bed, a dresser, a lamp. The colors were hunter green and dark wood, and they seemed to fade into the shadows until there was nothing but a pool of golden light when he laid her upon the bed. He sat beside her, looking down at her, his dark hair falling past his cheeks, his blue eyes seeming brighter than usual.

"Are you okay with this?" he asked.

She nodded; she couldn't have spoken to save her life. Her breath seemed to have become lodged in her throat, and her heart was beating harder than usual. Every muscle in her body felt warm and heavy, as if she were melting.

"They say that facing death makes people want to affirm life."

That shook her out of her languor. "Damn it, Quinn, shut up. You can analyze this to death later."

A sudden smile lit his face, and a chuckle escaped him. "Act now, think later?"

"Exactly. Because if we really start thinking, this'll never happen." Mike. Oh, God, she couldn't think of Mike now!

But before Mike's memory could fully intrude and send her into a tailspin of guilt, Connor leaned over her and stole her breath, her heart and her mind with a simple kiss.

Deceptively simple, because it seemed to reach deep within her and pluck at her very soul. She felt soft, then softer, yet her arms were able to reach up and wrap about his broad shoulders to draw him close.

He swung his legs up onto the bed and lay half over her, sprinkling kisses on her cheeks, her chin, her nose, her mouth. His weight felt almost like a blessing, and she wanted more, wanted to feel him bearing down on every inch of her until she sank into some other place where nothing mattered except a lover's touch.

"Sweet Katy," he whispered, his mouth beside her ear as he held her close. "Did you love our hideaway as much as I did?"

"Yes... Oh, I wish it was real!"

"Just keep your eyes closed, sweetheart. Just keep them closed and imagine that this bed is warm sand and that you can hear the gentle lap of the waves. Imagine it just as we were writing it."

She didn't have to work hard to imagine it. In her mind, during their writing, the images had become an integral part of her view of Connor. Even at work, his presence had evoked those images of sky and sea and sand. Connor Quinn had become her getaway.

He kissed her ear gently, washing it with his tongue in a way that made her shiver helplessly. Then he slipped his hand up inside her sweater. The skimming of his fingers across her midriff made her shiver again, and she clung tighter to his shoulders, suspended in anticipation as she waited for the touch he had already given her by e-mail.

When his hand closed over her breast, even through her bra it felt better than her wildest imaginings. When he squeezed gently, it was as if the rhythms of the sea moved within her, rising…falling…rising….

He lifted her and tugged her sweater over her head. With a flick of his wrist, her bra disappeared. Shoes sailed across the room, slacks followed. She lay naked before him in the golden pool of lamplight and felt as beautiful, wanted and wanton as she had ever in her life felt.

His clothes went next. He stood over her so that she could watch with heavy-lidded eyes and devour the breadth of his shoulders, the strength of his arms, the coppery width of his broad chest. When he dropped his pants and kicked them away, she caught her breath at his beauty. He was all male, and he was ready for her.

The warmth of her clothes was quickly replaced by the heat of his body as he lay over her, rocking gently against her, building the sea-rhythms inside her until even her breath kept time. His lips trailed hot kisses on her skin, discovering the spot behind her ear that sent ripples of pleasure running through her. When he kissed the hollow of her throat, she shivered again, with purest delight.

Her own hands rubbed gentle circles on his back and painted fire down to his hips, feeling the way his muscles bunched and rippled as he rocked gently, so gently, against her. She wanted more of him, more, but he taunted her and teased her and offered other gifts first.

When his mouth closed on her breast, she arched helplessly and unleashed a low moan of need and approval. When he sucked on her, ribbons of pleasure twisted through her to her very center. She was lost, lost, riding a wave of pleasure that lifted her up…up….

Surprising her, he turned her over and began to sprinkle kisses down her spine, following the curve lower until he reached its very base. Everything within her went still with amazement, for no one had ever kissed her there before, and she'd had no idea. But the heat within her wouldn't let her pause long in amazement. It wanted her fullest attention on the building passion within her, wanted her to focus on nothing but the storm growing inside her.

Lower his mouth moved, kissing her gently on the cheeks, then on the backs of her knees. The sensation was so exquisite that it was almost painful, and she whimpered softly, helpless against the torment. He kissed the soles of her feet, and she suddenly felt better loved than she had ever felt in her life.

When he turned her over again, she was as ready as she had ever been for consummation. Part of her wanted to reach out to him and reciprocate, but he caught her hands in his as he propped himself over her, trapping her. She opened her eyes and looked into the piercingly blue depths of his at the very moment that he slid himself into her.

She whispered something—a prayer?—then gave a long, throaty groan of approval as he filled her, filled a place that had been more achingly empty than she had realized until this very moment. She was his. She was *his!*

"Ride with me," he whispered. "Ride the sea and follow the stars and come with me...."

No one before had ever talked to her at this point, and his whispers made her feel impossibly close to him, as if they were truly one flesh, not two separate people taking their separate pleasures in a joint act. That feeling of oneness lifted her even higher than the tumult of pleasure within her, made her feel freer than a bird on the wing, and when she finally tumbled into free fall, she knew she was not alone.

Not alone. Oh, God, to be not alone.

Connor rolled to one side and drew her with him, holding her close while their breathing steadied and their skin dried.

"I shouldn't have done that," he said.

She looked up at once, fear shadowing her gaze, and he felt like a bastard for teasing her. "Why not?"

"We work together. What will our colleagues think?"

"Fuck that," she said sourly.

He laughed, and she laughed with him. Sharing laughter, he thought, was even better than making love. Being able to laugh with a lover was more important than being able to weep together.

But at some point he saw the shadows come back into her eyes, and he knew she was thinking about her ex-husband. He didn't understand why she felt as if she, too, had to suffer because he was sick, and he certainly didn't want her to be suffering tonight. Not tonight.

"None of that," he said softly.

"What?" She lifted her gaze to his.

"No sad thoughts, no regrets, no guilt. We stole tonight just for us. The paybacks will take care of themselves." With a vengeance, he thought as he rolled away and went to find something for them to drink. With a vengeance. Because he had a funny feeling that tomorrow he was going to realize that nothing in his life had ever been as painful as not being able to trust this woman.

All he had was some orange juice and some cranberry juice. He pulled out a couple of stemmed water glasses and poured orange juice into one and cranberry juice into the other, and wished he had, for once in his life, bought a bottle of wine. After living with alcoholic parents, he wasn't too fond of the stuff, though he kept beer for his friends, but it would have been perfect to offer Kate the glass of white wine they had so often pretended to share on their imaginary porch.

Instead, he carried two goblets, one full of ruby-red liquid and one full of orange liquid, into the bedroom.

"Drink, madam?" he enquired. "We have a premier Florida orange juice of recent vintage, or a delightful Massachusetts cranberry beverage of slightly older vintage, for your delectation."

Kate laughed and pushed herself up against the pillows, tugging the sheet up over her breasts. He wished she hadn't done that; she had very pretty breasts. "Cranberry, please."

"What? A Floridian, and you ask for cranberry?"

"I drink my orange juice every day, sir. But this evening I prefer a more piquant taste." She took the glass, sipped, swished it around in her mouth and swallowed. "Ah, a very fine West Barnstable, September twenty-third...no, September twenty-seventh...of the past year."

He gaped at her and then let out a hearty laugh. "Just tell me, what's a West Barnstable?"

"A place on Cape Cod where they grow cranberries." She gave him a sweet smile and took another swallow. "I never was able to joke with... I mean, before. He...always took me seriously."

He felt a pang and resisted an urge to crush her to him. Instead, still stark naked, he sat on the armchair in the corner of the room and crossed his legs. Lifting his own glass of orange juice, he studied it for clarity, made a great show of sniffing it, then rolled some around on his tongue. "The best," he said with appreciation. "Although you'll have to pardon me for remarking that about the only way you can get decent orange juice anymore is to buy orange juice."

"What?"

"Well, look how hard it is to get a decent orange in the supermarket. I figure the good ones must all be sold for juice...so I threw away my juicer."

That startled a laugh out of her. "Really?"

"No, not really. I never had a juicer. In fact, I cook only to survive, so I make every effort to spend as little time in the kitchen as possible."

"Me, too. Cooking for one is miserable."

"Maybe we ought to form a cooking club. You know. One day I cook for both of us, and the next day you cook." And what the hell was he doing, making plans, even joking plans, as if the two of them could possibly have a future?

She looked briefly saddened, then shook her head and

joked back. "I know how that goes. In no time at all, the woman is doing all the cooking." She broke off abruptly and bit her lip. "Um, I really don't want to go there, because...well, you know."

He knew. Her ex-husband. The time bomb ticking in her background, coloring everything she did, felt or said. That was another reason he didn't want to get involved with her. Even if she never lied to him again, there would never be any room in her heart for him until she stopped devoting the whole thing to Mike.

Part of him wanted to confront her about it, try to talk some sense and realism into her head, but another part of him utterly despaired of the attempt. Besides, she had lied to him, and he would never be able to trust her again.

No, what he had to do was get them both through tonight and however many nights were ahead of them until this killer was caught. Then he was going to send her back to her own house and have nothing to do with her outside work. For now, though, they could play out their little Key West fantasy to its ultimate conclusion.

"Connor?"

He realized he had been staring rather grimly at her. She looked uneasy. "Did you really think I could be the killer?" he asked. God knew where that question had come from, because he sure as hell didn't.

She shook her head. "No. I mean, from time to time I'd get this uncomfortable little twinge, you know? Mark's suspicions would come floating back, but I was never really able to make myself believe it. Except when I saw all those pictures. They frightened me, and I couldn't imagine why you had them up there...."

He nodded. "I can see that. Mark Polanski would do better working for a tabloid." He drained his orange juice and set the glass on the end table. "Are you hungry? I am. I don't know why it is, but Chinese food goes through me quicker than sh—" He broke off abruptly, and suddenly grinned. "Never mind. I'm just hungry. Want something?"

"That depends." She gave him an arch smile. "I'm picky."

"I think I have a coffee cake out there."

"Mmm. That sounds really good."

"Be right back."

In the kitchen, he cut two huge pieces, knowing full well she wasn't going to want that much, but damned if he was going to cut a big one for himself and an itty-bitty one for her. Didn't seem right, somehow.

When he turned around to head for the bedroom, he found her standing in the kitchen doorway, wrapped in his sweatshirt. She looked a hell of a lot better in it than he did.

"We need to talk, Connor."

He nodded; he'd known it was coming. "Sit wherever you feel safest."

She picked his dinette, putting the table firmly between them. He started a pot of decaf and sat facing her. "Okay. Shoot."

"I'm going to be honest," she said, the faintest tremor in her voice. "You're dangerous to me."

"Dangerous?" Christ, he felt poleaxed.

"Not physically. Emotionally. It's..." She hesitated. "When I met Mike, he was already in the early stages of his illness. We never...we never..." She halted and drew a long, shaky breath. "We never shared anything like I just shared with you. We never joked, because he would so often misunderstand me. Sometimes he misunderstood me even when I thought I'd been perfectly clear, but when I was joking..." She shook her head.

He waited, and when she said nothing more, he asked, "Why is that dangerous to you?"

"Because...because it made me realize just how distorted my whole marriage was. I used to cling to the belief that it had been good before he got sick, but he was sick when I met him, and the good times were few and far between. I guess I thought I could—" She broke off.

"You thought you could save him."

Compressing her lips, she nodded. "I never could, you see. But I have to believe... I mean...I don't think I want to know what I missed, because it'll make me angry. And I don't want to be angry at Mike."

"Jesus." He just stared at her, unable to imagine any way in the world to get through that kind of denseness. "Why the hell shouldn't you be mad at him? Just because he couldn't help getting sick doesn't mean you can't get mad. Damn it, Kate, you have a right to get mad. The guy married you and turned your life into a living hell. And now that he's not doing it anymore, his family seems bound and determined to do it for him. Why in hell shouldn't you get mad?"

"Because he can't help it!"

"So fucking what! Maybe instead of being mad at him, you ought to be mad at yourself."

"Myself?" She looked stunned.

"Yes, yourself. After all, you didn't get the hell out of the marriage years ago. Instead of finding a normal life for yourself, you hung on past all reason, while he abused you and treated you like shit beneath his feet. When he couldn't even *care* about you. Why, Kate? Why did you do that? Were you seeking sainthood? Or were you just ridiculously loyal? Because believe me, sweetheart, he wasn't the guy you fell in love with anymore, and nobody can stay in love for long with someone who doesn't care about them."

She stared at him for a long, silent moment, then jumped up from the table and ran into his bedroom, slamming the door.

He looked at the coffee cake in front of him and pushed the plate away. He wasn't hungry anymore, and he had a feeling he was going to be sleeping on the couch tonight.

# 16

Connor stood at the sliding glass doors that looked out over his balcony and watched the first light of dawn etch the Tampa skyline first in pearly gray, then in a soft tangerine glow. In his hands he cradled a hot mug of coffee against the chill he seemed to feel any time the outdoor temperature dropped, regardless of how he heated his apartment.

He hadn't slept more than a few hours. That damn couch just wasn't long enough for him, but then, when he bought it, it had never entered his head that he might actually have to sleep on it.

But the couch was the least of his problems. The main problem was sleeping in his bed. At least, he hoped she was sleeping. She had come creeping back out last night, probably to apologize for locking him out of his own bedroom, but he'd pretended to be sound asleep. He'd felt her look down on him, then listened as she walked quietly back to the bedroom and closed the door. He felt like a cad, but he was damned if he knew why. Well, actually, that wasn't true. He *did* know why. There weren't very many people who appreciated being told they were beating themselves up for no good reason.

But it was the truth! And he was beginning to think this woman was in love with her own martyrdom. It wasn't that he thought she shouldn't visit her ex-husband, or that she shouldn't care about his condition and what had happened to him. But she shouldn't be committing suttee on the pyre of some illusory guilt.

What did she have to feel guilty about, anyway? It wasn't her fault Mike Devane had become ill— He stopped the thought in midflow, suddenly struck. Maybe she *did* feel she was somehow responsible. Of course. That was it. The profiler in him knew it at gut level. For all that she knew Mike had been sick when she met him and it was ridiculous to believe she had driven him mad, at some level she believed she had—or that, at the very least, she hadn't saved him from his madness.

And from what she'd said and what he'd heard about her husband's family, they were very busy reinforcing that guilt. God, what a bunch of nasty jerks. Maybe they were all a little paranoid, too. Maybe she was getting a constant barrage of shit because they had developed the delusion that she had indeed driven Mike mad.

But whatever their excuse, what they had done to her was unforgivable. And the shithead who'd been calling the paper...well, he'd better hope he never ran into Connor Quinn.

His new insight also gave him a clearer picture of Mike Devane. If the man had grown up in a family capable of such emotional abuse, then he'd probably been abusive himself. And Kate was probably an emotionally battered wife, whether she knew it or not.

Which explained a great deal about Kate Devane. He stood there, watching the sky lighten, and felt as if his own confusion had lightened, as if a great veil had been stripped away.

Abused women very often felt guilty and responsible for things that were totally beyond their control. They felt as if they were to blame for everything, at first because they were made to feel as if they were to blame, but then, before long, they were assuming blame all on their own. She had once said that Mike had believed she was trying to poison him when she gave him his medicine. Maybe he had believed other things about her, too, things that weren't so obviously crazy. Things she *did* believe as she tried to make excuses for his behavior, particularly before he became ill. It was so easy to fall into that trap and start feeling responsible for everything, whether the dinner met his approval, whether the day was too warm, or the traffic was too heavy....

He'd seen it plenty of times as a cop. He'd seen women apologize to their husbands for auto accidents when the husbands had been the ones driving. "It's my fault," the woman would say. "I never should have asked you to take me to the store." Or whatever. He'd seen men in the same condition, taking the blame for the actions of their shrewish wives. "She doesn't mean it." They were always making excuses, always taking responsibility.

The ultimate excuse would be mental illness. It would always be an excuse for the abusive person's behavior and would encourage a spouse to be placating. And once you started to placate, you started to feel responsible. Add to that the fact that the most innocent actions could set off a firestorm in the mentally ill person, until the spouse learned to tiptoe around all the time to avoid causing a problem...and there was the recipe for one hell of a mess of guilt.

He padded barefoot into the kitchen to get another cup of coffee. He was still naked, but he preferred to be naked. Clothes had always felt constricting, and now there was no reason to fear offending Kate's modesty. If she didn't like it, she could damn well say something.

Back at the window, he watched the sky brighten to a deeper orange. The water of the bay reflected the color, along with a deep purple in the troughs of the waves. It was going to be a cold, beautiful day.

Well, he found himself thinking, at least now he understood why Kate hadn't told him who she was on-line. Katydid was a free, laughing, teasing person who had no responsibility or guilt, because she wasn't real. In the realms of the Internet, Katydid didn't have to be responsible for anything.

But as soon as he brought Kate and Katydid together, in the open, Katydid had vanished. The woman he had made love to last night was Kate. Those shadows in her eyes had not belonged to Katydid.

He heard the bedroom door open, heard her soft footsteps behind him. *Connor, I'm sorry.* If he was right about what she'd been through and where she was coming from, those would be her first words.

"Connor, I'm sorry."

He turned, not troubling to conceal his nakedness, and took a sip of coffee, observing her over the rim of his cup. "Sorry for what?"

She colored faintly. "For locking you out of your bedroom and making you sleep on the couch."

He nodded. "Anything else?"

"For..." She looked down at her hands. It was a surprisingly vulnerable gesture. "For blowing up at you the way I did. I had no right."

"Oh, for Pete's sake," he said disgustedly. "You want some coffee?"

Her head jerked up, and she looked at him in confusion, but she nodded.

"I saved the coffee cake. Want some of that, too?"

"Uh...sure."

He returned a couple of minutes later, slapped two full mugs on the table, along with coffee cake in a plastic bag. He then went for a couple of plates and napkins, just to prove he wasn't a total barbarian.

She sat facing him and picked at the coffee cake as if she weren't really hungry. Of course not. She was wondering what the dragon was going to do to her next.

"Eat," he said gruffly. "And don't ever apologize for what you feel. You had every right to get pissed at me last night. Nobody likes to be told they're living a pointless martyrdom."

"Is that how you see me?"

"Frankly, yes. Because what you refuse to see in all this is that you are as much a victim of your ex's illness as he was. What you refuse to acknowledge is that you loved him too much, so you let him mistreat you in a thousand ways. What you're scared to admit is that your marriage was a living hell. What you're even more scared of admitting is that you couldn't do a damn thing about any of it except leave. It was out of your control, Kate."

She watched him, her lips trembling, but she didn't get mad, and she didn't storm away. She listened.

"You don't want to admit you devoted...what? Ten years of your life, to a hopeless cause. You don't want to admit that nothing you ever did could make it any better. And most of all, you don't want to admit that none of it was your fault. Because if you do, you're out of control, and that terrifies you. It was easier to put up with Mike's moods, his nastiness, his bad spells and his accusations, than to admit you couldn't stop them. You kept trying to be a good girl, thinking that if you were just good enough he would get well and love you again."

There was a white line around her lips now, but she was listening.

"Sweetheart, for whatever reason, the gods-that-be made Mike Devane ill. And other than getting him to doctors, there wasn't a damn thing you could do to drag him out of that abyss. *It was out of your control.*"

Her lower lip was quivering strongly now, but she continued to stare at him with dry eyes.

"It's a bitch, isn't it?" he said quietly. "But sometimes life just deals out rotten blows. You did everything you could for that man, got him the best medical care you could. There was nothing else you could do for him. But what about *you?* When are you going to start living up to your responsibility to yourself?"

He waited, hoping she would say something. Anything. He was beginning to feel as if he were beating her up. And maybe he was.

Finally he said, "Eat your coffee cake so we can go visit Mike."

Her eyes widened and flew to his.

"I said I'd take you," he said with a shrug. "I keep my promises."

Whether he knew it or not, Mike Devane was damn lucky he had a family that could afford to keep him at this place, Connor thought as he followed Kate into the sanatorium. The Cedars was a resort spa compared to the state hospitals.

The lobby whispered of elegance and money, with deep carpeting, and the waiting room off the lobby looked like a salon in some very wealthy person's home, with French doors opening onto gardens that were lovely even at the height of Florida's winter. They were closed now, against the cold of the day.

Kate left him there when she went up to see Mike. What she didn't realize was that he followed her. He wanted to see Mike, too. Wanted to know what kind of interaction the two of them still had. She never noticed that he was watching around the corner of the door frame; nor was the door ever closed during the visit.

Mike's room was pleasantly appointed, with curtains on the windows and a colorful spread on the bed. There were several chairs for visitors, but they looked as if they saw very little use. Mike himself sat in a chair by the window, the morning sun shining through the slats of the blinds to make bands across his face. He was a man who would have been strikingly handsome if he had had any expression or life to him at all.

Kate sat facing him, occasionally reaching out to touch his hand, talking quietly of things Connor couldn't hear. He wondered what she was saying. Not that it really mattered. The man for whom the words were intended didn't appear to hear them.

Finally Kate rose, gave Mike a kiss on the forehead and turned to leave. Connor didn't bother trying to conceal himself, and when Kate's eyes found him, she looked startled, but only briefly. Then something in her face softened, leaving him feeling as if he had done something wonderful.

They went together to see Mike's doctor. Kate surprised Connor by wanting him to be present, and he was even more surprised when the doctor allowed it.

The office was as elegant as the waiting room downstairs, deeply carpeted, furnished with a massive oak desk and chairs. It was, Connor realized, a place for this man to meet patients, and the families who were paying exorbitant sums for them to be here.

"Let me remind you, Mrs. Devane," the doctor said, "that Mr. Devane's family has asked me to keep you entirely out of this."

"I know that. But I'm worried about him."

"How so?"

Haltingly she explained her fear that Mike was living in some terrifying delusion but couldn't express it because of the drugs he was on.

The doctor shook his head. "No, my dear, that's not the case."

"But how can you be sure, if he doesn't talk?"

"Because he *does* talk."

Connor felt the impact of those words on Kate as if a bomb had been dropped in the room. He looked at her swiftly and saw that she had turned frighteningly pale. He had to corral an urge to pop the doctor on the jaw for dropping the news this way.

"He...talks?" Kate repeated in disbelief.

"Yes. In group. With the other patients. With me at our private sessions. With the nurses when he wants something."

"How...how long has this been going on?"

"Three or four months, I should guess." He paused and looked at her almost kindly. "My dear, initially I approved of your visits because he seemed much calmer after you came. I felt that being abandoned by you would only enhance his isolation. Lately, however—" He broke off and swiveled the deep chair, staring off into space pensively.

"Lately," he continued finally, "it's become apparent that you're part of his delusion."

"Me? In what way?"

"He believes you're his jailer. He believes you kept him imprisoned before you brought him here, and that you're responsible for his being imprisoned here now."

"Oh, my God..." Kate began to shake, and Connor instinctively reached out to clasp her hand. She squeezed back, hard.

"It's a delusion, Mrs. Devane. We both know that. And I'm sure, after all your experience, you don't need me to explain how this all works. For now, he's fixed on you as the source of his problems. In a few months he may be back to blaming aliens. Or perhaps he'll switch to the government. One never knows. But for now, you're the enemy. And that's why he's not talking to you. The only reason, as near as I can ascertain."

Kate nodded slowly, still trying to absorb the shock. Connor wished he could reach out and hug her.

"At any rate," the doctor continued, "I'm thinking about discontinuing the visits of his brother Charles. I suspect he may have had something to do with the shaping of this new delusion— Well, I believe you're aware how the Devane family feels about you."

"I certainly am!" Kate lifted her chin, and Connor could see the sheen of unshed tears in her eyes. "I wasn't aware Charles had been visiting him."

"He started a few months ago, as a matter of fact. About the time Mr. Devane started becoming more communicative. I initially thought Charles was a good influence, but I've begun to revise my opinion about that. I had just about made up my mind to have him barred."

"And me?"

"I'm not sure. I've been debating whether to ask you to break off for a while and see if this fear of you wanes.

On the other hand, he might get over it just as quickly if you continue visiting."

Kate surprised Connor then. With her chin high and her eyes dry, she told the doctor, "I'll stop visiting him."

"I'm not sure—"

She interrupted the doctor. "*I'm* sure. I'm very sure. I've been dancing to his tune since the day we met, and I'm through. I don't care how sick he is, I'm not going to visit him if he's ignoring me and blaming me for his problems. Not anymore. I've served my time in that particular dungeon."

Rising, she turned toward the door, then glanced back. "Tell him that for me, please. Tell him I'm through being blamed for his problems. Maybe it's time he heard the truth."

She walked out, and Connor hurried after her.

Kate didn't say anything all the way back across the bay, and Connor left her undisturbed. Finally, when they were nearing the *Sentinel* offices, she suddenly burst into angry speech.

"That son of a bitch!"

Connor quickly wheeled around a corner, detouring to a longer route to give her time to vent.

"I can't believe him. I don't care how sick he is, he damn well ought to remember how much I took care of him. How I protected him!"

"How you put up with all his shit?"

"Yes! That, too! And I did put up with his shit, Connor. Lots and lots of shit. God, I practically ate the stuff, trying to keep him happy and out of trouble. And for what? So that he could blame *me?*"

Connor took a chance. "He blamed you all along, didn't he?"

"Well, not for all of it. Sometimes he blamed the aliens. But he sure blamed me for a lot of stuff. He blamed me for making too much noise, for being too quiet, for not cooking the required food— Do you know, he went through this spell where he would eat only certain things because his aliens had told him not to eat anything else...except that I never knew what it was he was allowed to eat until he blew up and threw the stuff across the room and screamed at me for trying to pollute him?"

"Jesus." *Abusive* was exactly the word for that relationship, and it didn't matter an ice cube in hell that it was Devane's illness that had caused him to act that way. He wondered if Kate was beginning to see that at last.

"And Charlie! So help me, I could wring his neck! What does he think he's doing, planting ideas like that? How is that supposed to help Mike?"

"Maybe it's not supposed to help Mike. Maybe it's to get at you. Maybe this Charlie guy is the one who called the paper about you."

"It wouldn't surprise me," Kate said glumly, slumping in the seat. "Charlie's always been a few bricks shy of a full load. Sometimes I think he's getting sick like Mike. He's only twenty-two, and that was when it started to worsen in Mike."

"Have you seen Charlie recently?"

"Not in a year or so. He never liked me."

"So it probably *is* him."

"Maybe. It could be their dad, too. Oh, hell, they're all a bunch of certifiable nuts. I don't know why I ever thought they were interesting."

"You were young. Most of us are inclined to think the best of people before life kicks us enough times to make us more cautious."

"Yeah." Her head was turned, so he could only see the back of it. "I keep trying to remind myself that he's sick, so I shouldn't get so upset—"

"Horseshit!" he interjected ruthlessly. "How many times am I going to have to say it, Kate? Being sick may be his excuse, but you don't have to put up with it."

As a conversational gambit, it failed miserably. She didn't say another word. That night she slept on his couch.

"They nailed the son of a bitch."

Kate looked up from her work at Connor, her heart leaping into her throat. "The killer? They got the killer?"

"They got the guy who's been e-mailing you. Rick wants us to come over right away. Ben says it's okay. I think he's already counting the increased subscriptions when this thing hits the front page tomorrow."

The weather was still chilly from the recent cold front, and Kate stopped long enough to pull a Shaker sweater over her blouse. "Let's go."

The wind was blowing briskly when they stepped outside, and clouds were moving swiftly across the sky.

"The tourists are probably demanding refunds," Connor said as he pulled his collar up and stuffed his hands into his jacket pockets.

"Actually, this probably feels warm to somebody who's just come from up north."

"Pollyanna. It's *cold* out here."

She laughed—a tinny sound even in her own ears. She didn't feel like laughing. There was nothing on earth to laugh about. There was Mike, who hated her, and all the rest of the Devanes, who hated her, and this unknown person, who hated her. And then there was Connor, who was probably still mad at her for deceiving him, although he hadn't said a word about it. But why should he? What was there to say about it, anyway? She had deceived him, and deceit was something people tended to remember for a long time.

Dread. She was feeling dread again, the way she had before she went to visit Michael at the hospital. She didn't want to go to the police station. She had a feeling they were going to bring her face-to-face with the person who had been writing these notes. She couldn't fathom why they would want to do that, but why else would they want her over there?

"It's okay," Connor said. "There's no need to be scared."

"What do they want with me?"

"I don't know. But nobody's going to hurt you, trust me."

"But it's not like I can identify this guy."

"Of course you can't."

"At least they caught the killer."

"I'm not sure they did."

She turned her head to look at him. "Why not? I thought everyone was convinced!"

He shrugged a shoulder and shook his head. "I can't explain it. It's just this feeling...."

Want to or not, he'd begun to slip into the killer's mind. Last night, while Kate slept, he'd sat in his workroom for hours, looking at photographs, imagining the sequence of events that must have led to the killings.

The killer saw the victims dancing. Or maybe he just saw them walking in and out of the clubs where they worked. He spoke to them, and they spoke back. They felt safe with him, because they'd seen him around so often. Nobody ever believed that someone they saw all the time could be dangerous. Nobody. And this time the guy had the personality and looks to soothe any doubts.

So they knew him and trusted him. And for most of them he *was* harmless. Only for the ones who caught his eye was there a threat.

Shoes. Black shoes with spiky heels and ankle straps. Ankle straps with bows or rosettes on them. Flirty, sexy shoes. They'd all had a pair like that. Maybe that was what the guy saw that set him off. Maybe it wasn't the blond hair or anything they did while dancing, but the shoes. Dancer's shoes, shoes that would stay on the feet and not slip off...

Shoes. Black shoes. Blond hair. Women who showed themselves in public wearing nothing but G-strings.

Women he felt compelled to kill but didn't want to kill. The notes weren't threats. No, they were meant as warnings.

The realization speared him, and he must have made a sound, because Kate asked him what was wrong. He didn't answer, because he couldn't afford to break his concentration right now. With a gesture, he silenced her.

Warnings. The notes were warnings. He wanted to scare the women in the hope that they would run away, go to the police, take precautions. In the hope that the notes would scare the women into saving him from having to commit the crime. God, he must have been hoping that the notes would get him caught.

Then the phone calls. The warnings about the next victim were a cry for someone to stop him before he did it again. So when the notes hadn't worked, he had escalated to phone calls. Then to e-mail? No. No. It didn't fit.

Before they even met Rick Diaz, he was convinced they had the wrong man.

Rick took them into an interrogation room, away from the bustle of the busy sheriff's offices, and closed the door. They all sat at the table, and Rick opened a file folder. "We picked him up on suspicion, but right now I've got nothing to pin on him. Seventy-two hours and he's out of here."

"You've got the wrong man," Connor said flatly.

Rick cocked a brow at him. "Yeah. That's what he says. He's also got one hell of a high-powered attorney, which is making my life shit right now." He shoved a mug shot over to Kate. "Recognize the guy?"

She gasped, and the room seemed to spin for an instant. "Charlie!" she said. "It's Charlie!"

"Yup." Rick took the picture back. "Charles Andrew Devane. He says he used to be your brother-in-law."

"That's right."

"Christ!" Connor slapped his palm on the table and rose, pacing the room like a caged cat. "He's probably the son of a bitch who called the paper with those wild stories about you, too."

Diaz looked interested. "He called the paper?"

"You bet," Connor said. "Trying to make Kate look bad. First he tried one of the crime reporters, but when the guy wouldn't bite and write a story about her supposed misdeeds, he called the managing editor, probably to try to get her fired."

"Now we're cooking," Rick said. "Add that to this note that was supposed to convince you the Puppetmaster was after you, and we've got him for aggravated stalking. Thanks. That's what I needed. Now I can charge him." He looked at Kate. "What misdeeds?"

For the first time since she could remember, Kate didn't have any difficulty explaining. "I had my husband committed. He's schizophrenic."

Rick nodded. "Sounds like a wise move to me. What did he say in his earlier e-mails to you? Anything threatening?"

Kate slowly shook her head. She was still having trouble taking this all in. "Um...basically he said things like he knew who I was, he could find me any time of the day or night, he was watching me. That kind of thing."

Diaz nodded. "That's about what he says he was doing. Says he wanted to make you feel what you made his brother feel."

Kate whitened, and Connor wanted to reach out to her, but he restrained himself.

"Do you have any idea what he meant by that?" Rick asked her.

"I do," Connor answered, his jaw tightening with anger. "Michael Devane suffers from severe paranoia. The family believes Kate drove him insane—which is impossible. This brother is trying to do the same thing to Kate. He's certainly succeeded in making her feel paranoid."

Rick leaned back in his chair. "That's pretty much how he tells it, too." He tapped a pencil on the table before him. "And you really don't think he's the killer?"

"No."

"Damn it, Quinn!" Diaz threw the pencil down and rose, beginning to pace the other side of the room. Kate felt as if she were sitting between two tigers. "We spent all this time to get some flake whose worst crime will probably amount to aggravated stalking! Jesus!'' But he turned suddenly to Kate. ''Not to minimize what's been happening to you, but we've got a killer out there we need to catch, pronto!''

Kate nodded, feeling not in the least slighted. In any reasonable terms, it was more important to catch the killer.

''I expressed my doubts at the time, Rick.''

''Not very strongly.''

''I'm still trying to feel this guy out! He hasn't exactly been dropping clues on every street corner!''

''Maybe not. But there's gotta be something you can go on.''

''There is. This guy didn't do it. Charles Devane is out on a personal vendetta. That's the beginning and end of it. The man we want makes phone calls and leaves notes that are typed. He doesn't mutilate his victims, or assault them sexually, either ante- or postmortem. What he does is make them wear ropes and kneel. I suspect he uses the rope around the neck as a tool for disciplining them to make them do what he wants. So we have women crawling on their knees trying to placate him while he threatens to strangle them if they don't do exactly what he wants.

''But what does he want? As far as I can tell, all he wants is to make them grovel before he takes their blood. So they grovel to his satisfaction, and by this time, having been choked over and over again, they don't even argue when he ties them to the bed. They expect to get raped. They don't expect to have their veins sliced open and a cannula inserted. They don't expect to be bled to death. They don't expect that their own pounding hearts are going to be the instruments that kill them!''

''Jesus!'' Rick looked stunned. ''Connor...''

"No! You wanted to know. I'm telling you." But his face had become a frightening mask. "And the killer...the killer is hardly aware of their fright. He doesn't care if he scares them. He doesn't get off on their terror. What he wants, all he wants, is to perform his sick little ritual of...of purification.

"First he makes them dance for him, wearing nothing but a G-string and high heels. Black high heels with ankle straps. This dance symbolizes the evil he sees in them. Then he makes them strip and throw the G-string and heels into a corner, out of the way. He forces them to kneel and perform his rites of purification, crawling on their knees, groveling, begging his forgiveness. And when he's satisfied, he binds them to the bed and takes their blood.

"While they bleed to death into old milk jugs, he tastes the blood briefly. He smells it. He dabs some of it on himself so he can partake of their purity. And when it's all done, he goes home with the blood to complete his own purification."

For long moments, there was nothing but stunned silence in the room. Finally Rick cleared his throat, as if he wasn't quite sure what to say. Connor looked like a man trapped in a nightmare, and Kate wanted so badly to wipe the pain away. But how could she? She felt as if her own soul had been stained by the things she had just heard.

Connor's eyes looked hollow as he turned to Diaz. "You're looking for a man who frequents these bars and clubs. A man known to most of the dancers and considered to be harmless. They talk to him all the time. Not a one of them would hesitate to invite him into her home. They think they know him. They don't.

"He's nearly forty, drives a conservative car, has a

strong religious affiliation of some kind, is personable and very likable. He's attractive, but not exactly handsome. And I think you'll find that his mother used tying him up and choking him as a way to get him to behave."

"His mother?" Rick repeated, scribbling furiously on a pad.

"His mother. You'll find she was a strict religionist, but that he caught her once, maybe more, wearing nothing but panties and high heels for a man who wasn't his father."

Rick muttered something under his breath. Kate stared at him, wondering how he could draw so much out of so little. But she didn't doubt him.

"And that," said Connor, "is about all I can do right now. But there's more. I can feel it. Just give me a little more time. At least he hasn't called to tell us there's another victim being stalked."

"That doesn't mean much. He didn't warn us about the first two. But it's a starting place. Say, did you hear the one about the minister and the hooker?"

Connor shook his head.

Diaz opened his mouth, then glanced at Kate. "Damn," he said, "I forgot the punch line. Forget it."

A while later, as she and Connor walked out to the car, Kate said, "He didn't forget that punch line."

Connor flashed her a smile. "No, he sure didn't."

"It must have been raunchy."

"*Very* raunchy," he agreed.

"I guess this means I don't have to stay with you any longer."

He didn't answer until they were pulling out of the parking lot. "I guess so," he said.

Neither of them said another word.

# 17

Every paper in the area printed a front-page article announcing that a suspect had been arrested in the Puppetmaster killings. The *Sentinel,* however, went one step farther. In an article announcing that Charles Devane had been taken in for questioning and had been charged in an unrelated incident of stalking, the *Sentinel* printed a supposed profile of the killer.

Connor and Keith Shepherd had put their heads together on a proactive description designed to infuriate and upset the killer, in the hope that he would be driven to respond somehow. Kate wrote the entire article, but Connor's name, as usual, was on it.

The reaction was surprisingly swift. During the early afternoon, Connor got the first call.

"That's not him," said the voice he remembered.

"Who is this?"

"I told you, I dream about him. I see inside his head when I sleep. You've got the wrong idea. He's not like that at all. God, don't you see? If that's the man you're looking for, you'll never find him!"

"Then tell us what you know. Tell us how to find him."

"I can't. I don't know that."

"Then tell us what he's really like."

"I don't... I can't.... He's not the evil person you think at all. He doesn't rape them. I don't know how you could think he rapes these women. He doesn't rape them, and he doesn't beat them up, and he doesn't cut them...."

"But he chokes them, doesn't he? He wants to perform some profane ritual with their blood, doesn't he?" Connor held his breath, hoping he hadn't gone too far.

"No," said the voice. "No. You've got it wrong. Don't you see? He's seeking sanctity." *Click.*

*Sanctity.* The word stuck like a burr to Connor's mind. He couldn't shake it. He called Rick but Diaz was unavailable. A few minutes later, he played the tape for Keith Shepherd, and then slipped a copy of it into an overnight envelope for delivery early the next morning at Quantico. Keith thought that word was significant, too.

"Say," Kate said as he passed by her desk later, "why don't we go out investigating tonight?"

He paused, looking down at her, wondering if she missed him as much as he missed her, and wondering why he had to be so damn hung up on her stupid little lie. A lie that was perfectly understandable in the context of her past. One little lie that probably meant nothing, since as far as he could tell, she hadn't lied about anything else. But as he glanced down at her, he saw that the wedding ring was still on her left hand. Fuck it.

"Yeah," he said. "I guess we could. What are you planning to investigate?"

"Who this guy is that all these dancers know and like."

"Oh." He sat on the corner of her desk and looked

down at her. "You just have to take risks, don't you? What if you catch this killer's attention?"

She shrugged. "Who cares?"

"Oh, cut out the self-pity! So some damn paranoid-schizophrenic ex of yours is having some delusion that you're Attila the Hun. So fucking what? He's so disconnected from reality that I can't imagine how anything he thinks could count for shit. Be ready at eight, Kate. I'll pick you up at your place. In the meantime, ditch the pity gig."

Before she could say another word, he stalked away.

Just as Connor was getting ready to leave that evening, Ben asked him to take a couple of photo assignments the next day.

"Nothing major," Ben said, "so if something comes up on the Puppetmaster case, just let me know. We can reschedule these."

Connor scanned the paper, noting that one was at an nursing home in South Pasadena, and another was at the Clearwater Harbor, where some regatta was being planned. "Sure. No problem."

"Great. See you tomorrow."

He figured he would grab something to eat at the Italian restaurant up the street and go straight to Kate's. But first, as he always did, he phoned home to read his schedule for tomorrow onto his answering machine. He always did that, in case he left the itinerary behind somewhere—a constant risk in a mobile occupation like his. Now he could call in from anywhere and find out exactly what he was supposed to be doing and where.

Only tonight his machine didn't pick up. Instead, he got a busy signal. Thinking a trunk line was possibly busy, he waited a few minutes and called again. Still busy. Finally he called an operator and persuaded her to listen in on the line.

"The phone is off the hook, sir," she said. "I don't hear anything at all."

He was about to dismiss it when he realized that Sophie might have gone in to water his plants for him. If she had gotten sick while there, she might have tried to use the phone. God, the woman was in her eighties. She might have had a stroke, or a heart attack....

All thoughts of dinner fled as he hurried out of his office. Kate was apparently gone already, not that it mattered. She wouldn't be expecting him until eight, and by then he would have it all cleared up.

He sped over to his apartment as if he still had a shield he could put on the dash to avoid getting a ticket. He even slid through a couple of stop signs, but he didn't see a single police cruiser the whole way.

At his apartment building, the elevator seemed to take forever, so he turned and dashed up the stairs. He kept telling himself that he was overreacting, that he'd knocked the phone off the hook this morning as he was leaving for work, or Sophie had accidentally knocked it off when she came to check on his flowers. In his heart, though, he didn't believe it.

He jammed the key in the lock, twisting it forcefully in his haste. And then his heart climbed into his throat. He didn't hear the familiar thunk of the dead bolt sliding open. The door was unlocked.

His police training sprang to the fore. Twisting the doorknob gently to release the latch, he stepped to the side and flattened himself to the wall. Then, reaching out with one hand, he gently shoved the door open.

The hinges creaked a little, and he cursed himself for not keeping them oiled. The apartment was dark inside, and no matter how he strained his ears, he couldn't detect any sounds. Reaching cautiously around the doorjamb, he flipped the light switch.

The golden glow of light filled the living room, and nothing moved. He stepped through the door cautiously, wishing for the first time that he'd never left the police force, because if he hadn't, at least he would be armed now.

He moved farther into the apartment, glancing into the kitchen and seeing nothing. That left the workroom and the bedroom. He headed for the bedroom first.

He flipped on the light and felt as if a giant fist punched him in the stomach. Sophie lay on the bed, wearing her favorite crimson blouse and skirt. There was a red stain on her forehead and rope around her throat, a makeshift noose made with a slipknot. Rope trailed from her wrists, too.

He took it all in at a glance and knew that the killer had invaded his home. Before he let the anger touch him, he crossed the room in a couple of long strides and touched the side of Sophie's neck. He felt a pulse, slow but steady, and whispered a prayer of thanksgiving to whatever gods had been watching tonight.

"Jesus, Sophie," he whispered. "Oh, Jesus, I'm sorry."

The phone beside the bed was off the hook, and he hung it up, waiting a few seconds for the return of the dial tone. Then he called 911 and Rick Diaz.

The ambulance arrived in less than five minutes. When he let the emergency personnel in, he cautioned them that it was the scene of a crime and warned them not to touch anything except the patient. They knew the procedure. He waited a few moments, watching them check Sophie, deciphering that they thought she had a serious concussion and a possible skull fracture. That was when he noticed that neither her wrists nor her throat showed any abrasions from the rope.

So the killer hadn't treated her as he had his other victims. Either he'd broken into the apartment and startled Sophie, or Sophie had walked in on him, but either way, he'd done only enough to shut her up, and then he'd left the ropes as a message.

A message about what, for God's sake? He was getting sick to death of cryptic, useless messages from this creep. Grabbing a pair of the latex gloves he kept around for handling negatives, he put them on and looked around the workroom.

Here was a museum of the killer's trophies. Pictures that probably gave the bastard a thrill in his gut. He half expected to find some of them gone, taken to appease the guy's need to relive his killings.

But they were all there. They didn't even look as if they'd been touched. Maybe he hadn't even come in here. Maybe Sophie had given him such a scare that he hadn't carried out his original intention, whatever it was. But why had he come here when he knew Connor had to be out? What had he hoped to accomplish?

The St. Petersburg police arrived swiftly to take control of the crime scene. Connor faced the inevitable questions that indicated that he was a suspect. Of course he was: The woman had been found beaten in *his* apartment, in *his* bed. Plus, he had a roomful of pictures of the earlier crimes. Nor did being a former cop help him a whole lot.

Rick Diaz must have broken every speed limit racing across the bay. He arrived with Ray Matucek twenty minutes after he received Connor's call. Bill Kittrick wasn't far behind.

"Christ," Rick said, "a live victim! And here. What the hell is he doing hitting an old woman at *your* place, Connor? And what the hell was *she* doing here?"

Connor was sitting at his dinette, taking care to touch nothing. He waved at the row of plants lined up in front of the balcony doors. "She's my neighbor. She drops in every now and then to check on my plants for me, because sometimes I forget them."

"Who is she?"

"Sophie Butler. An artist."

The medical personnel wheeled Sophie out of the bedroom on a stretcher and headed for the door. They'd established an IV, put a collar on her neck and removed the ropes.

God, thought Connor, Sophie, who always seemed larger than life to him, looked so old and frail right now, with her bloodstained hair all over the pillow, and her face so slack and empty.

"Do you know her next of kin?" one of the medics asked him.

"A son who lives in Trenton. Kyle Butler."

"Phone number?"

Connor shook his head. "I don't know."

"We'll be checking out her apartment," one of the officers said. "We'll let you know if we find it."

Christ, Connor thought, the endless paperwork. Always the damn paperwork. He rose from the table and went to stand beside Sophie. Bending, he touched her hand. "You're gonna be okay, Sophie. I'll come down to see you in a little while."

Nobody argued with him.

"Okay," Rick said. He, Ray and Bill gathered at the

dinette with Connor, pads and pens at the ready. "Give me the story."

"Not a whole hell of a lot to tell. I called home to leave my schedule for tomorrow on my answering machine, only the line was busy. I asked an operator to check it, she said the phone was off the hook. I almost ignored it until I remembered that Sophie might have come by to water the plants. She's in her eighties, Rick. I was afraid she might have had a stroke or a heart attack and been unable to call for help. So I came hotfooting it home and found her on my bed, knocked out, with ropes around her neck and wrists."

"The same kind of ropes and knots?"

"Exactly the same. I mean...there's no doubt. It was him. She wasn't abraded by the ropes, however, so I'm assuming they startled each other—she walked in on him or he walked in on her—and he knocked her out, then decided to make a statement with the ropes."

"What kind of statement?"

"Damned if I know." Connor rubbed his eyes with his hands and sat back in his chair. "I checked my workroom to see if he'd taken any of the crime-scene photos for souvenirs, but it didn't look like anything was touched in there. I'm thinking he got startled before he did whatever it was he intended to."

"But he still left a message."

"But he still left a message," Connor agreed.

"Why here? Why your place?"

"That's easy. We put that phony profile in the paper this morning. Did you get my message that he called me this afternoon?"

"No shit!" Rick looked excited. "No, I didn't get it." He turned to Ray. "Remind me to read somebody the riot act."

Ray nodded. "My pleasure."

"So what the fuck did he say?"

"Basically he told me that we didn't understand this guy at all, and if we don't understand him, how are we ever going to catch him? Then he said something really interesting. He said the killer is seeking sanctity."

"Sanctity?" Rick repeated the word disbelievingly, and Bill Kittrick snorted. "Have you ever seen anything more unsanctified in your life?"

"It doesn't matter what *we* think," Connor reminded him. "But it puts an interesting spin on the guy's thought processes. Yeah, we figured he was engaging in some kind of ritual, and I was pretty sure it had something to do with purification, but now he says *sanctity.* That's an interesting word...."

He trailed off, letting his chin drop to his chest while he thought. Then he pushed his chair back from the table and headed for the kitchen. "I need coffee. Anybody else want some?"

A chorus of *Yeah*s reached him from all the assembled officers.

"Be careful what you touch," Bill called after him.

"That's why I'm wearing these damn gloves—" He broke off sharply and swore mightily. Immediately people hurried to the kitchen doorway.

There, sitting beside the sink, was a washed coffee cup. Just like at all the other scenes. But not even that grabbed him as much as what he saw next: A glow-in-the-dark cross had been tucked into the corner of the counter by the fridge, the only reason he hadn't seen it when he first entered the apartment.

A signature. A cross. There had been a cross at every one of the scenes.

He turned to the others suddenly and said, "I know who the killer is."

# 18

"Anybody could have left a cross," Rick argued. The four of them were once again gathered at the dinette.

"Hell, yes," Bill agreed. "You can buy them all over the place, at Christian bookstores, church thrift shops… everywhere. It doesn't mean anything."

Connor leaned forward, tapping his finger on the table to emphasize his point. "On the face of it, I'd agree with you. But we have a guy who claims he isn't evil, who says he's seeking *sanctity*. Then we've got a minister who shows up at Josephine Gumm's place, supposedly to say a prayer for her. He says she's a member of his congregation."

"Maybe she is," Bill argued.

"Did anybody check it out? And what if she is? He has to find these women somehow, and Gumm was well out of his usual hunting ground. Are we to think he's just expanding, or did she come to his attention through the church?"

Rick shook his head. "Maybe. But it's not enough."

"Not enough for a conviction, but sure as hell enough for a direction. Look, time and again these guys come back to the scene. It's an opportunity for them to relive the killing, to relish it. And the fact that this guy is a minister doesn't change that. It merely fits in with the other stuff—the crosses, his claim that he's seeking sanctity."

But the faces were still uncertain.

"Look," Connor said, "this guy kills these women so he can steal their purity."

"Now wait one minute," Rick said. "Purity? From exotic dancers?"

"Wait. Just wait and let me finish. This guy takes a class of women he sees as sinners. One of them triggers his particular interest. Maybe she looks like his mother or resembles an old girlfriend. Whatever. The point is, he's trying to save her. He ties her up and forces her to her knees. Forces her to do penance for her sins. And when he considers that she's done enough penance, he kills her so she can't sin again. *He saves her soul.*"

"Jesus," muttered Ray.

"And once she's saved, he takes her purified blood to purify himself. Mark my words, this guy bathes in it. He washes himself in the blood of an innocent lamb."

Absolute silence settled over the table. Then Rick looked at Bill. "Can you get someone to check on Gumm's church affiliation?"

"Right now."

"Ray? Call in and get someone to check on Whitmore, Eppinga and the first one. I want to know what church these women attended. And tell 'em to step on it. I want the information yesterday."

While they were waiting, two detectives from the St. Petersburg homicide division arrived. Connor listened with one ear as the others filled the detectives in, wandering into his workroom to look around. The guy had to have done something else, left some kind of message other than the cross and the ropes on Sophie.

Closing his eyes, he let himself sink into the mind-set of the killer. He had come here to do something. Something that was important enough for him to risk detection by breaking into an apartment during busy hours when people were awake and coming and going. He wouldn't have left without completing that task.

He'd meant to leave a message of some kind that didn't involve Sophie. Would he have let that glitch stop him? Why should he? Once the woman was unconscious, he'd had plenty of time to carry out his original plan. What was it?

And suddenly he remembered what the guy had said on the phone that afternoon: "You've got the wrong idea. He's not like that at all. God, don't you see? If that's the man you're looking for, you'll never find him!"

He wanted to be found. He had come here to do something that would help Connor find him. Or just to plead his case.

"He's not the evil person you think at all." That was the other thing he'd said. He wanted to plead his case. He wanted to explain himself.

Connor turned suddenly to his computer. It had a feature that shut it down whenever it was inactive for a while, but restored the system to exactly where it had been at the time it shut down. If the guy had left a message there...

He leaned forward and hit the switch, then waited impatiently for the system to boot and restore. His heart had begun to thud heavily with excitement. He was sure it would be there. Absolutely sure.

And suddenly there it was, on the Windows Notepad screen.

> I didn't want to hurt the old lady. She got in the way. But I didn't hurt her badly. She'll be okay.
>
> But you don't understand. You've got to try to understand. I'm not evil. I'm trying to be holy.
>
> God is the Puppetmaster who directs us all, and he has directed me to be like Him, to exact penance, to make these women holy.

Connor felt an icy shiver trickle down his spine as he read the word *penance,* one he had used himself so recently.

> And when they are holy, He directs me to save them so they can never sin again. I am doing His work, and in their blood He purifies me.

It terrified Connor to be so close to the truth. The dread that filled him now had little to do with the possibility that other people might die. It had everything to do with the idea that if he could come so close to such a twisted mind, then he must be twisted in some way, too. That such horrible things couldn't occur to any normal person. He felt befouled.

But there was no time to indulge himself now. What he wanted to do, what he *had* to do, was catch this son of a bitch. He could worry about the state of his own immortal soul later.

He called the others in and let them read the note. While they did, he stared out the window at the dark, cold night and wondered if two sides of the same coin were so very different after all.

Then the call came. Judy Eppinga had belonged to the Church of the Holy Fellowship, and the pastor's name was Peter Masterson.

"That's him," Connor said without turning around. "That's the guy who was at Gumm's place when I was out there."

"It's also the same church that pickets the exotic lounges. That's enough," said Rick. "I don't need to hear any more. We're going out to talk to this guy right now."

The crime-scene team was arriving just as they were leaving. The two St. Pete detectives had to stay, but Rick promised them a full report. They went in two cars, Rick and Connor in one, and Bill and Ray in the other.

The Church of the Holy Fellowship was on the north side of Tampa, in the Temple Terrace area. The church itself was a conservative yellow brick building with a white wood steeple, and was surrounded by a neatly trimmed lawn and older trees. The parsonage was across the street, a single-story ranch-style house with white paint and green shutters. No one was there.

Connor suddenly wanted to kick something. "I'm going in there," he said.

"We don't have a warrant."

"And I'm not a cop. I'm a damn newspaper photographer. You guys go away somewhere, and I'll go in there and find something to get you a warrant."

The three policemen exchanged looks.

"No," Rick said. "Too many people know you're working on this with us. We'd wind up with some damn defense attorney screaming that you were a de facto cop, acting on my behalf, and anything we got on the warrant would be thrown out as fruit of the poisoned tree."

"God damn it." Connor shoved his hands in his pants

pockets and stood looking at the house. "We've got enough circumstantial evidence."

"We don't know exactly what we're looking for."

"Pictures of the victims. Items of women's clothing, locks of their hair, blood. Anything he might have taken. A diary. All that stuff is small enough that we'd be able to look everywhere. The plain-view doctrine would cover anything else that we see while we're searching."

"I don't like it," Bill said. "I want to nail this guy, so we'd better do it by the book."

"Besides," Rick said dryly, "there's more than a small chance this minister might be innocent."

"Yeah, right," Connor said sourly.

Nobody disagreed with him.

"Look," said Ray, "I'll go check on the church for a list of emergency numbers."

Twenty minutes later, a heavy middle-aged woman pulled up before the parsonage and climbed out of her car.

"Mrs. Hebert?" Ray said. "I'm Ray Matucek, with the sheriff's office." He showed her his shield. "We're conducting a murder investigation that involves a couple of members of the Holy Fellowship congregation, and we really need to get in touch with Mr. Masterson."

The woman nodded, looking suspiciously at the four of them. "Well, come inside while I check Pastor's appointment book."

She let them in the front door, into a cozy living room with furnishings that looked as if they'd been cobbled together by a Laura Ashley wanna-be.

"It's been just terrible," she said, closing curtains against the night as she turned on lamps. "We've tried so hard to save those girls, to bring them to a better life, and then this happens. What is the world coming to, I ask you? At least,'' she added, pausing to face them, ''I assume you're here about the girls?''

''Judy Eppinga and Josephine Gumm,'' Rick said.

Mrs. Hebert nodded. ''Such a tragedy! These were good girls, I want you to know. Very good girls. They just did an unpleasant thing because they needed money. Pastor Peter was talking about finding them better jobs, especially Josie Gumm. Judy was going to college, but Josie didn't have any real training at all. He was looking into secretarial schools for her, and the church was going to pay for it.''

''That's nice,'' said Rick, casting a significant look in Connor's direction. ''But I think exotic dancers make a lot more money than secretaries.''

''But they don't get the same respect, and Josie wanted to be respected. They do, you know. So many of these girls would dearly love to have normal jobs and lives. And here were these two, trying so hard, coming to worship every Sunday, and some terrible, terrible person killed them! It's appalling.''

Connor was getting the distinct impression that Mrs. Hebert didn't have much opportunity to express herself on these issues, because she was certainly eager to express herself now.

She bustled around, acting like a hostess who had been caught by unexpected guests. Rick had to remind her gently that they needed to contact the pastor.

She passed through a door in the living room, and Connor could see the study beyond, a room with a desk, several chairs and bookcases crammed to overflowing. She pawed around the desk and finally opened up a brown date book.

''Ah, here it is,'' she said. ''He has an appointment this evening with a patient at the hospital, but that was at seven. He ought to be back here soon. Would you like to wait?"

"Thank you," Rick said.

"Coffee? Tea? I'd be glad to make some."

Connor seized the opportunity. "Some coffee would be really great."

Mrs. Hebert beamed, as if she were truly glad to be able to do something useful. Following his lead, the others echoed a desire for coffee. As soon as she had bustled away to the kitchen, Connor rose and headed for the study.

"Remember the plain-view doctrine," Rick said quietly.

Connor nodded and stepped through the doorway into Peter Masterson's study.

The bookcases were overfilled, but orderly nonetheless. Alphabetized by subject, and then within subjects by author, Connor realized as he scanned them. Compulsive.

Working his way along them, he quickly absorbed the man's interests. Bible studies topped the list, followed by sociological and psychological studies. There was an odd assortment of other subjects, ranging from New Age to travel. Even a book on UFOs.

But then he came to a shelf of police books dealing with procedures and, perhaps significantly, crime-scene investigations. And below it was a shelf of true-crime studies of serial killers.

Connor felt his heart accelerate. The guy might have these books for any reason, of course. Maybe he wanted to write a novel. But in his heart of hearts he felt he had tumbled to the reason the Puppetmaster killer was able to leave such clean scenes behind him: he knew what to avoid.

To one side of the desk sat an IBM computer and a laser printer, and in one corner of the room there was a small typing table on which sat an IBM Selectric. The Selectric could easily have typed the notes they found. Curious, he bent over the machine and checked the type element: ten-point pica. The same as the notes, but so common as to be unidentifiable. The laser printer could probably reproduce something very similar. Unless there was a flaw in one of the letters that was identical to a flaw in a note sent to a victim, little could be proved.

Mrs. Hebert still hadn't returned with the coffee, so Connor sauntered over to the desk. A long time ago, he'd mastered the art of reading upside down, so he stood on the wrong side of the desk and began to scan what was visible. If Mrs. Hebert returned, he could easily claim to have been scanning the titles of the books on the shelves behind the desk.

The appointment book lay open, and he found it significant that nothing was scheduled from one o'clock that afternoon until seven this evening. Time blocked out to go to Connor's apartment?

He wanted to flip the pages and see what had been scheduled for the nights of the four murders, but he didn't dare. He couldn't explain that to Mrs. Hebert, if she caught him, and he doubted the plain-view doctrine would allow him to do that any more than it would allow him to open drawers. Essentially, plain view meant exactly what it sounded like: A cop who was anywhere he was legally entitled to be could seize as evidence anything he saw in plain view. Cops had been known to stretch that a little, and Connor wasn't above doing so if he thought he could get away with it. Certainly not in a case like this.

But both Rick and Bill were right to caution him,

because he was damned if he wanted this guy to get off because he, or anyone else, had violated his rights. Like most cops, he had chafed under the restrictions on search and seizure, but he also acknowledged their value. After all, if cops didn't need warrants to search a place, nobody, not even law-abiding citizens, would have any privacy. So it was best to play it like a game, in which you had to find a way within the rules to get what you wanted.

There was nothing out of line on the desk, or anywhere else, for that matter. He hadn't really expected that there would be. This guy was canny. But his attention kept getting dragged back to the shelf of crime books and police books, as if they were a flashing warning, telling him that he was hot on the trail.

Mrs. Hebert returned to the living room while he was still standing in the study. She put the tray down on the coffee table and regarded him suspiciously. "Is there something you need in there?"

He shook his head and came back to the living room. "I'm a bookaholic," he told her with a small smile. "That's a wonderful library. It drew me like a magnet."

She smiled back, relaxing. "Pastor Peter really is a bookworm. I think he spends most of his pocket money on books. Every so often we have to box up the ones he doesn't want anymore and give them away, or sell them at the bazaar. And he reads about so many things! A very brilliant man."

"With eclectic tastes," Connor agreed. Thanking her, he accepted a cup of hot coffee. The aroma was rich and good, and when he took a sip, his eyebrows lifted. "This is really great coffee."

The housekeeper nodded. "He's very particular about it. He buys a special blend, and he insists I make it just so.'' She gave a little laugh. ''He says coffee is the gas in his tank.''

Connor had a sudden vision of all the neatly rinsed coffee cups at the crime scenes. It fit. By God, it fit!

But he'd already made the housekeeper suspicious once, so he settled into an armchair and let the others handle the conversation for a while. It didn't take much persuasion to convince Mrs. Hebert to have a cup of coffee with them. She went back to the kitchen for another mug, then sat in the Boston rocker, with its battered, flowery cushions.

Rick spoke. ''Have you been with Pastor Masterson a long time?''

''Five years, ever since he came to Holy Fellowship. He's a good man, a kind, generous and warmhearted man. Everyone loves him, you know. I don't think I've ever heard a word spoken against him.''

''He has a particular interest in these women like Josephine Gumm and Judy Eppinga?''

''Oh, my, yes! He's always reminding us that Jesus defended a prostitute and asking us how we should think we're so much better than they. He's made it his personal ministry, you know. He says these poor women wouldn't take these jobs if only men would pay them enough in decent jobs. He says that it's a crime how much men will pay to see a woman undress and how little they'll pay for her honest labor.'' She flushed a little. ''Present company excluded, of course.''

Diaz turned on the charm and smiled. ''Of course. So he thinks men are the problem?''

''Oh, yes! But he says that it would be impossible to change all the men in the world, so the best we can do is save these poor girls one at a time.''

Connor felt the hair on the back of his neck rise. He

glanced at Rick and Bill and saw that they recognized it, too.

"So he saves them one at a time?" Ray said gently.

"It's all we can do. One at a time. Of course, we try to do more. Several times a week we go to picket these awful places of business, you know."

"I've seen you," Connor remarked pleasantly.

She nodded. "It's not much, but we'd like to think that we embarrass at least some of the men into going away. And, of course, we're always nice to the girls. We invite them to the church and tell them about our program to help them find other jobs." She paused, sipping her coffee, her eyes darkening with memory. "Some are more receptive than others, naturally."

"Naturally," said Rick.

Mrs. Hebert nodded. "Some are abusive to us, telling us it's none of our business. It's what you'd expect, though. As Pastor Peter says, they've become so hardened by their lives that there's very little we can do to help them."

Mrs. Hebert was a font of information, Connor thought, hoping she would continue. So the man picked his victims according to those who seemed receptive to being saved. A damn shame he didn't limit himself to saving their souls.

Mrs. Hebert went on at some length and in some detail about the various things the church did to help these girls. Pastor Peter, she said, had been trying to find members of the church who would help finance Judy Eppinga's education. And he'd been working on several members who owned businesses to agree to hire Josephine Gumm when she finished secretarial school.

"Of course," said Mrs. Hebert, "it wasn't as easy as you would think."

"What ever is?" Ray asked sympathetically.

"Nothing, I suppose, but when it comes to these girls...well! One man who originally thought he could provide a job for Josie changed his mind because of his wife. Now I'm not naming any names, mind you, but his wife told him that if he hired a stripper to work in his business, she'd lock the door on him and file for divorce. Pastor Peter tried to talk to her about it, to explain the point of the whole thing, but she wouldn't hear of it. Her husband wasn't going to spend his days with any stripper."

Rick clucked disapprovingly.

"There's a sorry lack of Christian spirit in the world today," the housekeeper continued with a shake of her head. "And that's why these poor girls have such a hard time of it. Now, if you ask me, it wouldn't have mattered to that woman if Josie had never been a stripper, because the poor child was just too beautiful and too buxom for her own good. I expect that wherever she went, she would have had bosses who tried to paw her and wives who wouldn't approve of her. It's such a shame that beauty can be such a curse, you know?"

Connor nodded in agreement.

"Especially," she continued, "a large bosom. And all these girls were especially well endowed. Why, we saved one just last year that we all nearly despaired of, because men couldn't seem to lift their eyes above her chest when they talked to her. And when men see blondes with large chests, they immediately think they're stupid. I finally took her out to buy garments that minimized her chest, and she found a job as a legal secretary."

"You're to be commended," Rick said.

Mrs. Hebert beamed. "We try."

"Did Pastor Peter ever have any contact with these women outside of the church?"

Mrs. Hebert's smile faded. "I'm sure I don't know what you mean."

"I mean, did he ever see them at any other time while he was trying to help them?"

"Well, he gave them religious instruction, of course. But I was always here when he did that. 'We don't want anyone thinking something improper is going on, Mrs. Hebert,' he said to me once. And he felt the young ladies would be much more comfortable if I was present, so I always made a point of it."

"Does he keep his own appointment book?"

"Well, yes. I write in appointments for him if he's not here, but he makes his own most of the time. Why?"

Rick hesitated almost imperceptibly. "I just wondered if he might have had another appointment after his hospital visit."

Connor glanced at his watch and realized with a start that it was quarter past eight. Kate must be getting pretty steamed at him by now.

"It's possible," Mrs. Hebert said, "but most likely the family showed up and he's talking to them, as well. The poor, dear woman is seriously ill and not expected to survive. But I'm sure he'll be here before much longer."

"Does he have a cellular phone with him?"

"Oh, no! He won't hear of it. He says the only private time he has is in the car." She laughed, and everyone obediently chuckled with her.

"Well, if you don't mind, then, we'll wait a little longer," Rick said.

"Oh, I don't mind at all!" And clearly she didn't. In

fact, if Connor had had to make a bet on it, he would have said she was enjoying herself.

He glanced at his watch again. His c-phone was in the car. "Excuse me, but I need to go out and make a phone call. I had an eight-o'clock date, and she's probably ready to kill me."

The woman smiled. "Just use the pastor's phone, if you want."

"I need to call St. Petersburg."

She waved a hand. "A quarter. Don't worry about it."

In the study, he picked up the phone and dialed Kate's home number. He got a busy signal. Aware that Mrs. Hebert was watching from the living room, he returned to his seat. "Busy," he said by way of explanation. "I'll try again in a few minutes, if that's okay."

"Of course. Being a police officer must make it very difficult to have a romance."

No one objected to her assumption that Connor was a cop. Rick filled the momentary silence.

"I'm lucky my wife hasn't left me," he said with a rueful smile. "I've missed more dinners, more parties, more outings with the kids...." He shook his head.

"She must be a wonderful woman," the housekeeper commented.

"Oh, she is. She says she never expects me until I show up."

"My wife couldn't stand it," Bill volunteered. "She took a hike years ago and married a doctor. She says at least she can expect him to come home alive."

Ray looked wryly at Connor. "I guess I should stay single."

"I probably won't have a choice after tonight," Connor joked, then felt a jolt when he realized that he really didn't want Kate to be mad at him.

"She'll forgive you," Mrs. Hebert said with certainty.

Connor found himself hoping so.

At quarter to nine, he went to call Kate again but still got a busy signal. She was probably so mad she'd taken the phone off the hook. And once again his eyes were drawn to the shelf of books dealing with serial killers. Behind him, he heard Rick and the others stir and begin to make leaving motions. They couldn't sit here much longer without turning this into something considerably more than a few casual questions about members of the minister's congregation. Mrs. Hebert would start to get really suspicious. Unfortunately, their having been here at all would probably serve as a warning to Peter Masterson that they were on to him.

"We'll call Pastor Masterson in the morning," he heard Rick say. "Tell him we're sorry we missed him, but it's nothing so important that we can't pick a more convenient time. Basically, we just wanted to know if he ever noticed these women with any suspicious men, if they had boyfriends they were scared of, that kind of thing."

Good cover, Connor thought, and wondered why he couldn't stop wanting to reach for those damn books. Morbid fascination? Or because they seemed so out of place in the study of a minister?

He turned suddenly and looked into the living room. Mrs. Hebert was just pushing herself up out of the chair. "Mrs. Hebert, I see Pastor Masterson is interested in police work."

She nodded and came into the room, smiling pleasantly. "He told me once that he used to wish he could be a police officer."

"Why couldn't he?"

"He felt called to the ministry. But he said he kept

on wishing anyway.'' She shook her head. ''It's kind of a shame, though. He might have gone and tried it one day, but then there was the accident.''

Connor was suddenly intently focused on what she was saying. A tension gripped the base of his skull. ''Accident?''

''Oh, it was terrible. He used to have a motorcycle, you know. Everyone thought it was such a cute thing, the minister on a motorcycle. The young people just loved it.''

''I can imagine.''

She nodded, then shook her head again. ''Someone ran a stop sign and hit him broadside. He was lucky to have lived. For a long time, we didn't think he would. He was unconscious for over a week. And ever since, he's had these terrible, terrible headaches that last for hours. They're so bad that he has to sit in a dark room and be completely undisturbed. Sometimes he goes to the hospital to get a shot. He'll never work as a policeman now.''

Connor felt ice slither down his spine. His eyes jumped past her to Rick, and he saw the same reaction there. Head injury. It fit the profile.

On impulse, he looked at the shelf again. ''Do you think he'd mind if I just looked at a few of his books? It's quite a library.''

''Oh, I know he wouldn't mind. He's always lending books to people. Book are to be shared, he always says. Help yourself.''

Connor looked at Rick. ''Five minutes.''

Rick looked puzzled, but nodded. ''Sure. We can wait that long.''

Like a man in the grip of some kind of spell, Connor walked over to the shelf that had caught his interest and pulled out the first book. The others went back into the living room.

He opened the book, scanning the table of contents, fanning the pages. Nothing. He put it back and reached for the next. He wasn't sure exactly what he was looking for. Perhaps underlining or highlighting? Or a chapter that seemed to leap out at him? He didn't know, but he felt compelled.

Another book, then another. It wasn't until the fifth book, a psychological study of five serial killers, that he found what he was looking for. As he pulled it off the shelf, Polaroid photographs fell to the ground.

Connie Sjorngren. Judy Eppinga. Marceline Whitmore. Josephine Gumm. All of them naked and kneeling, bound and blindfolded. All of them in their last moments of life. His stomach turned over.

"Rick? Can you guys come in here, please? Now."

They had found their killer.

# 19

Connor was late. At around eight-twenty, Kate tried to call him but only got his answering machine. She left a brief message, asking if they were still on for tonight.

When the doorbell rang, she went to answer it, sure it was him. Instead, she found an attractive man of moderate height standing on her porch. He wore dark gray clerical garb, with a Roman collar. His hair was blond dashed with gray, his eyes were a surprising blue, light and almost translucent, and his smile was pleasant.

"Ms. Devane?"

"Yes?"

"I'm Peter Masterson, pastor of Holy Fellowship Church in Tampa. I was wondering if I might take just a moment of your time."

Kate felt resistance stir. "I already have a church I'm very happy with...and I'm expecting a friend at any moment."

"Oh, this will only take a minute. And it's not about trying to convince you to come to my church." His smile faded, to be replaced by genuine sorrow. "It's about one of my congregation, Judy Eppinga. You wrote such a nice article about her, when everyone was suggesting such terrible things. I just wanted to thank you."

She could have just thanked him for stopping by and closed the door on him, but that would have been so churlish. The man had obviously cared about Judy, or he wouldn't be standing there trying to thank her. Connor ought to be here at any moment, and that made her feel safe. If this guy proved to be some kind of pervert, he wouldn't accomplish very much in a couple of minutes.

She stepped back and smiled. "Come in, Reverend. But I've only got two or three minutes until my date arrives." She added the latter for security.

"I won't need much time," said Peter Masterson, and stepped across her threshold. Then they sat facing one another in the living room, he on the couch, she in the armchair.

"Judy was such a wonderful young woman," Masterson said. "Going to school and working so hard to do it all on her own, without owing anything to anyone. You have to admire that kind of spirit."

"You certainly do," Kate agreed, wondering if she should ask to record their conversation. There might be a good article in this. "It's such a shame what happened to her. I can't imagine why anyone would do such a thing. Or how anyone would be capable of it."

He shook his head. "If there's one thing I've learned in my ministry, it's that people are capable of almost anything. Which is not to say it doesn't appall me. But we have to learn to forgive, because if we don't, we carry the burden of anger with us throughout our lives."

"I hadn't thought of it that way before." And inevitably she thought of Michael. Maybe what she needed to do was to forgive him. Maybe that would get rid of the anger and guilt. And if anyone deserved to be forgiven, it was Michael.

"I'm sorry," said Masterson. "You look sad. Did I say something wrong?"

Kate felt her cheeks heat a little. "Oh, I was just thinking about...my ex-husband, and what you said about anger."

"Forgiveness really does help, you know. It eases bitterness when nothing else will. It opens us up for the flow of God's grace and frees us to enjoy the blessings and joys that life offers."

"That's a very practical attitude."

He smiled. "A very selfish one, I suppose, but forgiveness seems such a pointless thing to most people until they realize that they benefit by it, too. I struggle with it myself, however. I'm struggling with it over Judy. It's so hard to forgive the monster who killed her."

"It would be," Kate agreed. She liked this minister, she realized. He wasn't all hoity-toity about what people ought to do; he was down-to-earth and practical. "Your congregation must like you very much."

He gave a self-deprecating laugh. "They keep paying my salary. Excuse me, but I have a terrible headache. Would you have any aspirin? Or a cup of coffee, possibly? It's some kind of migraine, and for some reason caffeine helps."

Kate glance at the clock and realized it was eight-thirty. Connor must have gotten delayed. "I can make a pot, if you don't mind waiting for it."

"If it wouldn't be too much trouble."

As soon as she left the room, he looked around and found the phone on the end table. It was a speakerphone and he punched the speaker button. At once he heard the dial tone, but he squelched it by turning the volume off. Now the phone was off the hook, but Kate wouldn't know it. Smiling with satisfaction, he sat back on the couch and waited.

Mrs. Hebert glimpsed the photographs and fainted. They sent for medical help at the same time that Rick radioed for backup. In fifteen minutes, the Temple Terrace police department had arrived and were setting up surveillance in the area. Two of their officers came inside.

"When he gets here," Rick said, "I want him."

They called the hospital and learned that Masterson had indeed visited the patient as scheduled, but had left just before seven-thirty. It was now just past nine. Where had he gone?

They put out an APB on his car and license tags across three counties, and officers were dispatched to question the family of the dying woman at the hospital about whether Masterson had given any indication of where he might be going next.

"He's hunting," Connor said. "Somewhere out there he's hunting his next victim. Start looking at the exotic lounges and other places like that."

More officers were dispatched in both Pinellas and Hillsborough counties.

"He won't be armed," Connor said. "It's not his style. And he'll come quietly. He wants to be found."

He was in the groove, he realized, feeling distanced from his surroundings, falling by instinct into the thought patterns of the hunter himself. He was feeling his way through Masterson's mind, and the worst part of it was that it felt right.

Later, he told himself. Later he could afford to think about what this was doing to him. Right now he had to keep his attention on the job at hand.

Pacing the room while people talked, radios crackled and Mrs. Hebert insisted to the paramedics that she was just fine, he tried to walk through Masterson's mind from the moment he had attacked Sophie Butler. The ritual had been only partially played out on Sophie, and must have left him very dissatisfied. He was struggling internally, fighting his own limbic urges, and it was most likely that the killer in him would win. He had managed to stop himself with Sophie, but she was far removed from his usual victim. God help the woman who next crossed his path who fit the type, however remotely. The urge was driving him, growing more powerful with each passing moment, and soon he would have to satisfy it.

"He's going to kill again tonight," Connor told Rick. "He has to. He's going into the cycle again, decompensating and disassociating. God knows how he managed to stop himself with Sophie—probably because the urge hadn't fully taken over yet. But it probably has by now. He's going to find a woman and kill her tonight, because he won't be able to stop himself."

"Jesus," Rick said. It was like a nightmare, knowing something horrible was about to happen and being helpless to stop it.

"Pastor Peter can't be the killer," Mrs. Hebert said from her chair, waving the paramedics away. "It can't be him. He must be trying to help the real killer. That's why he had those photos."

Connor looked at her, shaking his head. "I'm sorry,

Mrs. Hebert, but those photos were his souvenirs. We find things like that very often with serial killers. His head injury fits, too.''

She shook her head. ''No, it can't be....''

''He's not really responsible, you know,'' Connor told her gently. ''He's being driven by the animal part of his brain. When he had that motorcycle accident, something was damaged that allows his most primitive impulses to surface at times.''

Mrs. Hebert's face hardened. ''We're all responsible for what we do. That's what Pastor Peter always says.''

''I'm sure he feels that way before his brain goes out of whack.''

Rick arched an eyebrow at him. ''Sympathy for this scum?''

''I have to feel sympathy for him if I'm going to get in his head.'' He sat near Mrs. Hebert. ''Did he ever tell you anything about his upbringing? Was he abused as a child?''

She hesitated, pursing her lips, looking sorrowful and angry all at once. ''Well, when he was recovering from the accident, he mentioned once that he felt like he had when his mother beat him with a two-by-four.''

Connor nodded. ''Anything else?''

''Oh, I don't know if I should be discussing these things with you.'' She reached into her pocket and pulled out a lace-edged hankie to dab her eyes. ''I asked him once why he had never married, and he said...he said that he was afraid to have children. That his mother had been so abusive he was afraid he wouldn't know how to be a good father. I tried to tell him that as long as he was aware of that, he would be all right. He just shook his head and smiled sadly.''

"Did you notice any change in his personality after the accident?"

"He brooded more, and he wanted to be left alone more often. And sometimes he lost his temper. He never used to do that, but since he was hurt—well, frankly, he got quite a temper sometimes. He said once that he was afraid he was becoming like his mother."

"She couldn't have been all bad," Connor prodded gently. "She raised a fine son."

"That's what I thought. But, well, apparently she was a stripper in Miami, and she used to bring strange men home with her. I think that explains his interest in helping these young women."

And in killing them, Connor thought. The pieces of the puzzle were falling neatly into place. "Did he ever mention the Puppetmaster to you?"

She looked at him in amazement. "How did you know?"

"Who is he? The Puppetmaster?"

"The Puppetmaster is God." She shook her head. "I always thought that was a little strange, but he would talk about how God pulled all our strings and that we had to dance to His tune if we wanted salvation. I think that was something from his childhood. Something his mother used to say when he objected to her line of work and her men friends. That the Puppetmaster pulled her strings and made her do the things she did."

"Bingo," said Bill, who had been listening intently. "That's it."

Connor nodded, never taking his eyes off Mrs. Hebert.

She continued. "He used to say that God pulled our strings, and when we didn't listen, we got hurt. I don't think he saw it the same way his mother did."

"Probably not." Connor closed his eyes, feeling around inside himself as the new information settled in. It fit. Oh, damn, did it fit.

"I can't believe he hurt those girls," Mrs. Hebert continued, dabbing at her eyes. "He wanted so much to save them!"

"So much he got carried away," Bill said.

"He thinks he saved them," Connor said. "He really does."

"Somehow I don't think their families see it that way," Bill argued.

"Look," Connor said flatly, "I'm trying to get inside this guy's head so I can save the *next* woman. Stow the crap until later, will you?"

For a moment it looked as if Bill might erupt, but he controlled the urge swiftly. "You got it," he said, and turned away to see what the officers were finding in the study. Mrs. Hebert had given them permission to search the house, so they weren't waiting on a warrant.

Mrs. Hebert looked at Quinn with damp eyes. "Do you really think he's going to kill someone tonight? Really?"

Connor nodded. "I really do. He seriously hurt a friend of mine earlier today, and I think he's..." He trailed off suddenly as a fist of realization slammed into his chest. Jumping up, he went to the phone in the study and dialed Kate's number. Still busy. This time he called the operator and asked her to check the line. What he heard made him slam the phone down.

"Rick!"

Diaz stuck his head into the study.

"Kate Devane's phone is off the hook and has been

busy since a little after eight. Get the St. Pete police to her house—*now!*"

Rick swore savagely as he hurried to the phone.

"Can I have your keys?" Connor called to him.

"Wait one damned moment, will you? Bill? Call the St. Pete police for me. What's her address, Connor?"

Connor scrawled it quickly on a piece of paper from Masterson's desk. "He's there," Rick said. "Quinn and I are on our way. You follow."

"I'll be right behind you."

Rick and Connor ran out to his car and backed out of the driveway with a squeal of tires. Rick took the residential streets like a Grand Prix driver.

"How do you know?" he asked Connor. "How can you be sure?"

"I know. I just know."

"How, damn it?"

"He's mad at me because of that profile the paper published this morning under my byline."

"Well, that might explain Sophie Butler, but how would he know about Kate?"

"He's been watching me," Connor said with gut certainty. "He's been watching me. He must have seen me with her. Jesus God in heaven, the whole time she was staying with me to protect her from that damn brother-in-law of hers, I was exposing her to this killer. Oh, Jesus."

"You can't blame yourself—"

"No?" Connor turned on him, every line of his body tight with rage. "If I hadn't been having this stupid, juvenile crisis about not wanting to wallow in this guy's filth, I might have figured out who he was sooner. Damn it!'' He slammed his hand against the dashboard, wishing he could smash something.

''Look, you'd had enough of it. You were close to cracking after that last case. Christ, Connor, you're only human. Why would you think this guy was watching you?''

''Because I was setting myself up as bait. I was doing everything I could to get him to keep in contact with me. To confront me. Instead, all I did was make it possible for him to hurt everyone I care about! Damn, damn, *damn!*''

''So...'' said Rick after a couple of minutes. ''Are you coming back to the force?''

Connor didn't bother to reply.

''I didn't think so. Look, you can't be sure about this. Maybe Kate just accidentally knocked her phone off the hook.''

''I was supposed to meet her at eight. Don't you think she'd be waiting for a call from me?''

This time it was Rick who didn't answer. He just pressed harder on the accelerator.

Kate made the coffee and waited in the kitchen for it to brew. She was beginning to feel uncomfortable talking with Pastor Masterson, which was ridiculous, because not very long ago she had made her living talking to people she didn't know. Maybe it was just that she felt uneasy discussing religion with people she didn't know very well.

And where the devil was Connor? She considered calling him but yanked her hand back from the phone. She'd already called his cell phone once but gotten no answer, and she was damned if she was going to seem like she was chasing him.

And wasn't that a joke? How could she ever have thought she wasn't playing with fire when she dared to get personally involved with a co-worker? How could she ever have convinced herself that there was a "safe" distance between her and Connor when they flirted on the Net? Even if her damn ex-brother-in-law hadn't been sending her those nastygrams, sooner or later Connor would have found out who she was. And once they started their lovemaking in cyberspace, how long had she thought it would be before they did exactly the same thing in real life?

How could she have been so deluded?

The coffee was finished, and she poured two cups, carrying them back to the living room on a tray with sugar and milk. She had already given him a glass of water and two aspirin tablets.

"Oh, my dear, thank you," Peter Masterson said as she set the tray on the coffee table.

Kate objected to strangers calling her "my dear," but she let it pass. "People who knew her had a very high opinion of Judy Eppinga," she said instead.

He nodded. "I thought of her as a soul filled with light. Kind and generous."

"And very practical, too, apparently."

He smiled. "I would have to agree."

She never knew what impulse made her ask, "Did you know any of the other murdered women?"

His face darkened, and for a second something flickered in his eyes that made her uncomfortable. It was gone almost before she was sure she had seen it. "I knew the most recent victim, too. Josephine Gumm. She had just started coming to our church."

"Really?" Something at the back of her neck prickled. "How...curious."

"You might think so, except that the members of my church have made a ministry out of trying to persuade these people to change their jobs. The work these women do is demeaning, and it hardens them in a tragic way. We have a program to help with retraining and job placement for them. Josie was interested in it, and we were trying to work out the details when she was killed."

As hot as the coffee was, he managed to down nearly a half cup in one draft.

"So tragic," he said. "These girls are taken advantage of by our society, you know. If men weren't so ready to pay exorbitant sums to see women undress, these women wouldn't be tempted down this path."

"So you hold men responsible for this?"

"Oh, indeed." He drained his cup. "Could I have some more?"

Kate went to get him more coffee, wondering what the hell had happened to Connor. Something about this visit was setting her nerves on edge, and she wished to hell Connor would just show up, showering apologies about having been sent on an assignment, and get this guy to go away. Because now that Peter Masterson was in her home, she didn't know quite how to suggest he leave.

Masterson had risen and was standing by the front window when she returned to the living room. "May I close this?" he asked, gesturing to the curtains. "It's dark out there, and a woman alone needs to be careful."

She wanted to object, but he was already closing the curtains. He took the coffee mug from her with a thank-you.

"I realize," he said, "that most people would blame these women for taking the jobs they do, but I don't agree. I see too many people tempted down dangerous or illegal paths because we don't pay enough for honest, unskilled labor. Not that I have a ready solution to offer." He shrugged and gave her a rueful smile. "The poor will always be with us."

"It *is* unfortunate. Will you excuse me? I need to call my date and find out why he's so late. It will only take a moment."

He stepped around the sofa, so he was only a few steps from the phone. "Please. Don't mind me. I need to be going, anyway. Thanks for your hospitality, Ms. Devane. I'll just see myself out." He put the coffee mug down on the tray.

She listened as he walked out to the foyer, and then she heard the door open and close. Thank God! The man was trying so hard to be pleasant, but there was really no reason for him to be here. And the way he was talking...she couldn't put her finger on it, but it had made her uncomfortable.

She reached for the receiver of the phone and cursed softly when she realized it had been off the hook. She must have bumped it earlier. Or maybe the minister had. Hanging it up, she waited for a few moments so that she could get the dial tone.

Just as she was reaching for the receiver again, she felt a prickle of apprehension, as if a chilly breeze had blown across the base of her neck. Then, with a suddenness that totally astonished her, something dropped before her eyes and a rope wrapped around her neck, drawing so tight it hurt. Almost immediately, stars appeared before her eyes. Reaching up, she clawed at the rope, trying to pull it away, as she struggled to draw a whistle of breath into her constricted throat.

"I'm so sorry, my dear," Peter Masterson said gently into her ear, "but I need to save you. You *do* want to be saved, don't you? You seem like such a nice girl, but you've been living in sin with Connor Quinn. The Puppetmaster sees everything, my dear. Everything. But don't worry. I'll save you."

*This can't be happening!* Stars continued to whirl before her eyes, and the edges of her vision were going black. It was hard to strangle someone, she remembered reading somewhere. Hard to strangle them or hang them. But she was being strangled right now, and when her knees gave way, it only got worse. A long, dark tunnel reached out for her and swallowed her up, until the last pinprick of light disappeared.

It had never taken so long to get to St. Pete. Hell, it had never taken so long to get across Tampa onto 275. They came down Busch Boulevard from Temple Terrace and hit heavy traffic. Rick reached for his flasher, then tossed it disgustedly back on the seat. Apparently there had been some big deal at Busch Gardens that evening, because the road was clogged in both directions. Out-of-state plates were everywhere, and too many of the drivers were driving like people who weren't sure where they were going. The on-ramp for the southbound interstate was on the right side of the road. Some guy from Maryland tried to cut over from the left lane across three lanes of traffic at the last minute and nearly collided with two cars. Traffic slowed even more, and horns blared. Cars coming off the northbound lanes used the same ramp, and one jerk in a pickup didn't want to let Rick onto the ramp.

"Christ," Rick swore, "if I had the time I'd get somebody to give that asshole a ticket."

"We don't have the time."

Rick glanced at him as they rounded the cloverleaf. "No, we don't."

At the top of the ramp, somebody in a Cadillac had come to a complete halt, waiting for an opening in traffic. This time it was Rick who pounded his hand on the steering wheel. "You know," he said, "I've got this theory. Any time a cop is in a hurry on a matter of life and death, every stupid driver in the whole damn bay area comes out of the woodwork to slow things down."

Stopped on the ramp, the guy in the Cadillac might have to wait until midnight to find a hole big enough to get into in the heavy highway traffic, most of which was racing by at about seventy miles an hour. Rick didn't wait long, although it seemed like a lifetime to Connor, before he jammed down the gas pedal, passed the guy on the right and accelerated to sixty on the shoulder, merging smoothly with traffic.

"You're not supposed to do that," Connor remarked with a lightness he didn't feel.

"Fuck all assholes," Rick replied tautly.

Connor used his cell phone again to try to get Kate. The line was still busy. Swearing, he cut off the call.

"Thirty minutes, tops," Rick said. "And I can probably do a hell of a lot better than that."

"In thirty minutes he could bleed her to death."

"The St. Pete guys will be there any minute."

"Yeah." Any minute was too many minutes. Too damn many minutes.

Then they hit Malfunction Junction, the interchange between I-275 and I-4. Traffic slowed sharply as two lanes of merging vehicles from I-4 tried to cut into the three lanes of I-275. An eighteen-wheeler pulled over sharply, and Rick had to jam on the brakes.

"Damn it," said Rick, "when I retire I'm going to move to Key West, where I can walk everywhere."

The mention of Key West gave Connor a strong pang. "Have you ever tried to stroll down Duval Street during tourist season?"

"And while we're at it, damn tourists. And damn truckers. Those idiots drive like they're the only vehicles on the road."

"Who's going to argue with them?"

"Fuck 'em." He slowed down to let in a Volvo that was going to either come over or take the side off the car. "Where did these people learn to drive?" He jammed on his brakes again as the Volvo braked sharply to let in a car ahead of it.

"Put up your flasher."

"That'll only slow 'em down more. They'll think I'm going to ticket them."

That was unfortunately true. Connor had seen it countless times when he was speeding to a call in a cruiser. The minute folks saw a cop, they slowed down. It never occurred to them to just get out of the way. He knew that, but he was just so damned impatient that he was willing to try anything.

The bottleneck began to clear out as they pulled past the merge lanes and traffic began to pick up speed again.

Rick started darting among the lanes, trying to get past the slower traffic.

"So," he said as they pushed past fifty-five, "when are you going to marry her?"

It took a minute for the question to register. Connor felt an uncomfortable lurch in his stomach. "Marry who?"

"Kate."

"I'm not going to marry Kate. I'm not going to marry anybody."

"Yeah, right."

Connor shrugged, trying to fix his attention on the passing city, resisting an urge to press his foot to the floorboards as if he could make them go faster. "She's still hung up on her ex."

"Everybody's hung up on their ex, if they have one."

"Well, this guy's in a mental hospital, and she still visits him every week."

"So? I don't see how he could be much competition if he's out of his head."

"I'm not worried about competition."

"Then what's the problem? She seems like a really nice person, and she sure has a great body." He gave a descriptive wolf whistle. "Better yet, you're both in the same business. That ought to help a lot. I mean, you wouldn't have to explain if you were late getting home."

"Do you have to do a lot of explaining?"

"I spend my whole life explaining. Adela understands, but damned if the kids do. I was supposed to be at a soccer game tonight."

"Sorry."

"You can say you're sorry when you're the scumbag

I'm trying to catch. In the meantime, lay off the damn guilt."

Lay off the guilt? Now that was an interesting idea. Just what guilt should he lay off? Guilt that he hadn't figured out who this guy was sooner?

"I should have known it was Masterson when he showed up at Gumm's house."

"Yeah. Maybe. If you're into mind reading. It's not like curiosity seekers don't show up at crime scenes for no better reason than that they want to see where it happened. And it's not as if the guy didn't have a legitimate reason to be there. It wouldn't be the first time a minister showed up to say a prayer. Those guys thrive on guilt, too."

"Guilt." Connor repeated the word as another piece of the puzzle fell into place. "He *does* feel guilty."

"About killing them?"

"And about not being perfect. He thinks he should be perfect. Godlike."

"God giveth and God taketh away, you mean?"

"That, too. He's playing god with these women, exacting penance for what he sees as their sins, granting them forgiveness, killing them. But he doesn't see himself as God with a capital *G*. It's the sympathetic-magic thing. By acting like God, he feels more godlike."

"So who twisted this guy's brain this way?"

"I don't know. Who can say why one abused child with a head injury turns into a serial killer while another manages to be a perfectly decent citizen?"

"But you still think the brain damage played a major role?"

"Absolutely. It does in a lot of these cases. These guys have lost the civilized barrier that controls our worst impulses. In many of them it comes over them almost like a seizure, and they can't stop themselves. But who's to say they're any worse than Aztec priests who ripped the living hearts out of sacrificial victims? Primitive impulses, magical thinking, ritual activities. The only difference is that society frowns on that shit these days, and these guys structure their own rituals, rather than following an established one."

Rick's phone rang, and he picked it up. "Diaz. Yeah. Yeah. Yeah? Okay, got it. Thanks, Ray." He put the phone down. "They found the blood. It's in a freezer in the garage, under packages of frozen meat. God knows how he was going to explain it to Mrs. Hebert if she ever ran across it."

"I can hardly wait to hear what he does with it."

"I wish I didn't have to know. You're not the only guy who gets nightmares from these cases. Adela swears she's going home to her mother if I don't close this case soon. I get to tossing around so bad she has to get out of bed."

"I get so I can't sleep at all. I pace for hours." Connor took out his phone again and called Bayfront Hospital to get a status check on Sophie. The nurse on duty didn't want to give any specific information, so he passed the phone to Rick, who identified himself and twisted her arm.

They were on the Howard Frankland Bridge now. The water was choppy, and moonlight sparkled on it. At any other time, it would have been beautiful.

"She's in surgery," Rick said, handing the phone back. "Skull fracture and subdural hematoma, whatever that means. Her condition is stable."

Connor didn't know whether to be thankful or to

swear. "Can you call the St. Pete police and find out what the hell is going on?"

"Sure."

He glanced at the speedometer and saw that Rick was doing eighty now, zigzagging among the cars on the bridge. Still, a red sports car sped past them.

"He wants to die young," Rick remarked as he waited for the dispatcher to connect him to someone who could answer his questions.

"Yeah," he said suddenly. "Rick Diaz. How you doing, Skip? Yeah. Listen, can you tell me if your men have gotten to Kate Devane's house yet?" He listened. "Okay, thanks. I'll be there within twenty minutes." He gave Skip his number and hung up the phone.

"The police have the place surrounded. The SWAT team is on the way. They're going to treat it as a hostage situation."

*Kate.* Everything inside him ached with fear for her.

"You know," Rick said, "this is going to be one hell of a PR mess if you're wrong about this."

"Screw PR." He dialed Kate's number again, and again got the busy signal. He listened to it, gripping the phone so tight his fingers ached. Answer it, Kate. Just answer it. Make this damn nightmare go away.

They were off the bridge now, speeding past the Feather Sound area.

"It's fastest to go this way, right?" Rick asked suddenly. "Or should I have gotten off on Ulmerton?"

"Just keep going. Take Thirty-eighth Avenue North across to Sixty-sixth."

"Got it."

This part of I-275 gave the impression that they were driving through the countryside. No one would guess how heavily populated the peninsula was. No one would guess the nightmares that were out there. Jesus, let Kate be all right.

But Rick's phone remained silent, and he could only guess what was going on at Kate's house.

# 20

Kate came to lying facedown on the carpet. Her throat hurt and burned, and when she coughed, pain sliced through her esophagus.

"See there?" said a voice from above. "I can hurt you. That's why you have to be a very good girl."

With a jerk, the rope around her throat tightened. "Get up. Now."

She cried out as the rope tightened and struggled to obey, driven by a need to survive that reached through her confused mind and galvanized her. As she struggled to her knees, the room spun, and she nearly blacked out.

The rope, which had loosened, tightened again, choking her briefly.

"Come on, be a good girl," the voice said. "I don't want to hurt you. I want to save you."

She was on her hands and knees now, more frightened than she had ever been in her life.

"Up. Now."

The rope tightened again, but not quite as hard. Just a warning. Breathing hurt, and she was panting from fear, each breath slicing her throat. She made it to her knees, then to her feet. Peter Masterson was behind her, and as she rose he shortened the rope, keeping just enough tension to remind her it was there.

"Please..." she whispered hoarsely, and hated herself for the sound of it. Begging. She didn't want to beg.

"I won't hurt you if you do exactly as I say," he told her. "Really, I don't want to hurt you. I want Quinn."

She tried to turn to face him, wobbling on her feet, but he yanked the rope again.

"No. Don't turn. Just do what I say and you'll be safe."

"You...killed the other women," she said as her mind began to slip into gear. One rope around her throat. There had to be something she could do to stop this. But the instant she tried to raise her arms, the rope tightened.

"Don't make me hurt you," he said. "Don't. Just do what I say."

Then she realized there were already ropes tied around her wrists. "You're going to kill me."

"No. No. I don't want to do that. I don't do things like that. I'm..." His voice trailed off, and the longest seconds Kate had ever endured ticked by while she waited for him to speak. When he did, his voice held a flat emptiness that terrified her. He was fuguing in and out of his delusion, she thought. She recognized it. Oh, God, a madman held her life in his hands!

"It's all right," he said. "You're not like the others. You have an honest job. I don't need to purify you the way I purified them."

She was so terrified that she was shaking, but some spark of anger ignited in the pit of her stomach and made her say, "They had honest jobs, too. Just like anyone else, they worked for a living."

"It was indecent. They pandered to lust, and lust is one of the seven deadly sins."

"I thought you blamed the men."

"Not really. I blame the women who strip their clothes off for men. My mother did that, you know. She was a whore. Then she would beat me because I was a sinner. But she was the real sinner. She didn't have to take off her clothes for men or sleep with them for money. No one made her do it. It was her *choice.*"

She heard an edge creeping into his voice and held perfectly still, saying nothing. Her heart was slamming in her chest as if she had run a marathon, and every breath still hurt. The rope around her neck was tight enough to tell her that she would probably have bruises...if she survived.

"She tied me up," he said.

She moved her arms a little. "Like this?"

"She tied me up so that I had to kneel, with ropes on my wrists so I couldn't reach my throat, and a rope around my neck just like this one. She tied it through a ring in the ceiling so that I had to stay perfectly straight as I knelt or I would choke. Hour after hour she made me kneel, naked on the floor, and she would hit me until her arms got tired. She mostly whipped me with a belt, but sometimes she hit me with boards."

Despite her fear and anger, Kate felt a trickle of sympathy for him. "Nobody should treat a child that way."

"I agree. But you're not a child, are you? Kneel. Now."

"No—"

He jerked the rope, and she hastened to kneel before the choking sensation got any worse. But the rope didn't loosen. He kept drawing it upward while she gagged and choked.

"See?" he said. "That's what it was like. And it was

good for my soul. Suffering is penance, and the soul needs it to thrive. You'll thank me for this, Kate."

She was choking, and instinct made her strike out like a wildcat. The noose tightened sharply, and before she could find her tormentor with her nails, darkness claimed her once again.

They were barreling down Thirty-eighth, no more than five minutes from Kate's house, when the call came. The SWAT team was in position.

"They're checking out the premises right now," Rick told Connor as he hung up the phone. "Looking in windows— Hell, you know the drill. Lights are on in the front of the house. Then they'll knock."

"Tell them to wait until we get there."

Rick was so surprised that he jerked the wheel and the car swerved. "What? A minute ago you were so all-fired hot to get here because he could kill her in a matter of minutes!"

"He won't kill her, because he wants *me.* He wants to straighten *me* out. She's the bait to draw me in. If they bust in there, there's no telling what he might do. You'd better let *me* knock on the door."

"Come on, Connor! If he even suspects the cops are outside, he's not going to let you in. Just let them do their jobs."

"No. He wants me. He doesn't expect to get out of it this time. He wants to be caught. But the only way he can guarantee that he can get to me is through Kate. That's what he's doing. She's a hostage, all right. And *I'm* the payoff."

Rick wheeled them around a corner, tires screaming. "How can you be so damn sure? He might think this is just another victim and just another murder and that nobody's on to him yet. He can't be sure you'll show up."

"I can be so damn sure because I'm inside his head. The real message at my place was Sophie. He wants my full and undivided attention, and he's going to get it. Sophie was a way to let me know that he knows who I am and where I live and who I care about."

"That still doesn't explain why you're so damn sure he won't go all the way with Kate."

"Because Kate isn't his type."

"She's blond and stacked."

"But she's not a dancer or a whore. She's not his type," he repeated emphatically. "He won't kill her unless we make him. So tell them to wait, damn it."

Rick picked up the phone again and called Skip. "Yeah," he said, after explaining the situation, "our chief profiler is sure of this. Just do it, Skip. I'll take the flak if we fuck up."

"That was generous of you," Connor said when Rick hung up.

"Yeah, I thought so, too. But what the hell. Adela wants me to get into another line of work so my blood pressure will come down."

"What would you do?"

"Caddy at some country club. Hell, I don't know. All I know is how to be a cop. So do me a favor, Connor. Don't fuck this up."

"I don't intend to." He was ready to chew nails. Two more blocks to go. He could see himself arriving, could imagine walking up to the door and knocking. After that, he didn't know what the hell was going to happen. It was all dark.

Kate regained consciousness again, this time to find herself sitting in an armchair. Her hands were firmly bound to either side of the chair, and she could only move them a little. The noose was still around her throat, tight enough to be uncomfortable, but not enough to choke her.

Across from her sat her tormentor, looking not the least bit nervous or concerned. He was drinking a cup of coffee, and he even gave her a pleasant smile.

"Trust me," he said, "you'll be okay as long as you do exactly what I tell you."

"Why don't you let me go? Connor's not going to come here."

"Sure he will. I saw him go into Marceline Whitmore's house, right past the barricades, when they kept all the other reporters out. He was there at Judy's place, too, and they took him inside. They don't do that with reporters. I know he's working with the cops. Did he ever tell you he used to be the profiler with the Hillsborough Sheriff's Office? Oh, he worked as a crime-scene tech, but everybody I talk to tells me he was a natural profiler. He'll figure this out. And I made sure to leave him a clue."

His smile broadened. "He thinks I was fooled by that profile in this morning's *Sentinel*, but as soon as I talked to him on the phone, I figured it out. He was lying. He wanted to make me mad enough to do something stupid."

"And you don't think this is stupid?"

"No. It's over."

"Over?"

He didn't answer. His face changed, reflecting pain. "These headaches. Jesus Christ, I want to cut my head off sometimes!"

She didn't know which of his moods frightened her

more. The pleasant man who had just been talking to her was creepy, but when he spoke of violence, even violence directed at himself, she was terrified that he might take it out on her.

"The aspirin is in the kitchen cabinet, beside the sink."

His face changed again, swiftly, and he looked like an entirely different person. "You're very kind."

She seized on it desperately. "I have headaches, too. Terrible ones. I know what you're feeling."

"No, you don't. Nobody knows what this is like. Christ, those damn doctors don't even really believe me when I tell them how bad it is. It gets so I can't see and can't think and all I want to do is smash something."

"But it's not right to smash things, is it?"

"No...no..." His voice trailed off. Then he said, "Did you say there was some aspirin?"

"In the cabinet to the left of the kitchen sink."

"You don't mind if I make more coffee, do you?"

"No, of course not. Help yourself." Keep busy in the kitchen making coffee. Every minute she survived offered another chance to figure her way out of this.

As soon as he left the living room, she started pulling at the bonds on her wrists, hoping she could loosen them. Instead, they tightened, and she stopped for fear she would lose circulation and then be unable to help herself if an opportunity presented itself.

He returned a few moments later, smiling again. "I made more coffee," he told her, as if he were a host entertaining a guest. "It'll be ready in a few minutes."

"Will you let me have some? I'd really like a cup."

He shook his head. "I can't untie you, you see. And don't try anything, Kate. Peter gets so upset when I kill someone."

Kate nearly gaped at him. *Peter* got upset? Was this guy a multiple-personality? What the hell was going on here?

Her heart was still hammering, but some of the pain in her throat had eased. Her mind skipped around like a jackrabbit, trying to find some topic of conversation to keep him occupied so that he was distracted from thoughts of killing her. Not for one instant did she believe he wasn't going to hurt her, but the longer she could delay him, the greater her hope of finding a way to escape. The greater her hope that Connor might actually turn up and rescue her. Not for a moment did she doubt he could help her. He was a former cop, after all, and this guy didn't appear to have a weapon.

"He'll be here," Peter said, as if reassuring himself. "He'll come. It won't be much longer, Kate. And then it will be all over."

She shuddered and started praying frantically.

The SWAT team had the house surrounded, all right. In their dark clothes, they were just more shadows among the many shadows cast by the streetlights.

"I can't let a civilian go in there," Fred Wilcox argued. He was the officer in charge of the scene. "Christ, Rick, tell me you're kidding."

Diaz shook his head. "He's not really a civilian. Until six months ago he was a cop."

"He's still a civilian. And you can't expect me to hand over another hostage to this creep."

"I'm the one he wants," Connor insisted. "He'll let Kate Devane go if he has me."

"That guarantee isn't worth shit, and you know it."

"Then how about this? The only person who might die tonight is Peter Masterson. He doesn't want to hurt anyone else. He's hurt enough people, and he wants to be stopped. That's why he's doing this. If getting killed is the only way, he'll make a target of himself."

"Shit."

"I'll put it in writing that I'll take responsibility for anything that happens to me," Connor told him. "Will that help?"

"Fuck, no."

"Look, we've got to move to save the woman. Standing around here picking our noses and scratching our asses isn't going to get it done. There's not a doubt in my mind that this is the safest way to go, at least as far as Kate Devane is concerned."

Rick spoke. "I'll take responsibility."

"Hell, you're not even in my chain of command." Fred Wilcox hesitated another moment, but then nodded. "Okay, just do it. Christ, why do I feel like Pilate? Maybe somebody should give me something to wash my hands."

"You're not washing your hands of it," Connor said. "You're taking the most sensible course."

He walked toward the house, thinking about Kate being in there with a killer. The thought kept him moving even when every cell in his body shrieked that it would be smart to move in the other direction. But he was used to that feeling. He'd felt it countless times in tense situations when he was a cop, and he just ignored it and kept moving toward the door.

He was halfway up the walk when he realized that this time was different. This time he was more scared of what he might find inside than he was of what might happen to him. What if he was all wrong about this? What if Kate was already dead?

With a great mental shove, he thrust that thought

away. It would do him no good to start thinking such things. He needed to keep his head clear and calm.

When he reached the stoop, he turned and looked back. The cops had melted into the night, leaving the street clear. When Masterson looked out, he was going to see Connor Quinn and no one else. Good.

Raising his fist, he pounded on the door. "Open up, Masterson. I'm here."

The next few moments seemed endless. Maybe he'd been wrong. Maybe Kate had gone out somewhere on her own. Maybe Kate was already dead and Masterson had long since left. Maybe...

"The door's unlocked," a familiar male voice called out. "Come in."

He had expected it, but it still felt like a punch to the gut. The guy *was* in there with her. The nightmare was real.

He hesitated, then reached out and slowly opened the door. "I'm coming in," he called out.

"Just get in here and close the door," Masterson replied. "You wouldn't want to disturb the neighbors. We're in the living room."

"Okay." He closed the door behind him, making sure it thudded soundly, but kept the latch from catching by holding the knob. Then he left it open a couple of inches.

Wouldn't want to disturb the neighbors? Was it possible that Masterson had no idea the cops had the place surrounded?

He walked into the living room and felt a burst of white rage when he saw Kate tied to the chair, a rope around her neck. Masterson was holding the end of the rope, drawing it just tight enough that Connor could see it bite into her neck. Kate's eyes met his, imploring and terrified. Her face was as white as snow.

"Sit over there," Masterson said, pointing to the couch. "As long as you cooperate, Kate will be okay."

"Why don't you just let her go? We can talk it out without her."

"What kind of fool do you take me for? The minute she's out of here, you'll be all over me."

Connor sat on the couch, waiting. When the opportunity came, and it would, Masterson was going to be one sorry son of a bitch.

"Well, I'm here," Connor said. "What do you want from me?"

"I want you to retract the story you wrote today. I want you to tell the truth."

"That's easy enough. What *is* the truth?"

Masterson stepped out from behind the armchair, but he never let go of the rope he held, nor did he slacken it. It was going to be easy, Connor thought. Too easy. Unless the guy was armed, he wouldn't have time to hurt Kate before Connor could take him. Now all he had to do…

But hope died an instant later, when Masterson pulled out a long, sharp knife and laid it across Kate's throat. "Don't try anything."

"I won't."

"If you so much as twitch wrong, she'll be bleeding like a stuck pig. There won't be time to save her, understand?"

"I understand. So what's the truth, Peter?"

"You swear you'll print it?"

"Every word. Trust me." He pointed to Kate's microcassette recorder, sitting on the coffee table where she had placed it earlier. "Let me turn it on."

"Move slowly."

He did, punching the Record button and setting the recorder down again. "Okay. Talk."

A look of momentary confusion passed over Masterson's face, and Kate gasped as the knife pressed harder against her throat. "Ask me," he said finally. "Anything."

Connor looked at Kate. "Let up on the knife a little, please? You're terrifying her."

Surprisingly, Masterson did.

"Thanks. All right." He tried to think, tried to figure out how to ask things that would lead Masterson to get involved in telling his tale, so that perhaps he would move away from Kate, an approach that wouldn't somehow anger the man. Christ, he wished he had some training as a reporter, rather than a cop.

"Come on," said Peter, suddenly grinning, "you must have dozens of questions you've been wanting to ask."

"How do you pick your victims?"

"I don't know." His smile broadened. "Simple question, simple answer. I suppose a psychologist would say they all resemble my mother in some way. She was blond and busty, but that's where the resemblance ends. My mother was a goddamn whore. These women—well, except for Marceline—weren't whores, were they?"

Masterson shook his head, and his eyes grew distant, almost glassy. "He picks them because something feels right. Something...clicks. He *knows.* The hand of the Puppetmaster is upon him and moves him in mysterious ways."

Connor felt an uneasy prickle at the way Masterson changed pronouns, disassociating himself from the killer. This guy was really nuts. "Who's the Puppetmaster?"

"Oh, I think you already know the answer to that."

Connor glanced at the knife again and saw that it was still too tightly pressed to Kate's neck. If he didn't move fast enough... "You knew Judy and Josephine from church. But what about Marceline and Connie?"

Masterson shook his head. "You have it backwards. I found them all the same way. I was led to them. Judy and Josie just happened to come to the church." He shrugged. "But I knew them all beforehand. Even Marceline. I met her during a volunteer project at a hospital. She wanted to be a good person, you know. She wanted desperately to give up her whoring, but she couldn't stop herself. I think she was probably a nymphomaniac, but there was more to it than that. She needed to be treated like a slut. She needed the indecency of selling herself. She told Peter all about it, and he offered to help her." He shook his head.

"Help her how?"

Masterson smiled almost sadly. "It was such a shame, how afraid she was of herself and of being found out. But now she's purified, and her sins are all behind her. He purified her and then killed her before she could sin again. She doesn't have to be afraid anymore."

"So you were helping these women?"

"Of course. How many of us get to die in a state of sanctity?"

Connor nodded. "Few enough, I guess. Kate, are you all right?"

"Yes..." She whispered the word, her eyes fixed on him hopefully. Her face was still too pale, and her lips quivered, but her eyes told him that she was ready for whatever he might do.

He returned his attention to Masterson. "So you and Peter are two different people?"

A flicker of confusion, followed by a negative shake

of the head. The guy was losing it, Connor realized. If he could find a way to push him…

"We're the same person," Masterson said. "He knows what I'm doing, and I know what he's doing. But you know what, Quinn? He hates himself so much that he tries to pretend this part of him belongs to someone else. He can't face the fact that he gets high on the power."

"Power?"

"The power of life and death. Like Lucifer, he wants to be God, but he knows what happened to Lucifer. He's scared shitless of being sent to hell, but he can't stop me. He can't stop himself." A bitter laugh escaped him. "The Puppetmaster made me this way, you know. But Peter can't accept it. So he tries to cut himself off from me, but I am him. I'm inside him, part of him, an outgrowth of his own impulses. I was always here, but until the accident he managed to control me. He even tried to bury me by becoming a minister. He claims to prefer the namby-pamby way of going to God, but the truth is, he wants *all* the power. The power of life and death. The power to hold the strings and make the puppets dance. What he's afraid of admitting is that he's dancing on strings himself right now. We are what we are made to be."

In a horrible way, Connor understood. "Let up on the knife a little more, will you? If Kate dies now, she won't be in a state of sanctity."

An odd thing happened then. Something seemed to pass over Masterson's face, and Connor could have sworn that for just a few seconds the man didn't know what he was doing or where he was. Then his face set once again into harsh lines.

Connor pushed a little, testing. "How can you tell

yourself you're saving these women, when all you want is to kill them?''

''If we are to save these souls, we have to be harsh. The finger of the Puppetmaster is always harsh and cruel. Look at the Old Testament. Lot's wife was turned into a pillar of salt for the simple transgression of disobeying and looking back. There can be no room for mercy.''

Connor took a deep breath and took the plunge. ''Then there can be no mercy for someone who kills.''

''I'm only an instrument.''

''That's an interesting take on it, but I seem to remember the commandment that says, 'Thou shalt not kill,' and I don't remember any exceptions to that.''

''I purify myself in the blood of the lamb.''

''Like hell you do. You purify yourself in the blood of innocent victims!'' He held his breath, waiting, fearing that he had pushed too hard and that Masterson would take it out on Kate. Kate looked even more terrified, as if she, too, expected the knife to slash her.

Masterson's face went blank for a few seconds. Then he said, ''I purify myself in the blood of innocents. I am forgiven.''

''You steal the blood! You take it from them without their consent, and you do it while you are killing them! There's nothing holy in that.''

''They are holy and saved, and thus I am holy and saved.''

''Bullshit! Take a good long look at yourself, Reverend. You are nothing but a stinking, filthy, slimy, disgusting serial killer!''

The knife jerked away from Kate's throat, and Connor took advantage of it. He leaped up from the couch and took a flying dive across the room, catching Masterson around the knees in a classic football tackle.

He expected a struggle, a knock-down-drag-out fight with the man. But Masterson didn't resist. He looked stunned for a moment, then stared at Quinn. "Forgive yourself," he said gently.

Connor was startled and stared down into the man's almost beatific face. "Forgive myself? What the hell do I have to forgive myself for?"

"Forgive yourself for understanding me."

Connor felt as if he'd been stripped naked to the soul. Enraged, he struck one furious blow at Masterson and knocked him cold.

# 21

Masterson sat handcuffed on the couch. Kate sipped hot tea with honey in it to ease the soreness of her throat and insisted that she was just fine and didn't need the paramedics. SWAT team members milled around, getting ready to depart, while the regular cops took over.

Connor knelt by Kate's chair. "Are you really okay?"

She shuddered and gave an uneasy laugh. "Physically, I'm fine. But I'll never feel safe in this house again."

"So sell it."

"I think I will. Maybe I'll get an apartment."

"There's one available two doors down from me."

Her eyes flew to his, but he wasn't ready to meet her gaze. Not yet. Maybe not ever. It was his fault she'd been put through this hell. "You won't be alone tonight," he told her. "When the cops are through with us, I'm taking you back to my place."

Which was probably a mistake, he thought, when he remembered the blood all over his bed. "On second thought, we're getting a hotel room tonight. Think we can find anything on the beach?"

"At this time of year? I doubt it."

"I'll find something, somewhere."

"What's wrong with your place?"

"He hurt Sophie. Skull fracture. She's in surgery right now."

"Oh, no! That poor woman..." She put her cup down and shuddered. "I think," she said, her voice catching, "that I'm about to get hysterical."

"Nobody would blame you. But if you can hang on for a few more minutes, I'll get you out of here so you can do it in private."

She managed a nod as she bit her lower lip. God, thought Connor, she was brave. Brave or in shock.

"The paramedics should take a look at you before they leave," he told her. They'd already tended to Masterson, and they were milling around in the foyer, getting ready to depart. "Just let them check you out. For my sake."

"Okay." Her voice sounded weak and unsteady, but her eyes were still dry.

He went to get the medics, and while they talked with Kate, he looked over at Masterson. The man's face was still blank, as if he had gone to some place far away, where none of this could reach him.

Connor stood there looking at him, torn between an urge to rend the man limb from limb for what he had done and shame at having hit him out of anger.

Suddenly Masterson looked at him, and their eyes connected.

"It was me all the time, wasn't it?" Masterson asked, his voice hoarse.

Almost in spite of himself, Quinn walked over to the sofa and sat beside him. Masterson was sitting awkwardly, with his hands cuffed behind him, but he seemed unaware of the discomfort.

"Yeah," Connor said. "It was you all the time."

"I remember now." Then his face crumbled into a mask of ineffable anguish. "Oh, Jesus, Jesus, what have I done? What have I done?"

Connor looked away, feeling a pang of sympathy that he absolutely did not want to feel.

"I'm so sorry...." Masterson breathed raggedly, trying to stop tears. "Oh, God, forgive me, I'm so sorry...."

Connor couldn't look at him. He didn't want to see this man's human side. He wanted him to be a monster. Except there weren't any real monsters. They were all just us. And that thought caused him to put his arm around Masterson's shoulders and hold him while the man shuddered and shook with grief and horror.

The minister calmed finally, finding the serenity that came from a pain too great to endure. "They're going to electrocute me, aren't they?"

"Probably. But it'll be years yet. State law requires appeals."

"It can't be soon enough. I'm not fit to live."

For all that Connor believed Peter Masterson would never have been a serial killer except for his severe brain damage, he couldn't disagree. Society couldn't tolerate killers in its midst.

"This is the cup I've been given to drink," Masterson said. "I have to drink it to the bitter dregs."

Connor nodded and removed his arm from the man's shoulders as two policemen approached.

"Time to go," one of them said.

Masterson nodded and rose. Connor rose with him.

"It's okay," Peter said. "I deserve this as much as anyone has ever deserved this. Those poor girls..." He shook his head and looked away. "There can be no mercy for me, nor should there be any."

The minister started to walk away with the cops, but he paused and looked back over his shoulder. "Thank you."

Connor was surprised. "For what?"

"For understanding me well enough to stop me. Thank you." Then he walked away.

Rick entered the room. "Kate, can we get together tomorrow sometime and question you about what happened tonight? Do you think you'll be able to manage that?"

"I've told you everything."

"We still need to take a statement, and then the state attorney will probably want an affidavit." He gave her a rueful smile. "Once this guy talks to an attorney, his tune will change. We need all the testimony we can get."

"Sure. Tomorrow..." She trailed off and looked at Connor.

"Tomorrow afternoon," Connor said firmly. "I'm taking her away from this crap until then."

"Fair enough. Say two o'clock? Give me a call around eleven and I'll tell you where we're all meeting."

Connor nodded and watched as the police left the house, disappearing through the front door like water down a drain. Finally the door closed, and silence filled the house.

He looked at Kate. "Let me use your phone, then you can get as hysterical as you want."

"I'm not going to get hysterical," she said, managing a wan smile. "But I am going to get myself another cup of tea."

"I'll get it for you."

"I'm not an invalid, Connor. Really. I can do it."

So he let her do it, sensing that she needed to take control again, even in this small way. Then he reached for the phone.

Connor had her pack an overnight bag; then they took a cab to his place, where he packed one for himself. He forbade her to go into the bedroom with him until he had stripped the bedding and covered the bloodstained mattress with a clean sheet. He didn't want her to see it, and tomorrow he was buying a new bed. He called the hospital about Sophie again, and this time they told him that she was out of surgery and in satisfactory condition. She would be able to have visitors tomorrow.

They stopped at the supermarket, where he bought bread, cheese and a couple of bottles of wine. Then he drove them across the county and up the barrier islands along Gulf Boulevard. She never asked where they were going.

He pulled into one of the better hotels. He'd called from Kate's house and managed, despite its being tourist season, to find a room. A suite, actually. It was all that they had available, and it was going to cost him two arms and a leg, but he didn't mind. All his life he had found the rhythms of the sea to be soothing, and he hoped Kate would, as well.

After they checked in, he carried their bags up to the suite. They had a bedroom with two double beds, a sitting room pleasantly furnished in blues and greens like the sea, and a balcony with comfortably padded garden furniture. From the balcony doors he could see the ribbon of light cast by the setting moon on the black Gulf waters. The sound of the waves was audible and soothing even through the closed doors, but he opened them anyway and let the night in.

Turning, he found Kate standing in the middle of the sitting room, as if she didn't know where she was or what she was doing.

"Why don't you go get comfortable, and then we'll have some wine and cheese on the balcony?" If she didn't break down first.

She nodded and turned away, looking as if she might shatter at any moment. He stayed himself from reaching out to her and hugging her. She would come to him in her own good time, when she was ready. Until then, he had to wait.

He opened a bottle of wine and put it out on the balcony table with a couple of the hotel's water glasses. He put the packages of sliced cheese out there, too, but didn't open them. He had a feeling they weren't going to eat or drink for a while.

"Connor?"

He turned and found Kate standing in the doorway. Her lower lip trembled, and her eyes were filled with unshed tears.

"I think I'm getting hysterical."

He crossed swiftly to her, closing the door behind him and gathering her up in his arms, as if he could hold all the evil in the world at bay. He carried her to the couch and sat with her on his lap, holding her as huge sobs began to rip through her. He couldn't tell her anything that would help, because there *was* nothing. She had had safety and security torn from her by a madman. By two madmen, actually, but she would never acknowledge that. Frightened and alone, she had tried to face the world bravely, and the world had sent her a serial killer.

She had been seeking safety in the world they had

created in cyberspace and had believed anonymity would keep her safe. He could understand that, he realized suddenly. He could understand why she had been so afraid to let him know who she was.

He wondered if she would ever be able to trust a man again.

She cried for a long time, harsh sobs ripped from the deepest part of her. And when at last she grew quiet, he knew it was only exhaustion that stilled her. She had lost more tonight than the little bit of safety she had managed to build for herself. A killer had come into her house in the guise of a clergyman, and she would probably never again trust her judgment of another's character. Why should she? She had been wrong about her ex-husband, and she probably believed she had been wrong about *him,* too. And maybe she had been.

When she was calm and her eyes were dry, he eased her off his lap and went to get a warm, wet washcloth. Then he sat beside her and wiped the tearstains away from her cheeks and her throat.

She had changed into a black silk nightie with a plunging neckline that made her skin look like cream. He was suddenly aware that he was touching her, and his body responded with an instant rush of desire. He hated himself for it.

"Do you think you can eat something now?" he asked gently.

"No...no. Not yet." She sighed and looked down at her hands. They twisted together on her lap. "Can you...would you...just hold me for a while?"

He could, and he would, gladly. So he held her close while the moon sank in the western sky, while the horrors and fears of the evening past began to drift away on the tide of time. And with each breath she took, he wanted her more. He needed her more. He craved the affirmation of life, and he craved it from her.

But he felt like a jerk for even thinking of it, so he made no move. He wasn't worthy, for one thing. Dumb as it sounded, he didn't feel good enough for her, especially after he had nearly gotten her killed with his stupid machinations. Christ, would she ever be able to forgive him for that?

Her voice was little more than a sigh on the night air. "You knew he was coming for me."

"Not until it was almost too late. I didn't figure it out until we'd been at his house for more than an hour. Your phone was busy, and I kept calling...." God, he felt like an abject failure for not having figured it out more quickly. He should have come to her sooner. "I'm sorry. If I'd just done my job right, I'd have caught him days ago."

She astonished him by putting her finger to his lips. "Shh," she said. "Shh. Don't blame yourself. I wasn't blaming you. I'm just so grateful you figured it out. He knew you would. He kept telling me you would come...."

"He knew me better than I knew myself."

She tilted her head and looked up at him, her eyes dark with sorrow and something else. "That scares you, doesn't it?"

"It terrifies the shit out of me."

"It also terrifies you that you understand him."

"Yeah, it does. Nobody ought to understand a mind that sick and twisted."

She gave him a sad smile. "It terrifies me how well I've understood Michael sometimes. But being able to understand them doesn't mean we're like them. You may be able to walk in the shoes of a serial killer and pierce the veils of his mind, but that doesn't make you like him, Connor. It just means you have a gift."

"A gift? How about a curse?"

She shook her head. "For me, it was a gift. For the next dancer who might have been killed, it's a gift. For all the potential victims you have saved and will save, it's a blessing. I know it's like opening a wound inside yourself to do what you do, but it's a gift, and I am so very, very grateful for it."

"I almost got you killed!"

"I almost got *myself* killed. I let a total stranger into my house because he was wearing a clerical collar. When he started to make me uneasy, I had three or four chances just to get out of there. I didn't. It was my own foolishness that almost got me killed, and don't you ever forget that."

"You're not foolish. Just trusting." He looked away. "Are you suggesting I go back to police work?"

"Isn't that what you really want to do?"

He thought about it, really thought about it, and knew she was right. Taking photos for the paper satisfied the creative urge in him, but something more elemental and essential needed the work he did as a profiler. Something in him needed to make a difference.

He turned to her again. "How would you feel about that?"

"You going back to police work? Does it matter?"

"Believe me, Kate, it matters. It matters a hell of a lot."

The shadows suddenly left her eyes, and she smiled. "I'll think the world of you no matter what you do, Connor. It has to be *your* decision."

His cell phone, forgotten on the end table, shrieked

suddenly, jarring him. "Damn it, it's three in the morning." But because it was probably Rick, he answered it.

"Quinn," said the familiar voice of Ben Hyssop, "where the hell are you and Devane? I hear they got the serial killer tonight, and I want my exclusive."

"You'll get your damn exclusive. Tomorrow. There's no way in hell you could publish it in this morning's paper, anyway."

"I know that, but damn it, you two ought to be getting the info and writing it."

"We will. Tomorrow. And believe me, Ben, you're going to get a story that no one else will get. Now go away and leave me alone. We want to make love."

That stunned Ben into silence, and Connor had no qualms about disconnecting. And this time he turned the damn phone off.

"Make love?" Kate asked, her voice suddenly throaty.

"Make love," he repeated. "Here? On the bed? In the bathtub? On the chaise on the patio?"

She laughed. "All of the above. You pick the order."

So he carried her off to bed, where the warmth of their bodies and the heat of their passion blotted out all the evil that had touched them...for a little while.

Afterward they showered together, then went out on the patio to watch the birth of the new day. It was chilly, so they wrapped themselves in a blanket and squeezed onto the chaise together. Close didn't seem to be close enough.

The wine and cheese remained forgotten on the table, but neither of them cared. They were drunk on one another.

"It's not the Keys," Connor said suddenly.

"It's close enough." She was smiling dreamily, her

eyes closed. Last night would come back to haunt her again and again, but right now it felt as if it had happened to someone else, and she was content to have it that way.

"Next week," he said. "After we finish with the cops and we give Ben his story to end all stories, I'm going to abduct you and take you away to the Keys. We'll find a place to stay right on the water, and I'm going to get you a kitten to call Tigret."

"It's tourist season, Connor. We'll never find a place to stay."

"Just watch me." He looked into her eyes. "Will you come with me?"

"Have you forgiven me for lying to you?"

"You never lied. And you were only trying to stay safe. I don't have anything to forgive you for."

Her eyes darkened a little. "What about Michael?"

"You can visit him every week for the rest of your life if you want. I'll even go with you. But you need to make a new life, Kate. And so do I. If you think you can stand being married to a cop..."

"Married? Who said anything about marriage?"

"I just did. And I mean it. Of course, you might not feel the same." But he believed she did. That was one of the blessings of being a profiler.

She struggled until she freed her arms from the blanket, and, heedless of the chilly dawn air, she wrapped them around his neck and hung on tight. "I fell in love with you in cyberspace. Then I fell in love with you when you brought your geraniums in from the cold. Then I fell in love with you all over again when you hugged Peter Masterson."

He shifted uncomfortably. "I felt sorry for him."

"I know. And that takes one hell of a big heart."

He looked away for a moment. "I don't really know how to be married. I'd better warn you. My dad and mom fight like cats and dogs."

"So maybe you know what *not* to do."

He looked down at her and felt something inside him let go. It was okay. And suddenly he grinned. "You're an eternal optimist, aren't you?"

"I'm working on it."

"Okay, so we'll try. A week in Key West with no company but our own ought to be a good trial run, don't you think?"

"Sure." She snuggled closer and smiled. "If you really need one."

"Oh, what the hell. Why don't we get married the day after tomorrow?"

She laughed then. "Forget it. I want a wedding. Just a little one, with some of our friends. And I want it on the beach at sunset, just like all those notes we wrote to each other."

"You want to get married in the Keys?"

"Not necessarily. But beside the water. On the beach. Anywhere will do."

"Maybe I can even rustle up a heron."

"I'm sure you can."

And when he looked into her eyes, he believed he could, too.

# Epilogue

## He Wept For The Monster

*by Kate Devane*

*Sentinel* Staff Writer

The police described the scene as "secure," but for Pastor Peter Masterson there will never be any security again. The inner wall that separated the respected minister from the brutal serial killer crumbled, and Masterson beheld the monster in the flesh. He wept. Not for himself, but for the monster.

And so did I.

Last night, a task force of law enforcement officials from around the bay area...